YSABEL

YSABEL

GUY
GAVRIEL
KAY

SIMON &
SCHUSTER

London · New York · Sydney · Toronto

A CBS COMPANY

First published by Viking Canada, an imprint of Penguin Group (Canada), 2007
First published in Great Britain by Simon & Schuster UK Ltd, 2007
A CBS COMPANY

Epigraph on page vii from 'Juan at the Winter Solstice',
Complete Poems in One Volume, by Robert Graves. Reprinted with
permission of Carcanet Press Limited.

Epigraph on page 417 from G: *A NOVEL* by John Berger,
copyright © 1972 by John Berger. Used by permission of Vintage Books,
a division of Random House, Inc.

1 3 5 7 9 10 8 6 4 2

Simon & Schuster UK Ltd
Africa House
64-78 Kingsway
London WC2B 6AH

www.simonsays.co.uk

Simon & Schuster Australia
Sydney

A CIP catalogue record for this book is available from the British Library

Hardback ISBN-13: 978-0-7432-5250-8
ISBN-10: 0-7432-5250-0

Trade paperback ISBN-13: 978-0-7432-5251-5
ISBN-10: 0-7432-5251-9

Printed and bound in Great Britain by
CPI Bath

For

Linda McKnight

and

Anthea Morton-Saner

There is one story and one story only
That will prove worth your telling,
Whether as learned bard or gifted child;
To it all lines or lesser gauds belong
That startle with their shining
Such common stories as they stray into.

—ROBERT GRAVES

YSABEL

PROLOGUE

❧

The woods came to the edge of the property: to the gravel of the drive, the electronic gate, and the green twisted-wire fence that kept out the boars. The dark trees wrapped around one other home hidden along the slope, and then stretched north of the villa, up the steep hill into what could properly be called a forest.

The wild boar—sanglier—foraged all around, especially in winter. Occasionally there might be heard the sound of rifle shots, though hunting was illegal in the oak trees and clearings surrounding such expensive homes. The well-off owners along the Chemin de l'Olivette did what they could to protect the serenity of their days and evenings here in the countryside above the city.

Because of those tall eastern trees, dawn declared itself—at any time of year—with a slow, pale brightening, not the disk of the sun itself above the horizon. If someone were watching from the villa windows or terrace they would see the black cypresses on the lawn slowly shift towards green and take form from the top downwards, emerging from the silhouetted sentinels they were in the night. Sometimes in winter there was mist, and the light would disperse it like a dream.

However it announced itself, the beginning of day in Provence was a gift, celebrated in words and art for two thousand years and more. Somewhere below Lyon and north of Avignon the change was said to begin: a difference in the air above the earth where men and women walked, and looked up.

No other sky was quite what this one was. Any time of year, any season: whether a late autumn's cold dawn or midday in drowsy summer among the cicadas. Or when the knife of wind—the mistral—ripped down the Rhone valley (the way soldiers had so often come), making each olive or cypress tree, magpie, vineyard, lavender bush, aqueduct in the distance stand against the wind-scoured sky as if it were the first, the perfect, example in the world of what it was.

Aix-en-Provence, the city, lay in a valley bowl west of the villa. No trees in that direction to block the view from this high. The city, more than two thousand years old, founded by Romans conquering here—surveying and mapping, levelling and draining, laying down pipes for thermal springs, and their dead-straight roads—could be seen on spring mornings like this one crisply defined, almost supernaturally clear. Medieval houses and modern ones. A block of new apartment buildings on a northern slope, and—tucked into the old quarter—the bell tower of the cathedral rising.

They would all be going there this morning. A little later than this, but not too much so (two alarm clocks had gone off in the house by now, the one woman was already showering). You didn't want to linger of a morning, not with what they were here to do.

Photographers knew about this light.

They would try to use it, to draw upon it as someone with a thirst might have drawn from an ancient well—then again at twilight to see *how doorways and windows showed and shadowed differently when the light came from the west, or the sky was blood-red with sunset underlighting clouds, another kind of offering.*

Gifts of different nuance, morning and evening here (noon was too bright, shadowless, for the camera's eye). Gifts not always deserved by those dwelling—or arriving—in a too-beautiful part of the world, where so much blood had been shed and so many bodies burned or buried, or left unburied, through violent centuries.

But as to that, in fairness, were there so many places where the inhabitants, through the long millennia, could be said to have been always worthy of the blessings of the day? This serene and savage corner of France was no different from any other on earth—in that regard.

There were *differences here, however, most of them long forgotten by the time this morning's first light showed above the forest and found the flowering Judas trees and anemones—both purple in hue, both with legends telling why.*

The tolling of the cathedral bells drifted up the valley. There was no moon yet. It would rise later, through the bright daylight: a waxing moon, one edge of it severed.

Dawn was exquisite, memorable, almost a taste, on the day a tale that had been playing out for longer than any records knew began to arc, like the curve of a hunter's bow or the arrow's flight and fall, towards what might be an ending.

PART ONE

CHAPTER I

Ned wasn't impressed. As far as he could tell, in the half-light that fell through the small, high windows, the Saint-Sauveur Cathedral of Aix-en-Provence was a mess: outside, where his father's team was setting up for a pre-shoot, and inside, where he was entirely alone in the gloom.

He was supposed to feel cool about being by himself in here. Melanie, his father's tiny assistant, almost ridiculously organized, had handed him a brochure on the cathedral and told him, with one of her winks, to head on in before they started taking the test digitals that would precede the real photographs for the book.

She was being nice to him. She was *always* nice to him, but it drove Ned a bit crazy that with everything else she had to deal with, Melanie still—obviously—made mental notes to find things for the fifteen-year-old tag-along son to do.

Keep him out of the way, out of trouble. She probably knew already where the music stores and jogging tracks and skateboard parks were in Aix. She'd probably known *before* they flew overseas, googling them and making notes. She'd probably already bought a deck and gear on Amazon or something, had them waiting at the villa for just the right time to give them to him, when he looked completely bored or whatever. She was perfectly nice, and even cute, but he wished she didn't treat him as part of her job.

He'd thought about wandering the old town, but he'd taken the booklet from her instead and gone into the cathedral. This was the first working day, first set-up for a shoot, he'd have lots of chances later to explore the city. They were in the south of France for six weeks and his father would be working flat out almost the whole time. Ned figured it was just as easy to stick around the others this morning; he was still feeling a bit disoriented and far from home. Didn't have to *tell* anyone that, though.

The mayor's office, in the city hall up the road, had been predictably excited that they were here. They'd promised Edward Marriner two uninterrupted hours this morning and another two tomorrow, if he needed them, to capture the facade of their cathedral. That meant, of course, that any people wanting to go in and out to pray for their immortal souls (or anyone else's) were going to have to wait while a famous photographer immortalized the building instead.

As Greg and Steve unloaded the van, there had even been a discussion, initiated by the city official assigned to them, about men going up on ladders to take down a cable that ran diagonally across the street in front of the cathedral to the university building across the way. Ned's father had decided they could eliminate the wire digitally if they needed to, so the students weren't going to be deprived of lights in their classrooms after all.

Nice of us, Ned had thought.

Pacing back and forth, his father had started making crisp decisions, the way he always did when finally on location after the long buildup to a project. Ned had seen him like this before.

Barrett Reinhardt—the publisher's art director for the book—had been here in Provence two months ago, preparing a list of possible photographs, emailing jpegs back to Edward Marriner in Montreal, but Ned's father always preferred to react to what he *saw* when he got to a place he was shooting.

He'd pointed out a balcony off the second floor of the university, right above the square, opposite the facade, and decided they'd shoot with the digital camera from the ground, stitching a wide shot on the computer, but he wanted to go up to that balcony and use large-format film from there.

Melanie, following him around with her binder, had scribbled notes in different-coloured inks.

His father would make his photo selection later when he saw what they had, Ned knew. The challenge would probably be getting the tall bell tower on the left and the full width of the building into one shot. Steve had gone with the guy from the mayor's office into the university to see about access to the balcony.

A crowd had gathered to watch them setting up. Greg, using adequate French and a smile, was making sure the spectators stayed around the edges of the square, out of the shots. A gendarme had come to assist. Ned had watched, sourly. His French was better than the others', but he hadn't actually felt like helping. He'd left at that point, and gone inside the cathedral.

He really wasn't sure why he was in such a bad mood. On the face of it, he ought to have been really cool with this: out of school almost two months early, skipping exams (he did have three essays to write here and deliver in July back home), staying in a villa with a swimming pool while his dad and the others did their work . . .

Within the dark, high-vaulted cathedral, he abruptly removed his iPod buds and hit the off button. Listening to *Houses of the Holy* in here wasn't quite as clever as he'd thought it would be. He'd felt silly and even a little bit nervous alone in a place this shadowy and vast, unable to hear anything around him. He could imagine the headlines: *Canadian Student Stabbed by Led Zeppelin–Hating Priest.*

The thought amused him, a little. He'd put it in an email to the guys back home later. He sat down on a bench halfway up the central aisle, stretched out his legs, and glanced at Melanie's booklet. The cover photo was taken from a cloister. An arch in the foreground, a sunlit tree, the bell tower behind against a really blue sky. It was post-card pretty. It probably *was* on a postcard.

His father would never take a picture like it, not in a million years. Not of this cathedral. Edward Marriner had talked about that yesterday, while they'd watched their first sunset from the terrace.

Ned opened the brochure. There was a map at the front. The light was dim, but his eyesight was good, he could make it out. As best he could tell, from the map key on the facing page, this place had been built in a dozen stages over too many centuries by too many people who didn't care what had been done before they arrived. A mess.

That was the point, his dad had explained. The facade they were setting up to shoot was hemmed in by Aix's streets and squares. It was part of them, entangled in the city's life, not set back to be admired the way cathedrals usually were. The front had three styles and colours of stone that didn't come *close* to matching up with one another.

His father had said that was what he liked about it.

Remember why we're doing this shot, he'd reminded everyone as they'd piled out of the van and started unloading. Perfect cathedral facades like Notre Dame in Paris or Chartres were snapped by every tourist who saw them. This one was different, and a challenge—for one thing, they couldn't back up too much or they'd crash through a window into a university classroom and ruin a lecture on the eternal greatness of France.

Greg had laughed. *Suck*, Ned had thought, and reached for his earbuds.

That was when Melanie had fished the brochure from her black shoulder tote. The tote was almost as big as she was. The running joke was that half the missing objects in the world could be found in Melanie's bag, and she had a good idea where the other half were.

Alone inside, Ned studied the map and looked up. Where he was sitting was called a nave, not an aisle. *I knew that,* he thought, inwardly imitating Ken Lowery's exaggerated voice in science class.

As best he could tell, the nave had been finished in 1513 but the part just behind him was four hundred years older, and the altar ahead was "Gothic," whenever that was. The small chapel behind *that* had been built around the same time as the nave where he was sitting. If you looked left or right, the dates got even more muddled.

He stood up and walked again. It was a little creepy being alone in here, actually. His footsteps, in Nikes, were soundless. He approached a side door with two heavy old iron locks and a new brass one. A sign said it led out to the cloister and listed the times for tours. The black iron locks did nothing any more, the new one was bolted. Figured. Couldn't get out. That might have been a cool idea, sit in a cloister and listen to music. He didn't have any religious music on the iPod, thank God, but U2 would have done.

The cloister, Melanie's map informed him, was *really* old, from the 1100s. So was the side aisle where he was standing now. But the chapel up at the end of it was eighteenth century, the newest thing here. You could almost laugh. They could put a Starbucks somewhere in this place and it would fit as much as anything else did. Chapel of Saint-Java.

He walked towards that late chapel by the steps to the altar. Not much to see. Some fat white candles had burned down, none were burning now. People weren't allowed inside this morning: Edward Marriner was at work out front.

Ned crossed in front of the altar and worked his way back down the other side. This aisle was from 1695, the map told him. He stopped to get his bearings: this would be the north side, the cloister was south, his father was shooting the west facade. For no good reason it made him feel better to work that out.

This was a shorter nave, hit a wall partway down. Ned found himself back in the main section, looking up at a stained-glass window. He found another bench near the last side chapel by the bell tower. Saint-Catherine's, the brochure advised; it had been the university's chapel.

Ned imagined students hurrying here to confession five hundred years ago, then back across the road to lectures. What did they wear to school in those days? He popped in his buds again, dialing Pearl Jam on the wheel.

He was in the south of France. Well, forgive him for not doing cartwheels. His father would be shooting like a madman (his own word) from now to the middle of June. The photographs were for a big-deal book next Christmas. *Edward Marriner: Images of Provence*, accompanying a text by Oliver Lee. Oliver Lee was from London but had lived down here for the last thirty years, writing (Melanie had told him all this) six novels, including some prize-winners. Star English writer, star Canadian photographer, star French scenery. Big-deal book.

Ned's mother was in the Sudan.

The reports were of serious fighting again, north of Darfur. She was almost certainly there, he thought, leaning back on the bench, closing his eyes, trying to let the music envelop him. Angry music. Grunge.

Pearl Jam finished, Alanis Morissette came up next on his shuffle. The deal was, his mother would phone them here every second evening. That, Ned thought bitterly, was going to for sure keep her safe.

Doctors Without Borders was supposed to be respected and acknowledged everywhere, but they weren't always, not any more. The world had changed. Places like Iraq had proven that, and the Sudan was real far from being the smartest place on earth to be right now.

He pulled off the buds again. Alanis complained a lot, he decided, for a girl from the Ottawa Valley who absolutely had it made.

"Gregorian chants?" someone asked.

Ned jerked sideways along the bench, turning his head quickly. "What the—"

"Sorry! Did I scare you?"

"Hell, yes!" he snapped. "What do you think?"

He stood up. It was a girl, he saw.

She looked apologetic for a second, then grinned. She clasped her hands in front of her. "What have you to fear in this holy place, my child? What sins lie heavy on your heart?"

"I'll think of something," he said.

She laughed.

She looked to be about his own age, dressed in a black T-shirt and blue jeans, Doc Martens, a small green backpack. Tall, thin, freckles, American accent. Light brown hair to her shoulders.

"Murder? T. S. Eliot wrote a play about that," she said.

Ned made a face. Urk. One of those. "I know, *Murder in the Cathedral.* We're supposed to study it next year."

She grinned again. "I'm geeky that way. What can I say? Isn't this place amazing?"

"You think? I think it's a mess."

"But that's what's cool! Walk twenty steps and you go five hundred years. Have you seen the baptistry? This place *drips* with history."

Ned held out an open palm and looked up, as if to check for dripping water. "You *are* a geek, aren't you?"

"Can't tease if I admitted it. Cheap shot."

She was kind of pretty, in a skinny-dancer way.

Ned shrugged. "What's the baptistry?"

"The round part, by the front doors."

"Wait a sec." Something occurred to him. "How'd you get in? The place is closed for two hours."

"I saw. Someone's taking photos outside. Probably a brochure."

"No." He hesitated. "That's my dad. For a book."

"Really? Who is he?"

"You wouldn't know. Edward Marriner."

Her jaw actually dropped. Ned felt the familiar mix of pleasure and embarrassment. "You messing with me?" she gasped. "*Mountains and Gods*? I know that book. We *own* that book!"

"Well, cool. What will it get me?"

She gave him a suddenly shy look. Ned wasn't sure why he'd spoken that way. It wasn't really him. Ken and Barry talked that way to girls, but he didn't, usually. He cleared his throat.

"Get you a lecture on the baptistry," she said. "If you can stand it. I'm Kate. Not Katie, not Kathy."

He nodded his head. "Ned. Not Seymour, not Abdul."

She hesitated, then laughed again. "All right, fine, I deserved that. But I hate nicknames."

"Kate *is* a nickname."

"Yeah, but I picked it. Makes a difference."

"I guess. You never answered . . . how'd you get in?"

"Side door." She gestured across the way. "No one's watching the square on that side. Through the cloister. Seen that yet?"

Ned blinked. But he couldn't say, after, that any premonition had come to him. He was just confused, that's all.

"The door to the cloister is locked. I was there fifteen minutes ago."

"Nope. Open. The far one out to the street and the one leading in here. I just came through them. Come look. The cloister is really pretty."

It began then, because they didn't get to the cloister. Not yet.

Going across, they heard a sound: metal on metal. A banging, a harsh scrape, another bang.

"What the hell?" Ned murmured, stopping where he was. He wasn't sure why, but he kept his voice down.

Kate did the same. "That's the baptistry," she whispered. "Over there." She pointed. "Probably one of the priests, maybe a caretaker."

Another scraping sound.

Ned Marriner said, "I don't think so."

It would have been, in every possible way, wiser to ignore that noise, to go see the pretty cloister, walk out that way afterwards, into the morning streets of Aix. Get a croissant and a Coke somewhere with this girl named Kate.

His mother, however, was in the Sudan, having flown far away from them, again, to the heart of an insanely dangerous place. Ned came from courage—and from something else, though he didn't know that part yet.

He walked quietly towards the baptistry and peered down the three steps leading into that round, pale space. He'd gone right past it when he came in, he realized. He saw eight tall pillars, making a smaller circle inside it, with a dome high above, letting in more light than anywhere else.

"It's the oldest thing here," whispered the girl beside him. "By a lot, like 500 A.D."

He was about to ask her how she knew so many idiotic facts when he saw that a grate had been lifted from over a hole in the stone floor.

Then he saw the head and shoulders of a man appear from whatever opening that grate had covered. And Ned realized that this wasn't, that this couldn't be, a priest or a caretaker or anyone who *belonged* in here.

The man had his back to them. Ned lifted a hand, wordlessly, and pointed. Kate let out a gasp. The man in the pit didn't move, and then he did.

With an air of complete unreality, as if this were a video game he'd stumbled into, not anything that could be called real life, Ned saw the man reach inside his leather jacket and bring out a knife. Priests didn't wear leather, or carry knives.

The man laid it on the stone floor beside him—the blade pointing in their direction.

He still didn't turn around. They couldn't see his face. Ned saw long—very long—fingers. The man was bald, or had shaved his head. It was impossible to tell his age.

There was a silence; no one moved. *This would be a good spot to save the game,* Ned thought. *Then restart if my character gets killed.*

"He isn't here," the man said quietly. "I was quite sure . . . but he is playing with me again. He enjoys doing that."

Ned Marriner had never heard that tone in a voice. It chilled him, standing in shadow, looking towards the soft light of the baptistry.

The man had spoken in French. Ned's French was very good, after nine years of immersion classes at home in Montreal. He wondered about Kate, then realized she'd understood because, absurdly, as if making polite conversation—with a knife lying on the stone floor—she asked, in the same language, "Who isn't here? There's just a Roman street under there, right? It says so on the wall."

The man ignored her completely, as if she hadn't made any sounds that mattered in any way. Ned had a sense of a small man, but it was hard to tell, not knowing how deep the pit was. He still hadn't turned to look at them. It was time to run, obviously. This wasn't a computer game. He didn't move.

"Go away," the man said, as if sensing Ned's thought. "I have killed children before. I have no strong desire to do so now. Go and sit somewhere else. I will be leaving now."

Children? They weren't kids.

Stupidly, Ned said, "We've seen you. We could tell people . . ."

A hint of amusement in his voice, the man said dryly, "Tell them what? That someone lifted a grate and looked at the Roman paving? *Hélas*! All the gendarmes of France will be on the case."

Ned might have grown up in too quick-witted a household, in some ways. "No," he said, "we could say someone threatened us with a knife."

The man turned around, inside the opening in the floor.

He was clean-shaven, lean-faced. Dark, strong eyebrows, a long, straight nose, a thin mouth. The bald head made his cheekbones show prominently. Ned saw a scar on one cheek, curving behind his ear.

The man looked at them both a moment, where they stood together at the top of the three steps, before he spoke again. His eyes were deep-set; it was impossible to see their colour.

"A few gendarmes would be interested in that, I grant you." He shook his head. "But I am leaving. I see no reason to kill you. I will replace the grate. No damage has been done. To anything. Go away." And then, as they still stood there, more in shock than anything else, he took the knife and put it out of sight.

Ned swallowed.

"Come on!" whispered the girl named Kate. She pulled at his arm. He turned with her to go. Then looked back.

"Were you trying to rob something down there?" he asked.

His mother would have turned and asked the same thing, in fact, out of sheer stubbornness, a refusal to be dismissed, though Ned didn't actually know that.

The man in the baptistry looked up at him again and said, softly, after a moment, "No. Not that. I thought I was . . . here soon enough. I was wrong. I think the world will end before I ever find him in time. Or the sky will fall, as he would say."

Ned shook his head, the way a dog does, shaking water off when it comes in out of the rain. The words made so little sense it wasn't even funny. Kate was tugging at him again, harder this time.

He turned and walked away with her, back to where they'd been before. By Saint-Catherine's chapel.

They sat down on the same bench. Neither of them spoke. Across the echoing, empty space of the dark cathedral they heard a clang and scrape, then a bang again. Then nothing. He'd be leaving now.

Ned looked down at the iPod on his belt. It seemed, just then, to be the strangest object imaginable. A small rectangle that offered music. Any kind of music you wanted. Hundreds of hours of it. With little white buds you could put in your ears and block out the sounds of the world.

The world will end before I ever find him in time.

He looked over at the girl. She was biting her lower lip, staring straight ahead. Ned cleared his throat. It sounded loud. "Well, if Kate is for Katherine," he said brightly, "we're in the right place. You can do the praying."

"What the . . . ?" She looked at him.

He showed her the map, pointing to the name of the chapel. His bad joke.

"I'm not Catholic," she said.

He shrugged. "I doubt that matters."

"What . . . what do you think he was doing?" She'd seemed pretty confident, assertive, when she'd first come over to him. She didn't seem that way now. She looked scared, which was reasonable.

Ned swore. He didn't swear as much as some of the guys did, but this particular moment seemed to call for something. "I have *no* idea. What's down there?"

"I think they're just grates to let you look down and see the old Roman street. The tourist stuff on the wall also said there was a tomb, going back to the sixth century. But that's something I . . ." She stopped.

He stared at her.

"What?"

Kate sighed. "This is gonna sound geeky again, but I just *like* this stuff, okay? Don't laugh at me?"

"I'm nowhere close to laughing."

She said, "They didn't bury people inside city walls back then. It was forbidden. That's why there are catacombs and cemeteries in Rome and Paris and Arles and other places—outside the walls. They buried the dead outside."

"What are you saying?"

"Well, the info thing posted over there shows a tomb here from the sixth century. A little over from where . . . he was. So how did . . . well, how did someone get buried in here? Back then?"

"Shovels?" Ned said, more out of reflex than anything else.

She didn't smile.

"You think that's what that guy was? A tomb robber?" he asked.

"I don't think anything. Really. He said he wasn't. But he also said . . ." She shook her head. "Can we go?"

Ned nodded. "Not through the front, we might step into a shot and my dad would kill himself, and then me. He gets intense when he's working."

"We can leave the way I came in, through the cloister."

A penny dropped for Ned. "Right. That'll be how *he* got in, I bet. Between my seeing it locked and your finding the two doors open."

"You think he's gone out that way?"

"Long gone by now." He hesitated. "Show me that baptistry first."

"Are you crazy?"

"He's gone, Kate."

"But why do you . . . ?"

Ned looked at her. "History lesson? You promised."

She didn't smile. "Why are you playing boy detective?"

He didn't have a really good answer. "This is a bit too weird. I want to try to understand."

"Ned, he said he'd killed children."

He shook his head. "I don't think . . . that means what we think it means."

"And *that* sounds like a line from a bad movie."

"Maybe. But come on."

"This where the creepy music starts?"

"Come on, Kate."

He got up and she followed. She could have left by herself, he thought later, sitting on the terrace of the villa that evening. They didn't know each other at all that first morning. She could have gone out the way she'd come in, saying goodbye, or not, as she pleased.

They walked together down the three steps into the baptistry and stood above the grate, beside that inner ring of pillars. The light was beautiful after the dimness of the cathedral, streaming down through windows in the dome above the shallow well in the centre.

Ned knelt and peered through the bars of the grate. If it was supposed to be a viewing point, it wasn't much of one. It was too dark down there to see where the sunken space might go.

"Here's the bit about the tomb," Kate said. She was at the west wall, in front of some tourist information, a typed, laminated sheet, framed in wood. Ned walked over. Basically, it was just another map-key to this part of the interior. Kate pointed at a letter on the map, and then the text keyed to it. As she'd said, it seemed someone was buried there, "a citizen of Aix," in the sixth century.

"And look at this," she said.

She was pointing to an alcove on their left. Ned saw a really old wall painting of a bull or a cow and below it an almost obliterated mosaic fragment. He could make out a small bird, part of some much larger work. The rest of it was worn away.

"These are even older," Kate said.

"What was this place, before? Where we are?"

"The forum was here. Centre of town. The Roman city was founded about a hundred and something years B.C. by a guy named Sextius when the Romans first started to take over Provence from the Celts. He named it after himself, Aquae Sextiae. *Aquae*, because of the waters. There were hot springs until recently. That's why there are so many fountains. Have you seen them?"

"We just got here. The cathedral was built on top of the forum?"

"Uh-huh. There's a sketch of it on the wall. Where your dad is now was like the major intersection of the Roman town. That's why . . . that's why I still don't understand someone being buried here, back then."

"Well, it was hundreds of years after, wasn't it? It says sixth century."

She looked dubious. "It was still taboo, I'm almost sure."

"Google it later, or I will."

"Boy detective?" Kate sounded as if she was trying to tease but didn't actually feel like it. Ned could relate.

He shook his head again. He still wasn't quite sure what he was doing, or why. He looked at that faded bull on the wall. It sure didn't look like any church art he knew. This place was *really* old. He shivered. And perhaps because of that, *because* he felt scared, he walked quickly back, knelt again by the grate, put both hands on it, and pulled.

It was heavier than he'd expected. He managed to shift it a bit, making the scraping sound they'd heard before. The man had broken some clasp or catch, Ned saw. He just had to lift and slide, but . . .

"Help me, this sucker's heavy!"

"Are you insane?"

"No . . . but my fingers'll be crushed if you don't . . ."

She moved, to the part he'd levered up and, on her knees beside him, helped slide it over. There was an opening now, large enough for a small man, or a teenaged boy, to get through.

"You are *not* going down there," Kate said. "I am not staying to watch—"

"I bequeath you my iPod," Ned replied, handing it to her. And then, before he had time to think about it and get *really* frightened, he put his feet over the edge of the pit, turned so he was facing the side, and lowered himself. Just as he did he started thinking about snakes or scorpions or rats skittering through the dark, ancient space below. Insane wasn't a bad word to use, he decided.

His feet touched bottom and he let go. He looked down, couldn't even see his running shoes.

"You wouldn't by any chance have—"

"Take this," said the girl named Kate, in the same moment. She handed him a small red metal flashlight. "I keep one in my pack. For walks at night."

"Efficient of you. Remind me," Ned said, "to introduce you to someone named Melanie." He turned on the beam.

"You going to bother telling me *why* you are doing this?" she asked, from above.

"Would if I knew," he said, truthfully.

He shone the beam along the dark grey stones beside and below him. He knelt. The slabs were damp, cold, really big, like for a road—which is what she'd said they'd been.

On his right the foundation wall was close, below the grate. Straight ahead the flashlight lit the short distance to the sunken well, which was dry now, of course. He saw worn steps. The beam picked out a rusted pipe sticking out, attached to nothing. There were spiderwebs entangling it.

No snakes, no rats. Yet.

To his left the space opened into a corridor.

He'd been expecting that, actually. That was the way back towards the main part of the cathedral, where the placard on the wall had said a tomb would be. Ned took a deep breath.

"Remember," he said, "the iPod's yours. Don't delete the Led Zep, or Coldplay."

He bent low, because he had to. He didn't get very far, maybe twenty steps. It didn't *go* farther. It just hit another wall. He'd be right under the first nave here, he thought. The roof was really low.

His flashlight beam played along the rough, damp surface in front of him. It was sealed, closed off. Nothing that even vaguely resembled a tomb. It looked like there were just the two corridors: from the grate to the well, and this one.

"Where are you?" Kate called.

"I'm okay. It's closed up. There's nothing here. Like he said. Maybe this whole opening was just for getting down to fix the pipes. Plumbing. Bet there are other pipes, and more grates around the other side of the well."

"I'll go look," she called. "Does this mean I don't get the iPod?"

Ned laughed, startling himself as the sound echoed.

And it was then, as he turned to go back, that the bright, narrow beam of Kate's flashlight, playing along the corridor, illuminated a recessed space, a niche cut in the stone wall, and Ned saw what was resting in it.

CHAPTER II

He didn't touch it. He wasn't that brave, or that stupid. The hairs were actually standing up on the back of his neck.

"Another grate," Kate called cheerfully from above. "Maybe you were right. Maybe after they covered up the Roman street they just needed—"

"I found something," he said.

His voice sounded strained, unnatural. The flashlight beam wavered. He tried to hold it steady but the movement had illuminated something else and he looked at this now. Another recess. The same thing in it, he thought at first, then he realized it wasn't. Not quite the same.

"Found? What do you mean?" Kate called.

Her voice, only a few steps away and up, seemed to Ned to be coming from really far off, from a world he'd left behind when he came down here. He couldn't answer. He was actually unable to speak. He looked, the beam wobbling from one object to the other.

The first one, set in an egg-shaped hollow in the wall and mounted carefully on a clay base, was a human skull.

He was quite certain this wasn't from any tomb down here, it was too exposed, too obviously set here to be seen. This wasn't a burial. The base was like the kind his mother used on the mantelpiece or the shelves on either side of the fireplace back home to hold some object she'd found in her travels, an artifact from Sri Lanka, or Rwanda.

This skull had been placed to be found, not laid to some dark eternal rest.

The second object made that even clearer. In a precisely similar hollowed-out recess beside the first, and set on an identical clay rest, was a sculpture of a human head.

It was smooth, worn down, as if with age. The only harsh line was at the bottom, as if it had been decapitated, jaggedly severed at the neck. It looked terrifying, speaking or signalling to him across centuries: a message he really didn't want to understand. In some ways it frightened him even more than the bones. He'd seen skulls before; you made jokes, like with the one in science lab, *"Alas, poor Yorick! Such a terrible name!"*

He'd never seen anything like this carving. Someone had gone to great pains to get down here, hollow out a place, fit it to a base beside a real skull in an underground corridor leading nowhere. And the meaning was . . . what?

"What *is* it?" Kate called. "Ned, you're scaring me."

He still couldn't answer her. His mouth was too dry, words weren't coming. Then, forcing himself to look more closely by the light of the flashlight beam, Ned saw that the sculpted head was completely smooth on the top, as if bald. And there was a gash in the stone face—a scarring of it—along one cheek, and up behind the ear.

He got out of there, as fast as he could.

THEY SAT IN THE CLOISTER in morning light, side by side on a wooden bench. Ned hadn't been sure how much farther he could walk before sitting down.

There was a small tree in front of them, the one on the cover of the brochure. It was bright with springtime flowers in the small, quiet garden. They were close to the door that led back into the cathedral. There was no breeze here. It was a peaceful place.

His hands, holding Kate's red flashlight, were still trembling.

He must have left Melanie's brochure in the baptistry, he realized. They'd stayed just long enough to close the grate, dragging it back across the open space, scraping it on the stone floor. He hadn't even wanted to do that, but something told him it needed to be done, covering over what lay below.

"Tell me," said Kate.

She was biting her lip again. A habit, obviously. He drew a breath and, looking down at his hands and then at the sunlit tree, but not at the girl, told about the skull and the sculpted head. And the scar.

"Oh, God," she said.

Which was just about right. Ned leaned back against the rough wall.

"What do we do?" Kate asked. "Tell the . . . the archaeologists?"

Ned shook his head. "This isn't an ancient find. Think about it a second."

"What do you mean? You said . . ."

"I said it looked old, but those things haven't been there long. Can't have been. Kate, people must have been down there dozens of times. More than that. That's what archaeologists *do*. They'll have gone looking at those . . . Roman street slabs, searching for the tomb, studying the well."

"The font," she said. "That's what it is. Not a well."

"Whatever. But, point is, that guy and me, we're not the first people down there. People would have seen and recorded and . . . and *done* something with those things if they'd been there a long time. They'd be in a museum by now. There'd be stuff written about them. They'd be on that tourist thing on the wall, Kate."

"What are you saying?"

"I'm pretty sure someone put them there just a little while ago." He hesitated. "And carved out the spaces for them, too."

"Oh, God," she said again.

She looked at him. In the light he could see her eyes were light brown, like her hair. She had freckles across her nose and cheeks. "You think for . . . our guy to see?"

Our guy. He didn't smile, though he would have, another time. His hands had stopped shaking, he was pleased to see.

He nodded. "The head was him, for sure. Bald, the scar. Yeah, it was there for him."

"Okay. Um, put there by who? I mean, whom?"

He did smile a little this time. "You're hopeless."

"I'm thinking out loud, boy detective. Got your cereal box badge?"

"Left it behind."

"Yeah, you left this, too." She fished his brochure out of her pack.

He took it from her. "You gotta meet Melanie," he said again.

He looked at the guide. The picture on the cover had been taken this same time of year; the flowers on the tree were identical. He showed her.

"Nice," she said. "It's a Judas tree. Who's Melanie?"

Figured, that she'd know the tree. "My dad's assistant. He has three people with him, and someone from the publisher coming, and me."

"And what do you do?"

He shrugged. "Hang out. Crawl into tunnels." He looked around. "Anything here?"

"Fresh air. I was getting sick inside."

"Me too, down there. I shouldn't have gone."

"Probably not."

They were silent a moment. Then Kate said, in a bright, fake tour-guide voice, "The columns show Bible tales, mostly. David and Goliath is over there."

She pointed to their right. Ned got up and walked over. His legs seemed okay. His heart was still pretty fast, as if he'd finished a training run.

He saw a linked pair of round columns supporting a heavy square one, which in turn held up the walkway roof. On the top square were carved two intertwined figures: a smooth-faced man above the much larger head and twisted-over body of another one. David and Goliath?

He looked back at Kate, who was still on the bench. "Jeez, how did you figure this out?"

She grinned. "I didn't. I'm cheating. There's another guide thing on the wall farther down. I read it when I came through from outside. The Queen of Sheba is on the other side." She gestured across the garden towards the walkway opposite.

Because she was pointing, Ned looked that way, which he wouldn't have done otherwise. And because he was standing where he was, he saw the rose resting against the two round columns of another pillar on the far side.

And it was then—just then—that he began to feel really odd.

It wasn't fear (that had been in him awhile by then) or excitement; this was like something unblocking or unlocking, changing . . . just about everything, really.

Slowly, he went around that way along the shaded cloister walk, past the door to the street that Kate had used to get in. He would have gone out that way with her a moment before. Only a moment, and the story would have stopped for them.

He went along that side and turned up the far one, opposite where they'd been. Kate was still sitting on the wooden bench, the green backpack on the stone paving beside her. Ned turned his eyes to the pillar in front of him, with the single rose leaning between the two columns. He looked at the carving.

It wasn't the Queen of Sheba.

He was as sure of that as he'd been about anything in his life. Whatever the printed sheet on the wall might tell you, that wasn't who this was. They didn't always know, the people who wrote brochures and guidebooks. They might pretend, but they didn't always know.

He was aware of Kate getting up and coming towards him now, but he couldn't take his eyes from the woman on the pillar. This was the only one of all the slender, doubled columns here that had a full-length figure on it. His heart was pounding again.

She was worn almost completely away, Ned saw, more eroded than any of the other, smaller carvings he'd passed. He didn't know why that was, at first. And then, because of what was opening up inside him, he thought he did know.

She had been *made* this way, barely carved into the stone, the features less sharply defined, meant to fade, to leave, like something lost from the beginning.

She was delicately slender, he saw, and would have been tall. You could still see elegant, careful details in the tunic she wore and the robe that swept to her ankles. He could see braided hair falling past her shoulders, but her nose and mouth were almost gone, worn away, and her eyes could barely be seen. Even so, Ned had a sense—an illusion?—of a lifted eyebrow, something ironic in that slim grace.

He shook his head. This was an eroded sculpture in an obscure cloister. It should have been completely unremarkable, the kind of thing you walked right past, getting on with your life.

Ned had a sense of time suddenly, the *weight* of it. He was standing in a garden in the twenty-first century, and he was sharply aware of how far back beyond even a medieval sculpture the history of this ground stretched. Men and women had lived and died here for thousands of years. Getting on with their lives.

And maybe they didn't always go away after, entirely.

It wasn't the sort of thought he'd ever had before.

"She was beautiful," he said. Whispered it, actually.

"Well, Solomon thought so," said Kate mildly, coming to stand beside him.

Ned shook his head. She didn't get it.

"Did you see the rose?" he said.

"What rose?"

"Behind her."

Kate dropped her pack and leaned forward over the railing that protected the garden.

"There aren't . . . there aren't any rose bushes here," she said, after a while.

"No. I think he brought it. Put it here before he went inside."

"He? Our guy? You mean . . . ?"

Ned nodded. "And he's still here."

"*What?*"

He had just realized that last part himself, the thought arriving as he formed the words. He'd been thinking, reaching within, trying to concentrate. And it had come to him.

He was scaring himself now, but there was something he could *see* in his mind—a presence of light or colour, an aura. Ned cleared his throat. You could run away from a moment like this, close your eyes, tell yourself it wasn't real.

Or you could say aloud, instead, as clearly as you could manage, lifting your voice, "You told us you were leaving. Why are you still up there?"

He couldn't actually see anyone, but it didn't matter. Things had changed. He would place the beginning, later, as when he'd walked across the cloister and looked at the almost-vanished face of a woman carved in stone hundreds of years ago.

Kate let out a small scream, and stepped quickly back beside him on the walkway.

There was a silence, broken by a car horn sounding from a nearby street. If he hadn't been so certain, Ned might have thought that the experience underground had rattled him completely, making him say and do entirely weird things.

Then they heard someone reply, eliminating that possibility.

"I will now confess to being surprised."

The words came from the slanting roof above and to their right, towards the upper windows of the cathedral. They couldn't see him. It didn't matter. Same voice.

Kate whimpered again, but she didn't run.

"Believe me," said Ned, trying to sound calm, "I'm more surprised."

"I guarantee I beat you both," said Kate. "Please don't kill us."

It felt so strange to Ned, over and above everything else, to be standing next to someone who was actually speaking words like *don't kill us*, and meaning them.

His life hadn't prepared him for anything like this.

The voice from the roof was grave. "I said I wouldn't."

"You also said you'd done it before," Kate said.

"I have." Then, after another silence, "You would be mistaken in believing I am a good man."

Ned would remember that. He'd remember almost everything, in fact. He said, "You know that your face is down in the corridor, back there?"

"You went down? That was brave." A pause. "Yes, of course it is."

Of course? The voice was low, clear, precise. Ned realized—his brain hadn't processed this properly before—that he'd spoken in English himself, and the man had replied the same way.

"I guess it isn't your skull beside it." Real bad joke.

"Someone might have liked it to be."

Ned dealt with that, or tried to. And then something occurred to him, in the same inexplicable way as before. "Who . . . who was the model for *her*, then?" he asked. He was looking at the woman on the column. He found it hard not to look at her.

Silence above them. Ned sensed anger, rising and suppressed. Inside his mind he could actually place the figure on the roof tiles now, exactly where he was: seen within, silver-coloured.

"I think you ought to go now," the man said finally. "You have blundered into a corner of a very old story. It is no place for children. Believe me," he said again.

"I do," Kate said, with feeling. "Believe me!"

Ned Marriner felt his own anger kick in, hard. He was surprised how much of that was in him these days. "Right," he said. "Run along, kids. Well, what am I supposed to do with this . . . feeling I have in me now? Knowing this is *not* the goddamn Queen of Sheba, knowing exactly where you are up there. This is completely messed up. What am I supposed to *do* with it?"

After another silence, the voice above came again, more gently. "You are hardly the first person to have an awareness of such things. You must know that, surely? As for what you are to do . . ." That hint of amusement again. "Am I become a counsellor? How very odd. What *is* there to do in a life? Finish growing up; most people never do. Find what joy there is to find. Try to avoid men with knives. We are not . . . this story is not important for you."

Ned's anger was gone as quickly as it had flared. That, too, was strange. In the lingering resonance of those words, he heard himself say, "Could we be important for it? Since I seem to have—"

"No," said the voice above them, flatly dismissive. "As you just put it: run along. That will be best, whatever it does to your vanity. I am not as patient as I might once have been."

"Oh, really? Not like when you sculpted her?" Ned asked.

"What?" cried Kate again.

In that same instant there came an explosion of colour in Ned's mind and then of movement, above and to their right: a swift, coiled blur hurtling down. The man on the roof somersaulted off the slanting tiles to land in the garden in front of them. His face was vivid with rage, bone white. He looked exactly like the sculpted head underground, Ned thought.

"How did you know that?" the man snarled. *"What did he tell you?"*

He was of middling height, as Ned had guessed. He wasn't as old as the bald head might suggest; could even be called handsome, but was too lean, as if he'd been stretched, pulled, and the lack of hair accentuated that, along with the hard cheekbones and the slash of his mouth. His grey-blue eyes were also hard. The long fingers, Ned saw, were flexing, as if they wanted to grab someone by the throat. Someone. Ned knew who that would be.

But really, *really* oddly, he wasn't afraid now.

Less than an hour ago he'd walked into an empty church to kill some time with his music, bored and edgy, and frightened beyond any fully acknowledged thought for his mother. Only that last was still true. An hour ago the world had been a different place.

"Tell me? No one told me anything!" he said. "I don't know how I know these things. I asked *you* that, remember? You just said I'm not the first."

"Ned," said Kate. Her voice creaked like it needed oiling. "This sculpture was made eight hundred years ago."

"I know," he said.

The man in front of them said, "A little more than that."

They saw him close his eyes then open them, staring coldly at Ned. The leather jacket was slate grey, his shirt underneath was black. "You have surprised me again. It doesn't often happen."

"I believe that," Ned said.

"This is still not for you. You have no idea of what . . . you have no *role*. I made a mistake, back there. If you won't go, I will have to leave you. There is too much anger in me. I do not feel very responsible."

Ned knew about that kind of anger, a little. "You will not let us . . . do anything?"

A movement of the wide mouth. "The offer is generous, but if you knew even a little you would realize how meaningless it is." He turned away, a dark-clad figure, slender, unsettlingly graceful.

"Last question?" Ned lifted a hand, stupidly—as if he were in class.

The figure stopped but didn't turn back to them. He was as they'd first seen him, from behind, but lit by the April sun in a garden.

"Why now?" Ned asked. "Why here?"

They could hear the traffic from outside again. Aix was a busy, modern city, and they were right in the middle of it.

The man was silent for what seemed a long time. Ned had a sense that he was actually near to answering, but then he shook his head. He walked across the middle of the cloister and stepped between two columns and over the low barrier back to the walkway by the door that led out to the street and world.

"Wait!"

It was Kate this time.

The man paused again, his back still to them. It was the girl's voice, it seemed to Ned. He wouldn't have stopped a second time for Ned, that was the feeling he had.

"Do you have a name?" Kate called, something wistful in her tone.

He did turn, after all, at that.

He looked at Kate across the bright space between. He was too far away for them to make out his expression.

"Not yet," he said.

Then he turned again and went out, opening the heavy door and closing it behind him.

They stood where they were, looking briefly at each other, in that enclosed space separated, in so many ways, from the world.

Ned, in the grip of emotions he didn't even come close to understanding, walked a few steps. He felt as if he needed to run for miles, up and down hills until the sweat poured out of him.

From here he could see the rose again between the two pillars, behind the carving. People said she was the Queen of Sheba. It was posted that way on the wall. How did he *know* they were wrong? It was ridiculous.

Directly in front of him the corner pillar was much larger than those beside it—all four of the corners were. This one, he realized, without much surprise, had another bull carved at the top. It was done in a style different from David and Goliath, and nothing at all like the woman.

Two bulls now, one in the baptistry, fifteen hundred years ago, and this one carved—if he understood properly—hundreds of years after that. He stared at it, almost angrily.

"What do goddamn bulls have to do with anything?" he demanded.

Kate cleared her throat. "New Testament. Symbol of St. Luke."

Ned stared at the creature at the top of the pillar in front of him.

"I doubt it," he said finally. "Not this one. Not the old one inside, either."

"What are you saying now?"

He looked over, saw the strain on her face, and guessed he probably looked a lot the same. Maybe they *were* kids. Someone had pointed a knife towards them. And that was almost the least of it.

He looked at the sculpted woman where Kate stood and felt that same hard tug at his heart again. Pale-coloured stone in morning light, almost entirely worn away. Barely anything to be seen, as if she were a rendering of memory itself. Or of what time did to men and women, however much they'd been loved.

And where had *that* idea come from? He thought of his mother. He shook his head.

"I don't know what I'm saying. Let's get out of here."

"Need a drink, Detective?"

He managed a smile. "Coke will do fine."

KATE KNEW WHERE she was going. She led him under the clock tower and past the city hall to a café a few minutes from the cathedral.

Ned sat with his Coke, watched her sip an espresso without sugar (impressed him, he had to admit), and learned that she'd been here since early March, on an exchange between her school in New York City and one here in Aix. Her family had hosted a French girl last term, and Kate was with the girl's family until school ended at the beginning of summer.

Her last name was Wenger. She planned to do languages in university, or history, or both. She wanted to teach, or maybe study law. Or both. She took jazz dance classes (he'd guessed something like that). She ran three miles every second or third day in Manhattan, which was not what Ned did, but was pretty good. She liked Aix a whole lot, but not Marie-Chantal, the girl she was staying with. Seemed Marie-Chantal was a secret smoker in the bedroom they shared, and a party girl, *and* used Kate to cover for her when she was at her boyfriend's late or skipping class to meet him.

"It sucks, lying for her," she said. "I mean, she's not even really a friend."

"Sounds like a babe, though. Got her phone number?"

Kate made a face. "You aren't even close to serious."

"And why's that?"

"Because you're in love with a carving in a cloister, that's why."

That brought them back a little too abruptly to what they'd been trying to avoid.

Ned didn't say anything. He sipped his drink and looked around. The long, narrow café had two small tables on the street, but those had been taken, so they were inside, close to the door. The morning traffic was busy—cars, mopeds, a lot of people walking the medieval cobblestones.

"Sorry," Kate Wenger said after a moment. "That was a weird thing to say."

He shrugged. "I have no clue what to make of that sculpture. Or what happened."

She was biting at her lip again.

"Why was he . . . our guy . . . why was he looking down *there*? For whatever it was? Could it have been the font, something about the water?"

Ned shook his head. "Don't think so. The skull and the carved head were the other way, along the corridor." He had a thought. "Kate . . . if someone was buried there, they'd have walled him up, right? Not left a coffin lying around."

She nodded her head. "Sure."

"So maybe he was thinking the wall might have just been opened up. For some reason."

Kate leaned back in her chair. "God, Ned Marriner, is this, like, a *vampire* story?"

"I don't know what it is. I don't think so."

"But you said *he* made that carving in the cloister. You do know how old that thing is?"

"Look, forget what I said there. I was a bit out of it."

"Nope." She shook her head. "You weren't. When he came down from the roof I thought he was going to kill you. And then he *said* when it was done."

He sighed. "You're going to ask how I knew," he said.

"It did cross my mind." She said it without smiling.

"Bet Marie-Chantal wouldn't bug me about it."

"She'd be clueless, checking her eyeliner and her cellphone for text messages. Am I bugging you?"

"No. Does she really get text messages on her eyeliner?"

Kate still didn't smile. "Something did happen to you back there."

"Yeah. I'm all right now. Since he left, I feel normal." He tried to laugh. "Wanna make out?"

She ignored that, which was what it deserved. "You figure it's over? Just something to do with . . . I don't know."

He nodded. "That's it. Something to do with I don't know."

He was joking too much because the truth was that although he *did* feel all right now, sitting here with a girl from New York, from *now*, drinking a Coke that tasted exactly the way it was supposed to—he wasn't sure whatever had happened was over.

In fact, being honest with himself, he was pretty certain it wasn't. He wasn't going to say that, though.

He looked at his watch. "I should check in before lunch, I guess." He hesitated. This part was tricky, but he was a long way from home and the guys who would needle him. "You got a phone number? We can keep in touch?"

She smiled. "If you promise no more comments on my roommate."

"Marie-Chantal? My main squeeze? That's a deal-breaker."

She made a face, but tore a sheet out of a spiral-bound agenda she pulled from her pack and scribbled the number where she was staying and her cellphone number. Ned took from his wallet the card on which Melanie had neatly printed (in green) the villa address, the code for the gate, the house phone, her mobile, his father's, the Canadian consulate, and the numbers of two taxi companies. She'd put a little smiley face at the bottom.

When she'd handed the card to him last night he'd pointed out that she hadn't given him their latitude and longitude.

He read Kate the villa number. She wrote it down.

"You have school tomorrow?"

She nodded. "Cut this morning, can't tomorrow. I'm there till five. Meet here after? Can you find it?"

He nodded. "Easy. Just down the road from the skull in the underground corridor."

She did laugh this time, after a second.

They paid for their drinks and said goodbye outside. He watched her walk away through the morning street, then he turned and went back the other way, along a road laid down two thousand years ago.

CHAPTER III

The morning shoot was wrapping when Ned got back. He helped Steve and Greg load the van. They left it in the cathedral square, illegally parked but with a windshield permit from the police, and walked to lunch at an open-oven pizza place ten minutes away.

The pizza was good, Ned's father was irritable. That wasn't unusual during a shoot, especially at the start, but Ned could tell his dad wasn't really unhappy with how things had gone this first morning. He wouldn't *admit* that, but it showed.

Edward Marriner sipped a beer and looked at Ned across the table. "Anything inside I need to know about?"

Even when Ned was young his father had asked his opinions whenever Ned was with him on a shoot. When Ned was a kid it had pleased him to be consulted this way. He felt important, included. More recently it had become irksome, as if he was being babied. In fact, "more recently" extended right up to this morning, he realized.

Something had changed. He said, "Not too much, I don't think. Pretty dark, hard to find angles. Like you said, it's all jumbled. You should look at the baptistry, though, on the right when you go in. There's light there and it is really old. Way older than the rest." He hesitated. "The cloister was open, I got a look in there, too."

"The important cloister's in Arles," Melanie said, dabbing carefully at her lips with a napkin. For someone with a green streak in black hair, she was awfully tidy, Ned thought.

"Whatever. This one looked good," he said. "You could set up a pretty shot of the garden, but if you don't want that, you might take a look at some of the columns." He hesitated again, then said, "There's David and Goliath, other Bible stuff. Saints on the four corners. One sculpture's supposed to be the Queen of Sheba. She's really worn away, but have a look."

His father stroked his brown moustache. Edward Marriner was notorious for that old-fashioned handlebar moustache. It was a trademark; he had it on his business card, signed his work with two upward moustache curves. People sometimes needled him about it, but he'd simply say his wife liked the look, and that was that.

Now he said, looking at his son, "I'll check both tomorrow. We've got two more hours cleared so I'll use them inside if Greg says the stitched digitals this morning are all right and we don't have to do them again. Will I need lights?"

"Inside? For sure," Ned said. "Maybe the generator, I have no idea how the power's set up. Depending what you want to do in the cloister you may want the lights and bounces there, too."

"Melanie said they do concerts inside," Greg said. "They'll have power."

"The baptistry's off to one side."

"Bring the generator, Greg, don't be lazy," Edward Marriner said, but he was smiling. Bearded Greg made a face at Ned. Steve just grinned. Melanie looked pleased, probably because Ned seemed engaged, and she saw that as part of her job.

Ned wasn't sure why he was sending the team inside. Maybe taking photos tomorrow, the sheer routine of it—shouted instructions, clutter, film bags and cables, lights and lenses and reflectors—would take away some of the strangeness of what had happened. It might bring the place back to now . . . from wherever it had been this morning.

It also occurred to him that he'd like a picture of that woman on the column. He couldn't have said why, but he knew he wanted it. He even wanted to go back in to look at her again now, but he wasn't about to do that.

His father was going to walk around town after lunch with two cameras and black-and-white film to check out some fountains and doorways that Barrett, the art director, had made notes about when he was here. Oliver Lee had apparently written something on Aix's fountains and the hot springs the Romans had discovered. Kate Wenger had just told him about those. She just about *forced* you to call her a geek, that girl.

For the book, Ned's father had to balance the things he wanted to photograph with pictures that matched Lee's text. That was partly Barrett Reinhardt's job: to merge the work of two important men in a big project. His idea, apparently, was to have smaller black-and-white pictures tucked into the text that Lee had written, along with Marriner's full-page or double-page colour shots.

Ned didn't feel like looking at fountains. He knew what he *did* need to do. Greg was going back up to the villa to upload the digitals from this morning and check them on the monitor. He was also going to confirm by phone the arrangements for shooting in Arles, about an hour away, the day after tomorrow.

Melanie handed Greg detailed instructions about that, printed in her usual green ink. Ned saw a smiley face at the bottom of the card. He was pleased to see he wasn't the only one she did that to.

He rode back with Greg in the van, changed into a faded-out grey T-shirt, and shorts, clipped on his water bottle and pedometer, put the iPod in its armband, and went for a run. He had essays to write here, and a training log to complete for his track coach. Both were homework, really.

The running was better.

Melanie had told him the night before that if he went down their laneway and turned right at the road instead of left towards town, then kept going as it curved back uphill, he'd end up eventually where the road ended at some area where people biked and jogged in the countryside. She said there was supposed to be an old tower up there to look at.

It irritated him, as usual, that she was organized to the point of planning his training routes, but he had no better idea where to go, and there wasn't a good reason not to try that path.

It was a steep downhill on their little road past the other villas, and then steadily back up for a long, winding way along the ridge above. Up-and-down was good, of course. Ned ran on the cross-country team, this was what he needed.

He'd begun to think he'd gone wrong before he finally came to the car barrier. On the other side of it he found the trail. There were arrows on a wooden pole pointing one way towards a village called Vauvenargues and in the other direction to that tower Melanie had mentioned. Someone went by on a mountain bike towards Vauvenargues. Ned went the other way.

The tower wasn't far. The trail continued down and around it towards the northern edges of Aix, it looked like. Ned didn't like to stop during a run, no one did, but the view from up here was pretty cool and so was the round, ruined lookout tower. He wondered how old it was.

This whole place was just saturated in the past, he thought. Layers and layers of it. It could get to you, one way or another. He took off the earbuds and drank some water.

There was a low, really lame fence around the tower. A sign said it was dangerous to cross and a bigger fence had been authorized and was coming, but there was no one in sight now so Ned went over the railing and then he bent and stepped into the tower through a crumbled opening in the honey-coloured stones.

It was dark inside after the sunlight. There was no door anywhere, just the one broken opening. He looked up in a high, empty space. He could see the sky a long way above, a small circle of blue-black. It was as if he were at the bottom of a well. There were probably bats, he thought. There must have been a stairway once, winding up, but there was nothing now. He wondered what this had guarded against, what they'd been watching for up here.

He felt himself cooling down too much in the shade, not good. You pulled muscles that way. He stepped back into the sunshine, blinking, and gazed down at the city. There was an aqueduct in the distance, on the far side of Aix, vividly clear. After a moment, Ned spotted the bell tower of the cathedral in the middle of town, and that brought him back to this morning. He was nowhere close to wanting that.

He turned and started running again, back the way he'd come, but with the stop and cooling down and jet lag, he had lost his rhythm. He found it harder going than he should have, past the car barrier and downhill now along the road. It was a good jogging route, though, had to give Melanie credit. Next time he could go the other way at the signpost, keep going, log his proper distance.

He was halfway back up their own steep road, leading to Villa Sans Souci at the top, when he realized something.

He stopped running, having actually shocked himself.

Why now? he had said, and the man in the grey leather jacket hadn't replied. Maybe Ned had an answer, after all. Maybe it even mattered, for the first time, that when she was alive his grandmother had told him some of her old stories.

Ned walked thoughtfully up the last part of the hill and punched the gate code to get onto the property. He paced up and down the terrace for a bit, stretching. He thought about jumping in the pool, but it wasn't that warm, and he went upstairs and showered instead, dropping his clothes in the hamper for the cleaning help. The villa had been rented with two women to work for them. Both were named Vera, which made for challenges. Greg had named them Veracook and Veraclean.

Pulling on his jeans, Ned went down and into the kitchen. He got a Coke from the fridge. Veracook, clad in black, grey hair pulled tightly in a bun, was there. She had baked some kind of hard biscuits. He took one. From by the stove, she smiled approval.

Greg was on his cellphone in front of the computer in the dining room, so the house line was free. Ned went back upstairs and into his father's bedroom and dialed the mobile number Kate Wenger had given him.

"*Bonjour?*"

"Um, hi, I'm looking for Marie-Chantal."

"Screw you, Ned." But she laughed. "Miss me already? How sweet."

He felt himself flush, was glad she couldn't see it. "I just came in from a run. Um, I realized something."

"That you *did* miss me? I'm flattered." She was sassy on the phone, he thought. He wondered how she was on IM or texting. Everyone got looser online.

"No, listen. Um, it's April thirtieth on Thursday. Then May Day."

Kate was silent. He was wondering if he'd have to explain, then heard her say, "Jeez, Ned. Beltaine? That's a *major* deal. Ghosts and souls, like Hallowe'en. How do *you* know this? You a closet nerd?"

"My mom's family's from Wales. My grandmother told me some of this stuff. We used to go on a picnic sometimes, on the first of May."

"Want to go on a picnic?"

"If you bring Marie-Chantal." He hesitated. "Kate, where were the Celts around here? *Were* they here?"

"Yeah, they were. I can find out where."

"I can, too, I guess."

"No, you leave the heavy lifting to me, Grasshopper. You just keep running and hopping. See you tomorrow after school?"

"See you." He hung up, grinning in spite of himself. It was nice, he thought, to meet a girl in a situation where he didn't have to explain her, or what was going down, to the other guys. Privacy, that was the thing. You didn't get a lot of it back home.

THEY HAD DINNER at the villa, French time: after eight o'clock. The clear understanding, Melanie explained seriously, was that they *had* to eat here every so often or Veracook would get insulted and depressed ("Veradepressed!" Greg said) and start burning their food and stuff like that.

Before they ate, Ned's father took a vodka and tonic out on the terrace while the others went into the pool. Melanie, tiny as she was, looked pretty good in a bathing suit, Ned decided. She made a big deal about the water being freezing cold (it was) but got herself in. Steve was a swimmer, had the long arms and legs. He was methodically doing laps, or trying to—the pool wasn't really big enough.

As Ned and his father sat watching them, Greg suddenly burst through the terrace doors, sprang down the wide stone steps, across the grass, and cannonballed into the water, wearing the baggiest, most worn-out bathing suit Ned had ever seen.

Edward Marriner, laughing, offered an immediate pay bonus if Greg promised to use their next coffee break to buy a new swimsuit in town and spare them the sight of this one again. Melanie shouted a suggestion that Greg could skinny-dip if he wanted to save the money. Greg, splashing and whooping in the frigid water, threatened to take her up on it.

"You wouldn't dare," she said.

"And why not?"

Melanie laughed. "Shrinkage in cold water. Male pride. End of story."

"You have," Greg said after a moment, "a point." Steve, who had stopped his laps, laughed aloud.

Up on the terrace, Ned looked at his father and they exchanged a smile.

"You okay so far?" his dad asked.

"I'm good."

A small hesitation. "Mom'll call tomorrow."

"I know."

They looked at the others in the water. "Veracook will have decided they are insane," Edward Marriner said.

"She'd have figured it out eventually," said Ned.

They left it at that. They didn't talk a whole lot these days. Ned had overheard a couple of his parents' conversations at night about "*fifteen years old*" and "*mood swings.*" It had made him think about being totally affectionate for a couple of weeks, just to mess with their heads, but it felt like too much work.

Ned didn't mind his father, though. It got old after a while watching people go drop-jawed, the way Kate Wenger had, when they learned who he was, but that wasn't anyone's fault, really. *Mountains and Gods* was one of the best-selling photography books of the past ten years, and *Passageways*, though less flashy (it didn't have the Himalayas, his dad used to say), had won awards all over the place. His father was one of the few people who took pictures for both *Vanity Fair* and *National Geographic*. You had to admit that was cool, if only to yourself.

When the others came shivering out of the pool to dry off, Melanie said, "Hold it a sec. Forgot something."

"What? You? Forget?" Steve said. His yellow hair was standing up in all directions. "No possible way!"

She stuck out her tongue at him, and disappeared inside. Her room was the only bedroom on the main floor. She came dripping back out, still wrapped in her towel, with another one around her hair now. She was holding a bag that said "France Telecom." She dropped it on the table in front of Ned.

"In case Ground Control needs to reach Major Tom," she said.

She'd gotten him a cellphone. It was, Ned decided, easy to be irritated with tiny Melanie and her hyper-efficiency, but it was kind of hard not to appreciate her.

"Thanks," he said. "Really."

Melanie handed him another of her index cards, with his new phone number written out in green on it, above another smiley face. "It has a camera, too. The package is open," she added, as he pulled out the box and the fliptop phone. "I programmed all our numbers for you."

Ned sighed. It was *too* easy to be irritated with her, he amended, inwardly. "I could have done that," he said mildly. "I actually passed cellphone programming last year."

"I did it in the cab coming back up here," she said. "I have fast fingers." She winked.

"Oh, ho!" said Greg, chortling.

"Be silent, baggy suit," Melanie said to him. "Unless you are going to tell me that Arles is up and running."

"Up and run your fast fingers over my baggy suit and I'll tell you."

Ned's father shook his head and sipped his drink. "You're making me feel old," he said. "Stop it."

"The house line is 1, your dad's 2, I'm 3, Steven's 4. Greg is star-pound key-star-865-star-pound-7," Melanie said sweetly.

Ned had to laugh. Even Greg did. Melanie grinned triumphantly, and went back in to shower and change. Greg and Steve stayed out for a beer, drying off in the mild evening light. Greg said it was warmer on the terrace than in the pool.

It wasn't even May yet, Ned's father pointed out. The French didn't start swimming until June, usually. There was water in the villa's pool only as a courtesy to their idiocy. The sun was west, over the city. There was a shining to the air; the trees were brilliant.

A moment later, the serenity of that Provençal sunset was shattered by a startling sound. Then it came again. After a brain-cramp moment, Ned recognized it: the tune from Disneyland's kiddie ride, "It's a Small World."

The four of them looked around. Their gazes fell, collectively, upon Ned's new phone on the table. Warily, he picked it up, flipped it open, held it to his ear.

"Forgot to mention," Melanie said from her own mobile in the house. He heard her trying not to laugh. "I programmed a ringtone for you, too. Tried to find something suitable."

"This," Ned said grimly into the phone, "means war. You do know that, don't you?"

"Oh, Ned!" she giggled, "I thought you'd *like* it!" She hung up.

Ned put the phone down on the glass tabletop. He looked out for a second at the lavender bushes planted beyond the cypresses and the pool, and then at the three men around the table. They were each, including his father, struggling to keep a straight face. When he looked at them, they gave up, toppling into laughter.

HE COULDN'T SLEEP.

How unsurprising, Ned thought, punching his pillow for the twentieth time and flipping it over again. Jet lag would be part of it, on this second night overseas. They were six hours ahead of Montreal. It was supposed to take a day for each hour before you adjusted. Unless you were an airline pilot or something.

But it wasn't really the time difference and he knew it. He checked the clock by the bed again: almost three in the morning. The dead of night. On April 30 that might have another meaning, Ned thought.

He'd have to remember to tell that one to Kate Wenger later today. She'd get the joke. If he could keep his eyes open by then, the way tonight was going.

He got up and went to the window, which was open to the night air. He had the middle bedroom of the three upstairs. His dad was in the master, Greg and Steve shared the last one.

He pulled back the curtain. His window was over the terrace, looking out at the pool and the lavender bushes and a clump of trees on the slope by the roadway. If he leaned out and looked to his right, he could see Aix's lights glowing in the distance. The moon was orange-red, hanging over the city, close to full. He saw the summer triangle above him. Even with moonlight, the stars were a lot brighter than they were in Westmount, in the middle of Montreal.

He wondered how they looked above Darfur right now. His mom would phone this evening—or tomorrow evening—whatever you said when it was 3:00 a.m.

The world will end before I ever find him in time.

He hadn't wanted to think about that, but how did you control what you thought about, anyhow? Especially at this hour, half awake. The mind just . . . went places. Don't think about pink elephants, or girls' breasts, or when they wore skirts and uncrossed their legs. Sometimes in math class he'd wander off in his thoughts for a run, or think about music, or a movie he'd seen, or what some girl he'd never met had typed privately to him in a chatroom the night before. If it *was* a girl: there was always that to worry about online. His friend Doug was totally paranoid about it.

You thought about a lot of different things, minute by minute, through a day. Sometimes late at night you thought about a skull and a sculpted head in a corridor underground.

And that was going to be *so* helpful in getting to sleep, Ned knew. So would brooding about what had happened inside him this morning.

After another minute, irresolute, he made an attempt to access, locate—whatever word would suit—that place within himself again. The place where he'd somehow sensed the presence of the lean, nameless man on the roof above them. And where he had grasped another thing he had no proper way of knowing: that the person up there, today—right here, right now—had made the eight-hundred-year-old carving they'd been looking at.

Kate had been right, of course: the man's response, hurtling down to confront them, white with rage, had told them what they needed to know.

But Ned couldn't feel anything inside now, couldn't find whatever he was looking for. He didn't know if that was because it was over—a totally weird flicker of strangeness in the cloister—or if it was because there *was* nothing to find at this moment, looking out over dark grass and water and cypress trees in the night.

There wasn't a whole lot of point standing here in sleep shorts thinking about it. He decided to go down for a glass of juice. On the

way downstairs, barefoot in a sleeping house, he had an idea. A good
one, actually. When you couldn't do anything about the strange,
hard things, you did what you could in other ways.

He had *warned* Melanie, after all.

She, the ever-efficient one, had rigged up a multi-charger station
for all the mobile phones on the sideboard in the dining room. She
had even been helpful enough to label everyone's slot. In green ink.

It was almost too easy.

Working quickly through the options on each phone, Ned cheerfully
changed Greg's ring to the theme from "SpongeBob SquarePants," and
showed no mercy for Steve, innocent bystander though he might have
been, rejigging his cell to play "The Teletubbies Song." He left his
father's alone.

Then he took his time, scrolling thoughtfully through the choices
on Melanie's phone a couple of times before deciding.

Afterwards, pleased with himself and his contribution to justice
in the world, he went and got his juice from the kitchen. He took it
out on the terrace, standing shirtless in the night. It was cold now.
His mother would have made him get a shirt or a robe if she'd been
up. If she'd been here.

He tried, one more time, to see if he could find something within
himself, feel attuned to anything. Nothing there. He looked out across
the landscape and saw only night: pool and woods and grass to the south
under stars. A low moon west. He heard an owl behind him. There were
trees all around the villa, plenty of room for nests, and hunting.

∞

As it happens, he is being watched.

In the small stand of trees beside the lavender bushes, the figure
observing him has long ago learned how to keep from being sensed

in any of the ways Ned Marriner might know or discover by searching inside himself.

Certain skills and knowledge are part of his heritage. Others have taken time and considerable effort. He has had time, and has never been fazed by difficulty.

He'd seen the boy appear at the open window upstairs, and then, a little later, watched him come outside, half naked, vulnerable and alone. The observing figure is amused by this, by almost all that has happened today, but he does think about killing him.

It is almost too easy.

Because of the day that is coming he holds himself in check. If you are in the midst of shaping something urgently awaited, you do not give way to impulses like this, however satisfying they might be. He is impulsive by nature, but hardly a fool. He has lived too long for that.

The boy, he has decided, is random, trivial, an accident, not anyone or anything that matters. And it is not a good idea to cause any disturbance now, among either the living or the spirits, some of them already beginning to stir. He knows about the spirits. He is waiting for them, diverting himself as best he can while he does so.

He lets the boy go back inside, alive and inconsequential.

The impulse to kill is still strong, however. He recognizes it, knows why it is building. When that desire comes, it is difficult to put away unslaked. He has found that to be so over time and is disinclined to deny himself.

He changes again—the skill he took so long in mastering—and goes hunting. Moonlight briefly finds his wings in flight, then they are lost again, entering the woods.

CHAPTER IV

When Ned came down to the kitchen in the morning, bleary-eyed from his disrupted sleep, the others had already gone into town. Second work session at the cathedral. There was a note from Melanie that said they'd be back by lunchtime. He'd neglected to put on a shirt and Veraclean, in the adjacent laundry room, smiled at him before pointedly glancing away. He'd forgotten about her. He quickly drank some orange juice and went back upstairs to dress.

Then he phoned Melanie.

Three rings.

"Yes?" A really frosty tone for one word, he thought. Impressive.

"Hi there!" he said cheerfully.

"Ned Marriner," she said, low and intense, "you are in *so* much trouble. You have no idea. You are pushing up daisies, meeting your Maker, joining the choir." He heard her beginning to laugh, fighting it.

"Damn!" he said. "I'm talented after all."

"Talented and dead. Sleeping with the fishes."

"But, Melanie!" he protested. "I'd thought you'd like it!"

"'The Wedding March'? 'The Wedding March' as a ringtone? We're in a goddamned cathedral! Greg is in hysterics. He's holding a pillar to stay upright. He is *peeing* on it! You will be made to suffer!"

She sounded pleasingly hysterical herself. It was all very satisfying.

"I'm sure. In the meantime, you might want to phone Steve and Greg when you get a chance."

She paused, lowered her voice. "Really? You got them, too?"

"Got them, too. See you at lunch."

He hung up, grinning.

On considered reflection, he decided to keep his new phone hidden away for the next little while. There wasn't much he could do if she decided to short-sheet his bed, but he doubted she'd like garden snails in *hers*, and an offhand mention of the possibility might stave off retaliation. He thought he could handle Greg and Steve. Melanie was the challenge.

He loafed around the house for the morning, energetically avoiding any thought of the papers he was supposed to be writing. He was still jet-lagged, wasn't he? Who could possibly be expected to write an English or history essay while time-warped?

Despite what Kate Wenger had said, he spent a bit of time online googling *Celts+Provence*, and scribbled a few notes. Then he went outside in the bright morning and listened to music on the terrace till he saw the van making its way up the hill to the villa gates.

He took off the iPod and put it on the table. He had a premonition of what was coming. He sat up in the lounger and waved an enthusiastic hello to everyone. His father waved back from the driveway. Melanie stood by the van, hands on hips, trying to achieve a withering glare—which was hard when you were barely five feet tall, Ned thought.

Greg and Steve, smiling benignly, came up to the terrace together. Still smiling, they grabbed Ned by hands and legs (pretty strong guys, both of them) and began lugging him down the steps and across the grass to the pool.

"SpongeBob, spare me!" Ned cried, perhaps unwisely.

He heard Melanie and his father laugh, which was pleasing, but by then he was flying.

It was cold in the pool, it was *really* cold in the pool. Gasping and coughing, Ned surfaced. He knew what to say. There were time-honoured male ways of responding to this.

"Ahh," he said. "Very refreshing. Thank you so much, guys."

NED CAREFULLY MENTIONED snails, over lunch outside—how he'd heard they had a creepy habit of ending up in people's beds here, especially in springtime.

Interestingly, it was Steve who grew thoughtful, hearing that. Melanie pretended to treat it as a dubious piece of misinformation. It was hard to tell if she was faking or not.

Ned's father, in a surprisingly relaxed state, said he'd shot some potentially workable images in the baptistry, shooting towards the dome with soft flash bounces. They'd also done some of the columns in the cloister, and a zigzag pattern he'd noticed out there on the walkway. Ned hadn't seen that, but he didn't have his father's eye, and he'd been just a bit unsettled the day before out there.

"I really liked your Queen of Sheba," his father said. "The colour's gorgeous. Like amber from some angles. We'll check the images later. But I think I'm going to want to have her. I'll go back if I need to before we go home, maybe try late in the day, too. Two good calls, Ned."

He was meeting Oliver Lee at a café in town this afternoon, just the two of them, first actual encounter. Barrett, the art director, was coming over from New York next week and had wanted to be there, but both men had decided to get together without an intermediary.

"I may or may not like him, but it doesn't matter in the end. We don't have to work together."

"And you know he'll love you?" Ned grinned.

The cold water had woken him up pretty effectively. Long-lost cure for jet lag: freezing pools.

"Everyone loves me," Edward Marriner said. "Even my son."

"Your son," said Melanie, darkly, "is a terrible person."

"Really," Greg agreed, shaking his head.

Steve kept quiet, possibly thinking about snails in his bed. Ned decided he was going to *have* to do the snail thing at some point, and live with the consequences.

IT TURNED OUT the three others were going to drop his father in town then drive east towards Mont Sainte-Victoire, which Paul Cézanne had apparently painted, like a hundred times. The painter had been born and died here. He was Aix's main celebrity and he'd made the mountain famous.

Ned remembered his father grumbling about Cézanne on the flight over, leafing through Barrett Reinhardt's notes: how it was almost impossible to get a picture of that mountain that wasn't a cliché or some sentimental tribute to the painter. He wasn't looking forward to it, but Barrett had said it was simply not possible to be in Provence working on a book of photographs and *not* shoot that peak. Especially if you were Edward Marriner and known for your mountainscapes.

"Simply not possible," his dad had repeated on the plane, imitating the art director's voice.

This afternoon's drive would be partly an outing in the country, and partly to check some places Barrett had marked on local maps as where they might set up. Ned's father would make that call himself, but the others were good at eliminating locations they knew he wouldn't go for.

"You coming?" Steve asked Ned.

"Ah, I have to be in town by five-ish, actually. I'm meeting someone."

"Who? What? How?" Greg demanded. "We just *got* here!"

Ned sighed. "I met a girl yesterday morning. We're having a Coke."

"Holy-moly," said Melanie, grinning.

Greg was staring. "A date? Already? Jeez, the boy's a man among men!"

"Don't rush him, or me," Edward Marriner said. "I feel old enough as is."

"We'll get you back in time," Melanie said, checking her watch. "But change into running shoes, Ned, we may climb a bit. Sandals are no good."

"Okay. But will you tie my shoelaces for me?" Ned asked. Melanie grinned again. He was glad the subject had changed. This date thing was not something he was easy with.

They dropped his father in Aix and then took the ring road around the city and headed into the countryside along a winding route Melanie said Cézanne used to walk along to find places to paint.

It was a fair distance to the mountain if you were on foot. Ned thought about that: in the nineteenth century, the Middle Ages, Roman times, people walked, or rode donkeys or something, and the road would have been way rougher. Everything was farther, slower, back then.

And at the beginning of the twenty-first century here they were, cruising these curves in an air-conditioned Renault van, and they'd be out by the mountain in twenty minutes or something and then back in the middle of town in time for him to meet Kate Wenger.

Cézanne, or the priests who had paced the worn walkway of yesterday's cloister, or those long-ago medieval students who'd prayed in the cathedral and then gone across the square to lectures, they had all moved through worlds with different speeds than this one—even if the students were late for class, and running. Ned wasn't sure what all of that meant, but it meant something. Maybe he'd put it in an essay—when he decided to think about his essays.

It was a brilliantly bright afternoon; they were all wearing sunglasses. Melanie's were enormous, hiding half her face; Steve's blond hair and tiny round shades made him look like a Russian revolutionary. Greg looked like a nightclub bouncer.

Ned, on impulse, took his shades off. He decided he wanted to see this landscape the way people had seen it long ago. He felt a bit silly, but only a bit. He thought about that round tower yesterday above the city, men on watch there, looking out this way.

He didn't know what they'd have been gazing east to see, squinting into a rising sun, but someone had feared danger from this direction or they wouldn't have built the tower there, would they? A more dangerous world than today's, he thought. Unless you were in the Sudan, say.

He looked out the window, trying to keep his mind here, not let it drift that way to Africa, across the Mediterranean. Not so far away, in fact.

Beside him in the middle row of the van, Melanie leaned over and whispered, "Your dad was really pleased with your two ideas, you know. He spent a lot of time getting the baptistry shots."

"He always takes his time," Ned said. "Don't try to flatter your way out of doom, woman. This is war. Think about snails in your bed."

Melanie shrugged. "I like escargot. And actually, if I compare the prospect to some of the men I've dated . . ."

Ned laughed. But then he felt kind of young, again. He also thought, not for the first time, that women could be awfully strange. If the men had been so dorky, why'd she date them, why sleep with them? He looked sidelong at Melanie, almost asked her. If they'd been alone he might have; whatever else you could say about her, Melanie wasn't evasive. She was funny and direct. And she didn't actually treat him like a kid, just as part of her job. She'd have answered, he guessed. He might have learned something. He was getting to an age where a few things needed to be figured out, one way or another.

"There we are!" Steve said, pointing. "Target acquired."

Their first clear glimpse of the peak, the upper part of it, above the pine trees between. The road curved again, they lost sight of the mountain, then got it again at the next switchback. Greg pulled over, put on the flashers, and they sat and looked. The triangle of the western face of the Sainte-Victoire rose commandingly above the plain and trees.

"Well, this is a 'Cézanne Was Here' kind of shot," Melanie said dubiously. "We could probably get permission from the owners of one of these houses to set up on their property." They'd passed a number of villas on the road.

"Okay, so, yeah, we know we can do this. What else is there, if the Man wants to go another way?" Greg said. He didn't sound excited either.

"That's why we're driving," said Steve.

Greg pulled back onto the road. After another few minutes winding back and forth they approached a village and saw a dead-straight double row of trees along another road meeting theirs from the right. A sign said "Le Tholonet." There was a chateau on their left. It looked like a government building now, with a parking lot in front.

"Stop a sec," Steve said. Greg pulled to the side. Steve put his window down, took off his own sunglasses, eyeballing those trees.

"Plane trees," Melanie said. "They're all over down here, to protect the fields and vineyards from the wind."

"Ze mistral! Ze mistral!" Greg cried, in mock-horror. "She has nevair been zo bad as zis year, *mes amis*! And ze wolves . . . !"

"Paradise has curses," Melanie said. "The wind is one of them here. And that is a *terrible* accent, Gregory." She was laughing, though. She had a nice laugh, Ned thought. Nice smile, too. But they were still at war. Mercy was for wimps.

Melanie leaned towards Ned's side, looking out his window. "Steve, what are you thinking?"

"Long shot from the top of that straight road? They're pretty gorgeous. Barrett didn't mark any of these, did he? Move us up a bit, Greg?"

After Greg did, Steve took out a pocket camera and ripped a couple of fast digitals. Quality didn't matter in these, Ned knew; they were just to let his father have a glance at what they were talking about.

Steve said, looking back at Melanie, "You say there are others like this? Maybe we check some out later? Ask around, where the best ones are. Is there anywhere the sun might set or rise along them? That might be—"

"Uh-huh," Greg said. He had pulled right off the road again, to where they could look along the double aisle of green. "Good thought. East-west, most of these. The big wind's north."

Ned, impressed, reminded himself that his father's people were always going to be competent, really good at their jobs, even if they might wear ridiculous swim trunks or write notes in green ink, with smiley faces at the bottom.

The line of plane trees marched away from them, evenly spaced, framing the road on both sides, the spring leaves making a canopy above.

He looked at them a moment out his rolled-down window, then shook his head. "Sorry, but you won't get a sunset or sunrise," he said. "Too many leaves by now, guys. That's a winter shot."

Greg and Steve slowly turned around together in the front seat and stared at him.

"Scawy," said Greg. "Vewy scawy! What if he turns out to be like his old man? Imagine *two* of them. And he's already picked up a chick here! I think I'm going to make Ned my new hero."

Steve laughed. "Replacing SpongeBob? That's a major commitment!"

"Wait till you see him on Rollerblades," said Melanie.

Ned shook his head at that one. Ack. What did you *do* with someone like Melanie? "Right," he said. "I blade *just* like my dad."

Greg laughed and started the car again while Melanie made a note of where they were. She leaned forward and added another note. She was logging distance off the odometer, Ned saw.

Just ahead was a T-junction. There was a largish restaurant on the right and a small café ahead, with tables on both sides of the road. That seemed to be all there was to Le Tholonet. They went straight through. A little farther along the road rose a bit, the screening woods gave way, and they had their first glimpse of the full mountain, no trees between.

Ned was impressed. Hard not to be. Seen this close, Mont Sainte-Victoire completely dominated the landscape. It wasn't huge, you weren't going to snowboard down it in winter or anything, but there were no other mountains or hills around and the triangular peak was crisp and imposing. At the very top Ned saw a white cross.

"Well," Melanie said, checking her notes, "Barrett's written 'money shot' just ahead, where there's a place to get off the road."

Greg saw it and pulled over. He turned the engine off and hit the flashers again. They all got out.

The triangle loomed above a long green field. There were trees to their left, but none were in the way here; it was a wide-open shot, easy to frame. The rocky slopes were lit by the afternoon light. The mountain looked primitive and astonishing. The four of them were silent awhile, staring.

"Boss man won't like it," Steve said, finally. He put his sunglasses back on.

"I know," Melanie said glumly. She sighed. "There's a pull-over-and-snap-a-picture thing going on here. They might as well put up a Kodak sign and picnic tables."

Ned wasn't so sure, actually. The stony bleakness above the green meadow didn't say "pretty" to him. It felt more powerful and unsettling than that. He was going to say something, but in the minute or so since they'd stopped and gotten out he had started to feel peculiar. He kept his mouth shut. Steve took a few more digitals.

"I'll make a note, but let's go on," Melanie said. "I'm gonna get worried about Barrett Reinhardt, if this is his idea of a money shot."

"The man wants to sell books," said Greg. "This is, like, a photo of a painting everyone knows. Comfort food."

They got back in. Ned swallowed, tasted something metallic in his mouth. He had no idea what this was. Veracook's lunch? Unlikely. It was more of a headache than anything else, and it had come on really fast. He never got headaches, if you didn't count the two times he and Barry Staley had drunk cheap wine at class parties and he'd thrown up on the walk home.

I really shouldn't have remembered that, he thought.

He did feel nauseous, actually. The road continued to twist and wind south of the mountain. The swinging movement didn't help at all. There were parking lots on their left where people could leave their cars and climb. He saw a big wooden signboard with a map of the mountain trails on it.

There was a kind of needle in his head now, as if someone had a sharp, small lance and was jabbing it into his left eye, repeatedly. A humming sound, too, high-pitched, like a dentist's drill.

The others were busy talking as they went, Greg stopping and starting the van, the three of them eyeing angles along this side of the mountain, approaches to a shot, foreground, middle ground. Melanie was going on about the history of the place.

It sounded as if they'd decided none of these spots by the road was going to work. They were all too close to the mountain, no way to frame it. Ned was hardly listening now. He was just happy the three of them were busy and hadn't noticed him leaning against his door, eyes closed behind the shades.

As if from a muffled distance he heard Melanie reading from her notes. History and geography. Maybe *she'd* write an essay for him. That was a thought. He could buy her some escargot.

He managed to open his eyes. There was a broad, green-gold plain ahead of them, stretching east and south, away from the mountain. Melanie was pointing that way. Ned couldn't follow what she was saying. He closed his eyes again. He tried to focus on her voice, ride over the stabbing in his head.

"The whole landscape will change now," Melanie was saying. "We're directly south of the mountain. Everyone thinks of it as a triangle because that's the side Cézanne mostly painted, but from here it's a long, long ridge, no triangle, no peak. And ahead, where we turn north, is Pourrières, where the battle was. Just past that we'll get to where he sent men for the ambush."

"We take a look there?" Greg said.

"The ambush place? Yeah, sure. Pain de Munition, it's called. Look for a sign. Maybe we'll climb a bit. A photo from where they waited? Oliver Lee wrote a bit about the battle, I think."

"Well, yeah, if there's a photo," Steve said. He didn't sound happy. The three of them tried hard to please his father, Ned knew. They joked a lot, teased, but it was pretty obvious they were proud to be working for Edward Marriner.

He put a thumb to one temple and tried applying pressure. It didn't help. He had no idea what Melanie was talking about. What ambush? What battle?

"Got a Tylenol?" he asked.

She turned quickly. "What's wrong, Ned?"

"Kind of a headache."

"Dork! The *guy* doesn't say that on the date!"

"Be quiet, Gregory." Melanie was fishing in the bottomless black tote. "Tylenol, Advil, Aspirin, which do you like? Advil's better for a headache."

Three choices. Figured. "Advil, please."

They were in a village now, twisting through it, then they seemed to be out and going north. She gave him a couple of pills and some bottled water. Ned drank, managed a wan smile.

There was no photograph worth taking here, either; they were east of the mountain now, heading north to double back home along the other side, but trees blocked their view.

"Here's your Painful Munitions place," Greg said.

"That's how I feel," Ned muttered. "Artillery in my head."

Greg followed a bumpy gravel road a short distance past a sign strictly forbidding entry, then braked to a halt. Ned was extremely happy when the car stopped.

"Okay, campers, out and scout," Greg said. "Let's get higher and see what's what."

"I don't think I'll climb up, if that's okay," Ned said. He was afraid he was going to be sick. The needle and drill had been joined by a hammer. "You guys do what you have to, I'll wait here."

He got out with them. Didn't want to throw up in the van. He found a tree stump and sat down, his back to the sun.

"I'll stay," Melanie said. "You two go up. Phone if you need me."

"You call if you need us," Steve said, looking at Ned.

"I'm fine. Melanie, go and—"

"You aren't fine. You're halfway to green. I like green, but not in guys' faces. Go on, you two."

"We'll be quick," Greg said.

Ned felt acutely embarrassed, partly because he was actually glad Melanie was staying. He had never fainted in his life, but it crossed his mind that he might. He closed his eyes again behind the shades. It wasn't that hot but he seemed to be sweating. His mouth was dry.

"Drink some more water," Melanie said, bringing him the bottle. She took off her big straw hat and put it on his head to block the sun. "Do you get migraines?"

"Never in my life. You?"

"Lots. Is it off-centre, behind one eye? You feel like there's an aura in your head?"

"What's an aura in my head feel like?"

She laughed a little. "Who's good at describing that stuff?"

He heard her walking around. "I don't think there's gonna be a photo up there, either," she said. "The mountain's just a treed slope from this side."

Ned tried to function normally. "Maybe he could shoot at sunrise from up on top of it? Looking down and out? The opposite of Cézanne, sort of? Or look, maybe Dad just does the mountain from Barrett's spot and the book *says* this is what Cézanne painted a hundred years ago."

"Your father be happy with that?"

"Maybe. Probably not." Ned swallowed some more water. Pressed the bottle to his forehead under the hat. "What was this ambush about?"

"You don't need a history lesson now, Ned."

"I need something to distract me. Have you ever fainted?"

"That bad? Oh, Ned! I'll call the others."

"No. Just talk. I'll tell you if it gets worse."

It *was* worse; he was waiting for the Advil to do something useful.

She sighed. "Okay. This area, right where we turned north, was like the *biggest* battlefield. One of those change-the-course-of-history things? A Roman named Marius beat this massive army of barbarians who were marching to take Rome. If he hadn't stopped them here they might have, people think."

"What kind of barbarians?"

"Couple of tribes joined together, migrating from the northeast. Celts, basically. The Romans called them barbarians, but they called everyone that."

"How massive?" He kept the bottle on his forehead.

"Really. The books say two hundred thousand of them died here, maybe more, and they had their women and children with them. The survivors became slaves. That's a lot of people. The Romans took a bunch of the leaders and threw them down a pit called the garagai up on top of the mountain. Marius had a witch or wise woman who told him to do that because it was like a sacrifice place, and so their spirits couldn't return and help the tribes. That town where we turned up was later named Pourrières, which means putre-faction. Ick. Think about two hundred thousand rotting bodies."

"I'd really prefer not to just now, thanks. Is this revenge, Melanie?"

"No! No, no, really! Oh, Ned, I'm sorry!"

But knowledge, however you got it, changed things, Ned Marriner thought. You couldn't go back to *not* knowing, even if you wanted to. And when you put what you'd just heard together with other things, specifically yesterday, the feeling he'd had in the cloister . . .

He felt it again, right now, that inward awareness. Unblocking, unlocking.

Abruptly, Ned pushed off the log and stood up. His heart was pounding.

"What?"

"Shh. Wait."

Afraid now, not just in pain, Ned took off his sunglasses. He opened his eyes in the too-bright light. Pain danced and drilled in his brain. But what he saw, looking out towards the mountain, was worse.

In what should have been the clear, mild light of spring, the trees and grass between them and the ridge of the mountain were bathed—were *saturated*—in a sickening, dark-red hue.

It was terrifying. As though he were looking through some lurid camera filter. The world lay drowned in the colour of blood. And suddenly he could smell it, too. Appalled, horrified, he felt as if he were tasting blood. It was in his mouth, his throat, sticky, thick, clogging and—

He turned away and was violently ill by the tree stump. Then again, and a third time, wrackingly, his guts turning inside out.

"Oh, my God, Ned! I should never have . . ."

"I don't think I like this place a whole lot," he said, breathing hard.

Melanie had her phone out.

"Don't call them!" he said. It was difficult to speak. "I'm just . . . just a migraine, I guess."

Too late. She was talking fast to Greg, calling them back. He couldn't honestly say he was unhappy about that. He needed to get away from here, to somewhere where he could try to deal with the undeniable fact that he seemed to be seeing and *feeling* the presence of massive, violent death. A slaughter, the world soaked in blood.

Yesterday, a carving from eight hundred years ago. And now this.

"When did . . . ?" He took a steadying breath. "Melanie, when was this battle?"

"Oh, Ned. Forget the damn battle! Here, wipe your face." She handed him one of those packaged wet-wipes. One more thing in her tote. He did what she told him, put his sunglasses back on. Sipped some water.

"When was it? Please?"

"Oh, hell." He heard her rummaging for her notes. His eyes were closed again. "123 B.C., I've got. Why do you want to talk about *that*?"

"Because I don't want to talk about throwing up, okay?"

Two thousand, one hundred years.

What happened when you fainted? Did your eyes roll up in their sockets? Could you die, like, if you banged your head on a rock or something?

He heard the guys coming down. He kept his shades on. He knew if he took them off he'd see that redness again, everywhere. A world defined by dark blood. The smell was still with him, like meat, a thick, rotting—

Helplessly, just as the other two arrived, Ned heaved again—dry, convulsive, nothing left in him.

"Jeez!" Greg said. "You're really clocked out, aren't you? Let's roll. We'll get you into Veracook's hands, and bed."

They got back in the van. Greg started it, geared up, and they continued north, then left at a junction back along the other side of the mountain.

Greg didn't slow down to look for photo spots now, he was driving fast, on a road not meant for it. Ned, leaning against his door, was aware of Steve and Melanie casting glances at him every few seconds. He wanted to be brave—the heroic invalid—but it was hard when you kept smelling blood, and the swinging motion of the van was no help.

And then, halfway back along that winding stretch of road on the northern shoulder of Mont Sainte-Victoire, he was fine.

He was absolutely fine. It was gone.

A really bad taste in his mouth from throwing up, but nothing more than that. Nothing but the memory. And he knew it wasn't the miraculous properties of Advil. Cautiously, he took off his sunglasses. No blood-red hue to the afternoon sky or the trees. Only memory. And fear. There was that, too.

"Almost home," Melanie said, in a worried voice.

"I'm good," Ned said. He looked at her. "Honestly. I am. It's gone. No aura, nothing."

"You serious?" Steve had turned and was staring at him.

"Really. I'm not lying. I have *no* idea what that was about." That last part was a lie, but what was he going to say?

"Food poisoning, migraine, jet lag." Melanie ticked them off. He could hear relief in her voice. It touched him, actually.

"Guilt? Over what you did to our phones?" Steve said from the front seat.

"Has to be that," Ned agreed.

"I'm still taking you home," Greg said. "You can postpone your date till tomorrow."

"No way," Ned said. "And it isn't a date. It's a Coke at five o'clock."

"Hah!" said Greg. He, too, was obviously happier now.

"Well, we'll stop at the villa anyhow," said Melanie. "You've got time and it's on the way. You might want to shower and brush your teeth. Think of the girl, please."

"Right. And you can check my fingernails and ears and tie my shoelaces again. Double knot?"

She laughed. "Piss off, Ned. I am *way* too young and cool for that." She grinned. "You should be so lucky as to have me kneel in front of you."

Ned felt himself flush.

Greg snorted. "You? Cool? With a bottomless bag like Mary Poppins? No, you aren't, Mel," he said. "Sorry to break it to you."

She leaned forward and hit him on the shoulder.

"Don't fondle the driver," Greg said. He started singing, "Spoonful of Sugar," and Steve joined him.

Ned rolled down his window. The air was crisp and clear. Wildflowers, yellow and white and purple, dotted the sides of the road. They crossed over a small bridge. The view along the ravine below was gorgeous. He saw Melanie checking it out, too. She scribbled something in her notebook. That had actually been a really sexy line, what she'd said.

Up front the guys were still singing that song from *Mary Poppins*. Melanie leaned forward and gave them each another futile whack with her notebook, then she sat back and crossed her arms and tried to look aggrieved.

She saw him looking at her, and winked. Of course. He had to laugh. Melanie.

CHAPTER V

"Blood? Like, *really* blood colour?"

Kate had another espresso in front of her; Ned had ordered orange juice this time. She'd arrived at the café about five minutes after him, a bit breathless. Her school was halfway across town. The two outdoor spots had been taken again; all around their small table the interior was crowded with people talking loudly, smoking, reading papers, shopping bags at their feet. Ned still wasn't used to the smoke; it was everywhere here.

He nodded. "Blood red. And I could taste blood when I swallowed. It made me sick. But only near that battlefield. It was over when we drove away."

She was staring at him, brown eyes, lightly freckled face. She had her hair pulled back today, was wearing torn jeans and a blue-and-white striped tank top with a man's white shirt over it, unbuttoned, sleeves rolled halfway up. She looked pretty good, Ned thought.

He said, "If you don't believe me, no one else is going to. I can't even *tell* anyone else."

Kate shook her head. "Oh, believe me, I believe you." She met his eyes and then looked away. "After yesterday, I'd believe it if you said you saw the aliens' mother ship."

"That's next week," he said. She made a face.

"You know anything about this Marius?" he asked after a moment. "The battle there?"

She bit her lip; he was used to that already. Then she looked down at the tabletop.

Ned laughed aloud. "Aha! Of *course* you know."

"I knew you'd laugh," she said. "Why is it dumb to be interested in things?"

Ned looked at her. "It isn't," he said. "Tell me. I'm not teasing."

"Well . . . I actually wrote an essay about this."

"Oh, God, Kate, you kill me! I *have* to tease you." He stopped. Thought quickly. "Wait—maybe I, ah, won't. Um, do you have it? Here? The essay?"

She raised her eyebrows, took her time answering. "Ned Marriner, I am shocked . . . Do you want to plagiarize my paper?"

"Damn right I want to plagiarize your paper! I have three essays to write in six weeks, or ruin my summer back home."

"Well," she said, leaning back and grinning now, "I'll have to think hard about that. I've been needled a whole lot here, and we just met, you know. You can't go around handing out 'A' papers to just anyone."

"I'll buy your coffees. I'll buy you a better shirt."

"This," said Kate Wenger, "is my brother's shirt, and I happen to like it a lot."

"It is great. Truly great. You look hot in it. A babe. Tell me about Marius."

"Do I really look hot?"

"Hotter than Marie-Chantal could ever dream of being."

"That," she sniffed, "is no achievement."

"Marius? Please?"

She sipped her coffee. She looked happy, though. Ned felt kind of pleased with himself. He was being funny, making a girl laugh. Around them the place was vibrant with the clatter of dishes and cups and the buzz of talk. One woman had a small dog under her chair; that wouldn't have been allowed back home. He liked it.

"Marius was Julius Caesar's uncle," Kate said. "Married Caesar's aunt. A general in North Africa at the time. Apparently a little guy, tough, smart, young when this happened—like maybe twenty-five or something? Well, what it was is these eastern tribes started moving this way. A *lot* of them, with their women and children, migrating, looking for a place to settle. They scared everyone, huge men, you know?"

"Blond dudes? Pumped iron, used steroids? Broke the home run record?"

"Pretty much. The Romans were small, did you know that?"

"I didn't know that. Why would I know that?"

"Well, they were. But *really* organized. Anyhow, these tribes, the Teutones and Cimbrii, hung around here awhile and beat up a Roman army, then half of them went west to Spain. But they came back again and decided what they really wanted was land around Rome, and they decided they were going to go kick ass there."

"Could they have?"

"Everyone seems to think so. That's the point of the story. Rome was terrified. This is before their empire, remember? Before Caesar. They hadn't even conquered here yet, just some Greek and Roman trading colonies on the coast . . . and Sextius had founded this city, Aix. Their first one."

"And so?"

"And so if the tribes got down into Italy it was probably game over."

"Melanie said more than two hundred thousand."

"Who's Melanie again?"

"My father's assistant. I told you yesterday. She has notes on everything."

"What a geek." Kate grinned. "Way, way more than two hundred thousand. Some people say half a million, with the women and children. Some say more."

Ned whistled softly. It seemed called for. Someone glanced over and he grimaced an apology. He tried to imagine that many people moving across a landscape and gave up. He couldn't visualize it: just got an image of computer-generated orcs.

"Anyhow," Kate said, "Rome ordered Marius here from Africa and he took charge. They'd been creamed by the tribes in that first battle, and all the soldiers were afraid of them."

"But he won?"

"Spoiling the ending, you. Yeah, he won. From what I gather, he steered them into a trap by the mountain. He had a better position, and when the fight started some of his men ambushed the Celts' camp where their families were. When they turned to defend them, the Romans just pounded on them from behind and it was a massacre. That's your two hundred thousand dead. Marius saves the day. They built him monuments around here, but they've all fallen down."

Ned looked at her awhile. "You're good, you know."

She shrugged. "Google is your friend."

"Nope. You're good." He finished his orange juice. "So, like, if he hadn't beat them, they'd have taken Rome?"

"Maybe. No Roman Empire. Celts settle Italy. Really different world. This battle was a huge deal."

Ned shook his head. "Why doesn't anyone know this stuff?"

"You kidding? People don't even know World War Two."

He looked at her. "I really need that paper of yours."

"I'll bet you do. I'll think about it." She hesitated. "I mean, no, of course I'll give it to you. But doesn't it seem pretty trivial after what—"

"Kate, it seems *completely* trivial! Essays? Are you kidding me? But if I think too much about this afternoon or yesterday I'll freak."

"There's . . . nothing now? Inside you?"

He faked a shrug. "I'm too distracted by that way-cool tank top of yours."

"No jokes. Tell me."

"I told you. Nothing today since we left the battlefield. Nothing yesterday from the time our guy walked out on us. N-O-thing."

"Have you tried to . . . ?" she trailed off.

"Tried to what?" He knew he was sounding irritated, and knew it was unfair. "Control it? You gonna play Yoda now? 'Use the Force, Young Ned'?"

"Stop joking."

"I *have* to joke or I'll go screwy with this. Be grateful you aren't dealing with it!"

She was silent a moment. "I am," she said. "I am grateful. But I was there too. I'm not trying to hassle you."

Ned felt ashamed. "I'm not being cool, am I? Sorry."

"Hard to be cool if you're tasting blood and stuff."

"Yeah." He couldn't think of anything else to say.

Kate waved her hand for the bill. "Okay, I'll take off. Call me tomorrow, if you like. After school."

"Don't go yet," he said quickly. She looked at him. "I . . . there's no one else I can talk to. I need to touch base. If you don't mind."

"I said call me. I meant it." She flushed a little.

He sighed. "I did try, actually, middle of last night, to see if I could feel anything. Problem is, I have no idea what I'm supposed to be doing, or controlling. Maybe I do need a Jedi Master."

"Not me, Young Ned. I can give you an essay, though. Want me to email it?"

"That'd be good." She took out her notebook and he gave her his hotmail address, and added his new cell number.

"Reminds me," she said. "You asked about Celts, where they were around here?"

"And of course you found out. Google is your friend?"

"Google is my midnight lover."

"I'm not sure I'm ready to hear that, actually."

She laughed. "They were all over the area. Which figured. There's one place I've seen that we can walk to if you want. Above the city."

The waiter came by and they paid for their drinks.

"Might as well," Ned said. "Can't tomorrow, we're going to Arles."

She nodded. "Day after? Thursday? Meet after school, say, outside Cézanne's studio? Can you find it? We have to go that way."

"I'll find it. Where are we going?"

"It's called Entremont. Where the Celts were based before the Romans built this city."

"Okay. I'll be outside that studio at five. I'll call you tomorrow, when we get back from Arles."

"Cool." She got up, stuffed the notepad in her pack. They walked out together. On the street he turned to her.

"Thanks, Kate."

She shrugged. "Down, boy. You may not like the essay."

"Now who's joking?"

She made a face. "Okay. You're welcome. Call me."

She gave him a little flip-wave with one hand, then turned and walked along the cobblestones. He watched her go.

꩜

Inside the café, the man in the grey leather jacket, two tables over from where they'd been, puts down his newspaper. There is no need to hide his face any more.

He might have learned something here, he is thinking.

A thread, a way into the labyrinth. This is a possibility, no more than that, but it *is* that. When you were in urgent need and time was very short and your enemy had most of the weapons—at this point— you used tools like these two children, and prayed to your gods.

In one way it is obvious; in another, the girl is entirely right: there are too many choices here. And from where he is—outside the fires—he has no easy way to narrow them down.

There are *still* too many places, that hasn't changed, but he's decided something, sitting here—and these two are at the heart of it, despite what he said to them yesterday.

The boy, from the start. From *before* the baptistry, since he's being truthful—and he always is, with himself.

He isn't certain about the girl. He'd waited and watched them from a distance yesterday, after leaving the cloister. Saw them walk here. Made an assumption they'd be back. If he'd been wrong, if they had met elsewhere, not after school, or not at all, he wouldn't have been unduly disturbed. Few things affect him that much any more. When he is in the world again, when he returns, his is an entirely *focused* existence.

He is only ever alive for one thing. Well, two, really.

At the same time, he wasn't surprised when they did show up here. Nor by what he heard the girl say, from behind the screening pages of *Le Monde*. They have no business going where they are going two days from now, but he might.

He might have many lives' worth of business there. Or not. He might lose this time, before it even begins. It has happened. It is unfair, an unbalanced aspect of the combat, but he has long since moved beyond thinking that way. What is *fairness*, in this dance?

His sitting here is, in the end, just a feeble reaching out for signs—from two children who have nothing to do with the tale. At the same time, he has learned (he's had a long time to learn) that little is truly coincidence. Things fall into patterns. You can miss patterns, or break them, but they are there. He'd acted upon that yesterday, and now.

He finds a few coins, drops them on the table, rises to go.

"Why didn't I know you were here?"

He looks up. His way out is blocked. He is actually startled. The sensation is truly strange, a lost feeling remembered. For no easy reason he suddenly has an image of his first time here, walking through the forest from the landing place, invited but uncertain. Afraid, so far from home. Then coming out of the woods, the lit fires.

He sits down again. He gestures. The boy is standing between the table and the door. He sits gingerly opposite, edge of chair, as if ready to bolt. Not a bad instinct, all things considered.

The newspaper lies on the table between them, folded back. He'd been reading the forecast. Wind, clear skies. There will be a full moon Thursday. He'd known that, of course.

The boy has spoken in English. The man says, gravely, in the same language, "You have surprised me again. Brave of you to come back. I take it you sent the girl away?"

Ned Marriner shrugs. He has dark brown hair and light blue eyes, a lean build, medium height, wiry rather than strong. Barely old enough to shave. His face is pale; he will be dealing with tension and fear. Fair enough.

Welcome to my world, the man thinks, but doesn't say. He doesn't feel welcoming.

"No, she just went. I don't send her places. I didn't know anything till I was outside. And besides, I'm the one feeling . . . whatever this is. If you're dangerous, there's no reason for her to be here."

"Dangerous?" He smiles at that. "You have no idea. I said I wouldn't kill you, but there are others who might view your presence differently."

"I *know* I have no idea. But what does 'my presence' mean? My presence *where*?" He stops, to control himself. His voice has risen. "And why didn't I know you were here until I got outside? Yester-day I . . ."

That last he decides to answer.

"I was careless. I was screening myself from you, after yesterday in the cloister, but I thought you'd gone and so I let it down."

"I *had* gone. I don't even know why I checked inside. I was halfway across the market square."

He considers that. "Then you are stronger than you knew."

"I don't know anything," the boy says again. His voice is lower now, intense. There was someone like this, long ago. A vague sense tugs at him. But there are too many years between. He has been here so many times.

Ned Marriner leans back, folding his arms defensively across his chest. "I have no idea who you are, or what happened to me yester-day or today, if you heard us talking about that."

He nods. The mountain.

"So what is this *about*?" the boy demands. He really shouldn't be using that tone. "You said we were an accident, had no role to play, but you followed, or waited for us."

He is clever, it seems. "Followed yesterday, waited just now. I took a chance you'd come back."

"But why?"

The waiter is hovering. He signals for another of what each of them was drinking.

A mild curiosity rises. He still has some of that, it seems. "You don't feel reckless, interrogating me like this?"

"I'm scared out of my mind, if you want the truth."

"But that isn't the truth," he says. Who *did* this one remind him of? "You came back by choice, you're demanding answers of me. And yet you know that I sculpted a column eight hundred years ago. No. You're frightened, but not ruled by it."

"I probably should be," the boy says in a small voice. "It isn't a column, either, it's a woman."

The quick, familiar anger. A sense of intrusion, violation, rude feet trampling in something private beyond words.

He makes himself move past it. By today's standards this one is young, can still properly be called a boy. In the past, he could have been a war leader at his age. Fit for challenging, killing. He has killed children.

The world has changed. He has lived through the changes, at intervals. Coming and going, enmeshed in the long pattern. Sometimes he wants it over, mostly he is terrified, heart-scalded that it might end. You could grow weary beyond measure, feeling all those things at once.

The waiter comes back: an espresso, an orange juice. The brisk, habitual motions. He waits until the man leaves.

He says, still speaking English for privacy, "Once this awareness comes to you, it can be a kind of anchor against fear. You know what you are feeling, know a new thing is in you. The fear lies in not understanding *why*, but already you're not the person you were yesterday morning."

He sips his espresso, puts the cup down, adds quietly, "You never will be again."

A cruel thing to say, perhaps; he isn't beyond enjoying that.

"That's scary too."

"I imagine it is."

He remembers his own first awareness of this boy, decisions made quickly. They look at each other. The boy glances down. Few people meet his gaze for long. He finishes his coffee. "Frightened or not, you came back. You could have kept walking. You're inside now."

"Then you need to tell me what I'm inside."

Another flaring within. "I *need* to do nothing. Use words more cautiously."

"Or what?"

Opposing anger across the table, interestingly. He really isn't accustomed to talking this much any more.

"Or what?" the boy demands again. "You'll stab me in here? Pull the knife again?"

He shakes his head. "Or I'll walk out."

Ned Marriner hesitates again, then leans forward. "No you won't. You don't want to leave me. You *want* me in this, somehow. What did we say, Kate and me, that you needed to hear?"

Someone else had once talked to him this way. That nagging memory still there. Was it centuries ago, or a millennium? He isn't sure; people blur after so much time, but he believes he killed that other one.

He looks across the table and realizes that he was wrong, in fact. This impudent tone isn't the same as that other, long-ago voice: with a degree of surprise (again) he sees that the boy is close to tears, fighting to hide it.

He tries, unsuccessfully, to remember when he felt that way himself. Too far back. Mist-wrapped, forest-shrouded.

This defiant anger is a boy's, in the end. Or perhaps in the beginning. Anger at helplessness, at being ignorant and young, not yet an adult and so immune (boys believed adults were immune) to the pain he is feeling.

Had he been a different man he might have addressed some of this. Ned Marriner has, after all, come to the edges of the tale, and he might even be an instrument.

But that is all he can be. You didn't confide in tools or comfort them. You made use of what lay to hand. He stands up, drops a few coins on the table. The boy lifts his head to look at him.

"I don't know if you said anything I need. It is too long to tell, and I'm disinclined to do so. You are better off not knowing, though it may not seem that way to you. You will have to forgive me—or not, as you like."

Then he adds (perhaps a mistake, it occurs to him, even as he speaks), "I wouldn't go up to Entremont on the eve of Beltaine, though."

The youthful gaze is sharp, suddenly.

"That was it, wasn't it?" Ned Marriner says. He doesn't look any more as if he might cry. "What Kate said? About that place?"

The man doesn't respond. He really *isn't* accustomed to answering questions. Never has been, if truth were told, even from when he entered the tale himself a little west of here, having come across the sea.

Everyone here has come from somewhere else.

He'd said that to her, once. He remembers her reply. He remembers everything she has ever said to him, it sometimes feels.

He walks to the café door and out into the late-April afternoon.

The dogs have been waiting, scuffling around the market nearby. They attack as soon as he reaches the street.

࿇

Ned heard a woman scream. There were shouts and—unbelievably—the snarling of animals in the middle of the city.

At the two tables outside people were scrambling to their feet, backing desperately away from something. Ned leaped up. He wasn't really thinking. Thought took too long, sometimes. He ran towards the door. On the way, he grabbed one of the café chairs.

It may have saved his life.

The wolfhound sprang just as he cleared the door. Purely by reflex, adrenalin surging, Ned swung the chair up. He cracked the animal on the head with all the power fear had given him. The impact knocked Ned into one of the outdoor tables and he fell over it, hitting his shoulder hard. The dog cartwheeled in mid-air, landed on the street. It lay on one side, didn't move.

Ned got up quickly. The lean man was surrounded by three other animals, all of them big, dark grey, feral. These weren't anyone's pets off leash, Ned thought.

People were still screaming from farther along the street and in the market square, but no one came to help. He did see someone on a cellphone. Calling the police?

He hoped. Again, without really thinking, he stepped forward. He shouted, trying to get the animals' attention. One of them turned immediately, teeth bared. *Wonderful,* Ned thought. When you got what you wanted, you really needed to be sure you'd wanted it.

But the man in the leather jacket moved then, swift and unnervingly graceful. He slashed at the distracted dog with his knife. The blade came out red, the animal went down. Ned moved forward, wielding the awkward chair, feinting with it like some ridiculous lion-tamer, facing one of the last two dogs.

He really didn't know what he was doing. He was a distraction, no more, but that was enough. He saw the bald-headed man leave his feet in a sudden, lethal movement and the reddened knife took another animal. The man landed, rolled on the road, and was back on his feet.

These were more like wolves than dogs, Ned realized. There was nothing in his experience of life to *fit* the idea of wolves—or wolfhounds—attacking people in a city street.

But there was only one left.

Then none, as the last animal showed its teeth in a white-flecked snarl and fled through the market square as people backed away in panic. It tore diagonally across, down a street on the far side, and was gone.

Ned was breathing hard. He put a hand to his cheek and checked: no blood. He looked at the man beside him. He saw him wipe the bloodied knife on a blue napkin retrieved from the ground beside a toppled table. Ned set down his chair. For no good reason, he righted the table. His hands were trembling again.

The man looked at him and grimaced. "Curse his soul," he said softly. "He thinks he is amusing."

Ned blinked. He shook his head as if he had water in his ears, like after a high-board dive, and he hadn't heard rightly. "*Amusing?*" he repeated, stupidly.

"He plays games. Like a wayward child."

People were approaching, cautiously.

"Games?" Ned repeated again, his voice high-pitched, as if it hadn't broken yet. He was aware that he wasn't holding up his end of this conversation very well. "I . . . that thing went for my throat."

"You did choose to come out," the man said. "We invite our fate, some of the time."

He said it the way you might comment on the weather or someone's new shirt or shoes. He brushed at his jacket and looked at the crowd around them. "I suggest departing, unless you want to spend an evening answering questions you can't answer."

Ned swallowed. The man looked at him another moment. He hesitated. When he did speak, Ned had to strain to catch it.

"She is worth it, always and ever," was what he heard.

Then, before Ned could say anything, or even begin to think of what he might say, the man spun around and began to run, north up the road towards the cathedral.

For an uncertain moment, Ned looked at the frightened, concerned faces around him. He shrugged, gestured vaguely, and then took off as well.

He ran the other way, across the market square, hearing urgent shouts in his wake. Someone even grabbed for him. Ned slashed the brief, restraining hand away, and kept going.

He sprinted until he was out of town.

Only on the Route de Vauvenargues, leading east towards the cut-off to the villa, did he settle into a proper stride. He was in jeans, wasn't dressed for a run, but he had his Nikes on, and he badly needed to be moving just now.

Somewhere along the way he started to swear under his breath, rhythmically. His mother hated it when he swore. A failure of imagination, she called it.

His mother was in a civil-war zone where people were dying every day. Ned's shoulder hurt, his cheek was banged up, and he was scared and angry in pretty much equal measure. He actually felt as if he might be sick for the second time in a day.

Amusing? Someone had meant that to be funny?

It occurred to him that the man—he really needed a name—had said pretty much the same thing about the skull and sculpted head yesterday.

Ned could almost smell the hot breath of the animal that had leaped for him. If he hadn't grabbed that chair on the way out—he had no idea what had made him do that—he'd have had teeth ripping into him.

How amusing. Just hilarious. Put it on *America's Funniest Home Videos* with all the other cute little animals and men falling over tables. And how extremely grateful that arrogant son of a bitch had been, come to think of it. Not a word of thanks.

We invite our fate, he'd said.

Whatever the hell that meant. Ned, rubbing his shoulder now as he ran, muttered a few more words that would have got him into trouble if either parent had been there to hear.

Well, they weren't. And they weren't going to be much good to him in this. Whatever this was, anyhow.

She is worth it, always and ever.

He was pretty certain that was what he'd heard.

As he turned off the main road, taking their own uphill lane, the words hit him hard, a different sort of blow. Tidings from that still-distant, really complicated adult world he seemed to be approaching. And from somewhere else, as well, a place farther away, that he also seemed to be entering now, like it or not.

A few dozen strides later it occurred to Ned Marriner that if he'd wanted to, or had been thinking clearly enough, he could have taken those last words as a thank-you of sorts, after all. A confiding, explanation, even an apology from someone not obviously inclined to any of those things.

As the villa came in sight at the top of their roadway, beyond a sloping meadow and the lawn, framed against the trees that sheltered it from the wind, he was thinking of a rose placed yesterday beside a sculpted figure that was not the Queen of Sheba.

CHAPTER VI

The others were on the terrace having a drink as Ned came up the gravel drive. The sun, west over the city, sent a long, slanting light. It fell on the cypresses, the house, the water in the pool, and on the four people sitting outside, making them look golden, like gods.

"You should see yourselves," Ned called, keeping his tone cheerful. "The light's amazing."

In a moment like this, he thought, you could get a pretty good idea of what people loved so much about Provence.

He kept on moving; he didn't want to get close to the others until he checked himself in the mirror. "I'm gonna shower, be right out."

"Dude," Greg called out, "you were supposed to phone me for a ride!"

"Too nice a day," he shouted back, going around the side of the house to enter through the front, not from the terrace doors where they were.

"Ned, are you all right?" his father called.

They'd told him about earlier, obviously. He supposed they'd had to. He'd been pretty sick.

"I'm fine," he said, not breaking stride. "Down in twenty minutes."

He passed Veracook in the hallway and she didn't seem too alarmed at the sight of him. He looked in the bathroom mirror upstairs. His shoulder hurt, he'd have a bruise, be sore for a couple of days, but nothing worse than what you got in a hockey game, and he didn't think his cheek looked too bad. They might not even notice.

"OH, MY GOD, Ned! What happened to your face?" Melanie cried, the second he walked out on the terrace with a Coke.

Melanie, he thought. He bet the three men wouldn't have seen a thing.

He shrugged. "Stupid accident. I got rushed by a dog near the fruit-and-veg market and fell over a café table."

"A *dog*?" his father said.

"Big one, too," Ned said, taking a chair and stretching out his legs casually. He sipped from his Coke and put it on the table. Larry Cato had told him years ago that when you lied you cut as close to the truth as you could or way far off. One or the other. It was aliens with ray guns, or a dog and a café table. Larry was the type who had theories about these things.

"What the hell?" Steve said. "Did you, like, get bit?"

"No, no, no. I just fell. He ran off when people yelled at him."

Melanie had gone into the kitchen. She came back out with ice cubes in a plastic bag, a dish towel wrapped around them. She handed it to him, wordlessly.

"My own fault, probably," Ned said. "I was jogging through the market and who knows what the dog thought I was. A terrorist or something." His father looked dubious. "I'm okay, really. A bruise. I'll live, Dad." He held the ice dutifully to his face.

"What about earlier?" his father asked. "On the drive?"

He really *did* have a lot to explain. "That was weird," Ned said. "And then it totally went away. Don't say food poisoning or Veracook will kill herself."

"We all ate the same food, anyhow," Melanie said. "I'm thinking motion sickness after jet lag."

Ned managed a grin. "You just keep thinking, Butch, that's what you're good at."

Steve laughed. Movie joke. Ned saw that his father was still eyeing him.

"I'm fine, Dad. Honestly. How did it go at lunch?"

Edward Marriner leaned back in his chair. "Very pleasant. Perfectly likeable man. Likes his wine. He said he saw the book as more mine than his, so I said the opposite and we got on like a house on fire."

"Where *does* that expression come from, anyhow?" Greg asked, of no one in particular.

No one answered. Ned relaxed a little. He heard birds from the slope above the house. Aix gleamed below them, down the valley in the late daylight.

"This," said Steve, looking the same way, "is pretty cool, have to say."

It was, Ned thought. There were at least a couple of more hours before sunset, but the light was already turning everything an amber hue and the shadows of the cypresses were falling vividly across the grass.

"I told you," he said, "you guys were a photograph up here—for your own albums." A thought occurred to him. "Dad, if you tried Barrett's money shot right around now the mountain would look pretty goddamned unbelievable."

"Language, Ned," his father said, absent-mindedly. "Your mother's calling soon."

"Right. And God forbid I swear within an hour of talking to her. She'll *know*!"

Steve laughed again.

His father grinned. "Touché. Steve said Barrett's would be a tourist shot."

"Maybe not at this hour," Steve said. "Ned could be right. And those plane trees we told you about—if you didn't shoot down the alley but across, from the west, with the sun on them, their shadows, maybe an hour later than this . . ."

"We'll have a look," Ned's father said. "One day when the light looks right we'll drive out. If I buy it, we can arrange to set up another time. It's only—what?—twenty minutes from here."

"Bit more," said Melanie. "Ned, keep the ice on your cheek."

Ned put the ice back. It was really cold. He knew what she'd say if he said that. How did someone with a punk look and green-streaked hair get so efficient, that's what he wanted to know.

"How was the hot date?" Greg asked. "Before the dog had to beat you off her."

"It wasn't hot or a date. But it was fine," Ned said, repressively. There were limits.

"Who is this?" his father asked, predictably.

Ned gave him a look. "Her name's Lolita LaFlamme, she's a stripper at the HotBooty Club in town. She's thirty-six and studying nuclear physics in her spare time."

Melanie giggled. Edward Marriner raised an eyebrow.

"I do sometimes forget," his father said slowly, brushing at his moustache with one hand, "that amid the blessings of my life, which are many and considerable, I am raising an adolescent son. Having had your brief moment of dubious wit, my child, could you enlighten me more cogently?"

His father talked like that to be funny, Ned knew. He wasn't actually upset. You had no doubts when his dad was really angry.

Ned sighed, rattled it off. "Kate Wenger, my age, here for a term
at school, exchange from New York. Met her yesterday. Student-geek
type. Giving me some help with one of my essays."

That last, he realized—too late—was a mistake.

Larry Cato would have shaken his head sorrowfully. *Dude, never
tell more than you need to,* he'd have said.

"Ah. Some help? I believe I know what that means. Are you going
to copy her paper?"

His father asked it mildly. His mom would have gone ballistic.

"Of *course* he's going to copy her paper!" Greg said. "Jeez, cut him
some slack, boss, he's in the south of France!"

"I do know his approximate geographic location," Ned's father
said, trying to sound stern. He looked at his son a moment. "Very
well. Here's our deal, Ned: you can get notes for *one* paper from this
girl, the other two you write yourself. Fair?"

"Fair."

It was, especially since they had no way of checking on him. Larry
would have called it a no-brainer, flat-out win.

"And no one tells your mother or we're both in trouble."

"You think *I'm* going to tell her?"

"I might," said Melanie cheerfully, "if some unnamed people aren't
nicer to me."

"Blackmail," said Ned darkly, "is a crime, threatening the peace
and security of the world."

On cue, the phone rang inside.

"Shall I get that?" Melanie said sweetly.

But even as she spoke, Edward Marriner was out of his chair and
moving through the terrace doors.

They all looked at each other. He'd gone in very fast. It made Ned think for a moment. He wasn't, obviously, the only one worried about his mother, waiting for that call.

After a bit, as the other three remained silent, he got up and went quietly into the kitchen. His father was at the table they'd set up against the wall in the dining room where the main computer and a telephone were.

Bending to grab an apple from the fridge, Ned could hear his father's voice. He washed the apple at the sink. Veracook smiled at him again.

Ned heard his dad saying, "That's not especially far from shelling, Meghan."

And after a pause, dryly, "Oh, fine then, if someone said they're going the other way."

Ned took a bite of the apple, unhappily. He heard, "I'm sorry, Meg, you have to allow us to worry. You can't stop that any more than we can stop you going."

He thought about heading back outside. Wasn't sure he felt good about hearing this. His stomach was tight again.

"Ned's fine," his father said. "A bit jet-lagged. Yes, of course he's concerned, tries to pretend he isn't." A pause. "I think he likes the set-up well enough. Who knows at that age? He's made a friend already, it seems." Another silence. "No, he hasn't started his essays. Honey, we've been here three days." He stopped again. "Yes, *I'm* working. Doesn't mean—"

His father stopped, and then, surprisingly, laughed.

Edward Marriner's laughter was different when he was talking to his wife, Ned realized.

"He's out on the terrace with the others," he heard, and moved back through the kitchen door, to be out on the terrace with the others.

Melanie glanced up. She didn't wink or anything, just looked at him.

A little later he heard his father call his name and he went back in and took the phone. His dad walked away.

"Hi, Mom."

"Hi, honey! How are you?" The connection was pretty good. His mother sounded the way she always did.

"I'm cool. Nice house. A pool and stuff. Come visit."

She laughed. "Wish I could. Send me jpegs. There's a satellite link at our base."

"Okay. So, hey, you all right?"

"I'm fine, sweetie. Busy. There's lots to be done."

"I'm sure."

"They badly need doctors here."

"I'm sure," he said again. "Well, all right, okay then, good talking. You take care."

"Ned?"

"Yeah?"

A little silence. "I really am fine."

"I believe you."

A small laugh; he knew that laugh. "Make your father believe me."

"Not easy, Mom."

And that was about as much as he intended to say. She was smart, though, she was really smart, and he could tell from the silence that she was trying to think how to reply. "Leave it, Mom," he said. "Just keep calling."

"Of course I will. Dad says you've made a friend."

"Yeah, I'm quick that way."

Another silence, he was a bit sorry about that one.

She said, as he'd been pretty sure she would, "Ned, don't be angry. Doing this is important for me."

"Sure," Ned said. "And you're doing a lot of good. Stay cool, keep phoning. Don't worry about us. I'll get started on my essays soon."

She was silent again, he could hear her breathing, far away, could picture her face right now.

"Bye, Mom," he said, and hung up.

It had become necessary to get off the line. He stared down at the phone and took a few deep breaths. He heard his father come back in. He turned around. They looked at each other a moment.

"Damn it to hell," said Edward Marriner.

Ned nodded. "Yeah," he said, quietly. "Exactly."

His father smiled crookedly at him. "Watch your language," he murmured. And as Ned smiled back, he added, with a rueful shake of his head, "Let's go for dinner. I'll let you have a beer."

THEY WENT TO A BISTRO on the road east, a place out of town towards the mountain, but not so near as to worry Ned about what had happened earlier.

Melanie had picked the place. She had about twenty restaurants in her notebook: phone numbers, specialties, hours. Probably all the chefs' names, Ned thought. In green ink.

Everyone else had some kind of special asparagus appetizer, and fish, but Ned stayed with steak and frites, a chocolate mousse after, and was happy enough. His shoulder hurt but he'd known it would. His father did actually offer him half a beer but Ned passed. He didn't much like beer.

His new cellphone rang as they were walking back to the car.

"Damn," said Greg. "Damn! I *knew* it was a hot date. How does he get chicks to call him so fast?"

"Better swim trunks," Melanie said.

"Right. And how would *she* know that?"

"Women know these things," Melanie said. It was dark in the parking lot, but Ned was pretty sure she winked at him.

The stars were out by then, winking themselves in a blue-black sky, and the moon, nearly full, had risen while they were inside. He walked away from the others, his sandals crunching on gravel, and answered the phone.

A woman. Not Kate Wenger.

"Hello, is this Ned? Ned Marriner?"

Not a voice he'd ever heard. Speaking English, slight British accent.

"It's me. Who is this, please?"

"It *is* you. I'm so glad. Ned, listen carefully. Did anyone hear you ask that question? You need to pretend you're talking to someone you know."

"Why do I need to do that?"

It was curious, he really had never heard this voice, but there was something about it, nonetheless. A variant, a riff.

"I'll answer later, I promise. Can you make an excuse to go out for a bit when you get home from dinner? Running, maybe? I'll meet you."

"How do you know I run?"

"I promise answers. Trust me."

"And how do you know this number?"

"The woman at the house gave it to me. I called there first. Ned, please? We need to meet, somewhere without people."

"That's a bad movie line."

She chuckled at that; it made her sound younger. "It is, isn't it? Meet me alone by the old oak tree?"

"Then why? Why with no one there?"

She hesitated.

He had, with every word she spoke, more of that sense of something almost recognized.

"Because I can keep track inwardly of anyone approaching," she said.

"*What*? How do you . . . ?"

"You know how I do that, Ned. Since yesterday."

That silenced him pretty fast. He walked a bit farther away.

His father called. "Ned! You're keeping people waiting. Bad manners. Phone her back from the villa."

He lifted a hand in agreement. "I have to get back to the others. And you still haven't said who you are."

"I know I haven't." He heard her draw a breath. "I'm nervous. I didn't want to do it this way." Another silence. "I'm your aunt, Ned. Meghan's older sister. The one who went away."

Ned felt his heart thud. He gripped the phone tightly. "My . . . her . . . ? You're my Aunt Kim?"

"I am, dear. Oh, Ned, where do we meet?"

HE WAS WALKING in the night under that nearly full moon. They'd dropped him at the bottom of the hill where their road wound through trees to the villa. He'd said he wanted to take a walk, it wasn't even ten o'clock yet. His mother probably wouldn't have let him, his father was easier that way. He'd reminded them he had the cellphone.

He couldn't jog, he wasn't wearing running shoes, which gave him more time to think. He listened for a car behind him. He'd given her the best directions he could. She'd said she'd find it. She might be ahead of him, too: he had no idea where she'd been when she called.

He was still in shock, he decided, whatever that actually meant.

He had believed her, on the phone.

Reckless, maybe, but there was no real way *not* to believe someone saying she was your aunt, the one you'd never met. And it fit with things he'd known all his life—adult talk overheard before

sleep, from another room. It also made sense of that feeling he'd
had that the voice—accent and all—wasn't as unknown as it should
have been.

It was close to his mother's, he'd realized, after hanging up.

Things like that could make you believe someone.

The road went up for a pretty fair distance, actually, when you
weren't running. He finally came to the car barrier again. There was
a red Peugeot with a rental licence parked there. No one in it. Ned
walked around the barrier, came up to the wooden sign again, under
stars this time, and turned left towards the tower.

After a few minutes he saw it, looming darkly at the end of the
path. He hadn't been able to think of any other place. It wasn't as if
he knew his way around here. She'd said she wanted to be where no
one could sneak up on them.

No crowds here, that was for sure. He was alone on the path. Or
he assumed he was. It occurred to him that it would have been smart
to bring a flashlight—and in the same moment he saw a beam of
light beside the tower. It flicked on and off, on and off.

His heart was beating fast as he walked towards it. Impulsively,
feeling a bit stupid, he tried to reach inside himself, to whatever had
let him sense the man in the cloister yesterday and again in the café
this afternoon.

He stopped dead in his tracks. He swallowed hard.

The awareness of a presence ahead of him was so strong it was
frightening. Once he'd looked for it, there was this glow in his mind
where she was: green-gold, like leaves at the beginning of spring.

"That's me, dear," he heard her call out. Same voice, same very
slight British accent. "Interesting you found me. I think it *must* be a
family thing. I'm going to screen myself now. I don't want them to
know I'm here yet."

"Why? And who? Whom?"

The man in the café had talked about that screening thing too. Ned started walking, towards the flashlight, and to where he could sense the glow of her. Not a shining so as to illuminate the night, but within him, placing her in the landscape like some kind of sonar. Then, a moment later, the green-gold went out.

"It's 'whom,' I think," she said. "Your mother was always better at that sort of thing. Hello, Ned Marriner. Nephew. May I please hug you? Is that unfair?"

She'd been sitting on a boulder beside the low barrier ringing the tower. Now she stood up and came towards him, and in the moonlight Ned saw his aunt for the first time in his life.

He wasn't sure, actually, how he felt about being hugged, but she opened her arms so he did the same, and he felt her draw him to her, and hold on.

He became aware, after a moment, that she was crying. She let him go and stepped back, wiping at her eyes with the back of one hand. She was slim, not too tall, a lot like his mother.

"Oh, dear," she said. "I promised myself I wouldn't cry. This is so uncool, I do know that."

He cleared his throat. "Well, aunts aren't usually cool."

He saw her smile. "I thought I'd try to be," she said.

She looked at him. For some reason Ned found himself standing as straight as he could. Stupid, really.

"You look wonderful," she said. "I haven't seen any pictures since your gran died two years ago."

Ned blinked. "Gran sent you pictures? Of me?"

"Of course she did, silly. She was so proud of you. So am I."

"That doesn't make sense," Ned said. "You never even knew me. To be proud or anything."

She said nothing for a moment, then turned and went back to the boulder and sat on it again. He followed a few steps. He wished there was more light so he could see her better. Her hair was very pale, could be blond but he was guessing grey. She was older than his mom, six or seven years.

She said, "A lot of things in families don't make sense, dear. A lot of things in life."

"Right," Ned said. "I get that. It's kind of in my face now."

"I know. That's why I came. To tell you it's all right."

"*How* do you know?"

Choosing her words, she said, "Yesterday you entered a space I've been in for some time. When it happened I became aware of it, of you, from where I was. The family thing, I guess."

"Where's that? Where you were?"

She wasn't hesitating now. "England. In the southwest. A place called Glastonbury."

"That's . . . where you live?"

"With your uncle, yes. That's where we live."

"Why? Why did you go away?"

She sighed. "Oh, Ned. That's *such* a long answer. Can I just say, for a bit, that I feel easier there than anywhere else? I have . . . a complicated connection to it? That isn't a good answer, but the good one would take all night."

"Fine, but why did you cut yourself off from . . . from us?"

It had happened years before he was born, before there'd been any "us," but she'd know what he meant.

She had clasped her hands loosely, was gazing up at him. It was weird, but even in moonlight he could see how much she looked like his mom. That gesture was his mother's, even, when she was listening, making herself be patient.

"I didn't, really. Cut myself off. We always kept track of you three through my mother, your gran. I told you, families are tricky. Meghan felt, rightly I suppose, that I'd done something totally unexpected in getting married so quickly to someone she didn't even know, moving to England right away. She felt I'd abandoned her. She was . . . very angry. Didn't want phone calls, or letters, or emails later. Hung up on me, didn't write back. She was only seventeen when I left, remember?"

"How can I remember?" he said.

He saw her smile. "Now *that* sounds like Meghan."

He made a face. "Sorry."

"Don't be, but you do know what I mean? Big sister marries a stranger, city hall, no proper ceremony, moves across the ocean, changes *all* her life plans? Without any warning. And there was . . . there was more to it."

"Like?"

She sighed. "That gets us to the all-night part. Let's say I was involved in something connected to what you felt yesterday. It runs in our family, Ned, on the maternal side, as far back as I've been able to trace, disappearing, showing up again. And in me it included some other things that turned out to be really important. And really, really difficult? That changed me. A lot, Ned. Made it impossible to be what I'd been before. Or stay where I'd been."

It sounded, weirdly, as if she were asking his forgiveness.

He thought about how he'd felt by the mountain earlier today, and in the cloister before. The impossibility of explaining, making sense of it. "I might be able to understand some of that," he said.

"Thank you, dear." She looked up at him. "I thought you'd be feeling afraid, and confused, so I came to let you know you aren't alone. Not the first. In this."

She stopped. It seemed she was crying again. She shook her head. "I'm sorry. I *swore* I wouldn't cry. Your uncle said I didn't have a hope. I actually bet him."

"You lose, I guess. Where is he? My uncle."

She wiped at her eyes with a Kleenex. "I don't know if I should tell you," she said.

Ned shook his head. "Too many secrets. Gets screwy."

She stared up at him. "You're probably right. Between us, Ned?"

He nodded.

"Dave is north of Darfur."

It took him a moment. "The Sudan? But that's . . . my mom is . . ."

"Your mother's there, yes. Your uncle's watching over her."

His mouth had dropped open, comically, like in a cartoon. "Does she . . . does my mom *know* that?"

His aunt laughed aloud. A burst of amusement that made her seem much younger. "Does Meghan know? Are you crazy? Ned, she'd . . . she'd *spit*, she'd be so angry!"

He honestly couldn't imagine his mother spitting. Maybe as a ten-year-old . . . but he couldn't picture her as ten, either. Or seventeen, feeling abandoned by her sister.

He said, really carefully, "Let me get this. My uncle is there secretly? To keep an eye on my mom?"

Aunt Kim nodded. "I told you, we've been keeping track of all of you. But she's the one I worry about."

"Why her?"

She was silent.

"Too many secrets," he repeated.

"This is your mother, dear. It isn't fair, this conversation we're having."

"So it isn't fair. Tell me. Why?"

Gravely, his aunt said, "Because I think Meghan does some of what she does—the war zones, choosing the worst places—as a response to what I told her I'd done, just before I went away. I made a mistake, telling her."

Ned said nothing. He couldn't begin to think of what to say. He felt shaky.

She saw that, went on talking, quietly. "She'd thought . . . I would be an ambitious doctor, try to do good in a big way. I'd talked like that to her when she was young. Big sister, kid sister, sharing my future. Then I . . . had that experience, and everything changed. I went off to some village in England to spend my life doing country medicine. Childbirth and checkups. Runny noses, flu shots. Everything scaled way down. After the one very big thing she never understood, or accepted."

"That's . . . what you do?"

She smiled. "Runny noses? Yes, it is. I also have a garden," she added.

Ned rubbed at the back of his head. "And you think . . . ?"

"I think Meghan's been showing me, and herself, what she believes I *should* have been like. What I rejected. Along with rejecting her. And she's proving she can do it better."

Ned was silent. After pushing to hear this, he wasn't sure he'd been right, if this was something he really wanted to know.

"Ned, listen. People do wonderful things for complicated reasons. It happens all the time. Your mother is a hero where she goes. People are in awe of her. Maybe you *don't* know that—she probably doesn't tell. But your uncle knows, he's been there, he's seen it."

"He's done this before?"

"Only when we knew she was going somewhere very bad." She hesitated. "Three times, before this one."

"How? How did you know where she was going?"

He thought he saw her make a wry face in the darkness. "Dave's talented at quite a few things. Computers are one of them. He could explain it better than I can."

Ned thought, then he stared. "Jesus! My uncle hacked Doctors Without Borders? Their server?"

Aunt Kim sighed. "I've *never* liked that word. Hacked is so illegal-sounding."

"Well, it is illegal!"

"I suppose," she said, sounding cross. "I've told him I don't approve. He says he needs to know what she's doing with enough time to get there himself."

Ned shook his head stubbornly. "Great. So he just drops his own life and goes there too. And . . . and what was Uncle Dave going to do if Mom was attacked or kidnapped by insurgents? In Iraq or Rwanda, or wherever? The crazy places."

The anger he lived with, the fear, dull as an ache, hard as a callus in the heart.

His aunt said, quietly, "Don't ask that until you've met him. Ned, you won't ever know anyone more capable of dealing with such places. Believe me."

He looked at her. "And he does this because . . . ?"

"He does it for me. Because I feel responsible."

There was something different in her voice now. Ned looked down at her, where she was sitting on the rock, hands still clasped.

"Wow," he said finally, shaking his head again. "*That* is controlling. I thought my mom was bad. Is it another family thing? Last I checked she was forty-something years old. And you still feel responsible for her?"

Her laughter again, rueful this time. "If I plead guilty to being a worrier, will you let me off with a reprimand? And please—Ned, you mustn't tell her!"

"She'll spit?"

"She'll want to murder me with a machete."

"My mother? Are you—?"

"Shh! Hold on!"

Her tone had changed completely; there was a command in it, startlingly. Ned froze, listening. Then he, too, heard a sound.

"Shit," whispered his aunt. "I wasn't paying attention."

"You swore," Ned pointed out, a reflex; it was what he did when his mother's language slipped.

"Hell, yes!" said his aunt, which wasn't his mother's reply. "We may be in trouble. *Damn!* My mistake, a bad one. But why would they attack us? What have you been doing here, Ned?"

"Why would *who* attack us?"

"Wolves."

"What? No way. Wolves are mostly vegetarian. I learned that in school last year."

"Then tell these to go find the salad bar," said Aunt Kim, grimly.

Ned heard a crackle of twigs and leaves from the woods north of them, near the place where the path sloped down towards the city.

"Do you have anything? A pocket knife?" Aunt Kim asked.

He shook his head. The question chilled him.

"Find a stick then, fast, and get back towards the tower." She flicked on her flashlight and played the beam on the ground between them and the trees.

Ned caught a glimpse of eyes shining.

He was very afraid then, unreal as it all seemed. As Kim ran her beam across the ground nearer to them Ned saw a broken branch and darted forward to claim it.

As he did, he heard his aunt, her voice hard, icy, speaking words in a language he didn't know, followed by silence from the darkness.

"What?" he mumbled, hurrying back beside her, breathing hard. "What did you just . . . ?"

"I asked why they've come to trouble the living."

"The living? You mean humans, right? Us?"

"I mean what I said. These are spirits, Ned, taking an animal shape. They have come early, they aren't as strong as they will be in two nights."

Two nights.

Right, Ned thought. He knew that part. *Beltaine*. Hinge of the year, when souls were abroad.

Or so his gran had told him, along with other tales of the old ways. His gran had been named Deirdre and had grown up in Wales, half Welsh, half Irish. The woman beside him now was her older daughter. Things he needed to deal with were coming really fast and he didn't know what any of it *meant*.

There was a green-gold presence inside him again, though, when he looked. That was Kim. She wasn't screening herself any more.

"Were you speaking Welsh?"

"Gaelic. Closer to what they'd have spoken back when. I hope."

"You speak Gaelic?" A dumb question.

"Took me long enough to learn. My accent's terrible, but they'll understand me if I'm right."

Back when. When was that? he wanted to ask. Sometimes when you had this many questions, Ned thought, you didn't have a clue where to start.

Another sound, to his right this time, back up the path. They were a long way from the car barrier and her car, from the road, lights, from anyone.

"You didn't answer me," Kim said. "Ned, what have you been doing to draw these to you?"

"Nothing on purpose, believe me. I met someone in the cathedral. Who . . . he . . . it's complicated."

"I'm sure," she said dryly. "It tends to be."

She motioned, and they moved together, stepping over the low rail towards the curved tower wall, backs to it, facing outwards. For the moment her words in that other language seemed to have frozen the creatures out there.

She flashed her beam at a sound again, found another wolf. Four of them, five? They were both peering in that direction when Ned heard a scrabbling sound to his left, beyond his aunt.

Without stopping to think, an entirely instinctive movement, he stepped past her and swung the branch up and around, hard, like a baseball bat.

He cracked the wolf on the side of the head. It was heavier than the dog had been this afternoon. It didn't spin or flip, but it went down. Ned cried out as his injured shoulder felt the impact.

His aunt swore again. Ned heard her snap something, almost snarling it herself, in the same tongue as before, and though he couldn't understand a word he felt himself go cold with the ferocity of what she said.

Cold in fire, he thought. There was a word for that, the sort of stupid thing you got asked on English tests.

Kim repeated whatever she'd said, same cadences, more slowly. Ned almost *felt* a collective intake of breath in the night, as if the very darkness was reacting to her. He was down on a knee, holding his shoulder. The wolf lay near enough for him to see it. It wasn't moving.

"Well done," his aunt said to him quietly. "Are you hurt?"

"Shoulder, not from now. I had to fight a dog this afternoon."

"What? Ned, what *have* you been doing?"

"I got mixed up in something. He said after that they were just playing games. With him, not me."

She was still a moment. Then, "Who said that, Ned?"

"The man from the cathedral. He's part of all this, I think."

"Well, of course he is. That's why you're being tracked. Can you reach him?"

"What? Like a text message?"

She actually chuckled, briefly. She *was* cool, he decided, even if aunts weren't supposed to be. "No, not that. Can you see him the way you saw me, looking inside?"

He hesitated. "I *have* done that. Seen him. Twice. He said he can screen himself."

"I'm sure he can. I can't see him. You try."

Ned tried. He had the same foolish feeling as before, though not quite the same, if he thought about it. His aunt was here, and he *could* sense the glow of her, within.

Only that, however. Not the scarred man who'd told them in the cloister that he had no name. He shook his head. "I have no idea what I'm doing," he said.

"Why should you?" she replied, gently. "That's a reason I came, to tell you it's all right not to know."

"That's why?"

She nodded. "And a few other things."

The wolves hadn't made a sound since she'd spoken, or since he'd cracked one of them with the branch.

"Have they gone?" he asked.

Kim turned and looked out. He had a sense she wasn't really looking, or not with her eyes.

"They're waiting," she said. "I really wish I knew what this was about. How's your shoulder?"

"Never play tuba again."

She made an exasperated sound. "How terribly funny. You are *just* like your mother."

"Mom joked like that?"

"At your age? Endlessly."

It was news to him, that was for sure.

"What are they waiting *for*?" he asked.

"We'll know soon enough. Keep trying to find your friend."

"He isn't my friend, believe me."

A sound behind them. A voice in the same instant.

"He is not. You would do well to remember it."

They whipped around together. To see something that never left Ned—even with all that was to come. What appears to us first on a threshold is often what lingers afterwards.

A very big, broad-shouldered man stood in front of the broken opening in the tower. He had long, bright hair, a heavy golden necklace, and golden armbands. He was clad in a tunic and a darker fur-lined vest, with leggings, and sandals tied up around his calf.

And he was antlered like a stag.

It wasn't a horned helmet or anything like that, which was Ned's first thought. He wasn't *wearing* a helmet. The antlers grew straight out of his head.

It was in that moment that Ned Marriner finally accepted that he had entered into a world for which nothing in life had prepared him. There was no denial left in him; he felt fear coil and twist like a snake in his body.

"How did you get in there?" he stammered.

"He flew down. Most likely as an owl," said his aunt, with what seemed to him an awesome calm. "Why not take your own form?" she added, almost casually, to the man-beast in front of them. "Playing at shapes is a game. And this form is disrespectful. Even sacrilege."

"Not wise the thought," the antlered figure said. They were speaking French to each other, in an oddly formal way. "In my own guise I am too beautiful for you, woman. You would beg me to take you, right here, with the child watching."

Ned bristled, clenching his fists, but his aunt only smiled.

"Unlikely," she murmured. "I have seen beautiful men, and managed to keep my self-control."

She paused, looking up at him, and then added, "I have also seen the god whose form you are copying, *and* his son, who commanded wolves far more deadly than these weak spirits." Her voice changed again. "You have some small shape-shifting power. I see it. Do not expect me to quail. I knew men and women with so much more than that, there are no words for the telling. Do not ever doubt me. I am offering iron-bound truths by moonlight at the edge of an oak grove."

Ned shivered. He couldn't help it.

This is my aunt, he thought.

The yellow-haired figure with the antlers of a stag stared at her for a long time. "If you speak of the wolflord or the god so carelessly, one or both might make you pay a price."

"True enough. *If* I did so carelessly."

The figure in front of them hesitated. "You are very sure of yourself, woman. Who are you? Why have you come into this? It is nothing to you, nothing *for* you."

Kim shook her head. "I haven't come into anything, except to guard my sister-son. He has no power, only the beginnings of sight, and is no danger to you. He is to be left alone."

"Ah! She makes a demand. And if I do not accede?"

Ned heard his mother's older sister say, quietly, "Then depend on it: I will summon powers that will blast you out of time to an ending. And you will never do what you have come to do."

Silence in front of them. Nothing from the wolves behind. Ned wondered if the others could hear the thudding of his heart.

"It is a wise man who knows his true enemies," Kim added, softly.

"You do not even know what this is about. What I am come to do." But there was doubt in the deep voice now. Ned could hear it.

"Of course I don't," Aunt Kim said crisply. "Nor do I care. Do what you must. I have told you my only purpose. Accept it, and we are gone. Do not, and you have only yourself to blame if all you dream of goes awry."

"The boy fought this afternoon beside a man I must kill."

"Then kill that man if it is your destiny to do so. But the boy is mine and will remain untouched. He has no wish to interfere."

"Is it so? Can he speak for himself, or does a woman do all for him, as for a suckling babe?"

Aunt Kim opened her mouth to reply, but Ned, angered, said, "I can speak just fine. I have *no* idea what that was this afternoon, but someone I'd had a drink with was attacked. Would *you* have stood by?"

Another silence. "The cub has a tooth," the man said, laughing suddenly, a deep-throated, genuine amusement. The rich sound rolled over them. "Of course I would not have stood by. Shame to my family and tribe, to do so. That does not mean you might not have died."

"He said you were playing games."

Another explosion of laughter, the antlered head thrown back in delight. It was thrilling, as much as it was frightening.

"Truthfully? Did he say that?" The fair-haired figure looked at Ned. "Ah, you give me pleasure! By all the gods, I am his master. He knows it with every narrow breath he draws. And as for you: children have died in games-playing."

"Games like that, I can imagine." Ned was still furious. "So tell me, give *me* pleasure now, did I kill your four-legged friend today? With the chair?"

He felt Kim's hand on his arm, cautioning him. He didn't feel like being cautioned.

The antlered figure said, "He was in a form he'd taken for the moment. No more than that. He is behind you now in another shape. Tell me, foolish child, what *do* you think this is about?"

"We told you," Kim snapped. "We don't know what this is. And will not claim any role. Unless you compel it." She paused, then added, her voice going colder again, *"Will* you compel me? *Shall I summon Liadon from his sacrifice?"*

Amazed, Ned saw the tall figure take a quick step backwards in shocked surprise, the head lifting again, the antlers caught by moonlight.

"You know a name you ought not to know," he said after a long moment. His voice had gone quiet. "It is guarded and holy."

"And I am one with access to it," Kim said. "And I *have* seen the one you mock with your horns."

"I do not mock," the man protested, but he sounded defensive now.

"Playing a game dressed in his antlers? No? Really? Are *you* the child, to be forgiven by your elders? Not yet come of age?"

The man before them said, "Have done, woman! I have been among these groves and pools, coming and going, returned and gone, for past two thousand years!"

Ned swallowed hard. He heard the man say, "Is that a child, to you?"

Ned was intimidated now, really afraid, wondering at his own recklessness a moment before, but Aunt Kim said only, "It can be. Of course it can! Depending on what you have done, coming and going. Show me otherwise: go from us, and not in his shape. I wish to return to my own home. This is your place, not mine. Swear to leave the boy in peace and I am gone from your games. And your battles."

The tall, glorious figure stared down at her, as if trying to penetrate through moonlight to some deeper truth. "What is your name?"

Kim shook her head. "I will not give you that tonight."

He smiled then, another unexpected flash of teeth, and laughed again. "A sorrow to my heart. I would give you the gift of mine, and freely, bright one, if I had a name here."

Kim didn't smile back. She said, "You are waiting for one?"

"She will name me. She always does."

"Both of you?" Kim said.

Ned had been chasing the same thought.

A hesitation, again. "Both of us." He looked down at her. "And *then* it begins, and I may kill him again, and taste the joy of it."

He looked at Kim another moment, ignoring Ned entirely now; then he lifted his great head and rasped words in yet another tongue Ned didn't know. They heard a growling sound in reply; twigs snapped on the ground behind them as the animals left.

"You will not enter into it?" the antlered man said again to Kim.

"Not unless you force me," she repeated. "You will have to live with that as sufficient surety."

His teeth showed again. "I have lived with less."

He turned, ducking through the opening into the round, tall tower, twisting his head so the horns could pass through.

They stood a moment, waiting. There was a quick, sharp sound and they looked up and Ned saw an owl fly through the open tower top and away, to the north.

They watched it go.

Kim sighed. "I told him to change his shape. He does like to play, I guess."

Ned looked at his aunt. He cleared his throat.

"That was extremely close," she murmured. She leaned against his good shoulder. "I haven't tried anything like that in a long time."

"What do you mean?"

Kim stepped back and looked at him.

"Oh, dear. Ned, did you think I could *do* any of what I said?"

He nodded. "Um, yeah, I kind of did."

She sighed. "Fooled you, then," she said.

He stared at her. He felt cold. "You were *bluffing*? Could . . . could they guess that?"

Her mouth twitched in an expression he actually knew well, from his mother. "I guess they didn't. But damn it all sideways and backwards, I so wish your uncle were here."

CHAPTER VII

Afterwards, Ned Marriner was to think of April 29 of that year, mostly spent in Arles among Roman and medieval ruins, as the last day of his childhood.

It was an oversimplification; such thoughts always are. But we make stories, narratives of our lives, when we look back, finding patterns or creating them.

We tend to change in increments, by degrees, not shockingly or dramatically, but this isn't so for everyone, and Ned had already learned in the two previous, difficult days how he seemed to be different. Most of us, for example, don't see our aunts as a green-gold light within ourselves.

On a sunny, windswept morning among the monuments of Arles, he wasn't actually dwelling on this. He was—although being of a certain age, he'd have hated to admit it—having a good time, nerdy as that might be.

The Roman arena was seriously, no-messing-around impressive.

He'd never been to Rome. He understood the Colosseum there was way bigger than this, but the one here would do fine for Ned. Twenty thousand people, two thousand years ago, watching men fight each other, or wild beasts, in a place this massive. And it was still standing.

Even Larry Cato might have had to concede it was cool, sort of.

They'd driven here first thing, about an hour in morning traffic. His father and the others had gotten busy immediately to use the early light, setting up an exterior shot where the high stone walls of the arena were being restored: gleaming, almost white on the right-hand side, revealing the grimy evidence of centuries on the left.

With plenty of notice from Melanie and Barrett Reinhardt, the city authorities had removed the scaffolding for them, leaving Ned's father a clear line. The spring sunlight was brilliant, intensifying the contrast between left and right, the untouched part and the cleaned-up side.

It was going to be a terrific photograph, even Ned could see it, and his father's body language as he moved around, setting up, gave it away anyhow. Edward Marriner was watching the clouds scud past in the breeze: he was going to try to time the shutter releases, to have one of them in the background, half in, half out.

Ned had left them to their work.

He'd gone inside the arena and wandered among the seats, looking out over the bright sand below. They used this place for bull-fights these days. Everything changed, nothing changed: huge crowds of people coming here to watch a battle.

In the Middle Ages, the guidebook said, there had been a kind of ghetto inside these curved walls, shabby, falling-down hovels within a structure that had celebrated the power of Rome. If you liked irony, this was for you, Ned thought. Larry would *definitely* have liked it.

He looked at an artist's sketch of that medieval slum in the book Melanie had given him. He wondered what that would have been like: to live in a world sunken so low, struggling just to stay alive, with the towering evidence of glory all around you, looming above your collapsing little walls and muddy alleys.

You sure wouldn't have a feeling that the world was progressing or getting better over the years, he decided. The book reported that one time, during a plague outbreak in here, the authorities of Arles had surrounded the arena and had killed anyone trying to get out of the slum.

The world might be a *little* better than that today, Ned thought. Parts of it, anyhow.

Making his way along the seats, he circled all the way around to the chute where they released the bulls. He was able to get down from there, jumping a barrier onto the sands.

There were people inside the arena—including a big Japanese tour group—but no one seemed inclined to tell him to leave. He saw people taking his picture. He actually thought about that sometimes: how we end up as background faces in some stranger's photo album or slide show.

Had he been a little younger he might have pretended to be a gladiator or a bullfighter, but not at fifteen with people watching him. He just walked around and enjoyed the sunshine and the size of the place. The Romans were engineers and builders, his father had said on the drive here: roads, temples, aqueducts, arenas. Whatever else you thought about them, you had to give them that.

Ned wondered if Kate Wenger had been here, had seen this place. He thought of calling her, then remembered it was a school day. Besides which, it was too soon, majorly uncool, for that kind of call.

Thinking of her sitting in some classroom made him grin, though. He'd have been in school himself back home at this hour.

Without wanting to actually give his father the satisfaction of knowing it, Ned had to admit this was way better.

He took out his own Canon and snapped a couple of pictures. He'd email jpegs to Larry and Vic and ask how biology class had been today and how much homework they had. Maybe he'd get Steve to take a picture of him in the pool at the villa to send. They didn't need to know it was freezing cold in there. With his friends, you had to grab the moments when you had the upper hand.

Ned considered that for a moment. Grabbing moments with the upper hand: Mr. Drucker would have labelled that a mixed metaphor and probably marked him down for it. Ned smiled to himself. Mr. Drucker was on the other side of the ocean.

They had lunch at a restaurant with a terrace overlooking the Roman theatre ruins, near the edge of the city centre. Oliver Lee, the writer for the book, joined them there. He lived in the countryside to the north.

Lee was in his sixties, tall, rumpled, and stooped, with pale, pouchy eyes, reading glasses on a chain about his neck, and long, not very disciplined silver hair that scattered in various directions and gave him a startled look. Every so often he'd run a hand through it, to mostly negative effect. He wore a jacket and a diagonally striped tie and smoked a pipe. There were ashes on his tie and jacket. It was almost as if he'd been *cast* as a British author.

He was funny, though, a good storyteller. It seemed like he knew a lot about wine and Provençal food. He also knew the chef, who came hurrying out to greet him with enthusiastic kisses on both cheeks. Lee's French accent and grammar weren't good—surprisingly, after thirty years here. He put almost every verb in the present tense. He was rueful about that. Called it Frenglish.

"Stubborn Brits, my generation," he said. "Still regretting we lost Calais back to the French five hundred years ago, too superior to take the time to learn any language properly. Point of honour, almost, to be ungrammatical."

"Why move down here, then?" Edward Marriner asked.

He was in a good mood again. The morning had gone well, obviously. He had switched to water after one glass of wine, startling the Englishman, but there was a working afternoon ahead for him.

Oliver Lee gestured towards the gleaming marble of the Roman theatre across the way, pine trees scattered among stones and dark green grass. "Sun and wine, ruins and olive trees. The ancient, all-knowing sea an hour away. And truffles! Have you *tasted* the truffles here?"

Ned's father shook his head, laughing.

Lee drained half of his third glass of wine and smiled affably, fiddling with his pipe. "Mostly it was the sun, mind you. Ever lived through a winter in Oxfordshire?"

"Try Montreal!" said Melanie.

Oliver Lee turned to her. "Had you been there to greet me, and had I been even ten years younger, my dear, I'd have willingly tried Montreal."

Ned blinked, and then did so again. Melanie actually blushed.

"Wow!" said Greg, looking at her. "That was impressive! I've *never* seen her do that."

"Be quiet, you," Melanie said, looking down at her plate.

"Interesting," Ned's father said, grinning behind a hand, smoothing his moustache. "Green hair streaks do it for you, Oliver? Do people *know* this about you?"

"Adornment has varied widely over the centuries," Oliver Lee said airily, waving a hand. "My own ancestors painted themselves *blue* long ago, with woad. Silly to be wedded—or woaded, shall we say?—to only one look as attractive." He chuckled at his own joke. "Green hair is *entirely* a matter of a woman's style and choice, and when she has eyes like your Melanie, she may make any choice she wants."

"Wow!" said Greg again. "Um, she's single, you know. And she's read some of your books."

"Shut *up*, Gregory!" Melanie said fiercely, under her breath, still looking down.

Ned had never thought about Melanie's eyes. They were green, he realized. He wondered if the stripe in her hair, maybe even her ink colour, had been chosen to match. Women did that, didn't they?

"Mr. Lee, you are much too nice. You'll make me lose focus this afternoon," Melanie said, looking up finally, smiling at the author. "And that's bad in photography!" She still looked flushed.

Lee laughed, and shook his shaggy silver mane. "I must doubt that, though it is kind of you to say. I'm just an old man in sunshine among ruins, paying homage to youth and beauty."

Do people actually say *that sort of thing?* Ned thought.

Evidently they did, in Oliver Lee's circles, anyhow. The waiter came for their plates. The others ordered coffee.

"I'll be heading home, get out of your way," Lee said to Ned's father. "Wouldn't want me tripping over your apparatus or meandering into a photograph."

Ned decided this was a role the man played, a public pose. Looking at his father, he saw the same assessment there, and amusement.

"You're welcome to stay," Edward Marriner said. "Melanie can help keep you from meandering. We're going over to Saint-Trophime, the cloister."

"Ah. Good. You'll want to photograph the eastern and the northern sides," Oliver Lee said, brisk all of a sudden. "If the other elements . . . light and such . . . are right for you, of course. The pillar carvings on those sides are the glory and wonder. There are legends about them."

"What kind?" Melanie asked, clearly pleased to have the subject changed. *Homage to youth and beauty.* Ned was going to have to remember that. Ammunition for later, in the war of the ringtones.

"The sculptures there are so lifelike," Lee was saying, "it was believed at various times that magic was used to make them. That the sculptor had sold his soul and been given a sorcerer's power to turn real people into stone."

"The Devil's work in the cloister of a church? Very nice." Ned's father smiled.

"That was the tale, for centuries." Lee finished his wine. "People have often feared very great art."

"What about the other two sides?" Steve asked.

"Ordinary work, done later. Pleasant enough."

The judgment was crisp, dismissive. It made you realize how much of an act the eccentric ancient was. In its own way, Ned thought, it wasn't so different from Larry Cato pretending to be bored by everything.

"I'll remember that," Ned's father said. "But I'll need Melanie to tell me which side is east or north."

Oliver Lee smiled. "A woman is often our guide. Guardian of portals, and all that." He lit his pipe, taking his time about it, then brushed some ash off one sleeve. "East is to your left, as you go in."

"You'll put me out of a job," Melanie protested. They laughed.

"What else will you do here?" Lee asked.

"That's all today," Marriner said. "Two set-ups is as much as we usually manage. We can come back later. What else should we look at?" He pointed. "The theatre here?"

"You might. But the cemetery, surely. Outside the walls. They always buried people outside the city walls, of course. Les Alyscamps was the most famous burial ground in Europe for a very long time. Ruinously pillaged by now, of course. Most of the marbles are gone, but if it is quiet, and it usually is, it is one of the most evocative places I know. Van Gogh painted it. There were Celtic, Roman, medieval . . . wouldn't even surprise me if there were Greek tombs there."

"Why Greeks?" Ned asked.

First thing he'd said over lunch. He wasn't sure why he'd asked.

Oliver Lee smiled at him through pipe smoke. "It was the Greeks who founded Marseille, about 600 B.C. Called it Massilia. They traded with the tribes up this way. The coastline was nearer here back then, it's changed."

"Traded? Did they . . . fight?" Ned asked.

"Oh, of course. There was always fighting here. Provence isn't the lavender-coloured paradise travel agents and romance books make out, you know."

"I know," Ned said.

His father glanced at him.

"But they did trade mostly," Lee said, as the coffee arrived. He fussed with his pipe, put the lighter to it again. "In fact the founding myth of Marseille has the captain of that first Greek expedition being chosen as husband by a chieftain's daughter, shocking everyone in the tribe."

"*She* got to pick?" Melanie asked wryly.

"Celtic women were a bit different, yes. They had goddesses of war, not gods, among other things. But I think it was certainly unexpected when Gyptis chose Protis. If it really happened, of course, if it isn't just a tale. Can't imagine the warriors of her tribe could have been pleased. Someone just pops in to the feast and is picked by the princess."

"Tough life!" Greg said, laughing.

For no reason he could put a finger on, Ned felt a chill, as if he was hearing more than was being said. But he had just about given up trying to have things make sense the past few days.

He was remembering last night's lonely tower, wolves and a stag-horned man. His bright mood seemed to be gone. How did you send dumb emails to classmates after that kind of encounter? He felt like going off again to be by himself but he had to wait for the others to finish.

Steve said, "When did the Romans get here, then?"

Oliver Lee enjoyed having an audience. "They were asked to come, by those Greeks in Massilia, when the fighting got worse a few hundred years later. Some of the Celtic tribes were trading with them, but others were unhappy about foreigners all along the coast and started raiding. Collecting skulls for doorposts."

"Skulls," said Ned, as noncommittally as he could.

"Ah! I knew a boy would like that part," said Lee, chuckling. "Yes, indeed, they did do that, I'm afraid. Skulls of enemies, skulls of ancestors, a complex religion, really. The Celts put them in shrines, hung them from their doors—a form of worship. They found scads of them at a site not far from here, and at another one, just by where you're staying in Aix."

Ned kept his expression neutral. "Entremont?" he asked.

"That's the one!" Oliver Lee beamed at him.

"I've heard about it," Ned said, as his father raised an eyebrow. "A friend of mine here said it was worth seeing."

"Well, you can walk around it, the views are pleasant enough, but it's been picked clean by now. The finds are in the Musée Granet in Aix, but that's closed up for renovations all year. Everything's in crates. Actually, there was a bit in the paper a few days back . . . a robbery in the storerooms. Someone nicked a couple of the finds, a skull, a sculpture . . . that sort of thing. Bit of hue and cry, valuable things, you know?"

"We didn't hear about it," Ned's father said.

Ned was controlling his breathing.

"Well, we're not listening to local news or anything," Greg pointed out.

"Ah, well, archaeological finds are always looted and pillaged," Lee said, waving his pipe. "First for gold and gems, then artifacts. Think of the Elgin Marbles in London, stolen from Greece. Wouldn't surprise me if these things from Aix turned up in New York or Berlin on the black market soon."

It would surprise me, Ned Marriner thought.

LEE EXCUSED HIMSELF after they paid the bill, to do some banking in town and then make his way home. He kissed Melanie's hand when they parted. Nobody laughed.

Ned arranged to meet the others at the cloister, then walked across the street to the theatre ruins. They were just reopening after the midday closing.

"Ned?"

He turned.

"Mind company for a bit?" Melanie asked. "They don't need me for the first half hour, setting up screens and lights."

It was windier now, she kept a hand on her straw hat.

"How could I refuse youth and beauty?" he said. He'd wanted to be alone, actually, but what was he going to say?

"You be quiet," she snapped, and punched him on the shoulder. He covered a wince; it was still sore from the day before. "Have you ever heard anything like what he said in your life?"

"Personally? I sure haven't. Which is a good thing, I guess. I know you get it all the—"

He stopped, because she punched him again. He wasn't actually in a kidding mood, anyhow. He was thinking about Greeks arriving among the tribes, back when, and objects stolen from a museum in Aix this week.

He was going to have to figure out what to do about that theft. He knew where those artifacts were, after all.

On the other hand, the person who had almost certainly taken them might not appreciate interference. There was even some question as to whether you could call him a "person," given that he'd had horns growing from his head and then changed into an owl in moonlight. In fact you could go further and say he had made it extremely clear he *didn't* want interference in whatever was about to happen.

If the joke in that underground corridor—and that is what both men seemed to consider it—was over now, would it be interfering to report that the objects stolen from the museum could be found under the baptistry in the cathedral? He didn't know. How could he know? He needed to talk to Kate. Or his aunt.

His aunt, all by herself, was another subject—object, person—that needed thinking about, big time.

The good news for the moment was that Melanie seemed preoccupied too, not in her chatty tour-guide mode, which he'd feared. She sat down on a grassy mound and took out a long green guidebook, but didn't open it. Nor did she seem unhappy to be left alone when Ned wandered away among the random pillars and what was left of the original theatre, which wasn't much. This site wasn't as well preserved as the arena was; grass growing among the ruins, and the quiet, made for a different sense of the past.

He glanced back at Melanie. He wondered if Oliver Lee's comments had upset her. Maybe she'd felt she was being teased, the only woman among five men—or four men and a kid.

Ned didn't think Oliver Lee had been teasing. He thought he'd meant the compliments, but these things were still a mystery to him.

So was trying to figure out last night.

AFTER THE WOLVES and the owl had gone away, he and Aunt Kim walked back from the tower to her car. Ned had kept his branch, but nothing troubled them on the path. He heard an owl as they approached the fork in the trail and it made him jump, but his aunt touched his arm.

"Not ours," she said. "That's a real one."

"How do you know?"

"Different sound. I live in the country, remember?"

He looked at her. It was hard to see clearly in the night, but her hair was really pale in the moonlight. He gestured to it.

"My mom colours her hair."

"I know. I've seen lots of pictures. She's lovely, Ned. She always was."

"Would it be like yours if she didn't? Colour it?"

She hesitated. "I doubt that."

They walked a bit farther. Ned saw the barrier and her car.

Aunt Kim stopped. "I'll drive you back, but first . . . Ned, listen to me, it would be unfair to you *and* to your mother for us to meet like this again. I don't want to put you in a position of having to keep secrets."

"Um . . . you think I don't keep secrets from my parents?"

She smiled faintly. "I'd worry if you didn't, but not this large, dear."

Ned was silent. He'd been thinking the same thing himself, actually, about everything here. "You going to leave? Go home?"

They were at the barrier. Her car was on the other side, but this seemed a conversation better suited to the night.

"Not immediately," Aunt Kim said. "I'm going to try to find out more about what's happening, if I can. For a day or two. Is my phone number on yours now? On callback? If you need me?"

He nodded. "Am I going to need you?"

Her turn to be silent. He had a sense she was dealing with real emotion. He felt it himself: this was his mother's sister, and he'd never seen her in his life and might never see her again. It seemed they shared something, too. Something complicated and difficult.

"I don't know," she said finally. "I hope you don't need me in the way you meant. I'm pretty sure he'll keep his promise, leave you alone."

"Pretty sure?"

She looked up at him. "What do you want me to say?"

"Um, 'absolutely positive' would do."

She laughed. "Your parents have done a good job, Ned."

He felt embarrassed suddenly. "Yeah, well, don't tell them."

He saw her smile, but she didn't reply.

Ned thought of something. "I should have asked before. Do you and Uncle Dave have kids? Have I got cousins in England I don't know about?"

She shook her head. "I'm afraid not. I never could have children."

Ned looked at her a moment. He might be young, but he knew enough to change the subject. "Ah, you really think my mom would be unhappy if . . . you called her, or wrote?"

Not the best subject change. "She always has been, Ned. It wouldn't be the first time I tried. Which is why she'd be so angry if she knew I'd called you."

That made sense. An end run, going around her.

"She'd spit?" he guessed. He was a bit fixated on that image, actually.

"Maybe not," Aunt Kim said, managing another smile. "Let's go. You need to be home before your dad gets worried."

"He's not the worrying type, except about my mom."

"I think I know that."

They walked around the barrier to her car. She started it up, switched on the headlights. He looked at her in the glow of the dashboard panel. She really did look an awful lot like his mother, but her hair, he now saw, wasn't silver or grey, it was entirely white.

"Do you colour it that way?" he asked.

"It's been like this since I was very young."

"Really? Must have been pretty cool, back then."

"I suppose. Your uncle liked it."

"I guess he must have."

She turned the car around and they wound their way along the narrow, twisting road back to the fork where Chemin de l'Olivette branched away. Ned had pointed and she'd stopped.

"I should walk up," he had said. "They'll see headlights from the house."

"I know. Tricky questions. You'll be fine tonight, but from now on, Nephew—and pay attention—you stay with the others after darkfall. Don't go wandering. I can't give you that 'absolutely positive,' so don't do silly things, okay?"

He'd thought of a joke, but didn't make it. Not after what had happened.

"I promise. But will you . . . if you figure anything out, will you at least let me know?"

His aunt had smiled at him. "You know I will. I'll call before I go home, regardless. Keep my number, Ned."

Ned had cleared his throat. "You know I will," he said.

He'd leaned forward and kissed her on the cheek. She brought a hand up and touched his face. Then he got out of the car. He'd stood in the darkness and watched her drive away. Started walking up their road and found himself working hard not to cry.

It had been a hell of a day, really.

He'd heard a grunting sound from the trees off the upward path. That would be the wild boars, *sangliers*, that came out to feed after sundown. Veraclean had told them about those. They didn't scare him. Other things might.

No one had asked any questions when he walked into the house. It wasn't all that late and he was fifteen, after all, not a kid any more.

THERE WASN'T THAT MUCH to see around the theatre of Arles. It was peaceful, though, in the sunlight and shade. You could imagine the past.

Ned wondered if that was the trade-off here in Europe: the major sights were impressive, and overrun with people. The smaller ones you could have to yourself.

He and Melanie were alone here except for three cyclists who had chained their bikes to the railing outside and were huddled over a map on the far side of the three columns left standing.

He walked back to Melanie. She'd put her guidebook down, had her knees up and her arms around them. She looked relaxed, but he wasn't sure she was.

"*Did* you match the streak in your hair to your eyes?" he asked, sitting beside her on the grass. He plucked some sprigs and tossed them up to blow away. It was windy now.

She looked at him from behind sunglasses. "Don't tease me, Ned."

"I wasn't. Real question."

She shook her head. "A dumb one, then. Of course I didn't. You think I'm too old to just like punk as a look?"

"Way too old," he said.

"I said don't tease. I'm twenty-five, for God's sake."

"Like I said, *way* too—"

She punched him on the shoulder again, but it was his good arm this time. He held up his hands in surrender. She gave an exaggerated sigh and they sat quietly awhile. There was a bird singing in one of the trees. The cyclists walked past, speaking German, and went out through the gate. Ned watched them unchain their bikes and pedal off.

Looking straight ahead, behind her shades, Melanie said, "I am five feet tall, you know. That makes just over a hundred and fifty damned centimetres. Which is short, any way you look at it. Do *not* make a joke, Ned."

"No? I have at least three."

"I know you do."

He glanced at her. "It really bothers you?"

Still looking towards the pillars, she said, "Not always. Not even usually. I mean, there are worse problems in life. But it's a pain. It's hard to be taken seriously sometimes. Like I'm a hobbit with a Daytimer. Just . . . cute."

He thought about it. "My dad takes you pretty seriously. I think Greg and Steve do. And I don't think you're cute, I think you're an anal-retentive, micro-managing pain."

She laughed this time. "Ah! Progress."

"I mean, you researched jogging paths here, Melanie."

She looked at him. "I like my job, Ned. A lot. I'm just trying to do it right."

He sighed. "I know. Makes *me* feel babied, though."

She shrugged. "Don't. You aren't a baby at all. I checked out music stores and jazz bars for Greg and found an indoor pool for Steve, you know."

He thought about that. "I didn't know, actually."

"Think you're the only man in my life here, sailor?"

His turn to laugh.

He would remember that exchange. Another moment from when he was still young. Melanie looked at her watch and tsked, and got up, collecting her gear. Ned went with her back to the main square. The famous church was there; a tour group was just entering. Melanie walked farther along to a side entrance that led to the cloister. *Another cloister*, Ned thought.

As they went in, through an arched, covered space, they saw a gendarme keeping people out so that his father could work. Melanie explained who they were; the policeman motioned them through. Ned let Melanie go ahead of him up a flight of steps.

He felt strange again suddenly. A disorienting intrusion of that other world he seemed to have accessed. Something was approaching, a vibration in the air almost. Presences. He could *feel* them. Not the man in the grey leather jacket, or the golden one from the tower. But whatever this was, it wasn't far away. Or *they* weren't.

He looked around him. He wasn't sure why this place was shaping awareness in him, but on some other level he did know: layers and layers of the past were here. A past that seemed not to be entirely finished with.

Was it ever finished? he wondered.

They reached the top of the stairs and saw another arch, with a green space beyond, in shadow and light.

He wished his aunt were here. And at the same time he was uncomfortably aware that there was something he hadn't told her last night before they parted at the laneway. And that it might be a mistake.

I'm going to cancel, anyway, he said to himself. *It doesn't matter.*

"You and I are still at war," Melanie said over her shoulder just before she walked into the cloister. "Don't kid yourself. That ringtone doomed you, Ned."

He couldn't think of a funny reply in time.

He watched as she went towards where he could see his father and the others standing in a brilliant light. From the dim, vaulted cool of the archway Ned looked in at them. He saw his father moving quickly, talking quickly, stopping to frame a view with his hands, going a few steps over to gauge it elsewhere. He saw that the brown hair was greying more now, though not yet the notorious signature moustache.

One day, Ned understood, that hair *would* be grey, or thinning, or both, and his dad wouldn't be wearing tight blue jeans and moving with such crisp, strong strides. Time would do what it did to people. Ned stayed where he was, looking at his father as from within a long tunnel.

Edward Marriner wore a green workshirt and his favourite tan vest with a dozen pockets. He had his sunglasses pushed up on top of his head. He was talking, gesturing, but Ned couldn't hear what he was saying. He seemed far away. An effect of acoustics, of light and shade. It frightened him, this sudden feeling of distance, of being on the other side of some divide.

There was a full moon in his mind, high among stars in the midst of afternoon.

Childhood's end.

CHAPTER VIII

There had been clouds throughout the night, hiding the moon much of the time, but the last day of April dawned windy and very clear.

A mistral was blowing, Veracook advised over morning croissants. They were sheltered here, tucked under the slope, but it would be fierce today up on Mont Ventoux, or in Avignon, or the hill villages like Les Baux or Gordes or Menerbes. Small children had been blown off cliffs, she said, shaking her head dolefully, when the mistral came down from the north.

That same wind was, however, a photographer's dream of light. It scoured the sky of anything resembling haze or mist, leaving it hard, brilliant, precise: a backdrop that rendered wildflowers, monuments, medieval ruins, bending cypresses electric with intensity.

Edward Marriner had been here before in a mistral. He wasn't about to try going up any cliffs with their gear, but he did change plans for the morning over his second cup of coffee.

Melanie scribbled fast notes and got busy on the telephone. Greg, designated driver, carried his mug into the dining room where the maps were spread on the table and bent over them, plotting routes. Steve started loading the van.

They were now going east, an hour or so, to some monastery called Thoronet. In this light, the stones of the abbey would almost come alive, Ned's father told him. They were alone at the kitchen table.

"It's ironic," Edward Marriner said, "and it pleases me. There are a lot of things to like about the medieval Cistercian monks, and a few not to like. They started by opposing church wealth and ostentation, but they also detested learning, study, books themselves. And even worldly beauty. Bernard of Clairvaux, who shaped the order, would have hated the idea that people find their abbeys beautiful now. They weren't supposed to be. That would have been a distraction."

"From what?" Ned asked.

"God. Prayer. Silence and work in the most remote places they could find. They came down here for the solitude."

"From where?"

"East of Paris, I think. Don't quote me."

Ned made a face. "As if. This isn't an essay, Dad."

Edward Marriner ignored that, sipped his coffee. "Thing is, Provence has *always* been seen as a kind of paradise, and that attracts people. For their own reasons."

"The Greeks? Like he said yesterday at lunch?"

"Oliver? Yes. In a way, everyone who's ever come here has been a stranger trying to *make* it theirs. There are footprints and bones all over. Some places are like that."

"Isn't everywhere like that?"

His father looked at him. "Maybe. Even Greenland and the Hebrides have been fought over, but it's happened in some places more than others. This is one of those. Being desired can be a mixed blessing." He grinned suddenly, as if he'd amused himself. "This morning, my son, in this light, I am going to make an old, cold abbey look so gorgeous the bones of Bernard of Clairvaux will spin in his grave, wherever it is."

"Nice of you," Ned said.

"Damn right. Want to come see?"

Ned realized, not for the first time, that his father loved what he did. For reasons he decided not to elaborate upon, he declined the invitation. He'd do some reading on the terrace, he said, music, a training run . . . he'd keep out of their hair and out of trouble. Might even work on one of his essays.

Melanie, coming to report the van loaded, reminded him that their cell numbers were on his auto-dialer. Ned came to attention and saluted. She laughed.

He watched them drive off. The two Veras were busy, upstairs and in the kitchen. He did read for a bit outside: a novel Larry had said was really scary. Reading supernatural horror didn't have quite the same effect after last night. Ned wondered if Stephen King had ever encountered a figure with stag horns under a watchtower. Maybe he had. Maybe that was how he got his ideas.

Ned doubted it. He was too distracted to read, though. Kept looking up and watching the trees on the far side of the pool bending in the wind.

He went back in and checked his email. Nothing from home, but Kate had sent him her essay.

He read it over, decided it was perfect. Too perfect—she wrote way too well. Ned's own schoolwork was okay, but he never took enough time to be *that* good.

He opened the attachment and spent some time dumbing it down a little so Mr. Drucker wouldn't hear alarm bells going off in his bald head.

It was good to have something ordinary to think about. He stayed at the keyboard till he had the thing shortened and simplified enough to read like an essay Ned Marriner would do while on holiday in France. He added a couple of typos and misspelled some proper names.

Almost as much work, doing it this way, as it was writing a paper, he thought. Not quite, though. He was going to have to write the other two essays properly. He'd promised, and he personally doubted Kate Wenger would give him another essay without expecting something in return.

He wondered what that might be. She was cute, in that skinny, runner, ballet-student kind of way. Her being so geeky didn't bug him as much over here, with the guys not around to needle him about it.

The guys were where Mr. Drucker was. Let them suffer.

He downloaded the Arles pictures and sent a couple with emails to Larry and Ken, pretending to feel sorry for them.

It was too windy to go in the pool. Below the house, away from the sheltering slope, he could see the mistral ruffling the water and swaying the cypresses. He checked his watch. Not even noon yet. Time to kill. He wasn't due to meet Kate till after five.

His father's weren't the only plans changed, however. He would meet her, but they weren't going up to those ruins. Not today.

He'd made that decision in Arles. It was one thing to be adventurous, another to be an idiot. He'd figure out something Kate would go for: they could tour that studio where they were meeting, then have pizza or Chinese in town. She could tell him all about Cézanne, she probably *knew* all about Cézanne.

He'd tell her about what had happened last night. Maybe.

A part of him was torn about that. Kate was in on this, had been from the beginning, but she hadn't been around when the dogs attacked, and what he'd seen later with Aunt Kim by the tower was so outside whatever you wanted to call normal that Ned wasn't sure *how* to talk about it.

It wasn't that he didn't trust her. Kate Wenger was a "trust me" kind of girl. He'd already decided that. But Ned was the one with the burden of whatever was going on inside himself, that strangeness near Sainte-Victoire, sensing people as an aura inside his head, knowing things he should never have known . . .

In a way it felt like some kind of honour demanded he keep silent about what he seemed to have found. Aunt Kim had talked that way about her own experiences, whatever they were. It wasn't a word—honour—that you heard people use a lot any more.

There was also the considerable possibility that if he tried to talk about this with others, people would think he was flat-out nuts. That was B-movie stuff, of course. The guy who sees the aliens land, or the mutant giant killer spiders, and everyone thinks he's drunk or stoned.

Kate Wenger wouldn't think that way. Ned knew that much.

He just didn't know for certain what, or how much, to say.

He'd play it by ear, he figured. Sometimes planning too hard messed you up. His father had had plans for today and had shifted them with a gust of wind. You needed to be able to do that, Ned thought. React, be on your toes.

He decided to go for a run. He was under orders from his coach to keep to his routine and log it, anyhow. He went up to change, kept his phone with him. Aunt Kim had told him to do that. She was someone that still needed figuring out.

She'd said her hair had gone white—the way it was now—when she was young. As much as anything she'd said or done, it was that hair, the absolute whiteness of it, that made Ned feel certain she'd really gone through whatever it was she'd hinted at. She was another "trust me" kind of person, he thought.

She hadn't *told* him what it was she'd done back then. That had to do with the honour thing, he guessed. Partly being fair to his mother. He made another guess: it sounded like she'd told Ned's mom, her sister, before going away to England. And everything in their relationship had gone to hell.

Maybe you got careful after that. Maybe you learned a lesson.

He clipped on a bottle of water, put some euros in his pocket, grabbed a couple of power bars, and waved goodbye to Veracook. At the end of the drive he pressed the gate code and went through. He did his stretches there, getting used to the wind, then started jogging down the slope of their road, loosening up.

Halfway down, where the trees on the left opened out to a long, flat meadow beside the road, Ned stopped.

There was a boar, a really big one, in the middle of that field.

Ned held his breath and wished he were better hidden. Not from fear—the animal wasn't that close—but so he could watch it without scaring it away. They were morning and evening feeders, Veracook had said. They slept through the day. This one was a contrarian, it seemed.

On impulse, he reached out with his mind. He'd encountered a few animals lately that weren't what they seemed. He sensed nothing, however. He wasn't sure what he'd expected but it did seem as if what he was looking at here was just a really massive, grey-white boar, rooting for food in an open field in the middle of the day.

On the other hand, today wasn't an ordinary day, if Ned under-stood anything of what he'd been learning. He'd become suspicious of coincidences. And while he was thinking this, standing quietly in the roadway, the animal lifted its head and looked at him.

Boars were supposed to be nearsighted, relying on smell and sound, but this one sure did seem to be staring at Ned. Neither of them moved for a long time. Ned thought he'd feel foolish, holding the gaze of an animal, but he didn't.

Then the boar turned, not hurrying, but as if determined, purposeful, and went into the woods on the far side of the meadow.

Carrying a message? Had it been waiting here for him? Or was that way, *way* too paranoid a thought? Did everything have meaning today out here in the woods and fields, or would you go a little crazy—or a lot—if you let yourself think that way?

He shook his head. How could you sort out what had significance when you didn't *understand* anything? The answer was: you couldn't. And because of that, he told himself, you stayed out of it.

That was why he was going to tell Kate Wenger that they weren't going up to the ruins of Entremont today. Not on Beltaine eve, when the Celts believed the gates between the living and the dead lay open after the sun went down.

An artist's studio and a walk and wonton soup in town sounded just fine to Ned, thanks very much.

He watched the space at the edge of the woods where the boar had gone in, but there was nothing to see. He shrugged, and started jogging again. At the bottom of their road, without even thinking about it, he turned left and then right, heading towards Aix. There was traffic, it wasn't nearly as pleasant a run, but he couldn't handle Mont Sainte-Victoire to the east, and he was *not* going back up to the tower again.

Melanie had told him about a stadium and track on the edge of the city. A street sign pointed left to the "Stade" before he reached the ring road. It wasn't far. A track would be ordinary, familiar, uncomplicated. You went around and around, no surprises.

There were a few older guys running there, in blue T-shirts and shorts. Ned joined them, doing laps in the wind. His shoulder was still sore. It turned out they were from a military school down the way. Ned thought of a bad joke about French armies and learning how to run, but decided it wasn't a smart idea to tell it.

A couple of them were moving pretty well, and Ned fell into stride with them. He wasn't sure they were pleased that a younger kid was staying with them. They probably thought he was American, too, which would make it worse, he guessed, so he grunted a few things in French about the weather and trying to keep up his training while over here, and that seemed to help some. They didn't try to sprint away—or jump him and beat him up, for that matter.

Most of the students peeled off across the field when the teacher's whistle blew, but one of them did two extra laps with Ned and waved a goodbye when he ran after the others.

It felt good to have even that simple gesture of connection.

What he had to think of as normal life was still going on. He had essays to write, mileage to log, he would email more jokes and jpegs home. Maybe he'd find these guys here again, or different ones. Maybe he'd skateboard—he could see ramps south of the track. Later maybe he'd download some new songs from iTunes. In fact, he should do that today: he had a monthly download allowance from his mother, not used up yet, and this was the last day of April.

You could treat the fact as dark and mystical, full moon and spirit stuff, or just remind yourself that you had four songs owing to you, in the life you actually lived.

He was stretching and walking to cool off, drinking water from his bottle, when his phone rang.

He checked the number on the readout and flipped it open.

"Hello, babe," said Kate Wenger. "Watcha doing?"

Ned blinked. *Babe?*

"And whom might this be, please?" he said. "Nicole? Mary Sue? Marie-Chantal?"

She laughed. "Screw Marie-Chantal," she said. "Not literally, though. She's got two zits on her chin today, anyhow. Gross. How are you?"

Her voice sounded different. Sassier, older.

"I'm cool. Just finished a run on this track east of the city. With some army types. Bit weird."

"I know that track. By the municipal pool? The guys are from the *école militaire*. Seen them, too. Yummy."

"What's with *you* today?"

"Nothing. I'm in a good mood, that's all."

"Yeah, 'cause your evil roommate has pimples."

"Maybe. And maybe because we've got an outing later. If you have nothing more important doing, *mec,* buy us some cheese and apples and a baguette, we'll have a late picnic up there."

"Um, Kate. I've been thinking about—"

"Gotta run, babe. Late for class. *Ciao!*"

She hung up.

Babe, again? Ned felt confused. If they'd gotten to this stage in two coffees, he'd sure missed it. Larry would call him an idiot and tell him to go for it: a girl who seemed to like him, a long way from home and prying eyes . . . *vive la France!* Wasn't this the real life he'd just been thinking about? Download songs, email a picture, see how far Kate Wenger would let him go after school?

He shook his head again. Trouble was, he kept picturing a sculpture in a cloister with a rose leaning against it, and an owl rising through the open roof of a tower at night. Maybe you did have to hang on to normal life, but some images could make it hard.

He was sweating, needed a shower. He went back to the intersection, then to the right up the road. He stopped at the bakery and bought a *pain au chocolat* and ate it as he walked. Better than the power bars, by a lot. He took the wide curve left and then their own path. When he reached the open field again he looked, but the boar hadn't returned.

Small, handmade signs at branching points along the road pointed towards the different houses on the way up. He saw theirs at the top. Someone—had to be Melanie—had stuck cute little Canadian flags to the small blue markers for Villa Sans Souci.

For the first time, kind of late, Ned thought about what that name meant. *No Worries*. Yeah, right. And *hakuna matata* to you, too.

HE WENT BACK out later in the afternoon, before the others returned. Left a note on the table telling his dad he was meeting Kate. They had his cell number, anyhow. The wind was still blowing but not as much as in the morning. It was steady and hard, though, unsettling.

Veraclean had said the mistral would always blow for three or six or nine days, but Veracook said that was just an old tale and they'd argued about it, insulting each other. It was kind of funny, actually.

Ned wondered how the shoot at the abbey had gone. If Bernard of Wherever was spinning in his grave yet.

It was a bit of a hike: half an hour to the ring road and then around it north towards Cézanne's studio. He thought of taking a bus, but he felt hyper and figured the walk would help. He passed the grocery store and the bakery again but he didn't buy a baguette or the apples and cheese. They were not going up to picnic, there was no point.

He found the studio easily enough. It was signposted on a busy street, not much charm or quiet around it. It would have been a lot different in Cézanne's day, he figured. This place would probably have been outside Aix, in the countryside.

Leaning against the stone wall in the wind, he watched the traffic whip by and tried to imagine this house overlooking fields, olive trees, maybe a vineyard. He'd seen another sign on the way here: Entremont was along this same road farther north. Kate had said that.

He'd taken a few minutes to google the name. It was pretty much as Oliver Lee had told them. A tough tribe of Celts and Ligurians (whoever *they* were) called the Salyans had built their stronghold up there. The Romans had taken catapults up in 124 B.C., smashed it to bits, killed bunches of Salyans, took the rest as slaves.

Then they'd built Aquae Sextiae, which became Aix-en-Provence, eventually. And now a cluttered cathedral covered their forum. So the Roman city was gone, too, he thought. There were Celtic ruins, Roman ruins, maybe even Greek ones somewhere around. And ruined medieval abbeys like the one his father was photographing today: they were all covered over, or tourist spots, or just old and forgotten. Most people couldn't care less. Couldn't even tell the difference between any of them, probably. What's a thousand years, between friends?

Ned, standing by the roadside, car horns blaring at intervals, mopeds whining past, tried to decide if it *should* matter, anyhow.

If Coldplay, or Eminem, or the Boston Red Sox, or Guild Wars online were the big things in your life, and you didn't give a thought to ancient Celts or Bernard the Spinner in his grave, was that so bad? Everyone lived in their own time, didn't they? Didn't they *have* to?

Well, really. If you left out the types like the nameless guy in a grey leather jacket who had apparently made a carving eight hundred years ago and was here now to put a rose beside it.

Did you have to *believe* him, anyhow?

Yeah, Ned thought glumly: with enough added to the story, you did, even if you preferred not to. Same with what he'd seen with his aunt.

He wondered where Aunt Kim was right now. He thought of phoning her, but that made him think of his mother, and *their* whole story—a different kind of past—and he left the phone in his pocket. His mom would be calling tonight. He knew one topic he wouldn't raise with her.

"Yo, miss me lots?"

He turned, in time for Kate, stopping in front of him, to rise up on tiptoe and kiss him on each cheek.

Well, they *did* do that here in France. But still.

"Ah, hi," he said, looking at her. "Yo. You've, um, got lipstick on."

"So do you now." She wiped at his cheeks.

"You didn't before," he said.

"Wow. An observant male-type person. Must make an entry in my blog."

"You have a blog?"

"No."

He laughed. But he was still unsettled. She looked good. Her hair was brushed out today, not tied back. She wore chunky silver earrings, and—he belatedly realized—she had some kind of perfume on. He decided not to comment on that.

"Montreal men," he said instead. "We're the observant ones. Finest kind."

"So you say. Where's the food, dude? I *asked* you . . ."

Ned took a breath.

"I, ah, thought we'd do things a bit differently. I haven't been in town much. Not at all, really. Thought we'd see this studio since we're here, then cruise Aix? I'll get you a caffeine fix, then we can eat Chinese or a pizza or something?"

Kate Wenger stepped back a bit. A car horn honked, not at them.

"Ned, I really wanted to show you this place. It is seriously cool. And it may tie in to the stuff we've been finding."

He cleared his throat. "Well, that's the thing. You're right, it may tie in. And tonight's not a real good night, if it does."

"Beltaine?" She smiled a little. She had some kind of eye makeup on, too, he realized. "Uh-huh. Montreal men, careful, cautious guys . . . little bit afraid?"

"Kate, there's a couple things I've got to fill you in on. And, yes, maybe I'm being a bit careful. I did tell you what happened by the mountain, remember?"

"Well, obviously if you start getting sick or whatever, we turn back. You think I'm an idiot or something?"

"No, but I think you're a little overfocused on doing this today." There. He'd said it.

She crossed her arms, looking up at him. "You really are scared."

Stung, he said, "Kate, I'm the one who went into that tunnel. I'm not exactly afraid of doing stuff."

Her expression changed. "I know you aren't." She shook her head. "But look, Ned, it's twenty after five. It only gets dark after eight. It's a fifteen, twenty-minute walk and we'll go right now, forget the studio. I'd like to show you Entremont, even see if anything feels funny to you or anything? Then we'll leave. I prefer Chinese to pizza, and I know where to get good hot-and-sour soup. So, come on?"

She took his hand and tugged.

He found himself falling into step. Her fingers were cool. It took a second or two—he hadn't done a whole lot of hand-in-hand walking with girls—for them to get their fingers sorted out. He felt briefly as if he had a few too many digits, then they did interlace and it was . . . pretty good, actually.

He seemed to be going north with her, after all. He caught another hint of that perfume. He wondered if they'd be alone at this place.

"As it happens," she said cheerfully, "I am more woman than you deserve. I still have two apples and half a baguette in my pack."

"Ew," Ned said. "For how many days?"

With dignity, she said, "Montreal men may do that sort of thing but New York women don't. Packed this morning."

They walked beside the road into the wind. It was rush hour, cars going by, a lot of students getting on and off buses, classes over for the day. Ned saw another sign pointing towards Entremont. Just past it the road became a minor highway as they left the city limits.

"So, what else happened?" Kate asked. "What'd you need to tell me?"

Her fingers were still in his. The guys, were they aware of this, would be saying things about how he had it made, make-out wise, heading off with a chick who had *started* the hand-holding and had even met him with a tiptoe kiss. He wouldn't have gotten far pointing out that sometimes even guys greeted each other with kisses on the cheek in France.

There was something about Kate today. Or maybe—new thought—maybe this was what she was *usually* like and the tour-guide geek stuff had been her manner with a stranger?

He didn't think so. Ned shrugged, inwardly. *Go with it,* he told himself. She was right about one thing: Beltaine wouldn't actually begin until dark, hours away. They'd be back in Aix.

"You aren't talking to me," she said.

He sighed. Decided to go halfway, but keep his aunt to himself— too many family things entangled in that. He said, "After you left the café, day before yesterday, the guy from the cloister showed up."

He felt her react. The thing about holding hands: you could tell right away.

"You saw him outside?"

"No. He'd been in there, two tables over. Behind a newspaper."

"Oh, Jesus Christ," she said.

Ned, in his current mood, found that funny. "Nah. I'm beginning to think this goes back *way* before him."

"Don't be cute, Ned. What happened? How did you find him?"

The hard part. Explaining this. "He let his . . . screen down, whatever, his guard, when you and I walked out. And the sense of him I had in the cloister when he was on the roof kicked in. I knew he was inside."

"And you went back?"

"Yeah."

She walked a few steps in silence. "I didn't mean it, you know, before . . . when I said you were scared."

That felt good, but it would be uncool to show it. He said, "Well, I'm obviously not careful. I'm being led into the countryside by some hot New York woman I hardly know."

"Hot? Ned Marriner! You coming on to me, babe?"

Again! There was no *way* she'd have said that before. He looked over at her. She was grinning, and then she winked at him.

"Ack!" Ned cried in horror. "No winking! Melanie winks all the time, I can't stand it."

"I refuse," said Kate Wenger, "to let my behaviour be dictated by the habits of someone named Melanie. I will wink if I wish to wink. Deal with it." She was smiling.

Then she pointed ahead. Ned saw a brown sign with the symbol for a tourist site and "Oppidum d'Entremont" on it. They had arrived.

It was at a branching of highways. A lot of traffic, still. They waited for a break and ran across. No sidewalk here, just grass by the highway. They walked a little farther north.

"Right here. Up the hill," said Kate. "It's pretty steep. Can you handle it?"

Ned didn't actually feel like joking.

They went up a dusty gravel slope. He couldn't see anything at first, then they were high enough above the highway—they always built high in those days, he knew—and he saw a small parking lot and a metal gate. The gate was open, the lot was empty.

"I've never seen anyone here," Kate said. "I've been twice. I don't even think the guard sticks around, probably just comes to lock up at closing." Closing, Ned saw on the gate, was at six-thirty. They *would* be out of here hours before dark.

Kate led him through, still holding hands, along a wide path between olive and almond trees. "That's what's left of the outer wall," she said. She pointed. "This was a city here, not just a fort."

The wall was on their right, three metres high in places, rough stones still in place. A little ahead of them it had crumbled a lot more; stones lay where they'd fallen or been dislodged. The Romans had brought catapults all the way up here, Ned remembered. It couldn't have been easy to do that.

It was very quiet now, two thousand years after. He heard birdsong. The wind was still blowing. The light was really clear, what his father had been talking about.

A little self-consciously, he stopped walking, unlaced his fingers from Kate's, and closed his eyes. Found nothing, though, no sense of any presence, and he didn't feel queasy or unwell or anything like that.

She was staring at him when he opened his eyes. He shook his head.

"Told you," Kate said. "It's an archaeological dig, a tourist site, that's all."

"So," said Ned, "was the cathedral."

She bit her lip. First time today she'd reminded him of the girl he'd met three days ago. They walked on. There were almond petals scattered on the ground, making it seem like snow had fallen. The gravel path reached the end of the high wall and turned south to an opening and Ned looked through and saw the long, wide, levelled ruins of Entremont.

And though he'd felt nothing and found nothing when he checked within, he still shivered, gazing out over low grey stones in the late-day light. His gran used to say shivering like that meant a ghost was passing. He didn't say that to Kate.

It was bigger than he'd expected, though he couldn't say exactly what he *had* expected. The path they were standing on ran alongside the ruins on their eastern edge. Ahead of them, a long way, Ned saw that the plateau ended in a cliff. To their left, the ground sloped down past trees into a meadow.

On their right and in front was Entremont, what was left of it.

He really didn't want to stay here. There were a lot of reasons not to stay. But he found himself walking forward with Kate, looking out over the stones. They weren't holding hands now; her own mood had grown quieter, less feverish.

That was the word, Ned decided. She'd been *feverish* before.

He stole a sidelong glance at her. She looked pale, like the stones, as if taken aback by what she'd done, where they were. She stopped, so he did.

They were entirely alone here. In the wind, among the ruins.

He looked left. The site ended, not far away, in that short slope down to olive trees and the meadow. Tall grass there, wildflowers. On their other side were the crumbled, excavated ruins. Beside where they'd stopped were low stones, barely knee high. The wall of a house, he realized; there were others like it all around, defining small rectangular spaces.

"This was the lower town," Kate said softly. There was no *need* to be quiet, but it felt right. "There's an olive press over that way, under the tree." She pointed past the low walls. Her manner was more like what he remembered.

Ned nodded. He walked past her, taking the lead now. They went farther south alongside what remained of those one-room houses. This had been a street once, he realized. It rose a little as they went. He could see, ahead of them, where the upper town began. There was a wider east-west roadway, big blocks of stone beyond it.

Just before they got there, he stepped up on one of the knee-high house walls to look out over the site, and then he stepped down into the space that would have been a home for someone, with a roof and walls, over two thousand years ago. And as he did, as he entered, something happened inside him again.

Ned stood still. The wind was blowing, but they were somewhat guarded from it by the trees to the north and what remained of the settlement wall.

Kate looked at him from the path. "What is it?" she said.

He didn't answer. This wasn't like any of the sensations he'd had before.

"Ned, what is it?" he heard Kate Wenger ask again.

He took a breath. "There's just . . . a lot of power here," he said.

"What does that mean?" He heard her fear.

"I'd tell you if I knew."

It was true: he didn't understand this, only that from these stones a feeling like a heartbeat in rocks was coming into him. No sense of someone actually here, more a—

"It's waiting," he said abruptly.

Then, as he looked ahead, towards the higher ruins across the wide east-west street, he added, pointing, "What was that?"

Kate turned to look. She cleared her throat. "That was the guard tower at the upper town entrance. I saw a layout on their website. Beside it is where the religious sanctuary was. Just there. See the bigger stones? That was the tower."

Ned saw the stones. Thick, grey, heavy. Only the base was left, everything else was down, had been down a long time. But at some point back then, between the part where they were and the section ahead of them, architecture had changed.

You changed, as a people, bit by bit, learned things. Then someone brought war engines to your walls, and it didn't matter any more what you'd learned.

He went forward to look, almost involuntarily now.

Up on a low wall, back down, up and over another, and then he was on the dusty street that divided the upper and lower parts of Entremont. It ended to the east, he saw, on his left, where the slope ran down to the meadow.

This road was wider than anything behind them or ahead. *Main Street*, he thought. Just across it lay the base of the guard tower. He looked at the big stones, imagined a tower. Catapults and time, he thought. He still had a pulsing in his mind, as if the stones were trying to vibrate.

We should go now, Ned thought. He *knew* they should go.

Beside the tower base, to the right of it, was a large, rectangular space.

"What kind of sanctuary?" he asked.

"Well, Celtic, of course. They found skulls here," Kate said quietly. "You know they worshipped the skulls of their ancestors?"

"I heard. And the heads of their enemies, too. Preserved them in oil. Or made them into drinking cups," he said. "Nice people."

Maybe it was right that these walls had come down, if that's what they'd been like. Or maybe it wasn't. And maybe it didn't matter at *all* what Ned Marriner felt or thought about it, two thousand years later.

And then, finally—because they were quite close to it now—ahead of them, in the dusk, Ned noticed a column standing upright towards the back of that sanctuary space where Kate said skulls had been found.

It was as if he was being pulled that way.

He stepped over another low wall into what had been a holy place. He walked up to that column, stood before it, and looked more closely.

The pillar was about seven feet high. Tallest thing here, easily. Carved on it, from the base to the top, were a dozen primitive, unmistakable renderings of human heads.

Ned swallowed hard, and shivered again.

"Look at this," he said.

He heard Kate behind him. She was still on the roadway, hadn't stepped inside.

"Ned."

"Can you believe this?" he repeated, staring at it in the twilight.

"Ned," she said again.

He turned to look back. She was really pale now, ghost-like. Her arms were crossed tightly on her chest as if she were cold.

"Ned, this shouldn't be here."

"What? What does that mean?"

"I saw pictures . . . on the website. Of the dig. This was found here, but it was lying down, not standing, and . . . Ned, they *moved* it, into the museum, like fifty years ago. That's where it's supposed to be."

Slowly he turned back. The stone column wasn't lying down and it wasn't in the museum. It was in front of him, in the shadows of this quiet, gathering darkness.

Ned froze. He didn't breathe. He felt his heart begin to pound, very hard. His mouth was suddenly dry.

It took an effort to move his left arm, turn his wrist, so he could see what he already knew he would see. He looked at his watch.

It was just after six.

He turned to look at Kate.

"Why is it dark?" he said.

CHAPTER IX

After a blank, rigid moment, during which he could see her absorb what he'd just said, Kate put a hand to her mouth. She looked fearfully around her in the great and gathering dark—which had come down upon them hours too soon.

"Ned, what's happening?"

As if he'd know. As if he had any *hope* of knowing.

Gazing past her, still trying to accept the reality of this, Ned saw torches. He tried to swallow; it felt like there was sandpaper in his throat. His heart thumped again, so hard it was painful.

Fires were burning in the meadow east of the entrance through which they'd just come. Torches in a long line—a procession moving towards the ruins.

Unable to form words, Ned just pointed. Kate turned to see.

"Oh, God. What have I done?" she whispered.

No good answer for that. No time for one. Ned looked desperately around for a hiding place, but except for the one column beside him everything in Entremont was flat, levelled. Catapults and time.

He stepped quickly back out of the sanctuary, grabbed Kate by the hand and, bending low, started running east along that wide main street between the upper and lower towns. They went straight out of the site and down the shallow slope. He pulled her to the ground behind a tree.

They lay there, breathing hard.

He thought she was going to cry, but she didn't.

Ned lifted his head after a moment, cautiously, looking to his right, where the torches were. Twenty or thirty of them, he guessed. Some were inside the lower city now, others following. Coming in the way he and Kate had come themselves moments ago—in the sunlight of a springtime afternoon.

It was dark now. It was undeniably, impossibly, night.

He couldn't clearly make out the figures carrying those flames. *Beltaine*, he thought. The Celts used to light sacred fires tonight. He was looking at fires.

Kate lay beside him in the grass, up close, hip and thigh against his. He had to give her credit, she wasn't trembling or whimpering or anything like that. In the midst of everything, with the nearness, he was aware of her perfume again.

"This," she whispered suddenly, turning her mouth to his ear, "is kind of cozy."

Ned's jaw actually dropped again. So much for whimpering, or tears. "Are you insane?" he hissed.

"Hope not. But really . . . I never in my life expected to see anything like this. Did you never have dreams about magic?"

And what did *that* have to do with anything?

"Kate, get it together! I *met* some of these guys two nights ago I think. We could get killed here."

"Then stay close," she murmured, "and let's be real quiet." She shifted a bit so one arm was right against him.

"Quiet won't do it," he whispered. "They can *sense* things. If I can do it, they sure can. We need to get away."

He fished in his pocket for his phone. "Turn yours off," he rasped. "Last thing we need is a ringtone right now."

She moved to open her pack and do it. Ned flipped his phone open. Thank God, he thought: it was working here. He went to dial Greg and then stopped and swore savagely under his breath. Melanie's stupid, *stupid* joke. Greg had that idiotic, multi-digit auto-dial, and Ned didn't know his actual cell number. He punched "3" savagely. Heard two rings.

"Ned, what's up?"

He kept his voice very low. "Melanie, listen, I'm in a bit of trouble. I'll tell you later, but please get Greg to bring the van to the road below a place called Entremont. Quick as he can. I'll meet him there. You know where it is? You can tell him how to get here?"

She was brisk, unruffled. Had to give her that. "I do know. Just north of town? Ned, you okay?"

"I will be when he gets here. It's, ah, something like what happened at the mountain."

"Poor baby. Okay. I'll have him bring Advil. Hang in. He'll be on his way."

Ned flipped the phone shut and turned off his ringer. Put it back in his pocket. Lifeline to the real world, from wherever *this* one was.

He glanced at Kate, still right up next to him. "Is there another way back to the highway?"

She wasn't totally out of her mind. She whispered, "They had a stairway up the cliff, at the other end, but it's crumbled away mostly. It would go south down the valley, I guess."

"We may have to try it. This isn't close to safe."

He lifted his head again. More torches, at least twenty of them. Some had been planted along the path now: from the entrance to the site, lining the road all the way to—of *course*, he thought grimly— the sanctuary space where the one tall column stood.

It was directly in front of them, to the left of the main street. He couldn't make out the column from here, but he could see the flames clearly. The moon, he realized belatedly, was above them now. Full moon night.

"Well, I still have to say I like snuggling here," Kate Wenger said. Ned heard—amazingly—a huskiness in her voice.

Even more amazingly, amid his terror, he was starting to find this aspect of things, her scent, how close she was in the dark grass, unnervingly distracting.

"You gonna kiss me, or what?" he heard her say.

Oh, God, he thought. It made no sense at all. None.

"Forget that now!" he whispered fiercely. "Let's just *go*. We have to get down to the road. We'll try that other stairway, and hope. I figure it'll take Greg twenty minutes."

"No. Stay where you are."

Just behind them. A voice they knew.

Ned froze again, his neck hairs prickling. He felt Kate stiffen beside him.

"I have us shielded here," they heard. "If you go from me they'll sense you and they *will* kill you tonight. For violating this."

Well, *that* would change Kate's idiotic mood, Ned thought.

He heard a rustling sound. A figure crawled up beside him, to lie prone in the grass, as they were, by the tree.

"You followed us?" Ned whispered.

"I saw you arrive. I've been waiting for them." The man from the cloister and café looked at him. Same leather jacket, same cold, intense expression. "I *did* tell you not to come here today."

"I know," Ned said.

"He didn't want to," whispered Kate from his other side. "I thought it would be cool. I like your jacket, by the way." She smiled.

So much for changing Kate's mood.

The man ignored her, his attention fixed on the torches. Some were planted, others were being carried. Ned still couldn't clearly make out who was holding them.

"Why can't I see anyone?"

"They aren't entirely here yet," the man said quietly.

The matter-of-factness made Ned swallow hard again.

"They will be when he comes," he heard.

"When who comes?" Kate asked.

"Softly!" the man hissed.

"When who comes?" she repeated, more quietly. There was silence for a moment.

"The man I have to kill."

Ned looked at him. There were too many questions. He said, "I think . . . I may have seen him two nights ago."

The figure on his left said nothing, waiting. Ned doggedly went on, "I was at this tower, above our place, and . . . Does he have stag horns? Sometimes?"

"He can. Golden hair? A big man?"

Ned nodded.

The wind blew. In the moonlight Ned saw smoke streaming south from the torches. The man beside him shook his head. He said, "Ned Marriner, I have no idea who you are, but you do seem to have yourself entangled here."

"Not me?" Kate said, much too perkily.

"Perhaps," the man said, gravely. "You did bring me here with what you said. I used your words as a sign, lacking any other. You named this place, among all the possibilities. I am grateful beyond words. I'd have likely been elsewhere when she arrived and, as the gods are always witnesses, she would have made me suffer for it."

"She?" Kate said. "You said a man was coming."

Another silence. "She will be here. We are where we are. The barriers are down."

"Holy cow," Kate breathed. "Is he . . . is this guy, like, a druid?"

A sudden, involuntary movement on Ned's other side. "I hope not, or I am lost."

Way too many questions.

Ned asked the first one he thought of. "Why is it night?"

He heard a sound, almost amusement. "Why would you imagine time should follow a known course tonight? Here? I *told* you not to come."

"It shouldn't be dark for hours. We were going to be gone before—"

"You'd have been dead when the spirits came if I weren't here."

Blunt, not a voice to argue with.

"What's his name?" Kate asked. "This other guy . . . with the horns?"

An impatient voice from Ned's other side. "I have no idea yet."

"You aren't being very nice," Kate said, with a sniff. "Neither of you."

Ned still didn't get it: what was *with* her? But he saw the man on his left shift to look across him at Kate. He seemed about to say something, but he shook his head, as if rejecting a thought.

To Ned, he murmured, "I will go up when he comes. They will not be expecting me. He believes he has led me astray. All of them will be intent upon me. Go back along this field to where you came in, then *run* down the path. You will find your afternoon light again, beyond the gate."

Ned looked at him. "What will you do?"

Another shake of the head. "Accept my gratitude and your lives. Leave quickly when I go up."

In that stillness, wind blowing under moonlight, they heard a sound from the sanctuary ahead of them. Ned lifted his head. He gasped. The figures were visible now.

And more than that: the walls of the guard tower were back.

They were up, had risen again, as if they'd never been brought down, never known catapults.

The figures on the street in front of it had their backs to that tower. They were looking back along the path they'd just taken. Ned saw that they were dressed the way the man by the tower two nights ago had been, in variously coloured tunics, bright leggings, boots or sandals. Swords.

Swords?

These were Celts, Ned realized. And that meant they, and the risen tower, were over two thousand years old. *Oh God,* he thought again.

He wished he were home. *All* the way home.

And then he realized another strangeness, on top of all the others. He blinked, looked again. There was only moonlight, smoky torches, and yet . . .

He said softly, "Why can I see them so well? Even colours? Before, I couldn't at all. Now it's . . . too clear up there."

The man on his left said nothing for a moment, then he murmured, "You are inside the night yourself. In your own way. Be very careful, Ned Marriner."

"How do I do that?" Ned asked.

"By leaving. It matters. Beltaine can change you."

Whatever that meant.

The man looked away from them. When he spoke again his voice had changed again. "But see. See now. Here is the bright companion of all my days."

This, too, Ned Marriner would remember. The words, and how they were spoken.

He looked towards the entrance to the site.

Someone else was coming along the path.

No horns on his head this time, but Ned knew him instantly. Not a figure you forgot: tall, broad-shouldered, long-striding, the long, bright hair, same heavy golden torc about his neck. What seemed to be a sword at his side. He didn't remember a blade before. The others by the sanctuary were watching him approach, their torches high, waiting.

The man beside Ned whispered, "See how fair he is, the tall one, how brilliant . . ." Ned could feel him tremble. "I will leave you," the man said.

"You have no weapon," Ned whispered.

"They will give me one," he heard. "Remember, along this meadow, down the path, away."

"You said you weren't a good man," Kate Wenger said, almost accusingly.

"Oh, believe me," he whispered, staring straight ahead, not even looking at them now, "I told you truth."

Ned glanced at him. And, just as in the cloister, something was inside his head abruptly: a thought, whole and complete, something he should have had no way of knowing.

He heard himself say, before he could stop, "Were you at the mountain? Way back then? Sainte-Victoire?"

The man in the grey leather jacket shifted, as if being pulled from where he wanted to be. He gazed at Ned in the darkness for a long moment.

"It really would interest me," he said finally, "had we leisure enough, to learn who you are."

"I'm right? Aren't I? You *were* there?"

Ned could hear him breathing in the night. "We all were," the man said. "She was mine that time." He added something in a language Ned didn't know. And then he said, "Go when I go up. What will follow, you should not see."

He moved forward, low to the ground. Ned thought he was going to stand and walk up the slope right then, but he didn't. He stopped behind another, nearer tree.

Ned had a sense the man was feeling something too fierce, too charged with intensity, to have stayed beside them, with their questions and chatter and guesses: *Why is it dark? What's his name?*

He'd been patient. He was trying to save their lives. But now he needed to ready himself for what was coming.

Kate sighed suddenly beside Ned and slipped her left hand into his right, lacing fingers again.

They will kill you tonight. How did you react so much to the touch of a girl when you'd just heard that? Maybe, Ned thought, maybe such opposing feelings—fear, and the scent and feel of the girl beside him—could somehow go together, not be opposed after all. It was a difficult idea.

He looked up towards the site and the square, risen tower. The tall man had reached the sanctuary and those waiting there. He looked golden, godlike.

The others didn't bow, but they made a space for him in the wide street. His hair was unbound, lying on his shoulders. It was an axe at his belt, Ned realized, not a sword. Jewellery glinted on his arms and around his throat. A smaller, older man stood beside him, dressed in white.

"Wow," breathed Kate. "He's gorgeous!"

She didn't mean the little guy in white. A flicker of jealousy went through Ned, but her words were no less than truth, he thought.

There was a sense of waiting, of anticipation, on the plateau ahead of them, even now that this bright figure had come. They were all turned to the north, towards the torches planted on either side of the path. And because he was looking that way, as they were, across the low, long-levelled ruins, Ned saw when the white bull entered Entremont.

He felt, again, as if the world as he had always understood it was changing moment by moment, even as he lay hidden in the grass.

He saw that the animal was being led forward on a rope by three men through the moonlight of Beltaine eve. The bull was enormous, but it was also docile, moving quietly.

The torches were on stakes planted in pairs in the ground, and the bull—massive, otherworldly—passed between those fires. Ned somehow knew that there was a meaning to this going back so far he was afraid to think about it.

"Another bull," whispered Kate.

Ned shook his head. "Not another. This is the one the others were about."

The moon was shining and full and in that light the animal seemed to gleam and shimmer. Beside him, Kate was watching it in the same way Ned was, with awe and fear—and pity.

"They're going to kill it," she breathed.

"Yes," he said.

He saw the golden figure unhook the axe from his belt. A sound came from the figures around him.

This was a sacrifice, Ned understood. What else could it be? Tonight was the beginning of summer's season, hinge of the year in the days when these people and those who preceded and followed them—here and elsewhere—shaped their rites of goddess and god, fertility and death.

Here and elsewhere, Ned thought. Wales, too. His own people, his mother's. His grandmother's.

They would have to go quickly as soon as the man in front of them went up. Ned wasn't sure why he believed he could do that— just walk up—but what could Ned properly understand about this, anyhow?

He knew some things, but he didn't know *how* he knew them, and it didn't seem to be helping with anything that mattered. Once they got out, *if* they got out, it would matter less. Wouldn't it? It would be over.

"Hot-and-sour soup," he muttered.

In reply, Kate Wenger giggled, amazingly. Then, after a pause, she moved their linked hands up to her mouth and bit his knuckle. Ned's heart thumped, for different reasons than before.

"Behave, you," she said softly.

"Me?" he murmured, genuinely startled—and aroused.

But in that same moment he *did* have a new thought, and felt a hard kick of fear. Something slid into place: he was pretty sure he finally knew what was going on with Kate.

He was about to say it, but stopped himself. What was the point? He couldn't *do* anything about it. They just had to get out, for one more reason now, if he was right.

The three men leading the bull had now reached the one with the axe. They stopped in front of him. The white bull stopped. The smaller man in white stood to one side, holding something. There was silence.

Then Ned saw all the figures gathered there bow to the animal, as they had not bowed to the man.

The broad-shouldered figure spoke then, for the first time. Ned remembered that voice from two nights ago, rich and musical, deep as a drum. He said half a dozen words—Ned couldn't understand them—and when he paused, those around him, fifty of them at least, gave a response.

The man spoke, and then they did. The wind blew. Smoke streamed from torches held and those embedded in the ground.

The bull, eerily white in the moonlight, stood placidly, as if entranced by the chanting voices. It might be that, Ned thought. Or else they'd given it some drug.

The voices stopped.

"I can't watch," Kate whispered suddenly, and she turned her face against Ned's shoulder.

The man with the axe lifted it so that the weapon, too, glinted under that moon. And then, with a shout of joy, he brought it sweeping, scything, crashing down to strike the bull, overwhelmingly, between the great horns.

Ned felt Kate crying (only now, for the first time, for the animal). He forced himself to keep watching as the stricken, bludgeoned creature collapsed to its forelegs, and blood—strangely hued in the moon-silver night—burst forth, soaking all those close to it.

Barbaric, Ned wanted to say, think, feel, but something stopped him.

The man in the white robe stepped quickly forward holding a bowl to the spurting wound, filling it with blood. With both hands he extended it towards the one with the axe, the man Ned had last seen in the shape of an owl flying from a different ruined tower.

The big man let fall his bloodied axe. He claimed the bowl with two hands. Ned felt his pulse racing furiously, as if he were sprinting flat out towards some cliff he couldn't see.

The man raised the bowl in front of him, the way he'd lifted the axe a moment before. As he spoke, words of incantation, the white bull toppled to one side at his feet like some great structure falling, blood still flowing, soaking into the dusty ground. No one answered the words this time.

Beside the tree in front of Ned and Kate, a lean, scarred man stood up. He said something under his breath. It might have been a prayer.

In front of the sanctuary, the raised bowl was lowered by the golden man. He drank the blood.

"Oh, my!" said Kate Wenger suddenly, too loudly.

She lifted her head.

"I can't . . . I . . . What's happening?"

Her voice was *really* strange. She jerked her hand from Ned's, shifted away from him.

Ned stared at her. The man by the tree had heard. He looked back at them. Kate got to her knees, made as if to stand. Terrified, Ned pulled her back down.

"Kate!" he hissed. *"What are you doing?"*

She tried to pull away. "Don't! I need . . . I have to . . ."

"No," he heard the man just ahead of them breathe. "Not this one! She is too young. This should not be—"

Kate Wenger was writhing and twisting beside Ned, fighting to get away. She kicked him. Breathing in shallow gasps, she scratched his arm, then hit him in the chest with both fists.

And just then, in that same, precise moment, up on the plateau of Entremont under a full moon in a darkness that belonged only to this time between times when the walls were down, another voice was heard from the entrance to the site, beyond the paired torches burning beside the path.

"Ned? *Ned?* Are you here? Come on, I've brought the van!"

With his heart aching, and the first horrified glimmer of under-standing coming to him, Ned saw Melanie—small and clever and fear-less, with the green streak in her hair—take a hesitant step forward between the smoking torches, the way the bull had.

In that instant, Kate Wenger went limp beside him.

She collapsed as if released from a puppet-string, from a force that had been pulling, drawing, *demanding* her.

Several things happened at once.

The scarred man looked at the two of them a last time, then turned back to the ruins. As if he, too, was being pulled that way. And of course he was, Ned later realized: pulled by centuries.

And by love.

Ned saw him take a step himself and then another, up the small slope, and there he stopped, still unobserved, watching Melanie. Staring at her. He was completely exposed now, up on the plateau. He would have been spotted if any one of those gathered by the sanctuary had looked his way.

They didn't. The big man with the fair hair handed the bowl back to the one in white without even glancing at him. He stood very still, head high, hands empty at his sides, facing Melanie where she stood on the north-south path. They were *all* watching her, Ned saw.

She began to come forward, slowly, between fires.

Ned shifted to his knees so he could see better. He kept one hand on Kate's shoulder where she lay, face to the dark grass. But his eyes were on Melanie, along with everyone else's.

So he saw when she began to *stop* being Melanie.

She came along the straight roadway, past the low, ruined walls of ancient houses, towards the sanctuary and the figures waiting there, walking between nine pairs of torches. Ned counted them as she went. Each time she disappeared and reappeared through the smoke, she had changed.

The first time, Ned actually rubbed his eyes, like a child. After that, he didn't do it again, he just watched. With his unnaturally keen sight here, he saw when her hair began to change in that moonlight towards red, and then when it *was* red, and falling so much longer than before. And he thought, for the first time, how inadequate the words for colours could sometimes be.

Her clothing began to alter. Halfway down the row she was wearing sandals, not boots, and a calf-length, one-piece garment, with a heavy gold belt. He saw her come through another pair of flames with golden bracelets on her arms, and rings on several fingers. She was tall by then.

He watched her walk between the final torches.

The man who had summoned her—with the power of Beltaine and the white bull and the bull's blood—knelt in the roadway. So did all the others, as if they had been waiting for his sign, as if Melanie were a queen, or a goddess.

Ned could see, even from where he was, that the big man's face was alight with joy. And with need, or something beyond need, deeper. Whatever you thought of him, you couldn't see that look and not respond to it.

Melanie, who was not Melanie any more, stopped in front of him.

She was in profile for Ned, lit by the moon and the carried torches. She was more beautiful than any woman he'd ever seen, or ever imagined seeing.

He found it difficult to breathe. He saw her look up at the moon for a moment and then back down again, at the man kneeling before her.

He said something, in that language Ned couldn't understand. Melanie reached down then, slowly. She touched his yellow hair with the fingers of one hand. It was very bright where they were, as if they were on a stage, acting out motions from long ago, but also here now, in front of him.

Wherever *now* was.

Then the woman spoke for the first time, and Ned heard her say, in exquisite French, formal, very clear, "Change your words. Returned in this new time, shall we not speak in the tongue they use? We will have to, will we not, as the dance begins?"

"As you wish, my lady."

He was still kneeling. He lowered his head. It was difficult to see his face now, with the long hair falling.

"It is as I wish."

Her voice was harder to read, but it sure wasn't Melanie's. She looked around slowly. Grave, unsmiling, taking in those nearby, the risen, moon-touched tower.

"Only one of you?" she said softly.

"Only one of us," the kneeling figure said. "Alas."

He lifted his face again. Ned saw that he was smiling. He didn't sound distressed at all.

"Two of us," the scarred man said, from the edge of the plateau.

No more than that, and quietly, but everything altered with the words. Entremont and the night turned. They took on, they *accepted,* a weight of centuries, their place in a long story.

Or so it was to seem to Ned, looking back.

There came a cry of rage from the kneeling man.

He rose, took a stride this way amid shouts from the others behind him. Ned saw spears lifted, levelled. A sword was drawn by one enormous, bare-chested, nearly naked warrior. The figure in white lifted his hands, still holding the bowl, as if to cast a spell or a curse.

Amid all this, the man in the grey leather jacket walked forward, entering among them as if he perceived no threat at all, as if he hadn't even *noticed* any of this.

Perhaps he hadn't, Ned thought. Perhaps he was seeing only the woman. As if nothing else signified or had meaning.

She had turned to watch him approach, and so Ned could see her face clearly now for the first time. He closed his eyes, then opened them again. His mouth was dry.

"They tested you?" she said mildly, as the man stopped in front of her. He didn't kneel. She offered no other greeting.

He inclined his head in agreement. "They amuse themselves. As children do." They were speaking French.

"You think? Not only children, surely. I enjoy being amused," she said.

"I recall amusing you."

She laughed. Ned closed his eyes again for a second. "Sometimes, yes, my stranger." She tilted her head to one side, appraisingly. "You look older."

"You said that the last time as well."

"Did I?" She shrugged.

She turned away from him to the other one. The bigger man was rigid, tense, like some hunting animal. Ned had a sudden, sharp sense that violence was about to explode here.

Time to go, he thought.

"I remember that torc," the woman said.

Ned saw the golden-haired man smile. "And I that lapis ring, among the others."

She lifted one hand, looked at it briefly. "Did you give me this one?"

"You know I did. And when I did so."

She lowered her hand. "You will tell me what I know?"

He bowed his head. She laughed.

Kate was quiet now beside Ned, lying on the grass. He was still on his knees. He felt paralyzed by fear and fascination, by the horror of what had happened. And he couldn't take his eyes from this woman.

"We've got to get her back!" he whispered, feeling idiotic even as he said it. Who was he, to even think such a thing?

"Who went up? Who was it?" Kate murmured, finally lifting her head. She wiped at her wet cheeks.

"That's Melanie. She came herself. I have *no* idea why Greg didn't."

"That was going to be me," Kate said dully. "You know that?"

Ned nodded. He did know it. It was a difficult thing to get his head around. If Melanie hadn't come . . .

He looked away from Kate, up the slope. The man—*their* man— in his grey jacket was surrounded. He was weaponless. They will give me one, he'd said.

We should be going right now, Ned thought.

He stayed where he was.

"How is it you are here, little stranger?" he heard the golden one demand.

"Yes, how?" the woman added. "They *so* dearly wish to know! Look at them! You have spoiled the game." Music in her voice, capricious, amused.

"Children offer riddles they think are challenging," he said mildly.

Ned could see her face whenever she turned this way.

"Is that truth? A riddle solved?" she asked.

He hesitated. "It is a truth, love. But a woman also gave a hint they might be here for the summoning and I heeded her."

Love.

"Ah. A woman? And is she fair? Young, with a sweet voice? You have left me for another. Woe unto my riven heart."

There was a little silence. Beside Ned, Kate Wenger had gone still.

"I will never leave you," the man said quietly.

Ned Marriner shivered, on his knees in silver-green grass, hearing that.

"Never?"

Her manner had changed again.

The man's back was to them, Ned couldn't see his expression. They heard him say, "Have I not shown as much, by now? Surely?"

Her turn to be silent.

"I am a helpless woman," she said at length. "I must believe you, I suppose."

Helpless. Her tone and bearing made a lie of the word. "Tell me," she said, her manner altering yet again, "is that carving you made of me still down below, in the world?"

"It is."

"And do I look there as I do now?"

They could see him shake his head.

"You know you never did, in that stone. And time has worked its will."

She took a step back from him, withdrawing. "Ah? Time? And must I *accept* that? You have not gone to undo that will? Is this love? Am I well served, or do you merely offer words?"

He lowered his head, as the other man had done.

"I have not been back in the world for long, my lady. Nor have we arrived in an age when I may enter that cloister to work."

Her voice was scornful. "He offers an explanation! How gracious! Tell me, might a better man have done so?"

"That's not *fair!*" Ned heard Kate hiss sharply, beside him.

The figure in the grey jacket said only, "Perhaps so, my lady. I know there are better men."

Ned saw her smile at that. It was a cruel look, he thought.

The man added, softly, "But it had occurred to me then, as I worked, that no carving could come near to what you are. I shaped it to be only a hint, from the beginning, knowing it would become more so through the years, wearing away. One needs to have *seen* you—and perhaps more than that—to understand."

More than that. Ned drew a shaky breath.

The smile changed, and was not cruel any more. She lifted a hand as if to touch his face, but she didn't.

She turned to the other one instead. "And you? He says he will never leave me."

This one's voice was deeper, resonant. "My answer is as it was from the beginning, even before that night among the village fires. You left us when this began. You *began* this. It was always your right . . . but until the sky falls I will fight to have you back."

Kate sat up beside Ned in the grass.

The tall woman, red and gold as a fairy queen, said, "Indeed? *Will* you fight for me?"

He said, "I would prove my love in the stranger's blood tonight and always, with joy."

"And prove your worth?"

His teeth flashed suddenly; he pushed back his yellow hair, which was being blown across his eyes. He was magnificent, like a horse. Or a stag, Ned thought suddenly, remembering the horns.

"Have I ever been unworthy, Ysabel?"

They heard her laughter ripple across the ruins.

Ysabel.

"Ah," she said. "So that is my name this time?"

"The animal offered it, before it died. The druid said as much."

"Then I accept, of course."

Her amusement was gone. Another shift of mood, like a cloud across the moon.

She turned her head, looking down at the white bull lying in its own blood on the dusty, silvered street. She said something too softly for Ned to hear. Then she looked up again, from one man to the other.

"And now what happens? I name you both, is that it? And then a battle? That is why we are alive again?"

A challenge in her now, almost anger.

"That's why he couldn't answer before," Kate whispered. "About his name."

This time Ned reached out and took her hand. It lay quietly in his. They watched together. It was necessary to leave, he knew, and impossible.

The woman had turned this way again, towards the smaller man. The moonlight was on her face.

"What shall I call you?" she asked.

Her voice had lost that softer nuance again. She was controlling him, all of them. Wilful, teasing.

"Shall I name you Becan because you are small? Or Morven, one more time, since you came from the sea?"

"I had a different name when I did that," he said mildly.

"I remember."

"When I first came."

"I remember."

"And I . . . I have been . . . you have called me Anwyll."

She lifted her head. "*Beloved?* Do you presume so much? That I must name you thus, because I foolishly did so once?"

Not truly angry, Ned thought, but he wasn't sure.

"I only said that it was so, upon a time and more than once," the man murmured. He didn't lower his head. "You must not imagine I forget."

Kate Wenger made a small sound beside Ned. No one moved on the plateau. The torches burned, smoke streaming on the wind.

"More than once," the woman agreed finally. "Named so, or not. Before that scar and after. By the sea and from the waves."

And Ned Marriner, hidden in the darkness of their downslope and hearing this, thought that if, before he grew old and died, a woman spoke to him words like these, in such a voice, he might say he'd lived a life worth living.

The woman named Ysabel was gazing upon the man. She shook her head, slowly.

"'Anwyll' must be earned again, surely, by one of you. Or neither, perhaps. But I will not name you Donal here: not a stranger again after so long. Little one, lean and alone, clad in grey, you shall be Phelan one more time. My wolf."

"This is all Celtic," Kate whispered.

"I know," Ned murmured.

He was thinking *wolf,* how it suited.

The moon was high, so much sooner than it should have been. But what did *should have been* mean tonight? He watched the woman, who was not Melanie any more, turn to the other man.

"Gwri for your hair?" she said, that teasing tone again. "Allyn, or Keane, handsome one? Briant, for strength . . . Would you like one of those?"

It was as if she was testing, tasting names on her tongue. Playing with them. One long leg was thrust out to the side, a hand on her hip, head tilted, looking him up and down.

"You have cause to remember that last," he replied, and threw back his head, laughing at his own jest. Ned thought she'd be angry again, but he was wrong. She laughed too. He didn't understand her at all, he realized.

"Let me kill him here," he said, gesturing with his hand in a wide sweep. "Grant us leave to fight. This is a sacred place tonight."

Ned couldn't see her face, but he heard the smile in her voice. "Ah. And so we are given your name," she said. "Take it. Cadell you are and have always been, my warring one."

Wolf and warrior. There was a silence where they stood, like figures in a tableau. Ned saw a shooting star, a fireball, streak slowly across the western darkness of the sky beyond and disappear. Like a child, in need, he made a wish upon it.

"Very well. That is done. Thank you, my lady. If we are to battle now, might someone be good enough to offer me a blade?"

It was the lean one speaking, brisk, matter-of-fact, the man they could now call Phelan. Ned swallowed, hearing that, the crisp courtesy of the words. But there was so much beneath them. The night could explode right now, a red, electric violence.

Go now! an inner voice was crying.

"A sword? Of course. With joy," said the one called Cadell. "I cannot tell you how much joy." He paused, then added, almost gravely, "You know that I will kill you."

"I know that you will try."

Someone—the small figure in the white robe, Ned saw—stepped forward holding an unsheathed sword across his palms like another offering. He'd handed the stone bowl to someone else. It was as if he'd been waiting for this, as if he'd known it would come. Perhaps he had. Phelan came forward to claim it and begin.

But in that moment a very long dance—the torment and the glory of it—was altered on that plateau. It would be a while before Ned Marriner realized that this was so, and longer still before he understood why, and by then it was almost too late.

"No," said Ysabel.

Phelan stopped, a hand extended towards the hilt of the offered sword. He didn't touch it. Both men looked at her.

She said, quietly, "Not a combat. Not this time. And not by armies gathered to you. It pleases me not."

"I *need* to kill him, love," said Cadell. There was urgency in the words. He pushed a hand through his hair again. "Now that you are among us it is on me as destiny, as a longing."

"Then master it, if you are a man," she said bluntly.

His head snapped back, as if the words had been a slap to the face.

"My lady, we are brought back to fight for you," said Phelan softly. "We have always known this. It is what we are."

She wheeled on him this time. Ned could see her again, the fury in her.

"You are brought back to be *deserving* of me—the one more than the other—in my eyes! Will you deny that? Will you challenge it?"

He shook his head. "You know I will not."

Silence again. It was time to go, Ned knew. It was past time. He didn't want to die here.

He heard her say, "I have another test, of love and worthiness. Of . . . longing." She glanced towards the bigger man on the last word, and then back. "Tell, how do you long for me, my wolf?"

"I have told you," he said.

"Hai! Listen to the Roman! I will say it as many times as you are willing to hear my voice," the one called Cadell cried. "*Our* people—yours and mine!—do not squeeze words as coins from a miser's hoard."

The Roman. Yours and mine. Pieces of a puzzle, Ned thought. If he lived long enough to work it through.

Ysabel looked at Cadell and then back to the smaller man. She didn't smile this time. It was as if, Ned thought, she was waiting, expecting something now, because of what had just been said.

It came. Phelan spoke, looking across her at the other man, ice suddenly in his voice. "Words, did you say? I know your words. I remember some of them. Do you? These, perhaps: *Kill them all. God will know his own.*"

He stopped, letting the sound fade, drift like the smoke. Then he added, softly, "A hoard, is it? What sort of piled-up treasure, tell us all? Dead women and babes? Charred flesh? Blackened bone? A hoard such as that, perhaps?"

"Oh, God," Ned heard Kate whisper hoarsely.

Ned didn't get it. No time to ask.

The bigger man was smiling, even in the face of this—golden, beautiful, unshaken by that rage. Ned could see a wolf in him, too, suddenly.

Both of them, he thought.

"Poor little man," Cadell said mockingly. "My victory that time, wasn't it? I do think it was. A *difficult* memory? Can't escape? Trapped within walls? With those who so foolishly trusted you? And I never spoke those words. You know it."

"You acted upon them. You killed because of them."

The other man shook his head slowly, in elaborate mock-pity, then took a stride forward. "Will you chide me—will *you* do so—for deaths? Will you, Marius? For women and children? You will do that here? In *sight* of it?"

And with that name spoken, Ned understood.

Because of what Melanie had said before, beside the mountain. Telling of Pourrières, below Sainte-Victoire, and the world-changing battle there. An ambush behind the Celts, the supply camp, their families, wives, children . . .

Two hundred thousand bodies rotting. A redness in the world.

I am not a good man.

Two wolves here. Ned felt sick again. It occurred to him that these two could make a conflagration of the world in their war. That they already had.

But even as he shaped the thought, in sudden fear, Ysabel said, "No blades, no armies. It shall not be so. Hear my will. Hear me carefully for I will say this once. I am going to leave this place. You will not fight each other here. Cadell, you will release the druid and his spirits to their rest again when the needfires die. I have been summoned. They are not a part of this any more. Say to me now that you will release them."

She stared at him.

"I will release them," he said, after a pause.

"You will not change shapes to seek me. Swear it."

"I swear it. But what does 'seek' mean?"

Ned's question, too.

She looked from Cadell to the other man. "When morning comes—with sunrise and not before—the two of you will begin to look for me."

Phelan stared at her, said nothing.

She went on. "Call it a quest. Pretend you are gallant, honourable men, unstained by any sins. Who finds me first will prove his worth by doing so. I will be hiding and not easily found. Trust me in this. I do not *choose* to be easily found, or idly claimed." She paused. "You have three days."

"And if . . . we do not succeed?" Phelan's voice was low.

"Then do whatever you wish to each other, it will matter not. You will have failed me, both of you. I will have been shown to be unimportant to you."

She stopped, looked from one to the other, then added, in yet another tone, "I would prefer to be found."

First uncertainty in her voice, Ned thought. There was a silence up where the torches were burning.

"This is . . . you offer a child's game, my lady. I need to kill him." Cadell's voice was anguished.

"You *like* children's games, I thought." The hint of vulnerability gone, as soon as it had come. "And you are forbidden to kill now. It is my will. But there is this: who finds me first may sacrifice the one who fails. With my consent. And by my desire."

Dear God, Ned thought. *By my desire.*

"Swear to this, to all of this, then I am gone."

"You have only now come," Phelan said, barely loud enough for them to hear. "Am I to lose you so soon?"

"Find me," she said coldly, "and so keep me, if it matters so very much. Or wander off to make another carving. Stone instead of flesh, as you choose. But swear now, both of you. Three days. Find me. The loser is a sacrifice, for his failure."

She turned back to Cadell. "Will you call it a game?"

She was so hard, Ned thought. She was tall, and crimson as a fire, and terrifyingly cold. He felt small, inadequate; a child, listening. And he was all those things, in almost all the ways that mattered.

He heard the two men swear to her, one and then the other.

"Ned, we have to go," Kate whispered. "Before *she* leaves and they start looking around."

It was true.

I will never see her again, he was thinking.

"I need to get her back," was what he whispered, repeating himself, feeling stupid again even as he formed the words. *I need to.* What were his needs in this?

"Melanie? We'll try. We'll think how. But not here. Come on, Ned!"

Her hand was still in his; she tugged and he followed and they went from that place. From the woman whose name was in his head now, singing itself in that elusive, changing voice, never to leave. He knew it, even then, first night. That it would never leave.

It wasn't very hard to get away, in the event, slipping back north through the meadow past the wall. Phelan had been right.

When they were outside the site, on the gravel path again, the sky began to grow lighter as they ran. By the time they reached the iron gate and passed through it was late-spring daylight again, bright and fair.

Windy, the sun in the west, ahead of them, as if it had been waiting. The van was in the lot, the only car there. Ned stared at it. It seemed an alien, unreasonable object.

He walked over. Melanie's tote lay on the front passenger seat. It was difficult, confusing, seeing that. They had just been looking at swords and a sacrificial axe, a bull lying in the pool of its own blood after passing between sacred fires.

How did a Renault van come to exist in the world? How could Melanie *not* be here? He felt very shaky, thinking about that. And afraid.

Neither of them could drive and the van was locked; they'd have to walk. Ned heard traffic below, a strident car horn sounding. That, too, so impossibly strange. Kate tugged again and they started down.

It was difficult, his steps seemed to drag, even as she pulled him by the hand. He knew what he wanted. He wanted to go back into the lost moonlight behind them. *Find me*, she had said.

Ysabel.

PART TWO

CHAPTER X

He began to cry walking back to Aix. Amid the traffic noise and chaos as they approached the city came a delayed, after-the-nightmare feeling of horror. It was difficult to keep moving. He just wanted to stop somewhere by the side of the road; a bench, anything. He couldn't stop thinking about Melanie, the idea that she was gone. Like that. Taken over. And what was he going to say to his father and the others? How did you *tell* something like this?

Kate said nothing, which was a blessing.

Out of the corner of his eye, as they came to the ring road, Ned saw that she was biting her lip again, staring straight ahead. He thought about her, and what had so nearly taken place. Kate had been a heartbeat away—hardly more than that—from what had happened to Melanie. She had been leaving him, going up into the ruins. She *would* have walked between those Beltaine fires.

She is too young, the man they knew—Phelan—had said.

It would have made no difference. And fifteen wasn't that young in the days when this story seemed to have begun. You could be married by fifteen, have children. People had grown up faster once.

If he'd had Greg's phone number in his auto-dial, Ned thought, if Melanie hadn't come with the van instead, then Kate Wenger wouldn't be beside him now.

It didn't help anything, to think about that.

Above them, the sky was still bright with the late-day light. The mistral had died down, the sun was low. Traffic buzzed and rasped, mopeds whining through it.

Ned checked his watch. A quarter after seven. It had been night up at Entremont. How did you deal with that?

They crossed the ring road at a light and then stopped and looked at each other. Kate's eyes were puffy.

"What do we do?" she asked. People were all around them on the sidewalk, walking to wherever they had to go, wherever their lives required them to be.

She didn't call him *babe*. She wasn't going to do that any more, he knew. He also knew why she'd done it before: how Beltaine, like a tide, had been rising within her. She'd already been shifting towards becoming someone else when they'd met outside Cézanne's studio. Before that, even.

Then Melanie had come. And then Ysabel.

A car horn blared, and another in angry response. There was a traffic jam where they'd just crossed, Ned saw; the ring road was clogged, lanes blurred by cars undecided which one was quickest. Three buses were stacked in a row in the bus-and-taxi lane. The scooters darted dangerously in and out. Life in the twenty-first century.

"I don't know what we do," he said to Kate. "But I have to tell my dad."

She nodded. "I figured. I'll come with you. If you want? I mean, he may . . . he should believe it more, with two of us, right?"

Ned had had the same thought.

"You sure? It's okay? I'd appreciate . . ."

She shook her head. "Nothing's okay at all, but I'm not walking out on you. Two's easier for this."

It was. But that made him think of something.

"Three's better," he said, and took out his phone.

He turned it on, tabbed to the memory screen, scrolled, and had the cell dial automatically.

One ring only. "Ned? *What's happened?*"

She'd know there was something. He wouldn't have called, otherwise.

He cleared his throat. "Something bad," he said. It was tricky, controlling his voice. "I need . . . You think you can come up to the villa? I have no idea what to do."

Aunt Kim had the most reassuring voice. "Of course I can. Are you there now?"

"In Aix. Walking home. With Kate, the girl I met."

"Walking from where?"

"Entremont."

There was a silence. "Oh, Ned," she said. "All right, I'm west of the city, but not far, it won't take me long."

"Thanks. Really."

"Get yourselves home. It's the last house on that road? Where I dropped you?"

"Uh-huh. Villa Sans Souci. Melanie put . . . there are these Canadian flags. On the little signs."

"On my way."

He hung up. Kate was staring at him, waiting.

"That was my aunt," he said.

She blinked. "Because?"

He said, awkwardly, "She's . . . been here, done this kind of thing."

Kate's expression changed. "You're kidding me. And you *knew* that? Like, in the cathedral?"

He shook his head. "Met her for the first time in my life two nights ago. We saw . . . we ran into the big guy. Cadell? The one who killed the bull."

Kate bit her lip. "You didn't tell me that."

"I know. Complicated family story. Didn't want to start it on the side of a highway. And you were . . . in a pretty funny mood, you know."

She flushed. "That wasn't me," she said.

"I know."

"I mean, it *was* me, but I'd never do . . ."

"I know."

She smiled a little, first time since they'd come back down. "For a guy, you think you know a lot."

Ned tried to smile back and couldn't quite achieve it. "I don't know," he said.

She nodded slowly. "Okay. But, this is good, isn't it, about your aunt? I mean, she'll know what to do, right?"

"For sure," he said.

Maybe, was what he thought.

He wasn't at all certain there was anything they could do. He wondered about Melanie's family. He knew nothing about them. Imagined a conversation.

Hi there. Called to tell you your daughter's disappeared. She turned into some woman from more than two thousand years ago. Red hair. She's taller.

He took a deep breath. They started walking again, curving around to the left, beside the stop and start of the ring-road traffic, as if swimming upstream through time.

TIME COLLIDED HARD with the present when they reached the slope leading to the villa. Ned found his footsteps slowing between the trees, and not from fatigue. It was reluctance, resistance, a childlike wish that this state of in-between—when something had happened but it hadn't yet been told and made real, with consequences—might go on forever.

He told himself the feeling was irresponsible, even cowardly. That they couldn't start doing something about Melanie until he'd spoken about it. But he also knew how impossibly hard it was going to be to tell this story.

Kate was silent again, but beside him. He looked into the overgrown meadow on their right, when they reached it. Nothing there but butterflies and bees, birdsong. Wild grass, clover, a few poppies, some bright yellow flowers on the bushes at the edge of the woods.

At the villa gates he hesitated again, his fingers hovering over the code box that opened them.

Kate said, "We could wait here. For your aunt?"

He had been hoping, to be honest, that Aunt Kim might have been at the bottom of the road waiting to drive them up. He could have handed this off to her. Been there, done that? *You* tell them.

He looked at Kate, who had volunteered to help him, though she'd never even met Melanie, or his father or the others. She'd known Ned for only four days, and she was here.

He punched the code, the gates swung open. He punched it a second time, to lock them that way, and they walked through. Time moved again.

His father was on the terrace, at the little table, a tall drink in front of him. Steve was in the pool, doing his laps in the cold water. Ned couldn't see Greg. The gates clanged, as they always did when they opened. His father turned in his chair at the sound and waved.

"Yo!" Steve called, not pausing in his laps.

"You walked?" Ned's father called. "Better phone Melanie and tell her. She went down to get you!"

"Where was Greg?" Ned asked, walking across the grass. Kate trailed behind him.

"Fell asleep when we got back from the abbey. They were planning something dire for him when you called. I think you saved him. Why'd you phone if you were going to walk? And who's your friend?" He smiled at Kate.

Ned had a sudden, sharp awareness that this was the last moment of peace his father was going to know here. It was a hard thought: the terrible innocence of people before hearing news that could shatter their lives. The doorbell, a policeman on the porch at night in rain, news of a car accident . . .

He wasn't sure what had made him think of that.

He said, "This is Kate Wenger. Kate, my father, Edward Marriner."

"Hi, Kate," his father said. "Ned's told us about you. You sell essays for walk-around money?" He grinned.

"Hello, sir. No, not usually."

"Ned, have Vera set another plate. Kate can join us for dinner."

"I will," Ned said. He took a breath. "But I need to tell you something first. Something's happened."

It was awful, but he was actually afraid he was going to cry again.

His father's expression changed, but not in a bad way. He looked at Ned, then Kate. "Sit down, both of you. Tell me."

They sat. Ned took a couple of steadying breaths. Steve was still swimming. It had to be freezing in the pool. A black-and-white bird lifted suddenly from the grass and swooped across to the trees by the lavender bushes.

"It's about Melanie," Ned said.

"Oh, God," his father said. "The van? Ned . . . ?"

"Not the van! I would have phoned." He saw Kate biting her lip again.

"What happened, then? Where is she? Ned, tell me."

"She's gone, Dad."

"Melanie? She wouldn't leave us in a hundred years."

Maybe in two thousand, Ned thought.

"Is she joking again?" his father added. "Are you? Jesus, Ned, I'm too old for—"

"It isn't a joke, sir," said Kate. "Something bad happened and . . . it is really, really hard to explain."

She sounded earnest and intense, not even close to a practical-joke kind of person. Ned's father looked at her, and then back to his son.

"You're scaring me."

"I'm scared too," Ned said, "and I don't know where to start."

"That doesn't make me feel any better."

Ned took another breath, like the one before you went off the high board at a pool. An idea came to him, and he followed it before he had time to change his mind.

"Dad . . . do you know what story Aunt Kim would have told Mom, before she went away? Did Mom ever tell you?"

He had never seen anyone, let alone his father, look so astonished.

"Aunt Kim?" Edward Marriner repeated blankly. "*Kimberly?*"

Ned nodded. "Did Mom tell you anything about it?"

"Ned, Jesus, what does—"

"Please, Dad. Did she?"

He was pretty sure it was because Kate Wenger was beside him, worried and serious and biting her lip, that his father answered.

"She told me very little," Edward Marriner said, finally. "It happened before we met. She's almost never talked about it, or her sister."

"I know that," Ned said quietly. "I asked you once or twice, remember?"

His father nodded. "It was some supernatural story, I know that. Mystical. Very . . ." He clasped his hands together on the table. "Very

New Age, I guess. Things from Celtic roots your mother never liked, never believed in."

"And then Aunt Kim went away?"

"Uh-huh. Your grandmother used to keep in touch with her. Your mother wouldn't even let her talk about Kimberly. She was angry, hurt. I still don't understand all of it, but I learned not to ask." His gaze held Ned's. "Is your aunt involved in this, Ned? Whatever this is?"

"Sort of. Can I . . . may I ask one more question, first?"

His father's mouth moved sideways. "You're going to, aren't you?"

"Are you . . . do you . . . hate that New Age stuff as much as Mom does?"

Edward Marriner was silent a moment, then he sighed. "I don't believe any of us knows everything about how the world works. Go ahead and tell me."

Ned found that there were tears in his eyes again. He wiped them away. He said, "That's good, Dad. Thanks. I didn't expect . . ."

His father waited. Steve was still swimming, out of earshot. Ned said, "For the past three days, Kate and I have sort of stumbled into something off-the-wall weird."

"Where?" his father asked.

"It started in the cathedral. The baptistry and the cloister."

The blue eyes were direct now. "Where you sent me?"

"Yes." Ned took a chance. "Did you feel anything there?"

Another silence. "Leave that for the moment. Go on." His father was used to giving commands, Ned thought, but he didn't do it in a bad way. It was almost reassuring.

He looked at Kate. "We met, I guess that's the word, we met a man in there, and then later some other people who . . . who don't seem to belong in our time. Like, they're from the past? And it . . . it *is* a Celtic kind of story, I think."

"You think?"

"It is," said Kate. "We *know* it is. We're just really hesitant because it's scary and totally weird and people won't believe us. But today is, well it's May Day eve." She stopped.

"I knew that, as it happens," Edward Marriner said, after a pause. He looked at his son. "We used to go on picnics, when your grandmother was alive."

"I remember. And tonight was . . . is a really powerful night. For the Celts."

"Jesus, Ned." His father shook his head. "What are you trying to tell me?"

"Kate and I went up to a ruined site near here, called Entremont, this afternoon."

"It was my fault," Kate interrupted. "Ned didn't want to go."

"I *did* want to. But Aunt Kim said I—"

"You tried to stop us."

"But I went."

"Hold it," said Edward Marriner. *"Aunt Kim said . . . ?"*

Ned closed his eyes. He hadn't meant to do it that way. But if there was a good way to do this, he sure hadn't thought of it.

"I know. Mom will kill all of us. Or she'll get spitting mad. Aunt Kim says she used to get spitting mad."

"Ned. Please. Be extremely clear. Right now."

Ned nodded. "Aunt Kim called me when we were leaving that restaurant two nights ago. After I had that headache thing by the mountain? She realized somehow that I had connected to something she knows about."

"She called you? Your *aunt* telephoned you?"

That same look of disbelief, the one that should have been funny.

"Yeah. Remember, in the restaurant driveway? She was already here. She flew down because she realized something had happened to me. She *knew*, Dad."

"Flew down?"

"From England. She lives there. With Uncle Dave."

His father sighed. "I actually knew that. And she . . . ?"

"She met me that night. When I said I wanted to go for a walk?"

"Jesus, Ned." Third time he'd said that.

Ned still thought he might cry. It was embarrassing. "Dad, she's really great. And she was trying to *help*. To explain what had happened to me. That it was in her family, and Mom's. And she told me not to go anywhere that might involve . . . those guys. But I did."

"I made him go," Kate said again. "And we got trapped, and had to call for help."

"But it was supposed to be Greg."

"And if Melanie hadn't come when she did it would have been *me* who became . . . someone else."

Kate was the one who was crying, Ned saw. He watched his father register that.

"Why you?" Edward Marriner said quietly.

"There . . . needed to be a woman. Both men were there, they were calling her. They needed Ysabel. And I was supposed to become her . . . it was already happening. Then Melanie came, because we'd phoned."

Wordlessly, Edward Marriner picked up a serviette from the table and handed it to her. Kate wiped her eyes, and then blew her nose.

Ysabel. The name, spoken on a villa terrace, a bell-sound in the word. He could still see her. He could see Melanie, changing, between flames.

They heard a car changing gears on the steep slope of the road.

His father turned quickly, and Ned could see hope flare in his face: the heart-deep wish that this was Melanie in the van, that it had all been an elaborate practical joke, to be dealt with by a thunderous grounding of his only child.

Ned looked. He saw the red Peugeot.

"That's Aunt Kim," he said. "I asked her to come. We're going to need her, Dad."

His father stood quickly, scraping his chair, staring at the car as it came through the open gates. They watched it pull into the first gravel parking space. The engine was turned off.

A woman got out and looked across the grass at them.

Medium height, slender. White-haired. She wore a long blue-and-white flower-print skirt and a blue blouse over it, held a pale-coloured straw hat in one hand. She closed the car door. It made a *chunking* sound in the stillness.

Ned lifted a hand to her. She took off her sunglasses and began crossing towards them, walking briskly. His mother's walk, Ned thought.

Edward Marriner watched her come up the stone steps. He cleared his throat.

With real composure, given the circumstances, he said, "Kimberly Ford? Hello. Ned and his friend have . . . have been trying to explain what this is about. Thank you for coming. You do know what your sister will do to all of us?"

He extended a hand. Aunt Kim ignored it. She dropped her hat on the table and, stepping forward, gave him a long, fierce hug.

She stepped back, looking at him. "Edward Marriner, I have *no* idea why my sister lets you keep that silly moustache. I am so glad to meet you, and so sorry it is this way."

She stepped back, a brightness in her eyes. *She* was crying now. There seemed to be an epidemic of it.

Ned's father cleared his throat again. He handed Kim another of the serviettes from the table. She took it and wiped her eyes. She looked over. "Kate?"

Kate nodded. "Hi," she said in a small voice.

"Hi to you, dear. Are you all right?"

"Sort of, I guess. Not really. We were saying . . . trying to say . . . it was going to be me up there it happened to, if Melanie hadn't come."

Kimberly held up a hand.

"Stop, please. I don't know enough. And I'm sure Ned's father knows less. Back up, start with the cathedral, take us to what just happened." This crispness was his mother's, too, Ned thought. She took a chair.

Edward Marriner sat opposite her. He glanced meaningfully towards the pool where Steve was still swimming. Kimberly looked over. She turned to Ned. "Melanie's been changed? Into someone else? Is that it?"

Ned nodded. "Both men were there. The one Kate and I saw, and the one you and I met by the tower."

Aunt Kim closed her eyes. "Damn."

"I'm sorry," Ned said, miserably. "I know you told me not to . . . even Phelan told us."

She stared at him.

"He's the one we met first, Kate and me."

"He has a name now?"

Ned nodded. It was all really hard, sitting here above a swimming pool, holding images in his head of twinned fires and a slaughtered bull, that stone bowl held high, filled with blood. "The other one's Cadell. Melanie named them, after she—"

Aunt Kim held up a hand again, like a traffic cop. She looked at the pool, and then at Ned's father. "You still need to back up. But I think everyone has to be here," she said, gesturing towards Steve. "You can't keep it from him, if she's really gone."

"Is she?" Edward Marriner asked. "Gone? I mean, that's so . . ."

Kim nodded. "She's changed, anyhow. They wouldn't make this up."

Ned's father drew a slow breath, processing that. "Greg, too, then," he said, finally. "We'll have to wake him."

"I'll do it," Ned said. He needed an excuse to move.

He went into the house. Veracook smiled at him. He saw that she'd gathered some stalks of flowers and leaves, had laid them above the kitchen sink, sideways on the ledge, not in a vase.

She noticed his glance and flushed a little.

"Don't tell Vera," she said, in French, a finger to her lips. "She laughs at me."

"What are they?"

"Rowan. To protect the house. A special night tonight, very special."

Ned stared. He didn't say anything, just went upstairs to get Greg. He felt burdened, heavy with a weight of centuries.

IT WAS STEVE, surprisingly, who insisted they call the police.

He was almost shouting. Greg, perhaps still half asleep, perhaps not, was watchful and quiet after Ned and Kate finished their story. He was eyeing Aunt Kim and Ned's father, waiting to see what they did.

"They aren't allowed to kill each other?" Kim said.

Ned shook his head. "That's what she said. Not while they look for her."

"She gave them that set time to find her," said Kate. "Three days."

"It would be three," Aunt Kim said. "But she's doing something differently, I think. Sounds as though they would fight for her, normally."

"Maybe not," Kate said, hesitantly. "It seemed as if sometimes she just . . . chooses one, and then there's a war. In revenge, maybe?" They all stared at her. She flushed, looked at Kimberly. "But this was different. I think they were both surprised."

"So what does it mean, if it's different?" Edward Marriner asked.

"I'm not sure," Aunt Kim admitted.

"Then what do we do?" Greg asked.

"You *know* what we do now! This isn't goddamned Scooby-Doo!" Steve glared around the table. "We make a call, for God's sake! Melanie's been kidnapped and we aren't detectives!"

"She's been changed, not kidnapped," Kim said calmly. "Steven, Steve, the gendarmes will have no possible way of dealing with this."

"And we do?" Steve said, his voice rising. "I mean, way I make this, Ned and his friend saw some whacko cult, pagans or Wiccans or whatever, faking a ritual, and Melanie got grabbed when she walked in and interrupted them." He looked at Ned. "Admit it. You could have missed what really went down. You said there were fires and smoke."

"I wish," Ned said. He felt miserable. "Steve, I do. But too many things have happened. I mean, Aunt Kim and I *saw* the guy— Cadell—with stag horns, and then he changed into an owl."

Steve stared at him.

"And Melanie never disappeared," Ned added, after a moment. "I saw her all the way. I could see really clearly up there. I don't know why. She just changed, as she walked between the fires."

"Jesus! I'm supposed to . . . *we're* supposed to believe that?"

"I think we may have to, Steve," said Edward Marriner, slowly. "I don't like it any more than you do, but something inexplicable seems to be going on. I think we let Dr. Ford—Kim—guide us here."

"Why's that?" Greg asked, but quietly.

Kim looked at him. "I've seen this before," she said. "Long time ago. Not identical, nothing's ever quite the same. But I can tell you that Ned and I . . . our family . . . have a connection to this sort of thing."

"What sort of thing?" Greg again, still calmly.

"Call it Celtic, pagan, supernatural. Pick the word that works for you."

"And if *none* of them work?" Steve asked, but his voice had softened. Aunt Kim was pretty hard to yell at, Ned thought.

She smiled wryly at Steve. "Not even 'idiotic mumbo-jumbo'?"

Steve looked at her. His expression changed. "Maybe that one," he said. "That might do." He hesitated. "What do you want, then? How do we get her back?"

"Yeah. What do we do?" said Greg. "Tell us, we'll do it. Right now."

They were assuming they *could* do something, Ned thought. He glanced at Kate, saw her looking back at him.

The others hadn't seen Ysabel, or the two men facing each other among the ruins. Or the bull being led between flames. Ned wasn't sure about doing anything useful at all. He felt sick, thinking about that.

From inside the house, just then, as the sun was going down at the end of a day, the telephone rang.

Ned looked quickly at his watch. So did his father.

"Oh, bloody hell," said Edward Marriner, with feeling.

Listening to the ring, Ned corrected his earlier thought. *One* person could—probably would—find it extremely easy to yell at Aunt Kim, and disbelieve her, too.

He and his father exchanged a glance. Ned, feeling an emotion he couldn't immediately identify, said, "I'll get this one." His father, halfway to his feet, subsided into his chair again. In a way, that was a surprise. In another way, it wasn't: this wouldn't be a conversation he'd rush to have.

His heart beating fast again, Ned went in, crossed to the dining room, and picked up the phone.

"Hello?"

"Hi, sweetie, it's me!"

The connection to Africa was really good again. It was weird somehow; you expected a war zone to have crackly, broken-up phone lines.

Ned took a breath. "Hi, Mom. Listen. You have to listen carefully. We need you here. Fast as you can. Melanie's disappeared. Some totally weird things are happening. I can't even explain on the phone. Aunt Kim's come to help, but we need you. Please, Mom, will you come?"

It poured out in pretty much one breathless rush. In retrospect, he probably could have found a smarter way of telling her, but he was really scared, and wound up, and there wasn't an easy way to do any of this. And he hadn't expected to ask for her, not in that way, like a child.

There was a silence on the other end of the line, not surprisingly.

He heard her intake of breath. "Ned, did you just tell me that your *aunt* is there?"

He said, "Mom, what I said was that I need you. Did you hear that part?" Now that he'd said it, he realized he *really* wanted her here.

"Edward, where's your father?" She called him Edward only when it was *really* serious.

"On the terrace. We're trying to figure out what to do. Mom, I told you, Melanie's gone."

"Do I have this right? Kimberly, my *sister*, is with you? In France?"

She sounded a bit in shock, actually.

"Yes, Mom. We need her, too. With what's happening."

His mother swore. It was pretty remarkable. "Get me your father, please. Right away."

He took a breath again. "No," he said.

"*What?*"

"Not till you say you heard me, Mom."

"I'm hearing you just fine. I heard that—"

"Mom. I'm fifteen. I'm not a kid, and I'm asking for my *mother* to come help me. Think about that. Please."

Another silence. A release of breath from far away.

"Oh, dear. Oh, sweetie. Forgive me. I'm . . . pretty stunned. But all right, I'm on my way. Fast as I can get there. Soon as I'm off the phone I'll set it up."

For like the fifth time today or something he felt like crying. Maybe he *was* still a kid. "Jeez. Thanks, Mom. Really. I love you."

"I love you, too. Now will you get your father, please?"

"I think he's scared to talk to you."

"I'm sure he is."

He knew that tone. "I'll go get him. See you soon."

"Soon, honey."

He went back out. His father looked up, so did Aunt Kim. Both looked remarkably nervous.

"She wants to talk to Dad."

His father stood up.

"She knows I'm here?" his aunt asked.

Ned nodded. "I asked her to come."

They stared at him. Neither spoke for a moment.

"Is she?" his father said finally.

"She says so, yeah."

"How nice," Aunt Kim said, in a voice that was kind of hard to read.

His father went inside. Ned looked at his aunt. She was fishing a cellphone from her bag. "Uncle Dave?" he asked.

"God, yes," she said, nodding her head. "You have no idea how much I want him here right now."

Ned hesitated. "I might. You said so the other night. He wouldn't come if my mom had stayed there, right? He'd have stayed with her?"

Aunt Kim held her phone and looked thoughtfully at him.

"Ned Marriner, is *that* why you asked Meghan to—"

"No! I really want her. She's good, my mom, when things need figuring out. But I also thought, from what you said, that Uncle Dave . . . that we might need . . ."

He trailed off.

His aunt was staring at him. So were Steve and Greg. And Kate, he realized.

Aunt Kim smiled suddenly. She looked really pretty when she did, he thought. You could see what she might have been like when she was younger. She shook her head a little, seemed about to say something else, but didn't.

She took her phone and walked along the terrace towards the sunset. They heard her greet someone, then she went around the corner of the house and they couldn't hear any more.

There was a silence around the table. It was chillier now, with the day ending. Steve was bare-chested, wrapped in his towel. He had to be cold. Ned looked at the eastern trees beyond the driveway and the red car and the green wire fence. The moon would rise soon. For the second time.

"Do we tell her parents?"

It was Greg, and after a moment Ned realized the question was addressed to him, as if he was the one who should know, or decide. Steve was looking at him, as well, waiting for an answer. That was pretty tough to deal with. So was the worry on their faces. You had to call it fear, really. He didn't know the exact relationships among his father's team, but Melanie would be someone they cared about. A lot.

"Um, we'll see what Aunt Kim says, but I think—"

"I think we have to wait three days," Kate said, unexpectedly. "If we can."

"Three, because . . . ?" Steve asked.

Kate looked pale and anxious, but determined. "Three, because what are you going to *say* to them? And because that's how long she gave the men to find her."

"And why does that decide it?"

It was difficult, knowing this, but he did seem to know it. He had been there, on the plateau. "Because if we have any hope of getting Melanie back, it's by finding her before either of them does."

"Christ!" snapped Steve, standing up in his towel and bathing suit. "Is this hide-and-seek or James Bond? What do we do if we find her? Ask her pretty please to change back, and don't forget the green streak in her hair?"

Ned glared at him. "How the hell do I know? What do you want me to say?"

Greg looked from one to the other of them. He held up his hands in a "T" for time out. "We'll fall off that bridge when we cross it," he said.

Ned managed a shrug, but he was still mad. Really. What did they *expect* from him?

Steve was looking at him. "Sorry," he said, sitting down again. "My bad. I'm freaked. I have no idea how to act."

"None of us do," Kate said. "Unless maybe Ned's aunt?"

"It's like going to war," Greg murmured. He scratched his beard. "How can you know how you'll behave, or anything like that?"

They heard a footfall. Ned's father was in the doorway to the kitchen. He stood there, shaking his head. "I have no idea what you said," he murmured to Ned, "but she *is* coming. And she didn't explode."

"Not on the phone," Ned said.

His father considered that. "Right. Not on the phone."

"How's she getting here?" Ned asked.

"She thinks she can get to Khartoum tonight on a UN food plane, then to Paris in the morning. Then down here."

"So, like, late afternoon? Evening?"

"That's right," his father said. "She'll phone."

"I'm missing something," Greg said. "Why would Dr. Marriner explode? That's not her style."

Another footfall, from the far end of the terrace. Aunt Kim walked back. They all turned that way. The sun was behind her, almost down.

"Dave's coming," she said. "He's going to try for a military flight to anywhere in Europe tonight. Then connect." She stopped as she saw them staring at her.

"Ah," she said. "And Meghan's on her way?"

Edward Marriner nodded.

"How nice," said Kim, again.

CHAPTER XI

N ed had forgotten about the van. They had to go back for it. Greg had a second set of keys, Aunt Kim had her car.

Ned said he'd go with them.

His father looked as if he wanted to veto that, but Ned was the one who knew where the van was, and it was getting dark. The approach of night made them decide to take off right away.

"Please come straight back. Would you like to sleep here tonight?" Edward Marriner asked his sister-in-law.

Kim nodded. "I think I should. Kate, do you want to stay with us? Or have you had enough of this?"

Kate hesitated, then shook her head. "I'll stay. If there's room for me? I can call and say I'm overnighting with a friend." She gave Ned a look, and shrugged. "Marie-Chantal does it all the time."

"She'll be jealous," he said, half-heartedly. He was thinking that it was Beltaine eve now.

"Only if I say it's with a guy," she said.

"It definitely *isn't* with a guy," Edward Marriner said firmly. "You and Kimberly can have Melanie's room on the ground floor, if you don't mind sharing?"

Aunt Kim smiled. "'Course not. It'll make me feel young."

"And maybe we'll have her back tomorrow," Ned's father added.

Kimberly looked at him, seemed about to say something, but didn't. Ned realized that she'd been doing that a lot.

"Let's get your van," she said.

SHE DROVE QUICKLY and well. Traffic had thinned out. It didn't take long to get there. Ned found that unsettling.

You were sitting where you could grab a Coke from the fridge and listen to U2 on your headphones, and then you were in a place where a bull had just been sacrificed and a man had drunk its blood and summoned a woman to life, between fires. No transition space between those things.

He'd thought about distance and speed and the modern world a couple of days ago, on the way to the mountain. He'd even had a notion to write a school essay about it, saying clever things.

The memory felt absurd now, another existence entirely. He looked at Kim in the glow of the dashboard lights. He wondered if that had been the feeling that had driven her from home after whatever had happened to her. Could you be drawn so far into this other kind of world that your own—the one you'd known all your life—felt alien and impossible?

"Just ahead on the right," he said, as the headlights picked out the brown sign for Entremont.

She saw it, and turned, a little too fast, the wheels skidding briefly.

"Sorry," she said, downshifting as they climbed.

"That's how I drive," Greg said.

He'd been quiet, had taken the back seat so Ned could navigate. Ned was impressed with him, and grateful: Greg had been a lot easier than Steve about accepting their story. He wondered about that, too. What made some people inclined to believe you and others to react with anger or shock? He realized he didn't know a whole lot about Greg or Steve. Or Melanie, for that matter.

The headlight beams, on bright, picked out the closed gates and the parking lot to the left of them. Kim swung into the lot. The van was alone there.

They all got out. Greg punched his remote and the doors of the van unlocked. Kim opened the passenger side.

"Her bag's here."

"Figured. Okay, let's go," Greg said, going around to the driver's side. "I've got the creeps here, big time."

Ned heard him, but he found himself walking the other way, towards the gates. They were locked, but could be climbed pretty easily. Kate had said the security guy came just to open them and lock up. Ned looked through, saw the wide path that led east to the entrance.

Trees mostly hid the northern wall of the site from here, but he knew it was there, and what was on the other side. The wind had pretty much died down now.

"Ned, come on!" Greg called.

He heard his aunt's footsteps coming over.

"They're probably still in there," he said, not looking back. "She told them to give her all night. Not to start looking till morning."

She sighed. "If I had any real power, dear, I'd go in with you, see what we could do. But I don't, Ned. We won't get her back by getting killed there on Beltaine."

"Would they do that?"

She sighed again. He looked at her.

"I've no idea," she said. "I wasn't here. If they thought we were going to interfere, from what you've told us . . ."

"Yeah," he said. "If they thought that, some of them might."

"And we are," Aunt Kim said. "We are going to try to interfere."

"How?"

He saw her shake her head. "No idea."

"Come on!" Greg shouted again. They heard him start the engine.

"He's right. We don't want to see them tonight. Or have them see us. You two head straight home," Kimberly said. "I'll meet you there. I'm just going to stop at the hotel for my things."

Ned was still looking through the gates towards that other world beyond. Greg honked the horn. It sounded shockingly loud, intrusive. Ned turned and walked back and got in the van and they drove away.

He and Greg didn't say much to each other. Aunt Kim was ahead of them on the way back to Aix and halfway around the ring road before she pulled into a hotel driveway. Greg stopped by the side of the road until a doorman opened the car door for her and she went into the lobby. Then—still not speaking—he pulled back into traffic and continued around the ring to the road east.

He took the now-familiar left after the bakery and grocery store and the small aqueduct, and then swung right onto their upward-slanting lane. Ned had his window down, for the cool air. Country road, a mild night, the risen moon ahead of them above the trees.

Greg swore violently and slammed on the brakes. The van skidded, throwing Ned against his shoulder belt. They stopped.

Ned saw the boar in the road, facing them.

We don't want to see them tonight.

We don't always have a choice, he thought.

"Melanie will kill me if I hit an animal," Greg said. "Maybe it'll scoot if I go slow, or honk."

"It won't," Ned said quietly. "Hold on, Greg."

"Huh? What do you mean?"

"I've seen this one."

"Ned, what the hell . . . ?"

"Look at it."

Scoot wasn't a word you would ever really apply to what they were looking at. The boar was enormous, even more obviously so than before, seen this close. It was standing—waiting—with arrogant, unnatural confidence squarely in the middle of the roadway. There were a few high, widely spaced streetlights along the lane, half hidden by leaves, and the van's headlights were on it. The rough, pale grey coat showed as nearly white, the tusks gleamed. It was looking straight at them.

They really *weren't* supposed to have good eyesight.

Someone parted the bushes to the right and stepped into the road.

"Oh, Jesus!" Greg said. "Ned, do I gun it?"

"No," said Ned.

He unlocked his door and got out.

He wasn't sure why, but he did know he didn't want to run, and he didn't want to face this sitting down inside the van.

He'd also recognized who had come. He swung the door closed, heard the *chunk* sound. Loud, because there were no other noises, really. No birdsong after darkfall. Barely a rustle in the leaves, with the wind almost gone. He shoved his hands in his pockets and stood beside the van, waiting.

The druid, he saw, was still wearing white—as he had been among the ruins when he'd caught the bull's blood in a stone bowl.

Ned knew it was a druid. He remembered Kate asking Phelan if his enemy—Cadell—was one, and Phelan's horror at the very thought. Druids were the magic-wielders. This was the one, he was almost sure, who'd shaped the summons that had claimed Melanie, turned her into Ysabel. Cadell had been waiting for tonight, for this man to perform the rite. So had Phelan, for that matter.

It was necessary to remind himself that he was looking at a spirit, someone almost certainly dead a really long time, taking shape now only because it was Beltaine.

He was also pretty certain this particular spirit could kill him if it decided to. He wondered how far behind them his aunt was, if she'd taken the time to check out of the hotel or just grabbed her stuff and followed.

The druid was a small figure, not young, stooped a little, salt-and-pepper beard, seamed face, long grey hair, a woven belt around the ankle-length robe. He wore sandals, no jewellery. No obvious weapon. Ned thought they were supposed to carry a sickle or some-thing and hunt for mistletoe . . . but he might have gotten that from an Asterix comic book, and he wasn't too sure how much to rely on that source.

You could laugh at that, if you wanted to.

He said, in French, "Is the boar yours? Watching us?"

"Where has the woman gone?"

A thin, edgy voice, angry, controlling, accustomed to being obeyed.

Ned heard the other van door open and slam shut.

"That's a real good question," he heard Greg say. "Way I get this, you answer it for *us*. Where the hell is Melanie? Tell, then you can crawl back into your dumpster."

"Easy, Greg," he murmured, more afraid by the minute.

"There is no person of such a name any more," the druid said. "Not since she walked between needfires. I require you to say where Ysabel has gone. You will not be harmed if you do."

Ned lifted a hand quickly, before Greg could speak again.

"Couple of things," he said, working really hard to stay calm. "One, I heard her say you were to stay up there tonight *and* that the two guys were to search alone. Any comments?"

The man looked almost comically startled. "You were there? During the rite?"

"Damn straight I was. So, like, I know the book on this."

"You understand you can be killed for that?"

"Nope. I understand that the woman—Ysabel—laid down the rules. You hurt us here, we go missing, you think Phelan's not gonna know about it, and *tell* her? You want to ruin this for Cadell? Think he'll be happy?"

He heard the bravado in his own voice and wondered where it came from. But he was *not* going to show fear to this guy. He didn't seem to be the same person, dealing with these people. Fifteen wasn't a kid in their world. Maybe that was part of it. And it still seemed to him he was seeing too clearly in the darkness, as if everything was *sharper* tonight.

The druid was staring, saying nothing. Ned cleared his throat. "He's your boss, isn't he? Your chief? Whatever. So what are you doing here, screwing things up for him?"

"You are ignorant, whatever else you are," the figure in front of him said. His eyes were deep-set under thick eyebrows.

"Maybe, but why do *you* care which one of them wins her? You're dead again by morning, aren't you?"

He didn't know if that was so, actually. He hoped it was.

Another silence, and then: "She was one of us. The world began to change when she made her choice and left." The druid lifted his voice. "She *belongs* among us. Changes can be undone. This is not just about the three of them."

He looked briefly towards the trees, then back.

Ned had a thought, hearing that raised voice. On impulse, he tried the inward searching he'd used before to find Phelan twice, and his aunt by the tower.

Something registered, a glow within. Not the druid.

Ned smiled thinly. It was *really* weird, but though he was scared to the point that his hands were trembling, he also felt excited, alive, charged with something, *by* something, that he couldn't explain.

The boar had gone now—off the road, back into the dark field or the woods beyond. It had been here to stop them; it had done that, and departed.

Ned said, "I had two questions, remember? Here's the other one. You say you didn't know I was up there before. What are you doing *here* then? Why did you think I'd have a clue about this? How did you know me at all, or how to find me?"

He knew the answers, but wanted to see what the other guy did.

He was aware that Greg was looking at him, a kind of awe in his face. The van's headlights were illuminating the road and the white-robed figure. Insects darted through the light.

The druid lifted his head. "By what right do you question me?"

"Oh, fine," Ned said. "That's cool. I'll just wait for your friend to climb out of the bushes and ask him."

He saw the reaction to that. He turned to his right, towards the trees by the road. "There are mosquitoes up here, man, they must be worse in there. You getting bitten?"

He waited. There was a stirring in the trees.

Out of the darkness beyond the twin arcs of the headlight beams a red-gold figure emerged. Ned's heart started pounding when he saw him.

Cadell had the stag horns growing from his head again. Ned heard Greg swear softly in disbelief.

"Who are you?" the big Celt said, stepping up onto the roadway.

Where the druid had been angry, Cadell sounded almost amused. His voice was as before: deep, carrying. You could follow that voice into battle, Ned thought.

He needed to be careful, though. It was true, the thought he'd had looking through the barred gates by the parking lot: if these guys thought he and Greg were a problem, they would do something about it.

If they could ignore his questions, he decided, he could do the same with theirs. He said, "Tell me, since this guy won't, you really think Phelan won't let her know you broke the rules? Like, broke them immediately? I heard you swear an oath."

Cadell said, "It is Beltaine, she said to release them when the night ended." The voice was still amused, diverted. It hadn't been, Ned remembered, when Phelan walked up into the site, after Ysabel had come.

"True," Ned admitted. Beside him, Greg was breathing hard. "But I also heard her say *you* were to stay there, start searching in the morning."

The big man smiled down at him. His easy manner didn't feel faked to Ned. "But I'm not looking for her," he said. "I was looking for you."

"Cute. You willing to take a chance she'll buy that? Risk everything on it? Is she the type to be cool with that kind of scam?"

Cadell's expression did change then, which was kind of satisfying. There was a silence.

Ned nodded his head. "Thought so. And anyhow, why *were* you looking for me?"

"She called your name—the small woman—when she came up, before she went through the fires."

Oh. Right, Ned thought.

And Cadell would have known his name, who he was, from by the tower with Aunt Kim. He'd made the connection. If Ned was

understanding any of this—which wasn't a dead certainty—the guy
had been alive, on and off, for more than two thousand years. He'd
had time to get clever. Learn how to grow stag horns, change into an
owl, control wolves and dogs.

Piece a few clues together.

In the middle of the roadway, the druid was muttering to himself,
angrily rocking back and forth like some wind-up toy ready to
explode. Ned ignored him.

"You saw us come back for the van?" he guessed.

Cadell nodded. "I had someone watching it."

"Smart of you," Ned said. "One man against one man, but you get
the ghosts?"

"He seems to have you," Cadell said softly. "Doesn't he?"

Ned hesitated.

"No one has us," Greg snapped. He took a step forward. "We have
nothing to do with this. We want Melanie back, then you can all go
off and screw each other for all we care!"

"An unappealing notion," Cadell said. He smiled. "What Brys
told you is true, the woman you call Melanie doesn't exist any more.
You need to understand that. There is no reason for you *not* tell us
where Ysabel might be, if you know."

"You bastards!" Greg shouted. His hands were balled into fists.
"By what goddamned right do you—"

"Hold it, Greg," Ned said. He moved over and put a hand on the
other man's arm. "Hold it."

Ned took a breath. He was pretty upset himself, trying not to let
it show. They couldn't lose control here, though, they needed to
know too much more.

He said, "Why should we have any idea where she is? Why would
you even think that?"

The druid said something swiftly in that other language.

Cadell looked at him and shook his head. Replied curtly in the same tongue, then turned back to Ned.

"You can be told this much. But you must believe I am not your enemy, and Phelan is *not* your friend. Or anyone's friend." He paused, as if reaching for words. The druid was still muttering.

That one, Ned thought, *wants to kill us.*

Cadell said, "Ysabel changes. Each time we return. Each time, she is altered a little by the summoning. She carries something of the woman brought for her."

"This has happened before, then? Someone else becomes . . . ?"

"Always."

Ned was getting a headache trying to concentrate, to remember all of this. He was going to have to tell Aunt Kim. Maybe she could make sense of it. If they got out of here. The villa was so close, but it felt *years* away. He had to keep Greg from exploding. He could feel the other man's tension beside him.

He said, "She changes? You two don't?"

Cadell shook his head, the antlers moving. "I am as I have always been, from the first days. And so is he, may the gods rot his heart."

"So why? Why does she . . . ?"

Again the druid, Brys, snarled something at the bigger man, and again he was ignored.

Cadell wasn't smiling now. "She alters so that her choice alters. You are not expected to understand. I am giving you these answers to show goodwill. I am not your enemy."

"*Goodwill?*" Greg shouted. "After what you did to her? Are you insane?"

Ned grabbed for his arm again. He could feel Greg trembling, as if he wanted to charge forward, start swinging fists. He'd get cut to pieces if he did.

"I don't understand," Ned said. "You're right. Maybe I don't need to, but believe me—and this is the truth—we have no clue where she is."

Cadell stared at him a long moment, then he sighed, as if surrendering something—a hope?

"It was always unlikely." He shrugged. "Very well. Your road is clear now. Leave us to our search. Keep away from this. The woman by the tower, she swore that you would."

That was Aunt Kim. "Uh-uh. No dice. She promised," said Ned, "*before* you took one of us." He pointed a finger, was pleased to see his hand was steady. "You changed things, not us." He paused, took a chance. "Would you surrender someone who mattered to you, just like that?"

"It is not the same," Cadell said. But he'd hesitated.

"Yes it is!" Greg snapped. "You want someone you lost, so do we!"

Ned looked at him. So did Cadell.

"Ysabel is never lost," the big man said. "That is the nature of this. She is in the balance. And I have someone to kill."

"Then play all that out without Melanie," Ned said. He gambled again. "My aunt will be coming up this road any minute. She knows the one you're mocking again with those horns. She's *seen* him, remember? You want her in on this? Risk losing Ysabel because you chose the wrong woman to change and got tangled with us?"

Cadell was looking away now, up towards the trees and sky. So was the druid, Ned saw. He wondered if he'd made a mistake, mentioning Aunt Kim.

He knew what they were doing. He did the same thing himself, closed his eyes, reaching inward and then out for her. No presence, no sign of her pale, bright glow. She was screening herself, or too far away.

"I do not mock him," Cadell said, looking at Ned again. "When I am in the woods, it . . . pleases me to honour him with the horns he wears."

Ned shook his head, angry again, and scared. It was getting to be a bit much. He heard himself saying, "Oh, sure. Right. Do you honour a king by wearing his crown?"

And where had that *come from?* he thought.

The druid stopped rocking. Cadell blinked. Greg was staring at Ned again. Ned realized he still had a hand on the other man's arm. He let it drop.

"Who are you?" Cadell said. He'd asked that already.

"A friend of the woman you took," Ned said. "And nephew of the other one. The one who matters. So you need to just reverse whatever you did to Melanie, and you'll get us all out of your hair."

There was another silence. "That cannot be," the druid said.

Cadell nodded his head. "Even if I wished it. You *saw* the bull die, and the fires." He looked at Ned a moment. "And would it be honourable for you to reclaim your woman and have someone else be lost in her stead?"

No good reply to that, actually.

"She isn't my woman," Ned said lamely, feeling like a high school kid again, even as he spoke. That was what you said when guys teased you about a girl, for God's sake.

Cadell smiled. A different sort of expression. It made you realize—again—that this man had lived a very long time.

"The roadway is clear," he repeated, gently enough. "We will go back to the sanctuary and wait for dawn, as she commanded. As it happens, you are right . . . I don't trust him not to tell her, and she may choose to let such things matter. I have learned, at cost, not to anticipate her. Go your way." He paused, then added, again, "I am not your enemy."

Ned looked at him. In the headlights, under moonlight, wearing those horns, the man looked like a god himself, with a voice to match.

A week ago, Ned had been worrying about his frog dissection in biology and a class party at Gail Ridpath's house and the hockey playoffs.

He shivered, nodded his head. What did you say to any of this, anyhow?

"Screw you," was what Gregory said, and added an extreme obscenity.

"I would be more careful," Cadell said, calmly.

Greg repeated exactly what he'd just said, word for word, and strode forward—towards the druid. "We're not going anywhere and neither are you," he snarled at the one called Brys. "You handling this stuff? You *handle* it, man—change her back before I break your face!"

Sometimes a suspended moment boiled over into action just a little too fast.

"Stop!" cried Cadell.

Ned saw the druid raise both hands as Greg approached, moving fast. He thought the man was warding a blow. He was wrong.

Greg's head snapped backwards. His whole upper body lifted, as his feet kept moving—almost comically—forward for an instant. Edward Marriner's assistant, a solid, heavy-set man, went flying backwards through the air and landed hard in the road, flat on his back in the glare of the van's headlights.

He didn't move. His body looked awkward, crumpled, where it lay.

"Oh, Jesus Christ!" Ned said.

"I *said* stop," Cadell snapped at the druid. And added something savagely in their other tongue.

Ned's own anger came. A force such as he couldn't remember feeling in his life. He wheeled towards the big Celt, heard himself scream, wordlessly, with fury and fear, and without knowing what he was doing, without a clue, his right hand swung up and across, *scything* through the night air, aimed towards Cadell, a good three metres away.

There was a sizzling sound, like steak first hitting a barbeque or electricity surging. Ned cried out again. Something *leaped* from his fingers like a laser—and sliced through the stag horns, severing them halfway up. The big man roared, in shock and pain.

Then there was silence.

Cadell, still twisted in the act of ducking, stared at Ned. A hand went to his horns. What was left of them. The sliced-off, branching part lay beside him in the road.

Ned turned to the druid. The white-robed man lifted his own hands quickly, but this time clearly in self-defence. Ned could see fear in his face.

"Who *are* you?" the druid said.

His turn, it seemed. People were asking that a whole lot, Ned thought. It could get old fast, or be really, really scary.

"Did you kill him?" he demanded. Greg still hadn't moved.

"He's alive," Cadell said. "I blocked most of it. Brys, be gone now. You disobeyed me. You heard my command."

The druid turned to him. Speaking slowly, a watchful eye on Ned, he said, "Command me not. I have a task here, for *all* of us. This is not only the three of you."

"Yes it is," said Cadell flatly. "It always is. Shall I unbind you, spirit from body, right here? Do you want to try journeying back to the other side right now? From this place? I will do it, you know I can. You are here only because of me."

Another moment of stillness, a night road between trees and fields, the moon risen. Brys said something in that other tongue, words laden with a bitterness so deep even Ned could hear it. Then the druid gestured—towards himself this time—and disappeared.

Ned shook his head. And in just about the same moment, he felt a glow within. He hadn't been searching for her . . . Aunt Kim was reaching for *him,* he realized, letting him know she was coming. He hadn't known that could happen.

He hadn't known much, in fact. His right hand was tingling, from the force, the fury, of what he'd just done.

He looked at Cadell again. The remnants of the broken-off horns were gone, he saw. The man stood, golden-haired, as he had at Entremont.

Ned felt an unexpected sorrow. A loss of something, of majesty. He swallowed. "I don't know how I did that," he said. "I didn't know you'd saved Greg."

"He'll be all right. Didn't deserve death so soon, though he's a fool."

"He isn't," Ned protested weakly. "We're way over our heads. We've *lost* someone."

Cadell looked at him, then lifted his head, as he had before, looking above the trees. Ned saw him register that Kim was coming. The big man shook his head.

"We all lose people. I told you truth. So did Brys, in this. She is gone. There is no such person in the world any more."

"How are we supposed to accept that, or explain it?" Ned asked.

The Celt shrugged. *Not my problem,* the gesture seemed to say. But Ned was too worn out, too spent, to be angry again.

"Carry on with your lives," Cadell said. Golden, magnificent, the resonant voice.

Ned remembered Phelan saying the same thing to them—him and Kate—just days ago. Cadell put a hand up and ran it through his long hair. "If you stray near to us you are going to be hurt or killed, or end up hopelessly between two worlds. You are close to that already, yourself, whoever you are." His voice was unsettlingly gentle again.

I am not your enemy.

They heard a car below them, changing gears to climb.

"Farewell," the big man said. He lifted one hand, straight over his head.

An owl was in the air where a man had been. It was flying away, north again, over hedge, field, towards the ridge beyond the houses set back from the road, then it was gone.

Ned looked at his hands. He felt like one of the X-Men, a comic-book freak. His fingers weren't tingling any more, but he didn't feel any kind of power, either.

Aunt Kim's lights appeared. The red car came to a stop behind the van. Ned heard her door open and close, saw her approaching, moving quickly, almost running. Her white hair gleamed in the headlights.

He had never been so glad to see anyone in his life.

His aunt looked at him and stopped dead.

"Ned. What happened? Who was here?"

"Cadell, and a druid. There was a boar blocking the road, they sent it, and then they . . ." It was pretty hard to talk.

"*Sent* it? Why, Ned?"

"They thought we might know where she is."

She looked around. "Where's Gregory?"

"Present, ma'am."

Ned turned quickly. Greg was sitting up, propped on one hand, rubbing at his chest with the other.

"Oh, God. What happened to *you?*"

"Got whomped by the druid guy. Good thing I'm way tough. Viking blood, all the way back."

Ned shook his head. "Cadell blocked it."

"You're kidding me."

"No."

"Why'd he do that?"

"Scared of our telling Phelan, Ysabel learning they were down here. Or maybe he's . . . not so bad."

"You mean I'm *not* way tough?"

Aunt Kim managed a smile. "I think you're tough as horseshoe nails, Gregory. But let's go up to the house. I don't like it out here after dark. Not tonight."

"Hold it," Ned said.

His hearing seemed to be sharper, too. But a second later the others heard it. Then they all saw the bobbing flashlight beam above them on the roadway.

"Ned? Greg?" It was his father.

"We're here!" Kimberly called. "It's all right."

The searchers appeared a few seconds later: his dad, Steve, Kate, hurrying down the slope. Ned saw that his father was carrying a hoe. Steve had a shovel. Kate held the flashlight . . . and a hammer.

"We saw the van's lights, then they stopped," his father said. "We got nervous."

"And charged to the rescue? Like that?" Greg said, standing up carefully. He was still rubbing his chest. "Jeez, you look like extras storming the castle in *Frankenstein*. All you need's a thunderstorm and accents."

Ned's father scowled. "Very funny, Gregory."

Kate giggled, looking at her hammer. "I couldn't find a stake," she said.

Dracula wasn't that far from the truth here, Ned thought, with risen spirits abroad.

This was all release of tension, and he knew it. They'd been scared, now they weren't—for a while, anyhow.

"Ned, you okay?" his father asked.

Ned nodded.

It occurred to him that no one had seen what he'd done to Cadell. Greg had been flat on his back, out cold. Ned decided to keep that part to himself. He looked at his aunt.

"What was the name of that figure?" he asked. "The one you mentioned. With the horns. From when we met Cadell."

Aunt Kim hesitated. "Cernan. Cernunnos. Their forest god." Her expression changed. "He had them again?"

"Yeah."

She shook her head. "So much for my powers of intimidation."

"He left when we felt you coming."

"As an owl?"

Ned nodded. "I think he *was* worried about you, or at least unsure."

Aunt Kim made a wry face. "Probably scared of Peugeots. Famous for bad transmissions."

They were trying to calm him down, Ned realized. He must look pretty freaked out. He managed a smile, but he didn't seem to be fooling anyone. He kept remembering what he'd done, the feeling of it.

"Let's go up," Kimberly repeated. "You two can tell us what happened, but in the house."

His father said, "Right. Greg, I'll drive. You can ride shotgun with this."

Greg eyed the hoe. "Thanks, boss. That'll make me feel *so* protected."

He had to be in considerable pain, Ned thought, remembering Greg flying backwards and that crumpled landing. He wasn't letting on, though. People could surprise you.

Ned wanted to smile with the others, joke like them, but he couldn't do it. He stared at his hands again. What he was feeling was hard to describe, but some of it was grief.

⟨∽⟩

This time, when he came downstairs in the middle of the night his aunt was in the kitchen, sitting at the table in a blue robe. He hadn't expected anyone—she startled him. The only light was the one over the stove-top.

"You get insomnia too?" she asked.

Ned shook his head. "Not usually."

He went to the fridge and took out the orange juice, blinking in the sudden light. He poured himself a drink.

"Kate sleeping?"

She nodded.

He walked to the glass doors by the terrace.

"Did you go out? It looks beautiful, doesn't it?" He saw the moon above the city.

"We're better off inside, dear. It isn't a night for wandering."

"But I *did* go wandering," Ned said, looking at the pool and trees. The cypresses were moving in the wind, which had picked up again. "And because I did, Melanie's gone. If we hadn't gone up—"

"Hush. Listen to me. The two of you went because Kate was halfway inside the rites already. She said so. *You* said so, how different she became. She was starting for the fires when Melanie came."

It was true. It wasn't a truth that made you happy.

"I could have said no."

"Not easy, Ned. Not in this kind of situation. You were in it too."

He looked at her. "Did you ever say no?"

His aunt was silent for a time. "Once," she said.

"And what . . . ?"

"Long story, Ned."

He looked away, towards the moon in the window again. He crossed back and sat at the table with her. He said, "Did you see that Veracook put rowan leaves on the window ledge?"

Aunt Kim nodded. "Probably outside all the doors, too, if we look. The past is close to the surface here, Ned."

"Which part of the past?"

She smiled faintly. "That's the problem, isn't it? Right now, from what you've said? I'd guess a lot of it, dear."

He drank his juice. "We're not going to get her back, are we?"

His aunt raised her eyebrows. "Oh, my! And which part of what family did *that* come from? Not ours, that's for sure. Is your father like this?"

Ned shook his head.

"Then stop it right now. We haven't even *begun* looking. You go get some rest. This is three in the morning talking in you. And remember, we have six good people here, and two more coming."

Ned looked at her. "Well, yeah, but if my mom kills you we're down to seven."

His aunt sniffed. "I can handle my baby sister."

He had to smile at that. "You think so?"

She made that wry face. "Maybe not. We'll see. But really, go back to bed. We're starting early."

They'd made their plans. Both cars, two groups. Aunt Kim, with Kate in her best geek mode, had chosen the destinations. It had seemed hopeless, even ridiculous when they'd discussed it. It seemed more so now, in this dead-quiet of night.

He said, "There's something I didn't tell you, from before."

She sat still, waiting.

"When the druid slammed Greg I thought he'd killed him. I got . . . I lost it, I guess. I'm *really* not sure how, but, like, I slashed sideways with my hand, from at least four, five metres away, and I . . . I cut Cadell's horns off. Halfway up. Like, with a light-sabre, you know?"

She said nothing, absorbing this. Her expression was strange, though. She reached out, almost absently, and finished his orange juice.

"You aimed for the horns? Not him?"

He thought about it. "I guess. I don't think I actually aimed at all. I had no idea I could even . . . " He stopped. It was pretty hard to talk about.

"Oh, child," Aunt Kim said.

"What do I *do* about it?"

She squeezed his hand on the tabletop. "Nothing, Ned. It may never happen again. It was Beltaine. You'd seen the boar, a druid, the fires. You were pretty far along that road. And you have our family's link to all of this. Maybe more than any of us. But you probably aren't going to be able to control it, and maybe that's just as well."

"So I just forget what happened?"

She smiled again, sadly. "You'll never forget it, Ned. But there's a good chance it'll never come back. Keep it, a reminder that the world has more to it than most people ever know."

"My dad said something like that."

"I like your father," she said. "I hope he likes me."

"You need my mom to like you a lot more."

"Meghan? She loves me. Like a sister."

Ned actually laughed.

"Go to bed," his aunt said.

He did, and to his surprise, he slept.

༄

Up in the wind at Entremont, middle of the night, he is remembering other times, watching the torches burn down. He is thinking about the forest, the first time he came here.

He'd been afraid of dying that day, so many lives ago, walking through black woods, following the guides, no idea where they were taking him, if he'd ever get back to the shore and sea, and light.

Even half lost in reverie, he is aware when the other man returns to the plateau, in his owl shape.

It isn't as if Cadell is making a secret of anything.

Phelan is looking away south, doesn't bother turning to see the other man change back. He keeps to himself at the end of the ridge overlooking the lights of Aix below. The sea is beyond, across the coastal range, unseen. He feels it always, a tide within, and the moon is full.

He is undisturbed by the other man's disregard of the rules she has given them. It isn't as if such behaviour is unexpected.

She is not going to make her choice because one of them has sought some advantage. They have fought each other or waged wars here for millennia. She is as likely to see Cadell's flying as evidence of a greater desire for her. Or not.

It is never wise, he has learned, to believe you know what Ysabel will think, or do. And this newly devised challenge is unsettling.

Cadell will be feeling the same way, he knows. (They know each other very well by now.) The Celt might even—the thought comes—have returned here because he's actually afraid she *might* let a transgression have consequence. She is capricious, almost above all else, unpredictable even after more than twenty-five hundred years. And she has altered their duel this time into something new.

Sometimes when he thinks the number, the length of time, *twenty-five hundred*, it can still catch him in the heart. The weight of it, impossibility. The long hammer of fate.

They never change, the two of them. She always does, in small, telling ways. She must be rediscovered, as a consequence, each and every time. Endlessly different, endlessly loved. It has to do with how she returns—through the summoning of someone else. The claiming of another soul.

His back to the other man and the spirits, looking out from the edge of the plateau, he is entirely unafraid. Cadell will not attack him here. That far he would never go.

He expects the Beltaine dead to be gone—as commanded—before sunrise, though the druid might not be. Brys is a wild card of sorts in this, always has been, but there is nothing to be done about that, really.

What he cannot alter he will ignore, for the next three days.

What he needs to do is find her. First.

He needs to concentrate on possibilities and there are too many. He reminds himself that she *wants* to be found. Tries to grasp what that means, in terms of where she might be.

It is possible that she'll move around, not stay in a single chosen place. They have done this return so many times, the three of them. She will know how to change garments, hide her hair, find money if she needs it. She cannot fly, but there are trains, taxis. This world will not frighten her any more than it has unsettled either of the men, returning to changes. There are always changes.

She is not limited, except by the range, the ambit of their history here, and that is wide, east and west and north, and to the margin of the sea.

In the moonlight, the land below, unfurling south, is bright enough for shadows. He holds the sound of her voice inside him and gazes out towards the changed, invisible coastline, remembering.

He was so afraid, that first time here.

Arriving with three ships to establish a trading post on a shoreline known to be inhabited, and dangerous. You made your fortune in proportion to the danger. That was the way of it. If the goods on offer were difficult to obtain back home, the rewards were that much greater.

He was young, already known as a mariner. Unmarried as yet, willing to take risks, shape the rising trajectory of a life. Not an especially genial man, by reputation, but no obvious enemies, either. A habit of command. They had made him leader of the expedition.

They put ashore, he remembers, on the coast a little west of here. The shoreline has silted up, is greatly changed in two millennia: logging for timber, wood burned for fires, irrigation systems, flood barriers. The sea is farther away now than it was.

He remembers seeing the trees from the boat, the forest coming right down to where they made harbour. A windbreak cove, small, stony beach. Looking from the ship at those oak woods, wondering what lay beyond. Death or fortune . . . or nothing of significance.

After all, it didn't *have* to be one or the other.

The Celts came to them two days later. Appearing silently out of the woods as they were putting up their first temporary structures.

Fear returning, the sheer size of them. They had always been bigger people. And the wildness: half naked, the heavy gold they wore, the long hair, bright leggings, weapons carried.

He knew how to fight, some of his seamen did. But they were traders, not truly soldiers. They had come in peace, in hope and greed, to begin a cycle: a rhythm of trade, seasonal, enduring.

To stay, if they could, eventually.

There was no language in common. Two of his men had been here before, farther east along the coast; they had twenty or thirty words between them in the barbaric tongue men spoke here. And it would have been laughable to imagine one of these giant savages speaking Greek. The tongue of the blessed Olympians.

Of civilized man.

They were far from civilization on that stony shoreline by the woods.

The Celts accepted gifts: cloth and wine, and cups for the wine, jewelled necklaces. They liked the wine.

And they made an overture, a promising one. From their gestures on the second encounter, two days after the first—motions of drinking, eating, pointing inland beyond the trees—he understood what they were conveying. He was being invited to a feast. No thought of not accepting.

You couldn't allow fear to control you.

He left, with one companion, the next day when they came for him. They followed ten of the Celts into the trees, darkness dropping like a cloak, immediately, even on a sunny day, the sea disappearing behind them, then the sound of it gone.

He remembers, on this high, open, moonlit ground, how frightened he was as that day's long walk went on. He had thought, for whatever reason, that this tribe lived by the water, but there was little reason for them to do so. These were not fisherfolk.

The woods seemed endless, enveloping, unchanging. A journey from his world into another one. A space out of time. Forests could be like that, in the stories, in life.

They heard animals as they went; never saw any. He was lost almost immediately as they twisted to follow a barely seen path, mostly heading north, he thought, but not invariably. He realized he was at their mercy; the two of them would never find their way back alone.

Your profits were in proportion to the risks you ran.

Towards sunset, end of a full day's travelling, the trees began to grow thinner. The faint path widened. The sky could be seen. Then torches. They came out of the forest. He saw a village, lit with fires for a festival. He didn't know, at that point, what the celebration was.

How could he have known?

They led him into that torchlight, across a defensive ditch, past bonfires, through an earthen wall, then a gauntlet of men—and women. Not hostile, more curious than anything.

They came into a circle, a wide space at the centre of small houses made of wood. A tall man, silver-haired, not young, stood up to greet them. They looked at each other and exchanged gestures.

He had liked the man from the first moment.

He was given a cup, one of their own. He lifted it in salute, drank. A harsh, burning liquor, unwatered. Fire down his throat. An effort (he remembers) not to shame himself, insult them, by coughing, or spitting it out. No civilized man would take liquor this way.

He was far from civilized men. He'd felt the drink affecting him almost immediately. A deep breath. A brief smile. He handed the cup back; a man of restraint, moderation. Chosen for these things as much as for courage and skill. A leader, responsible for his companion here and the others on the shore. The need to be diligent, careful.

He saw her then. First time.

The world changing, forever.

Really that, he thinks, on the plateau of Entremont, two thousand six hundred years after: as near to forever as a man might know.

For good or ill, joy or grief, love or hatred, death or life returning. All those things. As much as a man might know.

He hears a sound now, someone approaching, stopping. He turns this time. He knows the footfall as he knows his own, very nearly.

"Did you enjoy watching?" Cadell asks. "Hiding down below?" He smiles.

"The bull?" He shrugs. "I never enjoy it very much. You've improved. The kill was clean."

The Celt continues to smile. "It always is. You know it."

"Of course."

They look steadily at each other. He wants to kill the other man. He needs to kill the other man.

The Beltaine spirits and the druid are a distance away, by the sanctuary and the still-burning torches. He and the other one might easily be alone here in the night. The wind had lessened earlier but has returned now. Clouds and stars overhead.

"I know where she is," Cadell says.

"No you don't," he replies.

CHAPTER XII

I n the brightness of morning, driving west again with his father
and Greg in highway traffic, Ned was fighting a heavy-eyed lack
of sleep and the sense that he was a useless, irresponsible person.

He was trying to make himself concentrate on what they were
doing, on all that had been discussed last night, but he kept thinking
about Kate Wenger as she'd looked before going to bed.

Ned had been alone at the dining-room table leafing through
a guidebook—the section on the history of Provence—amid the
scattered notes and papers they'd put together earlier.

They wouldn't have been scattered if Melanie had done them,
he'd thought. She'd have stacked and sorted and filed the pages.
With coloured tabs. Of course, if Melanie had been around they
wouldn't have *needed* those notes, would they? He'd just finished
looking up something and was feeling even more depressed and
confused.

"What'd you find?" Kate said, coming over.

He glanced up. She was barefoot, wearing only one of his own oversized T-shirts. He said, "I've been meaning to ask you about that bit up there, before, 'God will know his own.' "

"Oh. Right." She made a face. "Siege of Béziers? It's west of here."

"Yeah, I found it. In 1209. 'Kill them all.' Pretty unbelievable."

In the muted light and the quiet, her body under the T-shirt and long legs below it were suddenly way too distracting. You weren't supposed to be thinking about that at a time like this, were you?

Steve and Greg had been at the other end of the room, slumped on the big couch watching television—*The Matrix*, dubbed into French, which might have been pretty funny any other time. Ned's father was on the computer upstairs, emailing, and Aunt Kim was showering. Kate was just out of the shower herself, her hair still wet.

"They were after heretics down here," she said. "It was like a crusade. Those tended to be vicious."

"Yeah, but from what Phelan was saying, the one who spoke those words—"

"Was with Cadell, I know. And our guy was inside."

They looked at each other.

"Is he our guy?"

She shrugged. "I don't know."

"What does all this *mean*? Like, if they are supposed to battle each other for her, how do armies come into it?"

Kate looked away, out the window into darkness. "Maybe sometimes they fight and one gets killed, but sometimes she makes a choice, and they both live, then the other one goes to war?"

"You're just guessing."

She looked back at him. "Well, of course I'm just guessing."

He sighed. "Sorry. Sit down, eh?"

"No way. This shirt's too short. This is all the leg you get."

He smiled. "Want my sweatpants?"

She shook her head. "I'm going to bed."

"Uh-huh. I should make a bad joke now, right?"

"Probably. Wet T-shirt or something."

"It isn't wet."

"I was careful. I'm a good girl. And you're obviously the kind of guy who'll do *anything* to get a woman to sleep over."

"Oh, yeah. Druids and blood. My usual. Never fails. You call Marie-Chantal?"

She nodded. "She was shocked."

"Really?"

"No, idiot. But she did want to know what you looked like."

Ned blinked. "What'd you tell her?"

"I said you looked Canadian. G'night, Ned."

She turned and went towards what had been Melanie's room the night before. Ned was left at the table, images lingering of how clean and fresh she'd looked, her wet hair and her dancer's legs.

Then he thought about Melanie, and the lean, fierce man he'd first seen in the cathedral. Imagined that one leading a red slaughter by the mountain, then casting men alive down a pit, the way she said Marius had done. He could see it, that was the problem.

I am not a good man.

And if he was understanding anything at all, the other one, Cadell, had burned a city, Béziers, eight hundred years ago, with Phelan inside—and maybe Ysabel, whatever her name was that time.

Revenge? Was Kate right? Had Ysabel made a choice, picked Phelan that time, but Cadell hadn't died? Had he made that crusade, or just made use of it?

Might that be why one of the men *needed* to be killed, so her choice was made that way, or else this part of the world could drown in blood?

Had it been the same at Pourrières, where Ned had felt *he* was drowning in the slaughter? Or was this all so far off base it wasn't even funny?

And what did a Canadian look like, anyhow?

IN THE MORNING they'd gone back to Entremont first, on the off chance someone had lingered there. The gate was locked, though, the parking lot empty. It was the first of May, a holiday in France. But it didn't matter: Ned could *feel* it, there was nothing here. Whatever had been on this plateau during the night was gone. He wondered if the remains of the Beltaine fires would be there if they climbed the fence and went in.

He thought about the bull. How would the guard or the first tourists tomorrow deal with that? Not his problem, he supposed. His problem was a lot bigger.

It wasn't that he didn't believe in his aunt, but the hard fact was, if they were actually going to check out all the sites near Aix that had connections to Celts or Greeks or Romans, they were going to need months, not three days.

And they might not even *have* three days. There were others searching, after all.

The plan, such as it was, had been worked out earlier the evening before. Those had been the notes on the table. Kate, scribbling place names as fast as she or Ned's father or Aunt Kim could rattle them off, had begun biting her lip part of the way through, he remembered.

It was pretty unbelievably random, Ned had thought, watching the list grow.

GREG TOOK THE MOTORWAY EXIT for Arles and paid the toll. It was a fresh, blue-sky holiday morning, a day for a walk, a picnic, a climb.

They continued west for a bit but got off before the city to go north on a smaller road towards a low, spiky range of mountains.

Ned saw vineyards on both sides, and olive trees, their leaves silver-green in the light. There were signs showing where you could pull off to buy olive oil. It was beautiful, no denying it. He had no idea how any of them were supposed to enjoy scenery today, though.

Aunt Kim's plan had been that she and Ned, with their links—however imperfect—to the world of the rites that had taken Melanie, would each anchor a team. They'd use the van and her little red car to criss-cross towns and ruins and the countryside. If either of them got even the glimmer of a sensation, any kind of presence, they'd telephone the others and . . .

And what? That was the depressing part. Even if, by whatever miracle of intuition or luck, they actually found the place where Melanie-as-Ysabel was hiding from the two men, what were they supposed to *do*?

Ask her nicely to change back?

Ned remembered that he'd put the question more or less in those words the night before. He'd been sitting next to Kate, looking at the list she was making: *Glanum, Arles, Nîmes, Antibes, Vaison-la-Romaine, Orange, Fréjus, Pont du Gard, Roquepertuse, Noves, Narbonne, Saint-Blais, Hyères.* He'd stopped reading there, though Kate kept on scribbling.

Glanum—whatever that was—was their next stop this morning. The red car was going to Nîmes, farther west, and a couple of the other sites that way.

They were all pretty much just names to Ned. And there were way too many. It felt hopeless. There were even connections to Greeks, Romans, and Celts in Marseille itself, and Marseille had three million people. They could spend days there.

And what was the point, anyhow? Did they wander the streets calling her name like someone looking for a lost cat? And which name, even? Melanie or Ysabel?

It was Steve, surprisingly, who'd nailed him on this last night.

Steve's attitude had changed almost completely, right after Greg had added his voice to Ned's, explaining the events on the road, including the druid's long-range flattening of him. Greg had credibility, it seemed. Came with a bruised sternum. And he hadn't even seen Cadell change into an owl, Ned thought.

Ned had seen it. Twice, now. What did you do with *that* memory?

Steve had said, from by the terrace doors, "Ned, if we don't have anything better, this is what we do, man. If we find her, we figure out a next step. We're not going to just sit here, are we? Or go around taking photos as if nothing's happened?"

"No, we're not going to do that," Edward Marriner had said.

"And it makes no sense to be pessimistic," Greg added, sitting a little stiffly on a dining-room chair. "I mean, this whole thing is so off the wall, why shouldn't *we* do something off the wall and fix it, eh?"

Ned looked at him.

"You sound like Melanie," he said.

Greg hadn't smiled. "Someone has to, I guess," was what he'd said.

Ned was thinking about that, too, as they continued north towards the sharp-edged mountains, passing tourist signs for a place called Les Baux. What *did* Melanie sound like? How did she think? What was there about her that he could try to sense, or locate?

Or did that even matter? Was it more a question of thinking about Ysabel, instead, reborn into the world so many times? So dangerously beautiful it could scare you. He did get scared, in fact, remembering how he'd felt last night, looking at her, hearing that voice.

Or maybe it was the two men, maybe *they* were what he should be searching for, inwardly? But what was the point? It was pretty clear they had no clue where she was—that was the whole idea of the challenge she'd set them. That's why Cadell and the druid had come looking for Ned, wasn't it?

He considered that for a bit. They drove past a farm with horses and donkeys in a meadow on their left. There were plane trees along a dead-straight east-west road they crossed. Another sign pointed the way to a golf course.

"She *wants* them to find her," he said.

His father turned around in the front seat.

Edward Marriner had insisted on being with his son today. It made sense, anyhow. Ned and Aunt Kim had to be in different cars. Kate was with Kim because she was the only one besides Ned who could recognize Ysabel—or Phelan, for that matter. Steve went with the two of them, as protection, for what that was worth. Ned had his dad and Greg.

His mother had phoned very early. She was taking a military plane from Darfur to Khartoum, then a flight to Paris and connecting to Marseille. She'd be with them by dinnertime.

"What do you mean, she wants them to?" Edward Marriner asked. His father looked older this morning, Ned thought. A worried man, lines creasing his forehead, circles under his eyes. He probably hadn't slept much either.

Ned shrugged. "Nothing brilliant. Think about it. Ysabel doesn't want to stay lost. This is a test for them, not mission impossible. She's *choosing*, not hiding."

"Which means what?" Greg asked, eyes meeting Ned's in the rear-view mirror.

"Means Aunt Kim's right, maybe," Ned said. "There *should* be a way to find some place that . . . connects up. Or makes sense. I mean, they have to do it, so we can too, right? There has to be some logic to it?"

"Well, it would be easier if we could narrow it to a bit less than twenty-five hundred years," his father said.

"Now you sound like me last night," Ned said.

Greg snorted.

"God and His angels forfend," his father said, and turned back to watch the road.

Edward Marriner was carrying two cameras, a digital and an SLR. More for comfort, Ned thought, than anything else. It had occurred to him, getting into the van, that on the viewfinder side of a camera you had a buffer between you and the world.

There were a lot of ideas coming to him these days for the first time. Looking out the window, he saw the turnoff for Les Baux coming up. Traffic slowed as cars made the left.

"Straight on, Gregory," Edward Marriner said, checking the map. "Road goes to Saint-Rémy, we pull off just before."

"I got it," Greg said. "It's on the signs."

"What is that?" Ned asked. "Up there? Les Baux?"

"Medieval hill town, castle ruins. Pretty spectacular."

"You've been?"

"With your mother, before you were born."

"On our list?"

"Not for this. Oliver and Barrett have it down for the book. Though it probably *could* be for this, too. Best I gather, the Celts were all over this place before the Romans came."

"It's way up there," Greg said. "Look close."

They were waiting for the cars ahead of them to turn. Ned looked out the left-side window. What appeared at first to be crumbled rock was actually the smashed-up remains of a long castle wall at the top of the mountain. It blended in almost perfectly.

"Wow," he said.

His father was looking too. "They used to throw their enemies from those walls, the story goes."

"Nice of them. When?"

"Medieval times. The Lords of Les Baux they were called. Louis XIII sent cannons up to the castle a few hundred years after. Blew it apart. Thought it was too dangerous for local lords to have a fortress that strong."

Ned shook his head. The Romans with siege engines at Entremont, same thing here with cannons.

"I thought you told me we were coming to a beautiful, peaceful place."

His father glanced back. "I'm sure I told you beautiful. I doubt I was so foolish as to say peaceful."

"Besides," Greg said in a joking voice, "when do fifteen-year-old dudes want it peaceful?"

"Could use some about now," Ned said.

They came up to the intersection, waited for the car ahead to go left, and carried on through.

"This next bit here's called the Valley of Hell," Edward Marriner said. "Melanie has a note it may have inspired Dante." He had her notebook, among the other papers he was carrying.

"He was here too?" Greg asked.

"Everyone was here," Ned's father replied. "That's sort of the point. There were popes in Avignon for a while, long story. Dante was an emissary at one time."

"I can see it," Ned heard Greg saying. "Valley of Hell, I mean. Look at those boulders." The landscape had become harsh and barren quite suddenly as they wound a narrow route between cliffs. A few splashes of colour from wildflowers seemed to emphasize, not reduce, the bleakness. It was darker, the cliffs hiding the sun. It felt lonely and desolate. Looking around, Ned began to feel uneasy.

"Barrett has this place down too," Edward Marriner was saying. "For the landscape. Another side of Provence."

But his voice had retreated, seemed somehow farther than the front seat. There was something else, inside, pushing it away. Ned took a deep breath, fighting panic. He didn't feel ill, not like at Sainte-Victoire, but he did feel . . . distant. And really odd.

"Can you stop for a second?" he said.

Without hesitation, without a word, Greg swerved the van onto the shoulder, which was not all that wide. The driver behind them—close behind them—blasted his horn and shot past. Greg came to a hard stop.

"What is it? Ned?"

His father had turned again and was looking at him. The expression on his face, a mixture of fear and awe, was unsettling. A father shouldn't have to look at his kid like that, Ned thought.

"Feeling something," he muttered.

He searched inwardly. Nothing tangible—only a disquiet, like a pulsebeat, a faint drumming.

"Does . . . do we have anything on what's here? What might have been around this place?"

Edward Marriner pulled a notebook from his leather case on the floor. There were labelled, coloured tabs separating it into sections. His father flipped through, found a page, skimmed it. He shook his head.

"There were quarries for bauxite, which gets its name from Les Baux. Those are finished now. She mentions the Valley of Hell. Dante. A quote from Henry James about driving in a carriage through here. She thought we might use it."

"Nothing else?"

Greg was looking back at him too. "You feeling sick?"

"Not that. But there's something."

Ned shifted to the right side of the van and opened the door. He got out. He stood by the side of the road, trying to understand what he was feeling. Traffic was lighter now, an occasional car went past. Greg had the flashers on. The high cliffs on both sides cast the road into shadow. It was chilly. The wind blew from the north. Not a mistral, but not comforting, either. Valley of Hell.

"You think she's *here*?" Greg asked through a rolled-down window.

Ned shook his head. "No. I think what I'm getting is older, from the past. I think I'm feeling something from back then, not from now."

"But not as bad as before, right?" Greg asked.

Ned looked through the window past his father at Greg, whose face was a lot like Edward Marriner's now. Fear, and a kind of diffident respect. It was a bit scary to realize it, but they *believed* him.

"Not as bad," he said. "Just the same sense of something still here. The same kind of . . ." He fought for the words. "Breaking through?"

"You mean from medieval times? The castle at Les Baux?" His father's forehead was really creased now, Ned saw. The struggle to make sense of this.

Ned thought about it. He walked away towards the cliff and looked up at it. Then he came back and shook his head again. "Can't tell. I'm no good at this, but I think it goes further back." He took another breath. "We'll ask Kate. Or look it up. But I think we can go on. I don't feel anything here from, like, now. This is just weird, that's all."

His dad looked as if he was about to disagree, then he sighed and shrugged. "I'm out of my league," he said.

Ned got back in and slid the door shut. Greg looked back at him for a second, then put the car in gear and started forward again.

They passed through that closed-in arid canyon in silence, came out of shadow into springtime fields and vineyards and sunlight again. Moments later they saw the Roman arch and a tower on the left side of the road—right beside it.

There was another brown sign pointing towards the ruins of Glanum down an angled, tree-lined path on the other side.

Greg pulled into a gravel parking lot directly in front of the arch. The lot was almost empty. Ned got out. He saw a couple of families spreading an early picnic on the grass beyond. Kids were playing soccer. He felt like an alien watching them, someone from a different world, just intersecting theirs.

Greg walked over to look at the arch, and the taller, oddly shaped structure beside it. Ned's father stopped beside him.

"Feel strange, looking at them?" Edward Marriner said, gesturing at the picnicking group.

Ned looked at him quickly. "I was just thinking that."

His father made another wry face. "Good, we can still share some things."

Ned thought about that, the distance it implied. Not just parents and kids growing up. There was more now. He swallowed. "I haven't changed, Dad. I just . . . I can see some things."

"I know. But that's a change, isn't it?"

It was. "I'm scared," Ned said, after a moment.

His father nodded. "I know you are. So am I."

He put an arm around Ned and Ned let him. His father squeezed his shoulder. He couldn't remember the last time they'd stood like this.

His father let him go. Edward Marriner managed a smile.

"It's all right, Ned. And it'll be better when your mom gets here."

"You think?"

"Yeah. I do."

"But what can she—"

"Your mother's one of the smartest people I know. You know it too. That's why you asked her to come, isn't it?"

Ned hesitated. "Partly, yeah." He looked down at the gravel by his feet.

His father said, gently, "You wanted her out of there?"

Ned nodded, still looking down. After a moment, Edward Marriner said, quietly, "So did I. Very much. We may have cheated a bit, but it was still the right thing to do. Melanie is gone, your mother can help. You'll see."

Ned looked up. "But Aunt Kim? And Mom?"

His father hesitated. "Ned, people have tensions. History comes back, even our own, not just the big stories. They'll sort it out, or they won't, maybe. But I don't think it'll . . . control what we have to do here."

"You don't think," Ned said.

"Certainty," his father murmured, "can be overrated."

"Whatever the hell that means." Ned looked away, towards the arch and the structure beside it. Greg was up close now, gazing at them. The soccer kids were laughing beyond.

"Where are we?" he asked.

"That's the oldest Roman arch in France," his father said. "Honours Julius Caesar's conquest here. If you go look you'll see carvings on it, Gauls in chains, dying. This whole area was in the balance, then after Caesar it's Roman. The other one's later, a memorial to Augustus' grandsons, or nephews, something like that."

Ned was thinking about the druid on their roadway the night before. *This is not just about the three of them.*

This arch recorded the beginning of something, and the end, he thought.

His father said, "These two monuments were the only things showing for hundreds of years. The ruins across the way were underground till the eighteenth century. They only started digging Glanum out eighty years ago."

"How do you *know* all that?" Ned looked over at him.

His father made a face again. "Did my homework, unlike some people I know. I read Melanie's notes last night. I couldn't sleep."

"Figures. Want to write an essay for me?"

His father smiled, but he didn't laugh.

They walked down together towards Greg. Up close, the arch was even bigger, dominating, only the one other tall structure beside it.

"The asylum where van Gogh committed himself after cutting off his ear is over there," his dad said, pointing. "Across the field, by the ruins."

Ned shook his head. *Everyone was here.*

It was true, wasn't it? Or damn near. He looked up at the arch, walking around it in silence. The carvings on the base and a little higher up were as his father had said. Battle scenes, some eroded or broken off, some pretty clear. Romans on horses hacking down at enemies, or fighting on foot. Gauls fallen, mouths open in a scream. There were chained captives, their heads bowed. He saw a woman in a Greek-style robe, different from the others. He wondered about that. He stepped back, thinking about the *power* this arch represented.

Everyone might have been a stranger here once, but did everyone who had come conquer and lay claim? Some visitors, he thought, killed themselves, like van Gogh. Or just went home, like Dante.

"Were the Romans good?" he asked suddenly.

His father looked startled. "You expect an answer to that?"

Ned shook his head. "Not really. Dumb question."

"Let's go across to the excavations," Edward Marriner said. "You can tell us if there's anything here that . . ." He shrugged. "You know what I mean."

Ned knew what he meant.

"They'll be closed," Greg said. "The holiday."

"I know. Everything's closed. I'm assuming Ned can get a read, or whatever, by the entrance."

"And if he does?" Greg asked.

"Then I'll do what I have to do," his father said. Ned and Greg exchanged a glance.

"Come on," Edward Marriner said.

He led them across the road, then along a path through trees. The Glanum site had a low wooden gate, which was locked, though it wasn't especially high. They could see the entrance building about a hundred metres down.

Edward Marriner looked at his son. "Haven't done this in a long time," he said. And placing a foot on the cross beam of the gate, he swung himself up on top, then down the other side.

"Not bad, boss," Greg said.

Ned didn't say anything, he just followed his father over. They waited for Greg to do the same, which he did, grunting when he jumped down—his chest had to be hurting, Ned knew.

They went up the path, alone amid morning birdsong, under the mild, bright sky. The low structure ahead was clearly new. Beyond it, visible now to their left, were the ruins.

Ned moved off the path towards the fence that surrounded the excavated area. In the distance he saw two tall columns. They reminded him of pictures of the Forum in Rome. *Well, yeah*, he thought.

The site was bigger than he'd expected. That was one thing.

But there was no other thing.

He couldn't feel anything. At Entremont earlier this morning he had *known* it was empty, the sense of vacancy had penetrated into him. Here, he just couldn't tell. He didn't know.

He stood by the fence, looking through it at those uncovered stones, and felt nothing but quietness. No awareness of anyone, living or dead, or returned. On the other hand, he knew by now that distance seemed to matter, for him at least.

He looked back at his father and shrugged. "Nothing I can tell. But I may have to get closer. Maybe I should go in. I can get over this fence with a boost."

In the same moment the door of the modern building opened ahead of them, and a guard hurried out, moving with an officious, self-important stride.

"Oh hell," Greg said. "Bet a euro and a pack of gum he's not real happy to be working a holiday."

"Double pay," Ned's father said. "Or more, in France."

Smiling broadly, calling a cheerful hello, he walked to meet the guard.

"At least we don't look like vandals," Greg said. He hesitated. "I think."

He combed a hand through his hair and beard and quickly tucked in his Iron Maiden T-shirt. Ned wasn't sure any of it was an improvement.

The two of them stayed where they were. Ned was entirely happy to leave this part to his dad. He turned back towards the fence and the site, trying, without success, to sense anything inside.

He looked over his shoulder. His father was chatting now—looking relaxed, it seemed to Ned—with the guard.

The guard didn't look quite so calm, but he wasn't blowing a whistle or shouting. Ned saw his dad take out his cellphone and dial it. He looked at Greg, who shrugged. Edward Marriner started speaking to someone, then he handed the phone to the guard, who took it, hesitantly. Comically, the man stood up straight as soon as he began speaking.

Ned looked at Greg again. Greg shrugged again.

The guard said something, then appeared to be listening to whoever was on the other end. It took a while. He nodded his head several times.

It was very quiet. They could just hear the traffic from the road. Ned tried to imagine this place two thousand years ago, a fully developed Roman town. Walls and columns. Temples and houses. He saw what looked to have been a swimming pool. Did the Romans have swimming pools? He thought they did. Kate would know.

There was a bird singing in a tree ahead of them. Wildflowers were growing along the fence, pale purple and white. Towards the south, at the far end of the site, the hills rose sharply, framing the ruins. The Valley of Hell was back that way, cliffs coming right to the shadowed road.

He tried again, still couldn't register anything within. It was possible, he thought, that even if he did, it might be someone entirely unconnected with what they were doing, with Ysabel and Cadell and Phelan, that story.

Once you acknowledged—as if he had any choice now—the existence of this other kind of world, who knew what else might be here? Lions and tigers and bears . . .

"Come on!" his father called suddenly, in French. "This kind fellow's opening up for us."

Ned started over, Greg beside him. The guard had already gone ahead. He was holding the door to the building for them. His manner as they approached was remarkably changed; you'd have to call it deferential.

"What'd you *do*?" Ned whispered to his dad. "Bribe him?"

"That was my next idea. I called the mayor of Aix. She gave me her cell number. I caught her making lunch for guests, but she spoke with this guy. I told her we were idiots to come here on the holiday but asked if she could help out."

"And she did?"

"Obviously. I'm due to take a portrait of her next week."

"Was that planned?"

"You kidding?"

"I thought the French were supposed to be rigid bureaucratic types."

"They are."

Ned actually laughed. His father looked pleased with himself, he thought.

They went in. There was a cash register and ticket counter, a lot of souvenirs—replica jewellery, books, T-shirts, toy soldiers, plastic swords, miniature wooden catapults. Ned saw a big model of the site under protective glass in a sunken area on their left, and laminated posters around the walls showing the excavations at various stages.

The guard led them to another pair of doors on the far side. He opened one, and smiled.

"I will escort you," he said. "I can answer questions if you like, *monsieur*. I even have some thoughts for photographs. It is a recreation of my own!"

"I'd be very grateful," Ned's father lied. "But first, a picture of you?"

The guard hastily buttoned his jacket. Edward Marriner framed and snapped a digital shot of him at the open door with the ruins beyond.

"Merci," he said. They walked through.

Ned paused, overlooking the site. It really was large, seemed even more so from here: not so much ahead of them, because the hills to the east came close, but running north-south along the narrow valley. It would have been open to the wind in winter, he thought.

"The older part is that way," the guard said, gesturing to their right. "The biggest houses, with their courtyards, are ahead of us, and the marketplace and the baths."

"Let me start with the baths and the big houses," Edward Marriner said. "Greg, will you keep the photo log for me? Ned, you can wander around . . . just don't get into trouble."

That had a bit more meaning than usual. His father was proving unexpectedly good at this.

He was going to say, *I promise,* but he didn't.

The other three went straight and then veered left, the guard—cheerful now, something to do on a boring day—was gesticulating and talking already.

Ned went alone to the right, towards the older part.

It didn't take long to begin. After no more than twenty steps he felt a pulsing inside. It came and went, then a moment later it was there again, on and off.

Someone was calling him.

It would be a whole lot smarter, he thought, to have Greg come over, but he couldn't think of a good excuse, given that his dad was supposed to be here working with his assistant.

His heart was beating fast again. He swore under his breath. Then he thought about Melanie, about *why* they were doing this, and he carried on, alone.

He passed two tall pillars he'd seen from the fence. The sign at the base said "Temple of Castor and Pollux." There was a coloured drawing of what it would have looked like two thousand years ago. Tall and handsome, wide steps going up, toga-clad people under a blue sky.

He felt the pulse again. He could place it now, around a corner to the left, just ahead. Another sign there said "Sacred Spring." There was one wall still standing on the north side, and open steps, crumbled and moss-covered, leading down towards a dark, shallow pool.

Cadell was sitting on the steps looking at the water.

Ned stared at him. He ought to feel more surprised than he did, he thought.

"Why did you call me?"

The other man looked up at him and shrugged. "I don't know, to be honest." He smiled. "I'm not the one who figures everything out. What shall I say? A moment of fellowship? Call it that. You will need to learn to screen yourself, by the way. You are visible to anyone here with any power at all."

"Yeah, well, I don't know how to do that. But I don't plan to stick around in your space very long."

The man smiled again. "It isn't mine, it is your own now, too. Are you going to pretend this never happened, after it is over?"

"Once we get Melanie back, yeah, I am. Maybe not pretend, but I have no interest in staying in this."

Cadell gazed over and up at him, the blue eyes bright. He was dressed today in black boots and torn, faded jeans with a bright red polo shirt. Half biker, half tourist. He still had the heavy golden torc around his neck, though the other jewellery was gone. His long hair was pulled back in a ponytail. Ned registered again how big he was.

"It isn't really a choice," the Celt said, gently enough. "Some things aren't. How did you come to be here?"

"In a van," Ned said. A smart-ass line, but he didn't feel like being polite. "Greg drove. Remember Greg? Your friend almost killed him last night."

"I don't name Brys a friend. I need him for some things."

"Sure. Whatever. Are they gone? The spirits?"

Cadell shrugged again. "Probably. He might not be. I did tell him to leave. Really . . . why did you come here?"

"Well, why are *you* here?"

"Looking for her. Why else am I in the world?"

The simplicity of that. Ned glanced away for a moment.

"Well, so are we. Looking."

Cadell turned back to the black water below. He'd been gazing at it when Ned came up.

In the distance beyond the ancient wall, Ned could see his father and Greg with the guard towards the other end of the site. It was a clear day; they seemed small but distinct. His dad was taking pictures, shooting this way. They wouldn't even hear him if he called. The sunlight was bright on them, but it didn't fall where Cadell sat, by the wall, looking at the shallow water of the pool.

The big man gestured. "This part was ours first, up to where we are. That's the goddess's spring below us. Glanis, her name was. Glanum's a twisting of it. Names change, given time. Over that way," he motioned to his right, "the Romans built after they drove us out."

"You lived here? Yourself?"

Cadell shook his head. "No. The Segobrigae were south, nearer the sea. Another tribe was here, a village. They allowed the Greeks a trading place just behind you, past the Temple of Heracles. That was a mistake."

He seemed very calm this morning, disposed to talk, even. Ned tried to picture a Celtic village here, but he couldn't do it. It was too remote, too erased. He kept seeing Romans instead, tall temples like the one across the way, in the picture, serene figures in togas.

The Greeks here, too, their trading place. Ned said, "Is that why you started looking here? Because you were all in this place?"

Cadell looked up again. "Started? I have been moving since daybreak. I am leaving in a moment. She isn't here, by the way."

"You thought she might be?"

"It was a possibility."

Ned cleared his throat. "We thought so too."

"So it seems."

Ned took a chance, pushed a little.

"There is . . . no way for you to do this thing, this battle, and then release Melanie?"

Cadell looked at him a long moment. "Is this the woman you love?"

Ned twitched. "Me? Not at all! She's too old for me. Why the hell does that matter?"

Cadell shrugged his broad shoulders. "It matters when we love."
Something in the way it was said. Ned thought about Ysabel, how
she'd looked under that moon last night. He tried not to dwell on the
image. And if *he* was shaken by the thought, what must it be like for
this man? And for the other?

He cleared his throat. "Trust me, we care. It matters."

Cadell's gaze was still mild. "I suppose. You were angry in the
road. Did you aim for my horns?"

Ned swallowed. He remembered rage, a white surge. "I didn't
know I could do that. I'm not sure I was aiming at anything."

"I think you were. I think you already knew something important."

"What?"

"If you'd killed me there—and you could have—both the others
would have been gone." His expression was calm. "If one of us dies
before she makes her choice, or we fight, we all go. Until the next
time we are returned."

Ned felt cold suddenly. He would have killed Melanie last night,
if his hand had sliced lower.

"I didn't know that," he said.

"I think you may have."

There was really no way to reply to that.

Ned said, remembering something else, "I think Phelan was
trying to find you, to fight you, before she was even summoned."

"Why would he do that?" Eyebrows raised. The question seemed
a real one. "She would never have come then."

"Maybe . . . maybe he's tired. Of the over-and-over?"

Cadell smiled then. Not a smile that had any warmth in it.
"Good, if so. I can grant him rest here, easily."

"You aren't tired of it?"

The other man looked away again. "This is what I am," he said
quietly. And then, "You have seen her."

How did a sentence carry so much weight?

Ned cleared his throat again. He said, "You didn't answer my question, before. You can't release Melanie and still have your fight?"

"I answered last night. Your woman passed between needfires at Beltaine, summoned by the bull, his death. She is Ysabel now. She is inside this."

"And so what happens?"

"I will find her. And kill him."

"And then?"

"Then she and I will be together, and will die in time. And it will happen again, some day to come."

"Over and over?"

The other man nodded. He was still looking down at the pool. "She broke the world, that first time, giving him the cup."

Whatever that meant. "Why . . . why just the three of you? Living again and again."

Cadell hesitated. "I have never given it thought, I don't think that way. Go find the Roman, if you want to play philosopher." But he didn't sound angry. And after a moment added, "I wouldn't have said it was just the three of us. We are the tale for here. I wouldn't imagine there are no others elsewhere, however their tale runs. The past doesn't lie quietly. Don't you know that yet?"

The sun was bright on the ruins, the day mild and beautiful, carrying all the unfurling promise of spring. Ned shook his head. He couldn't even grasp it. *We are the tale for here.*

In the distance, he saw his father talking to the guard. Greg had moved away from them a little, was looking this way. He could see Ned, but not Cadell down on the ancient, crumbled stairway, against the stone wall. Ned made himself wave casually. He didn't want Greg here.

Cadell was looking at the pool again. Glanis, water-goddess. The water looked dark, unhealthy. The Celt's large hands were loosely clasped. In profile, composed and seemingly at ease, he no longer seemed the flamboyant, violent figure of before.

As if to mock that thought, he looked up at Ned again. "I killed him here once, twenty steps behind you. I cut off his head after, with an axe, spitted it on a spike. Left it in front of one of their temples."

What did you say to that? Tell about beating Barry Staley in ping pong four games in a row during March Break?

Ned felt sick again. "You're talking about Phelan?"

"He wasn't named so then. But yes, the Roman. The stranger."

A flicker of anger. "He's still a stranger, after two thousand, five hundred years, or whatever? When does someone *belong* here, by you?"

The blue gaze was cold now.

"That one? Never. We are the tale revisited, the number of times alters nothing. She chose him when he came from the sea, and everything changed."

Ned stared at him. "You actually think the Greeks, the Romans, would never have settled if, if she . . . ?"

Cadell was looking at him. "I'm not the philosopher," he repeated. "Talk to him, or the druid. I only know I need her as I need air, and that I must kill him to have her."

Ned was silent. Then he drew a breath. "I saw some of that change," he said. "Across the way. The carvings on that arch."

Cadell turned and spat deliberately on the steps below himself.

Ned said, quietly, "Don't you get tired?"

Cadell stood suddenly. He smiled thinly. His eyes really were amazingly blue. "I need sleep, yes."

"That isn't what I—"

"I know what you meant. You said it already. Leave this. You do not understand and you *will* be hurt."

When he stood, you registered the man's size again. Ned's heart was pounding. He folded his arms across his chest. "I don't think we can," he said. "Leave this. Means giving her up."

"We all give things up. It is what happens in life."

"Without a fight? Aren't *you* still fighting?"

"This isn't your story. It is desperately unwise to enter into it. I am certain the Roman will have said the same."

"Wasn't he Greek, first?" Dumb reply, but he didn't feel like giving in here.

Cadell shrugged indifferently. "The same in the end. A way of knowing the world. Subduing it."

She isn't here, he had said.

It was obviously true. It was time to go. They had ground to cover. Ned felt cramped with tension. He didn't want that to show. Tough Canadian. He turned and started walking away.

After a few steps he looked back.

"We're going to Arles from here. You headed that way? Need a lift?"

He saw that he'd disconcerted the other man. Some small pleasure in that.

"Who are you?" Cadell asked, staring up at him now from down on those worn, moss-covered steps. "Really."

"I'm beginning to wonder. No lift?"

Cadell shook his head.

"Ah," said Ned. "Right. You're going to fly, and hope she doesn't find out? Risky." He was taking a risk of his own, talking this way: this man could kill him right here.

Cadell smiled, though, as if honouring the verbal thrust. "We do what we must," he said. And then, as if reading Ned's mind, "You amuse me. I don't feel I need to kill you, but it may happen." A silence, then he added something, in a different tone, in that language Ned didn't understand. And after another beat, "Leave this, boy. Heed me, I am giving true counsel."

"No," said Ned.

He walked away then, towards his father and Greg and the still-talking guard. He gestured as he went, pointing towards the road and the van across the way and the Roman arch, with the Celts in bondage on it, and taken in slavery.

CHAPTER XIII

They went back south through the Valley of Hell.

Greg drove past Les Baux again, turning right, heading for Arles. No one was talking as they approached the city. Ned had already briefed them, then he'd done it again on the phone with Aunt Kim.

He hadn't told any of them about Cadell spiking the other man's head on a stake, or threatening Ned if he didn't get out of the picture. What was the point? Was he going to leave? Fly home to Montreal and study for a math test? Melanie wasn't his love, or anything totally stupid like that, but you didn't have to be in love with someone to fight for them. He should have said that, back there.

The real point, Aunt Kim had just explained—and she'd repeated it to his father when Ned handed him the phone—was that if Cadell had been at Glanum, it meant that *their* plan wasn't so foolish. That was what they had to take away from this. If the two men—or at least one of them—were checking the same locations, they were on the right track themselves.

Well, yeah, the right track—plus a couple of euros—would get you a café au lait somewhere.

Ned hadn't said that part, either.

Kimberly and Kate, with Steve, had walked through Nîmes already, his aunt reported. The Roman arena, the Roman temple, quiet downtown streets with shops closed for the holiday. Aunt Kim hadn't picked up any sense of the others, even though Nîmes apparently had a long association with magic and sorcery.

They were in their car now, too, on their way to Béziers. Ned knew something about that now: *Kill them all. God will know his own.*

He was just as happy not to be going there. He wondered, abruptly, if he'd have had a reaction to that long-ago massacre, the way he'd had at the mountain. Not something he was anxious to repeat.

Greg pulled onto the ring road around Arles.

He stopped at a red light, then drove slowly, looking for a place to park. It was not quite noon. Traffic had been light coming in, but a flea market was set up inside the ring road. Hundreds of people were browsing it.

Wonderful, Ned thought. Like, we go up and down, dodge the pickpockets, and Ysabel will be buying sandals or hand cream or something.

He shook his head. Wrong way to think. Cadell had been at Glanum. They *were* doing the right thing. You had to keep telling yourself that.

Greg stopped quickly, put on his turn signal, and endured a blaring horn behind him till the vehicle he'd spotted pulled away from the curb. He slid the van into a spot Ned would have said was too small. They all got out. The street was shaded on this side; the flea market was in the light.

"What now?" Greg asked.

He was looking at Ned, not Ned's father. There was still something unsettling about that. How was *he* supposed to know?

On the other hand, who else but him, really?

Ned glanced at his dad. "We wander, I guess. Go through this thing, then back to the Roman sites?"

"They'll be closed. But, yeah. Are you . . . feeling anything?" Edward Marriner asked again. He got that apprehensive look on his face whenever he said that.

It should have been funny.

Ned shook his head. "No, but I'm really not good at this, and those guys know how to screen themselves. Believe me, I'll tell you if I get something."

"You didn't tell me back there."

Mild tone, but eyebrows raised, in a way that Ned knew very well. First "parental" comment of the day. He had been expecting more, actually. Things had changed.

"I told you, nothing happened till we were at opposite ends of the place. I couldn't, like, ask him to hang on a sec till I got my dad." He looked across the street.

It was noisy and crowded, cheerful people milling about on holiday. A guy in a truck was selling pizza slices and soft drinks, another one had ice cream cones. There were tables with knock-off shoes and shirts, old records, books, chairs, walking sticks, jars of honey, olive oil, skirts and bathing suits, kitchenware, pottery. A very tall, very dark man in a bright-red African robe was selling watches for five euros. Someone else had farm implements: shovels, hoes, rakes. A wheelbarrow. Ned saw a guy his own age holding a rusted old sword and laughing.

Why shouldn't he be laughing on a spring day?

"Okay, details! What kind of woman we looking for?" Greg asked. He pretended to take out a notebook, cop-on-the-beat style. "Describe the perp?"

Ned had been waiting for this, too, and sort of afraid of it. How did you describe Ysabel? How could you possibly?

He shrugged. "It won't work like that. You're not going to just spot her. But she's . . . tall, she's got red hair, I guess, auburn, chestnut? But that can be covered, right? She looks young, but not . . . really young, if you know what I mean?"

"That's *so* helpful, citizen," Greg said wryly. "Is she pretty, at least?"

Ned looked at him, and then at his dad. He was remembering.

"You have no idea," he said. He crossed the road into sunlight, cutting between cars, and the other two followed him.

೦๏

She has spent the night in the cemetery.

When the wind picked up and it grew cold, she wrapped the stolen shawl around herself, then went to enter a family vault she knew. The bodies were very long gone: caskets cracked open and raided for whatever of value might have been buried with the dead. But the old iron key turned out to still be hidden where it has been all these centuries.

Each time she has come here, she's expected it to be gone: found, lost, one or the other. Lost to her, because it has been found. Each time it is still under the stone.

The covering boulder was heavy, but she knew the trick of tilting it. On the other hand, the keyhole had rusted shut this time. She couldn't turn the key any more. She stood outside, under stars, and made herself accept another aspect of time going by. It happens, one way or another, each return.

She'd ordered this tomb built herself, for a maid of honour, and that dead girl's family had grown in significance in generations following, expanding the vault. She'd seen it, returning, in different lives.

Changes such as this, over the years, no longer disconcert her as much, though there was a time when they did. She has known too many by now. Other things might be difficult to deal with—the eyes of one man, the voice of the other, the memory of both—but not changes in the world.

Money had been a small problem when she first left the plateau in the night. The cache she went looking for was gone; the city had grown north, overrun the wood where she'd buried it seventy years ago.

And currency has changed, in any event. It wouldn't have even mattered if she'd found her cache. Francs weren't going to get her food or a taxi ride this year. *Euros.* She had allowed herself to be amused. There was always something new.

Cars were faster, and there were more of them. There was also more light when night fell. Telephones moved with you now, it seemed, unconnected to anything. Men and women walking the streets talking animatedly to someone who wasn't there.

But in the bright, crowded city women left purses carelessly hooked on chair backs in cafés under the plane trees (the same trees, same cafés, some of them), or they left their shawls, on a spring night, when they went inside to adjust their lipstick.

She'd taken her time, up and down the wide, remembered street, and chosen a purse at one sidewalk café near the statue of King René, and a green shawl outside another one, halfway back along the street. Green hasn't always been a colour she has favoured, but this time it seems to be.

She took the last bus to Arles, walked to the cemetery.

She bought a skirt and blouse very early in the morning, dawn just breaking, at the street fair as it opened, and returned to the cemetery. She had wondered if one of the two men might choose this as his own first destination but they couldn't *get* here by sunrise— unless Cadell flew, and she has told him he cannot do that.

He won't listen (she'd be startled if he did), but he won't want to be seen transgressing too blatantly in this new challenge she's set them. He'd fear her reaction. Rightly so.

She knows both men very well. Eyes of one, voice of the other.

Neither seems to be here. She is screened, of course. They will have to *find* her not just sense where she has gone. Both, at times, have been in this place (one made love to her here, she remembers), but neither likes the cemetery, for differing reasons.

They almost always have differing reasons. It is what they are about. She finds it serene here, herself. Serenity isn't what she lives for, but there are moments, especially when she's just returned, is coming to terms again with being in the world.

On the other hand, she is at ease with the idea that one of them might guess and come immediately here, and see the lock of the outer gate picked, and find her resting now on a stone bench in the shelter of the church doorway, past the oldest of the graves. Claim her this bright morning. Right away.

It excites her to imagine. She can picture either of them doing it. She hasn't yet decided which one she wants this time. She wants both, almost always. She never finds choosing simple, no matter what soul is within her. How could it be simple, by now? Sometimes she declines to choose; they fight, one of them dies, the other comes to her. She puts her hand to his face. Another kind of choice.

But it isn't as if she *wants* to stay lost. Seeing them, under moonlight at Entremont, brought everything to her again, as it always does. Right back to the first time, the defining night when they'd become the story of this world. This part of the world.

She is also excited by this new game, in truth. She is still learning who and what she is this time, how she is different. Has been testing that inwardly, through the night, defining herself. She is someone drawn to a green shawl.

The soul within her, each time she's summoned, alters her a little, makes her behave differently, which is why and how her desire, her *need*—over two thousand six hundred years—can change.

They never alter. They return each time as what they have always been, gloriously. There are no men alive like these two. How could it be otherwise? With centuries to grow deeper, know more, *become* more? What man with seventy too-swift years can match these two?

They are always what they are, at the core, but they also have more than before, each time. They bring something new to her. It took Cadell fifteen hundred years, almost, to learn to change his shape and fly. Blessed or cursed, this story? She's never been able to say. Does it matter? Would deciding affect anything at all?

Can it change, in any possible way, the fact that she came out from the shadows at the edge of the village one night long ago, into a weaving of firelight and smoke, brightness and dark, her hair unbound—in the sight of all the Segobrigae—carrying a golden cup for the man she chose to wed, and she had circled the circle of men assembled there, and saw two strangers? One stranger, really, his eyes.

And seeing him, she did what she did. So small a thing. A cup of water from the goddess's pool, extended towards a man. A guest at her father's feast. A stranger from the sea.

The morning sun is higher now. It is springtime in the world, bright and mild. There are flowers along the paths of the cemetery as she walks back through it: pale green leaves on the oaks, silver-grey on the olives.

There were no olive trees here when this story began. The strangers brought them later from across the sea. One of the things they brought. Olive trees, wine. Writing. Straight, wide roads. Eventually, though soon enough, conquest and subjugation.

Springtime. It is always spring when she comes back. Beltaine, fires, blood of the bull. She buries the useless key again, pushes back the boulder. She could throw the key away now, she knows, but doesn't want to do that. A small sadness as she passes the tomb. A girl who died too young.

She walks the quiet, shaded pathway to the outer gate. No one is there, cars pass by on the road. She slips out when there are none to be seen, clips the bolt shut.

Goes out into the world again.

She uses the forest-green shawl to hide her hair in the light. She could have cut it off during the night, but she doesn't like cutting her hair. Once it had been hacked off, when she was burned for a witch. Such things happened in plague years, when terror shaped the world. There are enough such memories.

She needs a taxi now. Finds a place where one stands waiting. But when she asks, it seems she wants him to take her too far, that she doesn't have a sum that will make it worth his time. It is vexing at first, then amusing. She laughs aloud.

When she does that, standing by his rolled-down window in sunlight, the driver changes his mind, agrees to take her where she wants to go.

Later, on the long drive back to Arles alone, he'll be unable to say why he did that—risking an illegal trip outside his licence zone, wasting a morning and half a tank of fuel on a one-way cut-rate fare—and not even talking to the woman. Just glancing at her in his mirror as she gazed out the window at Provence gliding by.

He can't say why he changed his mind. But he'll dream of her for a long time. The rest of his life, in fact.

6∿9

They walked through Arles for two hours. The street market, the area around the arena, circling it again, standing outside the barred entrance with irritated tourists who hadn't factored a holiday into their travel plans. Greg tugged at a few of the gates optimistically, unsuccessfully.

They went over the theatre again. Ned remembered talking with Melanie here, two days ago. It was difficult, carrying such images, standing here again. He looked at the grass where she'd been sitting. It felt, for a moment, as if she were dead. It scared him.

He didn't say anything.

They went on to the remains of the Roman forum on the central square. Everything was closed for the holiday. It was quiet. His father and Greg both kept glancing at Ned expectantly, like they were waiting for some light bulb to go on above his head or something. It could be aggravating, but he tried not to let himself feel that way. What else were they going to do?

He didn't see Cadell within himself again, or Phelan, or a woman who looked like a goddess with auburn hair.

They had lunch at the only open café near the remaining columns of the forum. The Roman columns were embedded in the front of a nineteenth-century building, weirdly co-opted as architectural support after almost two thousand years. That said something about Roman architects, Ned decided. Or maybe about nineteenth-century ones. The rest of the forum was under their feet, buried, like it was in Aix around the cathedral.

Van Gogh had painted their café, apparently. Ned thought he remembered seeing reproductions of that. His father had insisted they eat a proper lunch, but the food was tasteless. Tourist fare.

They phoned Aunt Kim from the table. The others were in Béziers now. Nothing. They were leaving soon. They would stop in Roquepertuse, a Celtic site like Entremont—skulls found there, too—then head home.

Ned's father paid their bill.

"What's left here?" Greg asked. He looked tired, too.

"Melanie could tell us," Edward Marriner said, with a sigh. "I'd say everything and nothing, if you know what I mean. We can go, I guess."

"The cemetery," Ned said, suddenly. "The one Oliver told us about."

His father looked at him.

IF THEY HADN'T LUNCHED with Oliver Lee earlier in the week, they'd never have gone to Les Alyscamps. Or even if they *had* done that lunch, but Lee hadn't mentioned the ancient cemetery with its long history.

Ned found that if he thought about things like that too much, the *accident* of it all, his mind started down unsettling paths. Like, what if he'd decided to stay in the villa after being sick on the mountain, the way the others had told him to? If he'd never met Kate in the café that afternoon, or Phelan, after she'd gone? If Kate had never mentioned the word *Entremont* to him?

Well, she couldn't have, if he hadn't been there, right?

And what if he'd gone shopping for music that first morning instead of thinking it would be sort of funny—a joke to email Larry Cato—to listen to *Houses of the Holy* inside a cathedral?

Could you make a pattern out of any of this? Stitch together the seeming randomness into something that had meaning? Is that what life was about, he wondered: trying to make that pattern, to have things make *sense*?

And anyway, how did you make sense of a man turning into an owl to fly from you? Call it a computer-generated effect and give thanks to George Lucas?

Les Alyscamps cemetery was a fair walk from the centre of town, along the ring road to the outskirts. It was empty when they got there, closed up, barred, like all the other monuments today.

Ned put a hand on the bars, looking through. He swallowed.

"She's been here," he said.

He knew his voice sounded funny. "She may still be here, for all I know. I don't know much." His dad and Greg were staring at him. That look again. Could you get used to it, he wondered.

It wasn't like before, the feeling he had. Not from the mountain, not from the valley this morning. Here, it was as if a scent was in the air, drifting. Flowers, but more than that, or less. An almost-recalled memory. Something unsettling that could reach in, change the rhythm of your heart as you stood by iron gates.

He knew there was nothing actually around them; the others would have noticed if there were. But he also knew what he knew, bone-dumb as that might sound, and Ysabel's presence was here, disturbing and exciting. He swallowed again, his mouth dry. He wished they had a bottle of water.

"Gate's padlocked," Greg said, yanking at the lock. "We could try to climb . . . ?"

The iron gate was well over their heads, and railings ran both ways from it, same height, all along the street front.

"Maybe you could boost me?" Ned said, looking upwards.

"Not so you go in alone," his father said flatly. "Don't even think it."

Through the bars they could see trees and a long, wide walkway, splintered with light and shade. There was a church at the far end. A ticket office a little way down on the left was shuttered. Ned saw smaller and larger trees, stone benches, grey stone coffins lying about as if discarded. He assumed they were empty. He hoped they were empty. It was really quiet here.

He stared through the bars, as if gazing could make her come to life in there. He pictured her walking towards him along that cool, light-and-shadow alley between trees and tombs.

"Stand behind me," his father said suddenly. "Watch the road. Let me see that lock." And a moment later, as they obeyed, "This is easy. It's been done before, I see the scratches."

"Jeez. You can pick locks?" Ned said.

He was looking out for cars, but glanced back over his shoulder, eyes widening. His dad had taken out a Swiss Army knife.

"You have no idea the things your old man can do," Edward Marriner muttered, flipping open a blade. "Which is probably a good thing."

"I'm not gonna *touch* that line," Greg said. But Ned could see that he was surprised too, and nervous. They were breaking into a major tourist site in broad daylight.

When was daylight *not* broad? Ned thought suddenly. What *made* it broad? Could you break in more easily in narrow daylight? Kate might have laughed if he'd said that to her. Or maybe not.

He wondered if the mayor of Aix was in the middle of her lunch party now. If she'd answer her phone again if they needed her. A Citroën went by, going too fast, and took the curve left towards town. The sun was high. It was windy, a few fast white clouds moving south. Ned heard a scraping of metal behind him.

"Got it," Edward Marriner said, satisfaction in his voice. "Inside, both of you, I'll close it behind us."

"Hold on!" Greg said. They waited for a pair of cars to go past. "Okay," said Greg. "All clear. Man, why do I feel like James Bond?"

They slipped through the gate. His father came in last, pulled it shut and quickly fiddled through the bars with the padlock so it looked closed again.

"Go on!" Edward Marriner said. "Out of sight of the road."

They walked past a stone coffin and the ticket office. It was cooler in the shade. To their right was a large monument. On the left, as they went ahead, Ned saw a locked-up tomb with an iron grate in a heavy door. Steps led down, behind the door.

Ahead, between them and the church, in sunlight, was an area of sunken excavations, roped off. "Those are the oldest graves," his father said.

Ned looked at him. "You've been here?"

His father made a face. "No. I told you, I read Melanie's notes."

Of course. You could almost laugh, except you couldn't because she was gone. And then you couldn't because you heard a sound behind you, in a place that was locked shut, with no one but them inside, and you turned, thinking it might be a security guard, and then you *really* didn't feel like laughing any more.

"I did tell you to leave this," a cold voice said.

Cold could make you shiver. It wasn't a guard. It was the druid, standing between them and the gate that led back out to the world where cars took curves too fast, or honked when you slowed to park.

Brys, who had almost killed Greg last night, was still wearing his white robe. Ned couldn't tell where he'd come from, where he'd been hiding as they walked in.

Or where the wolves had been that now padded up, seven of them, behind him. They sat on their haunches, watching.

The quiet didn't seem peaceful any more. Ned looked at his father. Edward Marriner stroked his moustache thoughtfully, taking his time. Calmly, he said, "I'm not quite sure why, but I feel a bit relieved to see you exist. You wouldn't understand that, I suppose."

The druid said nothing.

Ned's father went on, in a conversational tone, "My understanding is that you have powers that can be used to harm us. You used them last night on our friend here."

Powers? Ned was thinking. *Dad, pay attention! Those animals with the teeth! He doesn't need powers.*

A week ago, a little more, he'd been doing a half-assed science project on tectonic plates with Barry Staley.

He wasn't sure what his father was trying to achieve. This might be stalling, but he had no idea what a delay would accomplish. Could they summon the Marines? What Marines?

It occurred to him for the first time, with a clarity that almost buckled his knees, that they could die here in this cemetery among the looted tombs.

"That one?" The druid looked at Greg. "Cadell saved his life. He fears drawing attention, bringing people into this."

"And you don't?" Edward Marriner asked, still in his most relaxed tone.

"I don't have the time to pay heed to such things. I have very little time, when I return. Fear a single death? Have you any idea how many people have died in this?"

"Over the years? I'm beginning to. Are you proud of it?"

The small, grey-haired figure lifted his head. "Pride has nothing to do with anything. This one is insignificant. So are you. You do not *matter*."

"What does?"

Ned saw Greg's hand in his pocket. And finally he realized what this delay was about—and how pointless it was. Greg would be auto-dialing Aunt Kim, who was, like, two hours away or something. Or maybe he was calling the mayor of Aix at her lunch. Or whatever 911 was in France.

James Bond would have had a bomb built into the phone.

The druid was looking at Ned's father, as if trying to decide what to answer. This one, too, Ned thought: he's been part of this, or at the edges of it, all this time. The one who shapes the summoning.

Maybe he didn't *want* to stay at the edges.

"She must be claimed by Cadell," the druid said, his voice almost an incantation. "The stranger must be killed. Sacrificed. He must *end*. There may be ways it can be done, even now." One of the wolves got up, shifted over a bit, and settled again. "Then the two of them, the man and the woman, must be made to understand that this is not just their story."

"What is it, then?" Edward Marriner asked.

Greg had stopped fiddling in his pocket. Ned thought—couldn't be sure—he'd heard a distant voice from the cellphone. Aunt Kim? Greg moved closer to Ned's dad. Both of them were right in front of Ned now. He didn't think that was an accident. The phone would be on speaker, whoever Greg had dialed could hear this. Maybe.

If it mattered.

Maybe it did, he thought suddenly. If they were killed here, the others would at least know why. And how else would they ever learn? His hands were shaking. He saw Greg murmur something. Ned's father nodded, briefly.

The druid said, "There was a world here once. A way of knowing the world. It was torn from us, and it can be reclaimed."

Ned saw his father straighten his shoulders. He crossed his arms on his chest, in a gesture Ned knew. "Is that it? *That* is how you see this? You want to roll back two thousand years of Greek and Roman culture? Can you possibly be serious?"

Edward Marriner's relaxed, chatty tone was gone. You could say his voice was as cold now as the other man's.

The druid's expression flickered. Maybe he hadn't expected such a response. Ned sure hadn't, and he still wasn't there yet, wasn't getting it. He was trying to catch up, to understand what was being said.

"They would be near to immortal," Brys said. "More powerful than you can imagine, if this story were ended with that death. And if they understood their task, the *need* we have. Am I serious, you ask? A fool's question. The world can change. It always changes."

Edward Marriner's reply was quick, sharp with scorn. "A fool? I think not. I hear you. You just want to decide *what* it changes to. Aren't you being just a tiny bit arrogant?"

The druid's mouth tightened. "Believe me, I have known change shaped by others. I lived it. All my people did. I am unlikely to forget. Arrogant, you say? And the Romans were not?"

Ned's father looked away, past the other man. It was, Ned thought, a hard question. He was remembering that arch this morning: Romans on horses, wielding swords, Gauls dying or dead or chained, heads bowed and averted. He thought of the smashed walls at Entremont, siege engines. Or the enormous arena such a little distance from here, a twenty-minute walk through two thousand years of power.

Edward Marriner said, more softly, "The Romans? They were all about arrogance, and conquest. But yours is the greater, even so: the idea that two millennia can be run backwards. That they *should* be, whatever the cost."

"Cost? Measuring it out? A Roman thought."

Edward Marriner laughed aloud, a startling sound in that still place. "Maybe. Is it why they were able to destroy you? Because they worked that way? Weighed cost and gain? *Thought* about things?"

He was asking a lot of questions, Ned decided. He was pretty sure his first guess was right: his dad was stalling. Was that what Aunt Kim had said to Greg, to delay? For what? He was thinking fast: maybe Kate was dialing on *her* phone, as they stood here. Maybe she was calling 911, or whatever, here in Arles.

Something occurred to him.

He stepped forward and said, loudly, "Enough of this already! What the hell? You guys think because this is a cemetery you can just add new bodies to the count? Is *that* the gig here?"

Greg looked quickly over his shoulder at Ned, his expression stricken. *I was right*, Ned thought. *They wouldn't have known where we are!* The Marines or the cavalry riding, nowhere to go.

The druid's expression, also turning to him, was bleak. "Have a care," he said. He looked back at Ned's father. "We need only deal with the young one. He matters. I don't know why yet. You and the other are of no concern to me. I am content to have you walk away."

"Content? The young one is my son."

"Children die. All the time. You have others?"

"None."

"Ill-judged on your part."

"Screw yourself," Edward Marriner said, and added an even harsher string of words. The stalling part of this appeared to be over.

Greg moved to stand closer to Ned's father. They were right in front of him again. The druid made no movement at all, but the wolves stood up.

Showtime, Ned thought. Three wolves began circling wide, the others moved slowly forward.

By the tower with Aunt Kim he had grabbed a branch. There were no branches on the swept-clean ground here. And there hadn't been seven animals then, either. He remembered last night on their road, sweeping his hand, scything the horns from Cadell's head. He didn't remember *how* he'd done it, only the rage that had driven the motion. He tried to find that within himself. He knelt and scooped some gravel.

"Keep them off your face," Greg said quietly. "Punch in the throat if you can. Kick underneath. Then run past the guy. The gate's unlocked, remember. Get to the road . . ."

Punch in the throat.

A wolf. Real good plan.

"I say it again," Brys rasped. "Only one of you matters. The other two can leave."

Greg said, calmly, "You heard the man. Screw yourself."

Gregory was actually ready to die here defending Ned, trying to save Melanie, and Ned realized he knew hardly anything important about the man. A wise-cracking, burly, bearded guy who owned a truly ridiculous bathing suit and mocked his own bulk by doing human cannonballs into a swimming pool.

Ned's my new hero, he had said the other day, because Ned was meeting a girl for coffee. Some hero.

"She was here," Ned said suddenly. "Do you know it?"

The druid took a half-step backwards. He rattled a handful of quick words like pebbles; the wolves stopped. They sat down again, the flanking movement suspended.

"Explain!" Brys said. "Do so now."

Ned stepped up beside his dad. They wanted him behind them; he wasn't going to allow it. "Back to back to back," he murmured. "When they come."

That was how they did it in movies, wasn't it?

He made himself take his time, even smile. Time was the whole point. He thought of Larry Cato, improbably: shit-disturber, professional pain in the ass. Times when that might be useful.

He said, "You like giving orders, don't you? Especially when Cadell's not around. What would happen if he was here? Should I guess?"

The druid's mouth opened and closed.

"Same as last night, maybe? He gets pissed off. Sends you to your room without supper. Right? Which tomb here's yours?"

He was close to Greg now, speaking loudly. It was possible Aunt Kim hadn't gotten the first hint about where they were.

"Where is she?" the druid said doggedly, ignoring the mockery.

"Another question!" Ned said. "Why do you expect an answer from me? Should I just do to you what I did last night to him?"

He had no way of doing it, but maybe *they* wouldn't know that. "Grow some horns," he taunted. "I'll use them as targets. Or use the wolves, if you prefer."

"You cannot kill them all before they—"

"You *sure* of that? Really sure? You have no idea what I am." That, at least, made sense, since Ned didn't, either. "Tell me something else: if you're planning to off me here, why should I give you *anything* I know? What's my percentage, eh?"

The druid said nothing.

"I mean, you are really bad at this, dude. You need to offer something to make it worth—"

"If you care for your father's life, you will tell me what you know. Or he dies." The words were flat, blunt, hard.

Maybe, Ned thought, the guy wasn't so bad at this after all.

"I said they could leave," Brys went on. "But I can alter that. If you know she was here, you know where's she's gone."

"Are you stupid?" Ned said. "If I knew where she was, would I be *here*?"

That, too, was true, but it might not keep them alive. Did logic work with druids? Inwardly he was wishing he were religious, so he could pray to someone, or something. He was stalling for all he was worth, and had no idea what sort of rescue could come. He didn't think a bored gendarme arriving at the gates would stop—

He looked at those gates. The others did too, even Brys, because there was a sound from there. Then another. Something landed with a distant clatter on the shaded pathway.

And then, improbably, a really big man could be seen taking a hard, fast run from the edge of the road, propelling himself up the far side of the gate, arms and legs moving, and then—with what had to be exceptional strength—*vaulting* himself over the sharp, spiked bars at the top, in a gymnast's move.

Ned saw him in the air, looking like a professional athlete. The illusion of an Olympic gymnast held, briefly, but this man was way too big. He landed, not all that smoothly, fell to one knee (points deducted, Ned thought). He straightened and stood. It could be seen that he was wearing faded blue jeans and a black shirt under a beige travel vest, and that his full beard was mostly grey beneath greying hair.

"Goddamn!" the man said loudly, bending to pick up his stick. "I am *way* too old to be doing this." He was some distance away, but his voice carried.

Coming forward—favouring one knee—he proceeded to add words in that language Ned didn't understand. His tone was peremptory, and precise.

"Be gone!" the druid snapped by way of reply. "Do you seek an early death?"

The man came right up to the group of them and stopped, on the other side of Brys and the wolves.

"Early death? Not at all. Which is why I can't leave, if you want the truth. My wife would kill me if I did, you see. Ever meet my wife?" the very big man said.

Then he looked at Ned. A searching, focused gaze. Wide-set, clear blue eyes. He smiled.

"Hello, Nephew," he said.

CHAPTER XIV

Ned felt his mouth fall open. The jaw-drop thing was happening way too often. It was majorly uncool.

"Uncle Dave?" he said.

His voice was up half an octave.

The smile widened. "I like the sound of that, have to say."

The grey-bearded man looked over at Ned's father. "Edward Marriner. This would be even more of a pleasure elsewhere. I hope it will be soon."

Ned glanced at his dad, whose expression would have been hilarious any other time. It made him feel a bit better about his own.

"Dave Martyniuk?"

The other man nodded. "To the rescue, with a really bad landing."

"I saw that. You okay? I'm afraid the gate was open," Edward Marriner said. "We picked the lock to get in."

Ned's uncle's face became almost as amusing, hearing that. He swore, concisely.

"It *was* a dramatic entrance," Ned's father said. "Honestly. Bruce Willis would have used a stuntman."

The two men smiled at each other.

"Your wife's coming down on Air France 7666 from Paris," Dave Martyniuk said. "Flight gets her to Marignan around 6 p.m. Then, what . . . half-an-hour cab ride to your villa?"

"Bit more." Ned's father checked his watch. "We might have time to meet her." Neither of them was even looking at Brys, or the wolves, Ned saw. Edward Marriner hesitated. "How do you know the flight?"

Martyniuk shrugged. "Long story. Mostly to do with computers."

"I see. I think. You keep an eye on her?"

The other man nodded. He looked awkward, suddenly. "Only when she's . . ."

"I know. Kimberly told us. I . . . I'm very grateful." He grinned ruefully. "Assuming we get out of here alive, she will try to dismember you, very likely. I'll do what I can to protect you."

"I'd appreciate that. Meghan's formidable."

"Oh, I know. So's her sister."

"Oh, I know."

"Enough. We can kill four of you as easily as three," the druid said.

Ned turned to him. So did the others.

Assuming we get out of here alive.

Brys had shifted position so he could look at all of them, left and right.

Aunt Kim's husband—Ned hadn't pictured him as being nearly so *big*—shook his head. "I'm not sure, friend. You don't know enough about me, and you're a long day past Beltaine, losing strength. So are the spirits you put in those wolves."

"How do you know that?" the druid snapped.

"The spirits? Beltaine? Cellphone. Wife. Mentioned her. Knows a *lot*, trust me."

Then, abruptly, the exaggeratedly laid-back style altered. When next Dave Martyniuk spoke, it was in that other language again, and the voice was stone-hard. There was authority in it, and anger. Ned understood nothing, except for what sounded like names. He heard *Cernunnos* and something like *Cenwin*.

But he saw the impact on the druid. The man actually grew pale, colour leaching from his face. Ned had thought that only happened in stories, but he could *see* it in Brys.

"Go home," his uncle added, more gently, speaking French. "You should have gone last night. This is not the hour or the life for your dreams to be made real. My wife asked me to tell you that."

Brys was still for a moment, then drew himself up as if shouldering a weight. A small man, standing very straight.

"I do not believe she knows anything for certain. And in any case," he said, "why hurry back to the dark? I *will* learn what the boy knows. And he will not interfere any more. I can achieve so much." He gestured at the branch Ned's uncle had thrown over the gate and picked up. "You think you can fight eight of us with that?"

Dave Martyniuk, unperturbed, nodded gravely. "I think so, yes. And there is a reason for you to leave. You know there is. Will you risk your soul, and these? If we kill you here you are lost, druid. The three of them can return, but not you."

"How do you *know* these things?"

Something anguished in the question.

"Same answer. My wife."

With a sharp, startling movement, Martyniuk levelled the branch in front of himself and cracked it hard across his good knee, breaking the stick in two.

"Ouch!" he said, and swore again.

Then he threw half of it across the open space.

Ned saw it flying. It was actually beautiful, spinning into light, shadow, light again under the leaves. One of the wolves sprang for it, jaws wide, and missed—it was arced too high.

Ned's father caught the thrown branch with unexpected competence and then—*much* more unexpectedly—stepped straight forward and swung it hard, a two-handed grip, sweeping flat. He cracked the leaping wolf in the ribs as it landed. There was an ugly sound. The animal tumbled, to crumple against a grey, tilting stone.

No one moved.

"Nice throw," Edward Marriner said.

"They need not die here," Dave Martyniuk said quietly, turning to the druid again. "Send them back. Go with them. It is past the day. You have nothing to gain."

Brys stared at him. An equally blue gaze. Ned had a sense of suspended time, a long hovering. He felt the breeze, saw it in the rippling leaves.

"Measurement again? Calculation? It is not only about *gain*," the druid said. "The world goes deeper than that."

Then he spoke to the wolves in that other tongue and the battle began.

Ned Marriner learned some truths in the next few moments. The world might be deep, for one thing, but sometimes it was *fast*, too.

The second truth was that a Swiss Army knife was just about useless against a wolf. He had his blade ready in time—he'd had it open in his pocket not long after the druid appeared—but unless you were good enough to stab a hurtling animal in the eye your knife was a distraction, nothing more.

He wasn't good enough to stab it in the eye.

He feinted, realized he didn't have a hope, and rolled urgently away from the animal that came for him. He heard footsteps, a shout, then another thick, dull sound. When he rolled to his knees—ready to twist away again—he saw that his father had clubbed this one, too.

That was the third new thing he learned: that Edward Marriner, celebrated photographer, absent-minded father with chronically misplaced reading glasses and trademark brown moustache, was lethal with a branch when his only son was in danger.

Greg was already engaging another wolf. And the fourth truth was that Greg was actually strong enough to do the punch-it-in-the-throat thing he'd whispered—but not quick enough to do it without being hurt.

From his knees, Ned saw it happen: slash of claws, heavy fist short-stroked to animal neck, the wolf flopping backwards, blood bright at Greg's raked-open sleeve.

The sudden redness was shocking.

His dad was over there immediately.

Necessary, but with implications: principally, that Ned was now alone without a weapon with three wolves circling him. He scrabbled in the gravel again and threw a handful of pebbles at the eyes of the nearest one. Clever. Meaningless. The animal ignored it.

Then the animal died.

Afterwards, Ned would try to recapture what he'd felt when he saw his uncle *hammer* that wolf—that was the word that came to him—and then immediately send another one twisting frantically back and away from a second swift, swinging blow.

As the third wolf also retreated, Ned saw the druid lying on the gravel behind it. Brys's arms were outflung, one leg was bent awkwardly under his body.

He looked at his uncle again. A thought came, inescapably: *He's done this before.*

There was a difference between his father's determined defence of Ned and Greg, Gregory's own bravery, Ned's scrambling attempt to do something useful . . . and Dave Martyniuk's laying low of chosen targets.

You might possibly be born knowing how to do this, but more likely you learned in the doing. When and where, Ned didn't know, but he was pretty sure it had to do with the time his aunt's hair turned white.

The three remaining wolves had backed away from Ned's uncle, tails low. They didn't run. Not yet. They were watching.

Martyniuk went over to the druid.

"I didn't want to kill him," he said. "I hope I didn't."

He knelt on the path. Put fingers to the man's throat. The two of them were in the shade there, a plane tree in leaf between them and the sun. Ned saw his uncle shake his head.

"Damn it," he heard him say.

"He was here to kill Ned," said Edward Marriner quietly, walking over, entering into that shadow as well. "And the rest of us, if he had to."

Martyniuk didn't look up. "I know. We . . . your son got himself into a story."

Ned wasn't sure why he felt so much sadness, looking at the small figure of the druid who had summoned Ysabel. Leaves rustled; splinters of sunlight came through as they moved.

There was a world here once. It was torn from us. It is not just about the three of them.

He cleared his throat. "Uncle Dave, if he's . . . gone, does that mean Ysabel can't be summoned again? After this time?"

His uncle looked up. "Is that her name?"

Ned nodded.

Dave Martyniuk stood, wincing a little. He brushed dust from his knees. "I don't think that's an issue." He gestured at the wolves. "These are spirits too. I suspect there are other druids among the ones who come back on Beltaine night. This one . . . was stronger maybe. Kept his place in the story."

"He was trying to change the story," Ned said. "Or that's what I . . ." He trailed off.

"No, you're right. I think so too." His uncle looked at Gregory. "Whoever taught you to punch wolves?"

Greg was holding his left arm. Blood was bright through his fingers, but he managed a crooked smile. "It was an option in undergrad. I could have done economics, did wolf boxing instead."

"Extremely funny. Let's go," Edward Marriner said. "We'll find the hospital here."

Greg shook his head. "No. Dr. Ford can bandage this at the villa. I'm all right. This looks worse than it is."

"You'll need a rabies sequence, Greg."

"No, he won't," Ned said, surprising himself. "These are spirits in a wolf shape, remember? They won't be rabid."

Uncle Dave nodded. "He's almost surely right, Edward. They'd insist on the rabies course and he might be kept there. And we'd have a bit of explaining to do." He pointed to the druid. "This body . . . I don't think he'll just vanish right away."

"What do we do?" Ned's father asked. "With him?"

"Will he disappear later? I mean, go back to being disembodied, or whatever?" Ned asked.

"Maybe. Not sure. I never took that course in undergrad." Martyniuk smiled ruefully.

"Could we shift that?" Ned's father pointed to a stone sarcophagus beside the shaded alley. The lid was slightly askew.

Dave Martyniuk looked over. "Maybe," he said.

Ned watched his father and uncle walk over together. They each grasped an end of the heavy stone top. He felt a weird sensation, a kind of pride, watching them count off three then strain together, grunting, and slide the stone halfway off.

"That's enough I think," Greg said, holding his arm. "He's not that big."

He wasn't that big. The wolves watched, oddly passive now, as the two men came back and—quite gently—lifted the druid and carried him to the empty coffin. They laid him inside and, straining again, dragged the stone lid all the way back.

They looked down on it a moment, then Dave Martyniuk walked towards the wolves.

There were four left; the one Greg had punched had recovered and gone over beside the others. They didn't retreat this time.

Martyniuk said something in that ancient language—Welsh or Gaelic, whichever it was. The animals looked at him. And then, after a moment, they turned and loped away together towards the oldest graves and the church beyond. The four men watched them go past the sunken area, around the church, out of sight.

"What did you say?" Edward Marriner asked quietly.

He was stretching out his back. That stone lid would have been heavy, Ned thought. His father was not a man inclined to lifting and pulling. Or to swinging blows with a branch. He was doing things Ned couldn't even have imagined a week ago.

"I told them nightfall would likely see them home. I wished them peace on the journey back."

"That's it?"

Martyniuk nodded.

He picked up the nearest of the three slain animals and, limping, carried it out of sight behind the trees. He came back for a second one. Edward Marriner picked up the third. He looked surprised when he lifted it, Ned saw, as if it was too easy. He saw his father raise his eyebrows, and follow Uncle Dave among the trees.

"Some animals were harmed in the making of this coffee-table book," Greg said dryly.

Ned looked at him. "You okay?"

Greg was still holding his shoulder. His second injury in two days. "Been better, man. Could have been worse, I guess. Where are the stuntmen when you need them, eh?"

The other two reappeared. Ned's father was unbuttoning his shirt. He took it off. Ned fished quickly for his pocket knife again and opened the small scissors. His dad tried it, but the blade wasn't big enough. Edward Marriner grunted, handed it back, and then tore the shirt from the bottom most of the way to the collar. He ripped off the buttons and wrapped the whole thing around Greg's arm before tying it.

"That'll have to do till home," he said.

"Got a bullet for me to bite?" Greg said.

Edward Marriner, bare-chested, smiled briefly. "Tylenol in the glove compartment."

"Have to do," Greg said. "We live in a primitive age. At least you don't paint your chest, boss."

Another thin smile. "I may yet," Ned's father said.

Dave Martyniuk had a cellphone to his ear. He looked over. "Kim's in her car. She'll meet us at your villa. I said an hour?"

Marriner nodded. "About right. You'll follow me?"

"I'll follow."

The four of them walked out, past coffins, past the tomb on their right and the ticket booth, between trees and under leaves, out the gate and into light.

�’ꞁ

As soon as the villa gate clanged open and they drove through with Dave Martyniuk's Peugeot behind them, Ned saw the woman with red hair standing alone on the terrace, watching them approach.

His heart started pounding.

His father saw her, too. He pulled the car straight over to the visitor parking pad, not around to the driveway on the far side. He switched off the engine. The three of them sat a moment, looking up at her.

It was late in the day now, the sun over the city, light slanting back along the valley, in their eyes, the shadows of the cypress trees very long. The woman came down the steps onto the grass, then she stopped.

"I'll go," Ned said.

He got out and walked across the lawn. In the light, her auburn hair was gleaming. She looked amazingly beautiful to him.

"Hi, Mom," he said.

She wasn't crying. She wasn't the crying type. He was taller than she was now. Hugs were awkward. He was fifteen, wasn't he?

He liked the way she held him, though, and said his name: half reproving, half reassuring. And he liked her known scent. And that she was *here*. That she wasn't in a civil-war zone where people were being blown up, or hacked apart with farm tools—even if they wore armbands that marked them as doctors come from far away to help.

He'd gotten her out. But this *wasn't* just his way of drawing her from the Sudan. They needed her here. He was almost sure of it.

He was also sure trouble was coming, in a red car not far behind them.

"We didn't expect you till later," he said.

"Why, dear?"

A mistake. Already. His first words. Jeez.

"You said evening to Dad, didn't you? Yesterday?"

"Did I? I must have been guessing. I was able to bump onto an earlier flight from Charles de Gaulle. The only hassle was the taxi driver having no idea how to find this place. I had to call. The woman here gave him directions."

"Veracook?"

Meghan Marriner smiled. "That what you call her?"

"Have to. There's a Veraclean, too."

"That's fun." His mother withdrew, looking past him. "Hello, honey. Reporting for duty. Present and accounted for."

"Meg."

He watched his father come up. His parents kissed. His mom laid her head on his father's chest. There was a time when he'd have been embarrassed by that.

"You going native, *cher*?" His mother stepped back, eyeing his father's bare torso.

"Last of the Mohicans. It's a long story. We'll tell, but it would be good if you had a look at Gregory first. Do you have a kit? We've only got basic first-aid stuff."

"What happened?" Her tone changed.

"We ran into some trouble."

"Ed. What kind of trouble?"

Ned looked back; Greg was getting out of the car. You could see blood on his arm all the way from here. It had soaked through the shirt bandage.

Uncle Dave had driven his Peugeot around the far side of the house, to the driveway, out of sight. Ned heard a distant car door close, but Martyniuk didn't appear.

"Greg got clawed by an animal," Ned heard his father saying. "I wrapped my shirt around it."

"A wild animal? He'll need rabies shots. Where *were* you? Gregory, come and let me see that!"

Ned took note that his father didn't answer either question.

Uncle Dave still didn't appear. He must have entered the house through the main door on the other side, under the hill slope. Leaving us to our reunion, Ned thought.

Then he thought something else.

They hadn't expected his mom to be here yet. And she'd *know* him, from Darfur. They'd been there until yesterday. There couldn't be *that* many people associated with Doctors Without Borders in the Sudan. And this wasn't the only time he'd been where she was, either.

She would go, to put it very mildly, ballistic when she figured out what he'd been doing. More trouble. But there was no way around this one, was there? Unless Uncle Dave stayed out of sight all the time. He was doing that now, but there was no . . .

They heard another car, gearing down for the last upward slope of the road. Ned turned, saw the red Peugeot approach. It stopped, idling in front of the gates.

"I'll do the code," he said quickly, and ran back over.

He punched the numbers. The gates swung and clanged. Aunt Kim drove through. Ned saw Steve in the passenger seat. Kate smiled at him from the back. His aunt slid her window down.

"Ned. How's Greg?"

"He's okay. Aunt Kim, my mom's here. She's checking him out, and—"

But his aunt's gaze had gone past him. She was looking into the serene, end-of-day light towards her younger sister. Ned turned. His mother was still beside Greg but was looking back this way now, at the woman driving the red car.

They hadn't seen each other, he thought, in something like twenty-five years. There was an ache in his throat, a rawness. You could think about the endless story they'd stumbled into here and call twenty-five years nothing, a blink. Or you could know that they were a good part of two lifetimes, never to return or be reclaimed.

He thought of Brys. The latest body buried in Les Alyscamps. The druid had spent so long trying to get something back. It couldn't be done, Ned thought. Even if you thought you'd achieved it, what returned couldn't be the same as what had been taken away.

"I'll park the car," Kimberly said quietly.

Ned stepped back and watched as she drove around the far side. With everything that was happening, *this* felt like one of the hardest things. He wanted to fix it, but he was feeling like a kid again, and that was hard, too. It occurred to him that, in a way, this was what the druid had been doing: trying to fix something that couldn't be made right. How did you undo conquered Gauls on a Roman arch?

How did you undo twenty-five years of silence?

He watched his aunt walk back around the side of the house. Kate and Steve were behind her but they stopped. Kim went over the grass towards her sister. The two women looked so much alike—even with the entirely white hair and the dark red—seeing them together just made it obvious.

Ned started back that way. He saw his father's face, the apprehension there. Greg looked worse, actually, as if he could rattle off a dozen places he'd rather be just now. He made as if to back away, but Ned's mother, holding an end of the blood-soaked shirt-bandage, said sharply, "Hold still!"

"She needs a good look, Greg," said Aunt Kim, stopping beside them. "Do we have antibiotics here?"

"I do," said Meghan Marriner, uncovering the wound. "Hello, Kim."

"Hello, Meg. How does it look?"

"Fairly shallow. More messy than dangerous. Clean and stitch. But he'll need rabies shots."

"Uh-uh," said Greg. "Dr. Marriner, I don't, it was a scratch, not a bite. And we don't have time."

"I do love it when my patients treat themselves. Makes me wonder why I did seven years of medical training. You can guarantee with mortal certainty no saliva got on those claws, Greg? Really? You'll bet your life on it?"

Ned knew that tone of his mother's. He'd grown up with it. Her response to illogic.

Greg didn't waver, though. He kept on surprising.

"Can't guarantee that, but I do know, Doc—and the boss and Ned know, too—that it wasn't a rabid wolf."

"It was a wolf?" Meghan said, her voice rising.

They hadn't told her, Ned realized.

"Same ones we saw before, Ned?" Aunt Kim asked quietly.

He swallowed. "Maybe. I'm not so good at telling them apart, and it was dark the other time. They were spirits, though, from Beltaine."

"Oh, Christ!" his mother snapped. "I absolutely *refuse* to start in with—"

Ned touched her arm. She stopped. Looked at him. He could see fury in her eyes.

"Mom. Please. You *have* to start in. You have to listen, or you can't help. They were coming for *me*, Mom."

His mother stared at him. He saw anger slipping, replaced by something trickier to define. "What does that mean?"

Ned looked at his father for help. Edward Marriner said, gravely, "It was pretty clear they were there to kill Ned, honey. And that they were ordered to do so."

"*Ordered*? Ed are you—"

"Meg, I'm neither insane nor addled. I'm desperately glad you are here because we need your thinking, and in a hurry. But honey, you have to be thinking, not fighting us." He hesitated. "Meg, I killed a wolf today in Les Alyscamps. And it was going for our son. It was given orders by a druid, Meg."

Ned saw his mother's eyes widen. "Oh, my! A real druid? Did he wave his mistletoe at you?"

A small silence.

"No," her husband said. "He was killed when they attacked us."

He didn't say, yet, who had killed him.

Meghan looked at Ned again, then at Greg, wounded.

Greg shrugged. "I got in the way, ma'am. He's telling the truth."

Aunt Kim was still saying nothing. It was hard to read her expression.

Edward Marriner stepped closer. "Meg, this isn't some grand conspiracy to make you revisit your family history. Something's going on here, and that *may* mean that more than you think went on back then . . . but that isn't the point now. Please listen when I say this. Please look at me and believe me."

His wife stared at him. Her body was rigid with tension. Ned had never seen her like this. She turned to her sister.

"What have you done?" she said.

Aunt Kim stared back. It occurred to Ned, after, that if Uncle Dave had been beside them on the grass, she might not have reacted as she did. But he wasn't.

"Oh, how perfect!" Kimberly snapped. "A flawless question, Meg. What comes next? We revisit how I dyed my hair white to fool everyone? How I got married and ran away just to reject you? Are you still a teenager?"

Meghan Marriner didn't back down. "I never said *me.* I said your mother, too. Our mother. And you know it."

"Our mother did a very good job of keeping close, Meghan, to the end of her life. She visited us, and *you* know it. We spoke all the time, and wrote, and visited. You know that, too. You made a point of staying away when we did. And she never, ever told me she was hurt by anything I'd done."

"You'd expect her to *say* it? Mother? Oh, come on, Kim, you know better than—"

"I knew her as well as you did, Meghan. And she understood *me* a whole lot better than you did. I left because I *couldn't* pick up the life I'd lived. I wanted to, I thought I would. I couldn't. Too much had happened. You were the only person who mattered who didn't see that. Want to talk about hurting someone? Meg, I came down here when I realized what had *already* happened to Ned. I'm trying to protect him. And get Melanie back. This is *not* about you and me."

This is not just about the three of them.

The druid had said that, at least twice. He might even have been right. Just as Aunt Kim might be right, or not. Because maybe this was, in some hard way, about the two sisters . . . and him. Maybe there were places where the past didn't go away, and maybe there were people for whom it stayed.

Ned looked at his father. Edward Marriner had the posture of a man desperate to say something, but having no idea what words would do more good than harm.

Which was pretty much how Ned felt.

Aunt Kim was still angry. He hadn't seen her this way yet, either. "Meg, I said goodbye to my own mother in Toronto a full month before she died. I didn't go to her funeral because she asked me not to. Said it would be too hard for you if I were there. You want to think about that?"

Hearing this, Ned was suddenly even more certain there was nothing he—or anyone—could say. He wasn't even sure he wanted to *know* any more about it. Greg looked stricken, as if he very badly wanted to get away, over by Kate and Steve at the drive. Way out of earshot.

Ned watched his mother. She looked shaken. "No, I don't, actually," Meghan Marriner said. "Not right now. I don't want to think about that."

Aunt Kim shrugged. "You thought I just didn't bother to come. That I didn't care enough. Of course, I could be lying about this, too.

The way I lied about my hair. The way your husband and son are lying now about the wolves. You could decide that, Meg."

Ned's mother shook her head. "False choice, Kim. It doesn't have to be truth or lie for them. People make mistakes, people get misled."

"Mom!"

"Honey, that isn't—"

"Meg, why would I mislead them? Listen to yourself!"

A silence as the three overlapping voices subsided.

Meghan Marriner looked from one to the other. "I feel like I'm being ganged up on."

"You are," Ned said. "But Mom—"

"Dr. M., can I say one thing?"

They all looked at Greg, with the blood on his arm. "I *was* clawed by a wolf just now. And it was given orders by a little guy who *was* a druid. I know that last for sure because of something he did to me last night. And that same guy was killed about an hour ago, and three of the wolves."

Meghan Marriner looked at Greg for a long time.

"That was more than one thing," she said.

Greg shrugged. "Sorry."

Ned was watching his mother struggle with something embedded in herself. This was hard for him. He couldn't imagine what it was like for her. He said nothing. He really, truly, didn't know what he could say.

She drew a breath, finally. "All right. Fine." Meghan turned to her sister. "I'm too old, I guess, for a certain kind of fight. I'm not very good with changes, though. Too old for that, too."

"None of us are good with changes," Kimberly said, quietly.

Meghan looked at her. "You've grown into the white hair, at least."

Ned drew a breath. He saw Aunt Kim close her eyes. When she opened them, they were suspiciously bright. One sister might be the crying type.

"I like that red on you," she said.

His mother made a face. "Once a month. Jean-Luc on Green Avenue. I'd be sad and grey without him."

She looked around at the others. Something had changed. The rigidity was gone. "Let's get Greg cleaned up," she said, "then you'll tell me what's going on. I need to know about Melanie."

"All right," said Kim, "but there's a lot to tell. We'll need wine."

"I can do that," Ned's father said, almost too brightly.

Glancing across the grass, Ned saw Kate Wenger looking awkward and apprehensive, as if she felt she didn't belong here. He wanted to go reassure her, but he couldn't. Not yet. Something else, first.

"Can someone please ask Verawhatever to boil water?" Meghan Marriner said.

"I got that," Ned said.

He took the terrace steps two at a time. Inside, he gave Veracook the request and told her there'd be two more for dinner. Then he went looking for his uncle.

He found him in the main-floor ensuite, off the bedroom Kim and Kate had shared. Melanie's room.

He was shaving. *That* was why he hadn't come out.

Grey and brown hairs were in the sink and on the tiled floor. Martyniuk had laid down his scissors and was lathered up, using a razor on the stubble that remained. He was working too fast and had cut himself a couple of times.

"You really think that'll do it?" Ned asked from the bathroom doorway.

His uncle glanced at him from behind shaving cream. "We are all doomed if it doesn't, right?"

"Not me," said Ned. "You are. I had zip to do with this one."

"Abandon me to my fate?"

"With my mother? Damn right."

"What happened out there?" Dave Martyniuk was swooping the razor across his cheeks and neck.

Ned hesitated. "So far, okay. Better than I thought."

"No explosion is better than I thought. How do I look?"

"Almost as bloody as Greg," Ned said.

His uncle scowled at his reflection. "I'll deal with that. But do I look different enough?"

Ned nodded. "I think so."

"Give me five more minutes."

"They're boiling water to clean Greg's wound. Slow down, you'll attract sharks."

His uncle grinned. "I like it. I have a witty nephew." He suspended the blade a moment. "Only one I've got."

Ned looked at him. "Don't you . . . I thought you had a brother and . . ."

"Two nieces there. Older than you."

Ned swallowed. "And you and Aunt Kim never . . . "

Dave Martyniuk shook his head briskly. "No, we never did. Is it too late for me to teach you a post-up move to the hoop?"

Ned tried to smile. He was old enough to know there was more to this. "I'm not tall enough. Perimeter game, defence, that's my thing."

His uncle shook his head again. "Uh-uh. The good guards have to know how to post-up when they get a mismatch. We'll find a basketball net later."

"I know where there are courts here."

Martyniuk was shaving too rapidly again. "Good," he said. Then swore, as the blade nicked his throat. "Go on back, I'll be there in a few, unrecognizable."

"OH MY GOD!" Meghan Marriner said.

She had looked up from where she was treating Greg

at the dining-room table. "*Ivorson?* What are you doing here? I don't—"

She stopped, very abruptly. Ned could see her figuring it out. Already. You could almost chase succeeding thoughts as they crossed her face.

Dave Martyniuk, a dab of Kleenex on each of two cuts that hadn't stopped bleeding, paused in the doorway to the dining area. Aunt Kim hurried over to him. They hugged each other, hard, then she stepped back.

Ned's father's introduction died on his lips.

Greg was in a chair at the table. Meghan had been wrapping a bandage. Pots of boiled water stood on trivets beside clean cloths and white spools of gauze and tubes of antibiotics.

Turning from beside her husband, Kimberly straightened her shoulders and looked at her sister, as if ready for a blow. Ned, with Kate by the glass doors to the terrace, felt a massive surge of anxiety. They were a long way from being out of the woods on this. He looked at his uncle.

Unrecognizable.

Yeah. Sure. You're, like, six-foot-three, with *big* shoulders and hands, and blue eyes, and you shave your beard and no one will know you from Danny DeVito?

And Ned's mother was very, very quick. That's why they'd wanted her here in the first place. One reason, anyhow. The other reason had to do with machetes and guns and bombs, and they weren't going to talk about that. Although it was also why his uncle had taken that fake name—Ivanson, or whatever it was— and had been following her for years to places halfway around the world.

Ned waited for the explosion. It didn't come.

Instead, Meghan Marriner, who never did, began to cry.

"Oh, Meg," her sister whispered. "Oh, honey . . ."

Meghan held up a quick hand to stop her. Ned saw Kate Wenger biting her lip beside him, a gesture he knew pretty well by now.

His mother wiped at her eyes with the back of one hand. She drew a breath and looked up. She stared at Martyniuk for a long moment.

"Three times?" she said finally.

He nodded.

"Sierra Leone, the Gulf. Darfur? That's where I saw you?"

He cleared his throat. "Ah, four times, actually, being truthful. I was in Bosnia, but just for a few days . . . it didn't end up looking too bad. You may not have spotted me."

She was still staring, still thinking. "You found out when I signed up for missions and you went there, if you thought they were dangerous?"

He nodded again.

"Dropped everything in your life? Took a false name, false ID? In war zones?"

"That's about it," Martyniuk said. "It didn't happen often, really."

"Four times, you just said."

Martyniuk nodded again. He made a face. "Damn. Looks like I just got rid of a beard I liked."

There was a short silence. "You look better without it," Meghan Marriner said.

"I tell him that too," her sister murmured. "Meg, I—"

Again, Ned's mother held up a hand. "I'm going to cry again if you talk, so don't, Kim." She still hadn't taken her eyes from the big, capable figure of Dave Martyniuk in the doorway. "I need to be really clear on this. You left your work in England, your wife, you put yourself in danger around the world, you certainly broke laws, with computers and a fake identity, and why?"

He leaned on the doorframe, took his time. An unhurried man, Ned thought. "We felt a sense of responsibility."

Meghan closed her eyes for a second. "You thought I did these things because . . . ?"

Martyniuk's expression was grave. "Meghan, sister-in-law, I learned a long time ago, the hard way, that people do things for an amazing variety of reasons, some good, some bad. Even heroic things. Sometimes we don't *know* all the reasons for what we're doing."

"I'd say we usually don't," Edward Marriner said.

His wife looked at him.

"You knew about this, Ed? Do I have to kill you, too?"

He shook his head, but the threat, the joke of it, had already changed the mood. Ned could feel himself beginning to breathe properly again. "I heard about it two nights ago, honey."

From the doorway, Martyniuk murmured, "If you want me dead, just tell me to shave closer. I seem to have lost the knack."

"You were rushing," Ned said.

The adults turned to him, all of them.

"Right, Nephew," his uncle said. "The unchallenged expert of the family. You shave—what?—twice a week to show off?" He was grinning, though.

"Well, I know who isn't going to teach me *his* technique, anyhow," Ned said.

"Listen to the lot of you! Bandage me already," Greg interjected. "Is this how doctors treat wounded patients? Family arguments while we die on the table?"

"An under-reported statistic," Kimberly said soberly.

Ned was opening his mouth to make another joke, out of sheer relief, when he felt a flaring, imperative presence inside himself. Awareness flashed in his aunt's face in the same moment. He saw her look past him.

He wheeled around. And looking out through the glass doors he saw, in the late-day sunlight, a slender, bald-headed man in a grey leather jacket step onto the terrace and stand there, waiting patiently.

CHAPTER XV

He accepted a glass of wine from Ned's father at the table, dealing easily with the scrutiny of a large number of people, but Ned could see how tightly wound the man was. There was a sense that Phelan was keeping himself under control, but only just. As before, when he'd seen this man, had been with him, the world suddenly felt more intense. And how could that not be so, Ned thought—with what they knew about him?

Ned glanced at his mother, and saw Meghan Marriner's alert, appraising look at the newcomer. She kept still, watching. She'd finished with Gregory, wrapping his wound.

Phelan saw that. "An injury? How did this happen?" The low voice, precise.

He had spoken to Ned, even with the adults present, so Ned answered, "In Arles. Wolves."

"Cadell attacked you? Where? Why?" Eyebrows raised. Control at the brink of violence.

He hasn't found her, Ned thought. *And he knows time is running.*

He said, "The cemetery. But no, it was Brys. On his own."

A hard look. "On his own? You are certain of that?"

Ned nodded. "Yes. What are you doing here?"

The obvious question, really. He was pretty sure he knew the answer.

"Perhaps a proper introduction first," his mother said. Her voice was cool, but not hostile. "I've just arrived, and I'm missing some critical information."

Ned looked at Kate. The two of them were the only ones here who'd ever seen Phelan.

The Roman—the Greek, the stranger—smiled briefly at Meghan Marriner, a wintry smile. "I fear that, rude as it might seem, there isn't time for proper introductions. My name is Phelan." He looked briefly at Kate. "This time."

Aunt Kim crossed her arms on her chest. "But it was Protis, wasn't it? And she was Gyptis?" A challenge in the words.

Phelan looked at her, a different expression. "No, actually, though the tale produced those names eventually. It often happens that way. But they were never ours."

He paused and then, as if reluctantly, "And you are . . . ?"

"Rude as it might seem," Kimberly murmured coldly, "there isn't time."

Ned, instinctively, looked at Uncle Dave and saw his mouth tighten, as if he was aware they were playing with danger.

"I see," said Phelan, after a silence. He looked at her thoughtfully. "You have some power, don't you?"

"Some," Kimberly said. "Enough to recognize it."

Phelan nodded. He glanced at Ned. "You are related?"

"My sister's son." Kimberly gestured at Meghan.

The man in the grey leather jacket sipped his wine again. "This begins to make more sense, your presence among us." He looked at Ned again.

"Your presence among *us* doesn't, yet," said Edward Marriner. "And there *is* the matter of Melanie. We'd very much appreciate—"

They heard a knock at the front door.

Ned looked quickly that way, and swallowed hard. He knew who this was. Who it had to be. There had been no buzz to request admission from the locked gates.

Steve, who was nearest, opened the door. With no surprise at all Ned saw Cadell standing there. He smiled cheerfully and entered, dressed as he had been at the Glanum ruins in the morning.

The two men looked across at each other, one at the front entrance, the other by the glass doors to the terrace.

Ned tried again—and failed again—to get his head properly around how long they'd known each other, and fought with each other for the woman he'd seen between fires at Entremont. The past infusing the present here, entering, defining it.

It is not just about the three of them, Brys had said.

Brys was dead. Ned's uncle had killed him. But perhaps it really *was* about the three of them, Ned thought, and everything else was bound up in that.

"Am I too late for a glass of wine?" Cadell said in that deep voice, standing where Dave Martyniuk had been a moment before.

No one responded, no one had time.

The blurred motion with which Phelan drew the knife and threw it was quicker than any possible reply.

It was in that moment, really, that an answer to another unspoken question came to Ned. He'd been wondering how Phelan could ever have battled the other man—so much larger, so obviously a warrior—on even terms in any sort of combat.

He ought to have remembered the smaller man spinning off the cloister roof, flipping himself outwards and landing with so much grace. Speed and poise and effortless intelligence could serve in a fight as well as power, he thought.

Cadell swore, an involuntary outburst. Ned heard Kate cry out, saw Steve back away from the door, at speed.

With greater speed—almost impossibly so—Cadell took a step forward and seized a metal serving platter from the table. He hurled it like a discus across the room. Phelan twisted urgently sideways and the plate whipped past his face to smash loudly against the wall, putting a long, jagged crack in it between the glass doors.

"What the *hell*?" Edward Marriner exclaimed.

Cadell had a hand to his left shoulder now. The knife was embedded there. Ned had seen that knife before. The cathedral, very first moments. He looked at Kate. She'd remember it. Her face was pale.

Phelan's was white. That plate had been moving fast enough to shatter his face, kill him if it had hit his throat.

"A mild precaution," he said. "To keep you from being tempted again. You don't do well with temptation, do you? He's been flying," he explained, looking around the room. "Tracking me from the air. That's how he came here. As an owl. She made him swear an oath not to fly. When a man disregards a sworn promise, he needs to have it enforced for him, or chaos descends upon the world, wouldn't you say?"

It was a question, but not addressed to anyone in particular. He was looking at the Celt.

Cadell's face had lost its colour as well. "I can kill you even with a wound, you know."

Phelan smiled thinly. Ice in his eyes. "You can *say* it. There's a doctor here. I believe she's finished with one injury."

"Two doctors," Kim said quietly. "As I understand it, if you'd killed him here you'd have lost for this time and—"

"I have no interest in what you understand. Believe me, if I had wanted to kill, the blade would not be in his arm," Phelan said.

Ned believed him.

Cadell, across the table, was controlling his breathing, as if stepping down—carefully—from a towering, annihilating rage. If Aunt Kim was right, killing the other man with that discus would have cost him Ysabel now. And he *had* been throwing for the face.

Cadell looked at Greg. After a moment, he said, "Again? You seem inclined to injure yourself."

"Not before you guys showed up," Greg said.

"Who did this?"

"You really don't know?" Phelan said.

"I do not."

The Celt turned to Ned. They kept *doing* that. As if he had the answers here.

He cleared his throat. "I told you this morning that we were heading to Arles, remember? Brys was waiting at the cemetery, or he followed us. Don't know which."

"And?"

"He had the wolves go for me. The others . . . Greg . . . defended me."

Cadell's expression slowly changed. He shook his head. "I told him to leave you. I shall tell him again."

"Don't think you can," Ned said. "My uncle there killed him."

Another silence. Phelan and Cadell, from across the room, looked at each other.

"This is truth?" Phelan asked.

Ned, irritated, said, "Why would I lie? Just give us Melanie back and we'll get out of this, you know it."

"And you know that cannot be done," Cadell said, still holding his arm. "I told you this morning, and last night in the road. Now I tell you a third time." He paused. He smiled. "Why would I lie?"

"Well, I can think of reasons," Kate Wenger said, bravely. "You lied about flying, didn't you? We know that. Neither of you gives a damn about anything but Ysabel. You'd do anything to get to her first."

Everyone looked at her. Ned, instinctively, moved closer.

"Just about anything," Cadell agreed, gravely. It was hard, Ned thought, to disconcert these two. Probably came with the territory: if you had lived as many times as they had . . .

Cadell turned to Dave Martyniuk, standing not far away. Seeing them together made you realize just how big Martyniuk was. The Celt was large, broad-shouldered, rippling neck muscles and arms—and Uncle Dave was a bigger man.

"Brys was a druid, and a companion of sorts. I should kill you for this, I suppose." The words, lightly spoken, hung in the air.

"I suppose," Dave Martyniuk agreed. "But, as I told him, you don't know nearly enough about me."

Cadell did look surprised at that. His head lifted, as if to a challenge. "You are aware of how many times and through how many lives I have fought?"

"I've been briefed." Uncle Dave nodded towards Kim.

"Indeed," said Phelan, from the other side of the table, the logical one, piecing things together. He and Kimberly exchanged a glance.

Ned had never felt so many layers of tension in one place in his life. He was almost sick with it. On impulse he tried that inward search again: he found the three auras right away—his aunt, both men.

And a fourth—a pale, soft hue.

It shocked him, then he figured it out. It was *himself.* He was seeing his own existence in this other space. Still impulsively, he reached within and tried to close his presence down, screen it, the way the others could.

It was gone. Ned swallowed hard. He looked up and saw that Aunt Kim had now turned to him, questioningly. He managed a shrug. What was he going to say? It wasn't as if he had a clue, really.

Phelan reclaimed his wine. He had put it down when the knock came at the door. He'd have known who was there, who was about to come in. Of course.

Cadell was still staring at Dave Martyniuk. "You're being reckless," he said. "Relying on my goodwill at the wrong time. I'm not known for patience, and I dislike your manner."

"I'm sure you do. But not enough to risk losing the woman, I suspect. And as I said, you'd need to know more about me before we fought."

The Celt shook his head. "I have killed so many like you."

"No, you haven't," said Dave Martyniuk quietly.

Then he added, in that other tongue, words that seemed to slice the air in the room the way Phelan's blade had, and Ned heard those names again: *Cernunnos,* and the one that sounded like *Cenwin.*

"Wherever you have fought," his uncle added, in English, "and however many times, it was never where I did."

In the silence that followed this, they heard Phelan across the room say, "Ah," as if something important had been clarified.

For him, maybe. Not for Ned, that was for damn sure.

Cadell looked from Dave across to the other man.

"I'd call it interesting," Phelan said lightly. "I would."

He smiled again, the same tight-mouthed look. Ned tried to remember if he'd seen joy or passion in this man's face—other than when Ysabel had appeared up on the plateau.

He couldn't. But it *had* been there at Entremont. You couldn't have missed it there.

"I would be happy," Phelan added, still looking at the golden-haired Celt, "to watch you fight this one. I see nothing but diversion for me."

"No one is fighting anyone, especially not with a knife in his arm," Kimberly Ford said, a little too briskly. She scowled at Cadell. "You! Sit, we'll deal with that. We seem to be all set, anyhow." She gestured at the table.

Ned saw Uncle Dave lean back, casually, against the wall by the computer table. "I do have a bad knee from this afternoon. Not moving all that well. Evens things out. But the truth is, your druid was attacking my nephew—you'd *expect* me to deal with that. And I didn't try to kill him."

"Why not?" Cadell asked.

An odd question. Dave hesitated. "Too final, from what my wife said. I told him, all of them, to let their spirits go back. They shouldn't have been lingering after Beltaine."

"You know about that?" Cadell said.

"Kimberly does. I listen. Go on, man, sit down, let her treat that wound. Your fight isn't with me." His voice was relaxed, steadying. "And, by the way, we honestly don't know where she is. I assume that's why you're both here."

Cadell stared at him another moment, then turned to Ned again. Phelan had already done that.

"It's true," Ned said. "We're looking, you know it. We haven't seen her."

He hesitated, then decided not to tell about sensing her presence in the cemetery. They were *competing*, weren't they? This was a race of some kind, though he had no idea at all what they'd do if they won it. "I thought . . . I felt something in the valley north of Les Baux."

"Well, yes," Phelan said. "You would have. But it is very old."

Cadell's mood seemed to have changed. "I don't think my flying here will matter to her."

As if he was pleading, in a way.

Ned said, "You're wrong. It'll matter to Melanie. She cares about things like that. And she's *in* her."

They both stared at him. He felt anger flare again. "Well, she is, isn't she? That's the whole point of this. Isn't it? The summoning? So Ysabel changes a little each time, and you never know who she'll choose. And *don't*," he added, glaring from one of them to the other, "say 'Who are you?' again, because I don't *know!*"

Nobody said it.

Cadell abruptly sat down in the chair by Aunt Kim. He looked steadily across at his enemy. Two millennia and more, Ned thought. You could screw yourself up thinking about that.

"Tell me," the Celt murmured, "which oath-breaking will she count the greater? Flying to meet you here, or your wounding me when she ruled we could not fight? Seeking the edge you so much need, for later?"

Phelan didn't smile this time. "You really think that was it?"

"An advantage? By the gods, I do."

Again, Ned didn't see the movement clearly. He couldn't tell whether the second blade came from a boot top again or from inside the leather jacket sleeve as Phelan's arm swept downwards.

He saw the knife. Cadell sprang to his feet, twisting, chair scraping on floor tiles.

And then the blade was deep, in Phelan's own shoulder.

He'd driven it in, exactly where he'd struck the other man.

Ned felt an overwhelming confusion of feelings. It really was becoming way too much. He heard Kate stifle another cry. Then he heard laughter.

He looked across the table. Cadell had subsided into the chair again, his head thrown back. His laughter filled the room.

Ned glanced at his mother. She was staring at the smaller man, who had just put a blade in his own arm. She turned to Ned and met his eyes.

He saw her nod acceptance. Finally.

This, if nothing else, had made her acknowledge that something entirely outside their understanding was unfolding here. Happening right now, but also before this, over and over, and again when they were gone—from Provence, or the world.

"How very amusing," Cadell said, looking across at Phelan, finally controlling his laughter.

It wasn't the word Ned would have used.

"I have my moments," the other man replied quietly.

"Such a stoic Roman," said Cadell mockingly.

"I was Greek when we met."

"Roman soon enough."

"And then something else."

"No, never anything else."

The tone was blunt, absolute.

Phelan smiled mirthlessly. "How many years is one a stranger? Do the druids propose a number?"

"That's a Roman question. You live in a different world."

"We all do, now," Phelan said. "Answer. How long?"

"Here? A stranger? Some forever. You are one of those."

The other man shrugged, with one shoulder. There was a knife in the other. Violence, Ned thought, could come and be gone and leave only the memory—the blurred image of it—behind.

Phelan looked at his left arm and made a face. "I am sorry about the jacket. I like it." Then he clenched his teeth and pulled out the dagger.

That had to hurt, Ned thought. Blood followed the blade, staining the grey leather. Phelan looked at his knife, wiped it on his trouser leg, and put it away.

It *had* been in the boot.

Meghan Marriner was staring at him. "I won't even pretend to understand either of you," she said. Ned knew that voice. She turned to her sister. "I assume it wouldn't help us with Melanie if we let these two get infections, lose a unit or two of blood? Die or something?"

Kim shook her head. "It might. But probably not. I think if they're gone, she's gone."

"Melanie?"

"Ysabel, but same thing now."

Meghan took a deep breath. "You'll explain?"

There was a lot in that question, Ned thought. Twenty-five years' worth. There were different ways of measuring what could be called a really long time.

He saw his aunt nod once and then, with a smooth, straight movement, draw the other dagger from Cadell's shoulder. He showed no reaction at all.

"All that this exercise in idiocy proves," Kim Ford said grimly, as she began using the same knife to cut away the Celt's shirtsleeve, "is that not even two thousand years and however many lives can make men halfway intelligent."

Her sister laughed.

NED GLANCED SIDELONG at Kate Wenger. They had walked around the far side of the pool to the lavender bushes in the last of the daylight. No flowers there yet; late June, apparently.

The sun was gone. Purple and pink bands, beginning to fade, striped the sky above Aix. The moon was over the woods beyond the drive. He heard birdsong.

It was chilly. He'd gone upstairs and found his hooded sweatshirt for Kate. The sleeves were too long; her hands were inside like a little kid's, the cuffs dangling. He remembered looking that way himself. His mother used to buy him clothes a size too big, cuff or double-cuff sleeves or trousers.

His mother was inside, dressing a knife wound.

Someone had tried to kill Ned today. It could have happened, probably *would* have happened, if his uncle had been later arriving. He wondered if he would start reliving those moments tonight when he turned out the bedroom light.

Kate looked over at him. "Nice pool here."

"Really cold. They don't heat them in France."

"I know. They wait till summer. You've been in?"

He remembered the ringtone war, being thrown in there. That made him think of Melanie. "Once," was all he said. Then, as that seemed inadequate, "Steve's the swimmer. He's been doing laps. Has a trick knee, that's his exercise."

Small talk. Meaningless. Kate seemed to reach the same conclusion. She said, "Why do they keep thinking we know—*you* know—where she is?"

"Ysabel?" That was dumb too—who else could it be? "I'm not sure they do. I think . . ." He stopped, trying to phrase it right, trying to *think* it right.

"Yes?"

Ned sighed. "I think they are trying for just anything they can. We did get Phelan to Entremont. You did that."

Kate made a face. "I didn't do anything, I just thought you'd want to see it."

They started walking, came to the western edge of the property. Across the wire fence he could see dug-up earth, black soil exposed. Wild boars, rooting. The neighbouring villa was some distance off, mostly hidden among trees, a little lower down. Lights were on there, he saw. They were alone here in the wind.

"You going to tell me it was just an accident we went up?" he said.

"Well, it was!"

"And the way you were? Before, with me, on the way?"

She looked out across the fence. "That was completely an accident."

"Right. It was Marie-Chantal, you were channelling her." He shook his head. "Kate, these two guys don't think that way, so we can't. They think we've got some other kind of channel."

"You do, don't you?"

He sighed again. "Some. I guess Phelan was here to ask us, or me, and Cadell's kind of tracking *him*."

"Yeah. He wasn't supposed to fly."

"He wasn't supposed to throw a dagger at him."

They looked out over the valley at the city beyond and below. Lights coming on there too, now. It was pretty gorgeous in the twilight. Ned struggled to formulate a thought. "You think, in the old days, people would come out for a sunset?"

Kate shook her head. "Sunrise, maybe. Nightfall would scare them. Not something to enjoy. Time to get behind walls. Bar the door. Evil things abroad."

Ned thought about it. He remembered the round tower, only a walk from here. Guarding against an attack. People had been calling this place a paradise for a long time. You fought wars for paradise.

And for a woman. He was having a hard time keeping the image of Ysabel from filling his thoughts, shifting them. Men kneeling before her among torches. He looked at Kate, beside him in his outsized sweatshirt. So *ordinary*, and they were so far from that ordinary world here.

He said, "You know, occurs to me, you cool staying with us? I mean, this is getting rough. And it's . . . it isn't your . . ."

She looked at him. "Trying to get rid of me?"

He shook his head. "No, and you know it. But I have a feeling my mom's going to say this is way too dangerous. She'll—any bets she'll want to call your mother or something?"

Kate smiled at the thought. "And tell her what, exactly?"

"No effing idea, but . . . there was a knife in there, Kate."

"I saw. Two of them. Not thrown at me."

"That's not the point."

"Bad pun. Ned, thank you. But it's cool. I'm still the only other person here who can recognize Ysabel."

True, sort of. "I think my aunt would probably know her. You know. Inside. If she wasn't screening herself."

"Then we can have three groups tomorrow. With your uncle's car now."

She was quick. He hadn't thought that far ahead. He had just figured out his own accidental pun.

"Maybe," he said. "I'm not telling you what to do."

"Ned, Melanie's where I was going to be. You know it." She looked out over the meadow again, darkening to brown and grey in twilight. "I didn't sleep a lot last night, thinking about that. I can't walk away."

He'd thought about this himself. How hard it would be for her to have been inside, and just leave. He turned towards the field across the fence too.

"Okay," he said. "I'm glad, actually. I'm glad you're here." It seemed easier to say some things not looking at her. "Fair warning about my mom, though."

"I'll deal. What did he mean—Phelan—when he said of course you'd have felt something by Les Baux?"

Ned shrugged. "No idea."

"Where was it?"

"Just north. On the way to those Roman ruins."

"Glanum." Kate's voice was resolute. "I'll google it and check Melanie's notes tonight."

"You do that," he said. "Prepare a memo with footnotes." He looked at her, amused, despite everything.

"Don't you make fun of me!" Kate said, glaring.

"I wasn't." Though he had been. He hesitated. "You're pretty cool, anyhow." He managed to keep looking at her this time. It was nearly dark, which helped.

"I'm not cool at all. I'm a geek, remember? Someone to get essays from."

Ned shook his head. "No."

He left it at that, turned away again. After a moment she said, in a different voice, "Well, thank you. But don't you think this sweatshirt makes me look fat?"

Ned laughed aloud.

Kate was grinning.

"Yeah, McGill hoodies tend to. Everyone knows that." He took a chance. "I saw you last night, remember? All legs."

She chose to ignore that. "What's McGill?"

"Main university in Montreal."

"You going there?"

"Might. Probably. Haven't thought about it a lot. Thinking less about it just now."

"Yeah, I'm sure."

They heard a sound to their right.

Ned turned quickly. In the fading light he saw an owl flying north along the upslope of the hill behind the house. The bird was awkward, labouring, fighting to climb.

They watched it. For no reason he could have explained, Ned felt a lump in his throat. It was Cadell, of course, defiantly forcing himself to take wing despite a wound. Refusing to acknowledge what had been done to him, that it could change anything, make him behave differently.

"He'll . . . he's going to have to land," Kate said. Her voice was rough. "Change back."

Ned nodded. "I know. He'll wait till he's out of sight if it kills him."

They were silent, watching the bird struggle. They lost it, then Ned saw it again. Its left wing seemed to be hardly moving, though it was difficult to see in the last light, and that might just have been his knowing where the blade had gone.

After another moment the owl passed from sight, cresting the hill.

"He didn't have to do that," Kate Wenger said softly.

"Yeah, he did," Ned replied.

She glared at him again. "Your aunt," she said, with more anger than seemed called for, "was right, then. Men are idiots."

"I try not to be," Ned said.

"Don't even start with me, Ned Marriner."

A presence, a voice behind them. "Be fair. He hasn't done too badly."

Phelan walked up.

"We didn't hear you," Kate said.

The man they'd first seen in the baptistry shrugged a shoulder. The other would be bandaged, Ned knew, under the jacket. The jacket would be torn. It was too dark to make that out.

"I've had time to learn how not to be heard," Phelan said. "I came to say goodbye."

"Well brought up?" Kate said.

"Once, yes." He hesitated. "In Phocaia."

"I know. I looked it up. Eastern Greece. But your name wasn't Protis?"

He shook his head.

"You can remember being young?" Ned asked.

Another hesitation. He was being kind to them, Ned realized. "You never forget being young," he said. Then, "Do you have anything for me? Anything at all?"

A great deal of pride being overcome to ask that. Ned shook his head. "I'd have told you both, if I had."

He thought the other man's expression was pained, but that was probably his imagination. The bands of colour were almost gone in the west.

"I thought you might . . ."

"Be on your side?"

Phelan nodded. "You were, in the café."

"You didn't need me," Ned said. "You said I was stupid to come out, remember?"

"I remember." His teeth flashed briefly. "Men are idiots?"

"Yeah. You heard that?" Kate said.

He nodded again. "Inside and out here. A body of opinion, it seems."

"How's your shoulder?" Kate asked.

"Same as his, I imagine."

"But you don't need to fly."

"I don't, no."

"You do the screening thing, though, right?" Ned said. "You told me about that. Then you did it at Entremont."

"I did learn it, eventually, yes. As he learned the shape-changing."

"Why him, not you?"

A hint of impatience for the first time. "Why did they have druids and keep their elders' skulls, and their enemies', and believe the sky would fall to end the world?"

Ned said nothing.

"Why did we build aqueducts and cities? And theatres? And arenas and baths and the roads?"

"I get it. Why did you conquer them? Make them slaves?" That was Kate.

"Why were we *able* to do that?"

"What are you saying? Different ideas of the world?" Ned asked.

Phelan nodded. He turned to Kate. "He isn't an idiot, by the way."

"Never said *he* was," she retorted.

Phelan opened his mouth to reply, but didn't. He looked at Ned again. "Different ideas, different avenues to power. You've learned how to screen yourself?"

Ned nodded. "Just now."

"Remember to let it go unless you need it. You're still hidden. You don't need to be. It will kick back on you if you hold too long. You can harm yourself. I learned the hard way."

"Seriously?" Dumb question.

Phelan nodded. "It drains you, takes a fair amount of energy, though you don't even know it."

Hesitantly, Ned closed his eyes, looked within again, saw the silver light that was the man he was talking to and the green-gold of his aunt up in the house. Cadell's presence was too far away now, or blocked.

He released his own, like opening fingers in his mind, and saw his own pale hue reappear inside.

"Ah," Phelan said. "There you are. I'll leave now. This is"—he looked from one of them to the other— "farewell, I suspect. I will say that I am grateful—for the café, for Entremont."

"You saved us up there," Kate said.

He shook his head. "He was unlikely to have hurt you, with Ysabel watching."

"The others might have, and it was Beltaine," Kate said stubbornly.

Phelan shrugged again, with one shoulder. "So be it. I saved your lives. Doesn't make me a good man."

"I know that," Ned said.

Phelan looked at him for a long moment.

"You must understand, I have . . . no balancing in this," he said quietly, in the near-dark. "The air I breathe is her, or wanting her."

Ned was silent. He felt something pushing from inside himself, a kind of wish, longing. Last encounter, an ending, a world touched and receding.

He heard himself say, "I sensed her in the cemetery. No idea from when. It might have been long ago like the other place, but I did feel her."

Phelan's attention was suddenly absolute. "Ysabel herself, not just a sensation?"

Ned nodded. "Ysabel."

Saying the name himself.

The man's head lifted. He was looking down the valley, as if trying to see as far as Arles. He was a grey shape in moonlight, going away from them. The villa's lights were across the grass, up the stone steps, gleaming through windows, far away from where they stood.

"That would have been her now, if so. She knew Les Alyscamps. We all did."

"What does it tell you?" Kate asked, an edge in her voice. *She knows he's leaving, too,* Ned thought. This world they'd found.

"One thing or two," Phelan said. He looked at Ned. "Thank you, again."

"I'm not sure why I did that."

"Neither am I," Phelan said. "Because he cheated?"

"I cheat on things," Ned said. "I even took an essay from . . ." He didn't finish. It seemed too dismally stupid a thought.

He saw white teeth in the darkness. "Perhaps I charmed you with my sweetness?" Phelan laughed. He shook his head. "I'm away. Remember me, if this is the end."

He turned and started back across the grass. Ned discovered he was unable to speak.

"How are you going to . . . How did you get here?" Kate again.

Ned had a sense—same as in the cloister—that she was trying to keep him here, hold him with questions, not release him into the night.

"You'll hear," Phelan said, without turning back. He hadn't turned back in the cloister, either.

They watched him go past the pool and the lavender to the iron gates. They were closed and locked. The motion sensors kicked on as he approached, so they had a sudden view as he put both arms—one would be bandaged, with a blade wound—on the bars, and then propelled himself over without fuss, with an ease that seemed absurd, in fact.

They stood listening.

A moment later there came a motorcycle's snarl out on the dark road, and then they heard it going down and away. Ned reached inside, but eventually the silver-tinted light there faded, some-where—he guessed—near the bottom of the lane where it met the main road and the streetlights.

"Ned? Kate? You two okay?"

His mother, from the terrace. He could see her in the glow there.

"We're fine, Mom."

"Come on in. We're going to eat something, then talk."

"Coming."

His mom turned and went back in.

Ned had an image, like an old photo, of himself as a child playing with friends at dusk in summer, the light fading, his mother's voice—faint but clear—summoning him home. Bath and bed.

"Why did you tell him?" Kate asked, softly.

"Don't know. Maybe because he can't fly."

"Cadell can't either, now."

"I know."

Kate was quiet a moment. "I don't think you're an idiot, by the way."

He looked at her. "I can be."

"We all can," Kate Wenger said, and kissed him on the mouth in the windy dark.

Ned closed his eyes, but by then she'd already stepped back. He drew a breath.

"Um, was that Marie-Chantal? You possessed again, like before?"

She hit him, pretty hard, on the chest. "Don't you dare," she said. "Idiot."

"We going through that again?"

"If we have to."

"You . . . you taste of peppermint gum," he said.

"Is that good?"

His pulse was racing. "Well, I'd have to taste it again, you know, to give a proper opinion."

She laughed softly, and turned away, starting back up towards the villa. Over her shoulder she said, "The management has received your application and will consider it in due course."

Ned had to smile. Before following, he looked back out over the slanting field. It was fully dark now. The lights of Aix gleamed, sprinkled across the valley bowl. Above the city, Venus was brilliant, low in the sky. He turned back towards the house, saw Kate going up the stone steps to the terrace.

He shook his head, mostly in wonder. How did you move so fast from being uncertain and fearful about everything to this sudden feeling of happiness? And then back: because the image that came to him right then was of Melanie, on the shaded grass at the Roman theatre in Arles, speaking of how hard it could be to find love.

He thought of her, he thought of Ysabel. He went back up to the villa. His mom had called him for supper.

CHAPTER XVI

"I think," said Meghan Marriner, "it is time for me to get up to speed here. Who'll start?"

They had eaten, the dishes were cleared. Veracook was at the sink washing up. The kitchen doors were closed, and they were speaking in English. Vera hadn't—apparently—seen the knives earlier. Ned hadn't checked, but it seemed that Steve had. He'd gone towards the kitchen when the blade was thrown, and closed those doors.

Ned hadn't noticed any of that. It would have been awkward to have their cook gossiping about weapons, he thought. Greg's injury—scratched by an animal—was one kind of event in the countryside; violence in the villa would be something else.

Ned watched as his mother took some sheets of printer paper from beside the telephone and set them in front of her beside a cup of tea. She had her reading glasses on.

He usually had a decent idea of what his mother was thinking—it was important in life to have a read on your mother—but this was all new terrain. He kept glancing from her to his aunt, the red hair and the white. He saw his father doing the same thing, which made him feel better. Sometimes he didn't think they looked so much alike, then he'd realize they did, a lot.

Meghan looked around the table now, waiting.

Ned cleared his throat. "It's my story, I guess. Mostly. Kate and Aunt Kim can help as I go."

Kate was still wearing his sweatshirt, and fiddling with a pen. They hadn't called her mother in New York. Ned didn't know what she'd said to his own mom—he'd seen them talking before dinner—but it had evidently been enough. She was still here.

He saw Aunt Kim, at the far end of the table from her sister, smiling a little. "I remember that note-taking," she said, looking at Meghan. "You had these green notebooks with you all the time."

"Blue. Someone," Meghan replied, "needs to be organized here."

"Melanie was," Greg said.

"Then I'll try to be," Ned's mother said. "So we can get her back." She uncapped her pen.

Ned started in. He expected her to interrupt, challenge him. She didn't. Not at the skull and sculpted head, not at the rose in the cloister or Phelan jumping from the roof. Not when Ned was sick by the mountain or fought the dogs outside the café.

She took notes. She did look hard at her sister when Ned told of his aunt's phone call.

"I'd driven to London and flown down that morning. I'd become aware of Ned the day before," Kimberly said. "In my garden. Nothing like that has ever happened before, Meg. Not even back when. I knew who he was and where he was, a kind of explosion in my head. Then he was gone. But I was pretty certain what had just happened. He'd crossed into the space where I am." She looked at

Ned, then at her sister. "I think . . . I *know* it has to do with our family, Meg. Blood ties. It can't be anything else."

"Your grandmother?" Edward Marriner asked quietly, from the middle of the table, opposite Ned.

"Great-grandmother, if this means anything." It was his wife who replied. "The story was she had the second sight. And her father before her. People in Wales, Ireland, the west of England, they all tell those stories."

No one said anything.

"Go on," Meghan said to her son.

He told his own story. His mother wrote, neat handwriting, straight lines on the unruled paper. No challenges, no comments. He spoke of meeting his aunt by the roofless tower and Cadell and the wolves attacking there.

"What did you say? To make them stop?" It was Steve.

Kimberly glanced at her husband. "Some things about me, a place I'd been when I was younger. Someone I knew."

"And it scared him off?"

"Didn't scare him. Made him think. Gave him a reason to back away. He wanted Ned out of the story, didn't have any particular desire to kill him."

"But he would have, if he had to?"

Meghan, looking at her sister.

Kim said quietly, "These two have caused a lot of damage over the years, honey."

"Collateral damage?" Steve said.

"That's about it," Dave Martyniuk said. "It's all about the two of them, and Ysabel."

"Brys didn't think so," Ned said.

"Back up, Ned. You're still at that tower." His mother looked at him.

Ned backed up to the tower. Moved on towards Entremont. He was going to skip the walk up there, but Kate didn't let him. She held up a hand, like a good student in class, and he stopped.

"I was feeling weird all day," she said. "Like, as soon as I woke up."

"Weird, how?" Meghan asked, looking over the top of her reading glasses, a doctor in her office.

Kate flushed. She lowered her gaze. "That gets embarrassing."

"You don't have to—" Ned began.

She held up her hand again.

"I felt older, and . . . darker. Stronger. Not dark as in bad. Dark as in . . ." She trailed off, looked for help.

"Desire?" Aunt Kim said softly.

Kate nodded, staring down at the table.

Ned saw Kim exchange a glance with her husband. "I do know a little about that. It was Beltaine. You were connecting through Phelan. And maybe Ned."

"Why me?" Ned asked.

His aunt smiled gently. "That's the hard question in this, you know. Our family line, back a long way. We're *in* this." She looked at her sister. "That's what happened to me, Meg."

"But I was never like this before," Ned protested.

"Everything starts somewhere, dear."

"You never shaved before this year either, right?" Uncle Dave said helpfully.

His wife stared at him, her eyes wide. "My goodness. Thank you so much for the clarification, dear. That," she added, "is an amazingly silly analogy."

Uncle Dave looked abashed. "I, uh, have shaving on my mind, I guess."

There was a brief silence. No one laughed.

"You're walking up to Entremont," Meghan Marriner said, looking at her notes. "Kate's feeling strange. Go on."

"Forgot to say, Phelan had told me to keep away that night. He'd overheard Kate and me planning the outing in the café, told me not to go, just before he left, and then we fought the dogs."

"He tried to warn you?" Ned's father looked thoughtful, but not as if the thinking was getting him anywhere.

"Why *did* you go up?" Steve asked. Fair question. Melanie was gone because they'd done it.

"I made him," Kate said glumly. "Called him a wimp and stuff."

"Oh, well, that'll do it," Greg said. "Really, I dig it, you had no choice. When a girl says that . . ."

A couple of smiles around the table this time.

Ned said, "It wasn't far. It was just after five, maybe a quarter after. The place closed at six-thirty. Way before dark. He'd told me not to be there for Beltaine, and I figured it started at night."

"It does," Kate said. "But it got dark too soon."

They shared the story, tripping over each other a little. The moon, the fires, the bull. Cadell and the druid and the spirits that came. Phelan appearing beside them. Ned phoning the villa.

Melanie. Ysabel.

Around the table there was silence as they spoke and when they were done.

"I just *had* to fall asleep back here," Greg said bitterly, first to break the stillness.

Kate looked at him. "I'd be gone," she said. "I'd be Ysabel now, if you had come."

She began to cry.

Meghan pulled a handkerchief from her sleeve and passed it down. She looked at Ned, and nodded calmly. He carried on alone, to Cadell and Brys in the laneway with the boar. He kept the one thing back: what he'd done to Cadell's horns. He told of Brys attacking Greg.

"My first Purple Heart," Greg said. "My mom will be proud."

"After that," Ned said, looking at his own mother, "Dad and the others came and got us, and then we talked to you."

"And I called Dave," said Aunt Kim.

Kate had stopped crying. She was still holding the handkerchief.

"And Dave was minding me in Darfur. We *are* going to have to talk about that," Meghan Marriner said, looking at her brother-in-law.

"I know," said Uncle Dave. "Will I get a blindfold and last cigarette?"

"Doubt it," Meghan said. "Ned, you're up to this morning? While I was flying here?"

He finished, taking her through Glanum and the cemetery. His father joined in there, and then Uncle Dave.

As they were wrapping up, laying the druid in his coffin, the telephone rang.

It seemed an alien, intrusive thing. No one moved for a moment. Ned's father finally got up to answer it at the desk.

"Oliver!" he said, forcing cheerfulness. "How nice to hear from you. No, no, no, we ate early. North Americans, what can I tell you? What's up?"

Everyone around the table was looking at him in silence. Edward Marriner said very little for a time. "Really?" once, and then, "That *is* extraordinary."

And then, "No, no, of course it is interesting. Thanks for calling. I'll be sure to tell the others." And finally, "Yes, we might indeed think of a photograph."

He hung up. Looked at all of them.

"It was just on local radio. Someone on a motorcycle dropped a heavy bag an hour ago in front of a café on the Cours Mirabeau in Aix, and tore off."

"A bomb?" Steve asked.

Edward Marriner shook his head. "They thought so, obviously. Cleared the street. But when the police and dogs came, it turned out not to be." He looked at Ned. "It was the sculpted head and skull stolen from the museum."

Motorcycle. Ned looked at Kate. He couldn't begin to think of what to say.

"These are the two things Ned saw? Under the cathedral?" his mother asked.

"They have to be," her husband said.

Meghan sighed. "Fine. I've got a note, for what it's worth." She looked at Ned, and then at Kimberly. "Is that it? That takes us to this evening?"

"More or less," Ned said. "I mean, I'm sure I'll remember other things, but . . ."

His mother nodded. "But this is the story. Fine. A couple of questions?"

"I knew there'd be an exam," he said, trying to smile.

"I'm the one writing it," his mother said. "Or it feels that way." She looked at her notes. "Wolves, twice, by that tower and in the cemetery, but dogs in the city?"

Ned blinked. What did that have to do with anything? He nodded. "Yeah, that's right."

Meghan turned to her sister. "I'm playing along here, you understand? Don't imagine I am buying everything." She waited for Kim to nod, then said, "Do these . . . spirits *change* themselves into animals or take over real animals here?"

Kim thought about it. "I don't know. I think they were dogs in Aix because there are always dogs there, and wolves would obviously cause an alarm."

"Yes, I thought that. But you don't know which they do, change or . . . occupy?"

Kim shook her head.

Her sister was still looking at her. "Ysabel takes over someone, right? Someone real? Melanie, this time, it would have been Kate. Different women each time, before?"

Kim nodded slowly. "I see where you're going."

"Good."

Meghan removed her glasses and turned to Greg.

"Whatever else happens, young man, we are going to the hospital first thing in the morning, you and I. Rabies will kill you. The treatment's easy now, but it *must* start quickly. I'm not going to be argued with on this. Some things we may not be able to do anything about, but simple medicine and common sense we can use. If these Celtic spirits entered an existing wild creature we have *no* idea what its condition was before."

Greg opened his mouth. Meghan held up a finger.

"Gregory, hush. We will say you met an uncollared dog outside the locked cemetery gates. You like dogs, you knelt to pat it, it clawed you and ran away. End of story, end of questions. I show my Médecins Sans Frontières ID, I sign all their forms, and they give me the dosages to follow up. They like MSF here, they *founded* it. One immunoglobulin shot tomorrow morning and one vaccine, five over the next month. Not even *remotely* complicated. Guaranteed prevention. Are we done discussing this?"

"Yes, ma'am," Greg said meekly. Ned would have said the same thing. He felt an overwhelming sense of relief that his mom was here, and not just because she wasn't where she'd been yesterday.

Meghan Marriner made a precise tick mark on her first page of notes. She put her glasses on again and studied the page a moment, then looked up at her sister again.

"Same point. If Ysabel has become Melanie, or the other way round, what do we know from that? Is Melanie *there* in any way?"

Kim pursed her lips. "I think so." She looked at her husband. "I think Ned had it right, before . . . the men return as themselves, but she's *summoned* into someone, and she's a little different each time."

Meghan nodded, "So if she's different it's—"

"—Melanie that's the difference," Kate Wenger finished. "That makes sense."

Meghan Marriner smiled a little. "I try."

"But what do we know if we know that?" Steve asked.

Meghan took off her glasses again. "Well, for starters, imagine she wanted to steer this, to tell us something. What does Melanie know about Provence, about Aix, this whole area?"

Ned's brief excitement faded. He looked glumly at Greg and Steve, and then his dad.

Edward Marriner sighed. "Just about everything, honey. She spent half a year getting ready for this."

"She's worse than Kate, Mom. She's worse than *you*," Ned said.

"Well, really," said his father, half-heartedly, "I wouldn't go *that* far."

Meghan raised an eyebrow at her son and then looked at her husband. "Careful, both of you. You are both in potential trouble tonight."

"Why me? I didn't compare the supernatural realm to an adolescent shaving," Edward Marriner protested.

"I still think that was a good metaphor!" Uncle Dave complained promptly.

"That," said Kimberly, "just makes the point for us. Better to keep quiet. Nobody needs to *know* you still think that way."

"The management is taking the entire question of male idiocy under advisement," Kate Wenger said.

Meghan grinned encouragement at her. "You said it, girl."

Ned carefully avoided looking at Kate. He knew exactly what she was doing with that phrase. He'd either redden or laugh if he caught her eye, and neither would be useful just now.

He cleared his throat. "I hate to accuse my own mother of being frivolous, but is this really the best time to get into sisterhood bonding?"

"It isn't such a bad time," Aunt Kim murmured.

She was looking at Meghan. Ned blinked. Moods could change pretty fast, he thought.

Meghan shook her head, "Don't rush me, Kim." She paused, looked back down at her notes. "So you guys are saying we can't predict anything from Melanie being part of this?"

"Maybe we can," Kim said. "It's a good thought, Meg. I just don't know what, yet."

Steve lifted his hand. They seemed to be copying Kate's good-student gesture here. "You know, I'd bet a lot the reason there's a search and not a fight is Melanie."

"That makes sense too," Kate said. "They were really surprised by it. They didn't like it at all."

"Why?"

"They want to kill each other," Ned said.

Meghan hesitated, then made another tick mark.

HIS MOTHER HAD other notes, and other questions. None of them triggered anything close to a revelation.

She asked why Phelan had been going under the baptistry in the first place. What he'd been looking for down there. Ned didn't know, neither did Aunt Kim.

"If I was guessing . . ." Ned began.

"Might as well, honey," his mother said. "No marks deducted."

"He said something about finding him—the other guy—in time. And never being able to do it." *The world will end,* he'd actually said. "Maybe he wanted to kill Cadell before the summoning."

"But then she'd never appear," his father said, "if I understand this at all."

"I know," Ned said. "That's why I'm just guessing. I think . . . I think he's really tired."

There was a short silence.

" 'Who could have foretold that the heart grows old,' " Aunt Kim said. Then added, "That's Yeats, not me."

The air I breathe is her, or wanting her. That didn't sound like a worn-out heart.

"I think it's really complicated," Ned said.

"Uh-huh, I'll buy that," said Greg.

Ned's mother made a dash this time on her sheet, not a tick mark. She asked about when the sculpture underground had been stolen, and when it might have been made. The theft, they knew, was recent. The work, they had no idea. A tick mark, a dash.

Meghan wanted to know what had happened at Béziers. *God will know his own.* Kate answered that one. Good student. Another tick. More questions, varying marks on paper, the moon rising outside. Ned felt a sudden rush of love for his mother. Against the weight of centuries—against druids and skulls and wolves, rituals of blood, fire, and men who could grow horns from their heads like a forest god, or fly—she was trying to bring order and clarity to bear.

He saw her put down her pen, take off her glasses and fold them. She rubbed her eyes. This would have been, he thought, a long, amazingly hard day for her.

Kate excused herself to call Marie-Chantal's house and report she was spending another night away. Ned had the feeling they didn't worry a whole lot about their guest there, but he didn't ask questions. He was glad she was staying. There were—by now—a variety of reasons.

In the absence of anything close to a better idea, they decided to stay with today's plan: do the same searching tomorrow. Kate had been right—they arranged three groups.

"I want to go back to Aix," Ned said suddenly.

He hadn't planned to say that, but it was interesting how everyone simply accepted it, deferring to him. Even his mother. That went beyond "interesting" and reached "surreal," actually.

Veracook had gone home. Greg went into the kitchen to make another pot of tea. Kate and Kim and Uncle Dave stayed at the table, bent over a big map, sorting out routes. Ned's parents put on sweaters and went out on the terrace together. He could see them through the glass doors, their chairs close. His mom touched his father on the shoulder once, as Ned watched.

Steve had put on the television, a soccer game. Ned went and joined him on the couch. Eventually Greg brought his tea and sat with them. On the screen one team got a corner kick and someone headed the ball into the net. The player became very excited, so did the announcers and the crowd.

When it was time for sleep things got interesting in another way, since they were now short a bed. Ned had the two singles in his room, but he somehow didn't think Kate would switch up there.

Good call on that one. Uncle Dave came upstairs with Ned, Kate stayed in the main-floor bedroom with Aunt Kim.

Ned thought he might talk with his uncle a little. He had his own really long list of questions. Mostly about his family. But he was also flat-out exhausted and he fell asleep pretty much as soon as they turned out the light.

He woke in the middle of the night again.

Not jet lag this time. He felt disoriented, afraid. He sat straight up in bed, his heart pounding. After a minute he rose quietly and went to the window. He looked out over the grass and pool.

Nothing there that he could see. He checked his watch. It was past two in the morning.

"Ned, what is it?"

He hadn't been as quiet as he'd thought. "Don't know. Something woke me." His head was hurting.

That was what made him do the inward search.

Another good call. He found his own aura, and Aunt Kim's downstairs. But there was a third presence registering, gold as well, but shaded towards red now—and pulsing, bright and dim, bright and dim, like a signal beacon.

"I got it," he said to his uncle in the dark room. "Cadell's out there, not too far, and I think he's calling."

"Why?"

"How would I know?"

That was unfair, even if he hated these questions . . . And then, in fact, he realized that he did know, because he remembered something.

"I bet he's hurt. Kate and I saw him trying to fly when he left."

His uncle stood up, a large figure in the darkness. "Ned, he couldn't have. He'd had a knife in his shoulder muscle."

"Go tell him that."

There was a silence. His uncle sighed. "All right," said Dave Martyniuk. "Let's do that. You able to find him?"

"Don't know, but if he's actually calling me, I have a guess. Why do . . . why do we want to go out there?" He was scared, he'd admit it if asked.

His uncle was dressing. "Because we're adrift here, no good ideas."

"He is too. That's why they came to us."

Martyniuk shrugged. "Sometimes the blind do lead the blind."

"Yeah," said Ned. "Straight over cliffs." But he started pulling on his jeans and a shirt. "We should bring Aunt Kim. If I'm right, he'll need a doctor again."

"Kim, and your mother," his uncle said.

"Mom?"

His eyes had adjusted enough that he could see his uncle nod. "She still feels outside all this. Afraid of it. The story of your family. The reason we never met before today. You have to draw her in, Ned. Has to be you." He hesitated. "You might not have thought about this yet, but what's happened to you here isn't going to go away after we leave."

Ned hadn't thought about that.

They went quietly down the hall and Dave knocked softly on the master bedroom door.

His mother was a light sleeper. "What is it?" they heard.

"We need you, Meghan. I'm sorry. Can you come downstairs?"

They went down without waiting. Same knock at the bedroom below.

A few moments later there were six of them in the kitchen, with the stove light turned on, for muted light. Ned had had a quick, subversive thought that Kate would come out all T-shirt and legs again, but she'd pulled on jeans and his McGill sweatshirt.

Uncle Dave briefed the others.

"We can all get in the van," Ned's father said. "I'll drive."

Dave Martyniuk shook his head. "Too many of us, and no reason. I'll take Ned and the doctors. Edward, there's really nothing you can do up there, and certainly not Kate."

"I did have four years of karate?" Kate said optimistically. "Till I was twelve."

Ned smiled, so did the others.

Edward Marriner looked as if he was about to protest. Aunt Kim forestalled it. "Actually," she said, "Dave can drive us, but he stays by the car. Ned will take us up."

"That makes *no* sense," her husband said quickly. "Kim—"

His wife held up an index finger. "One, you can't even walk properly, *cher*. I'll wrap your knee again later. That *was* a bad landing." She lifted another finger. "Two, even with that, you could very easily start or be provoked into a fight. I saw the way you two were circling each other."

"I was not circling!" her husband exclaimed. "I, um, have a bad knee!"

His wife didn't laugh. "Dave, listen. If he flew it was to be defiant, show that Phelan couldn't stop him, and our orders not to didn't matter. But the wound did stop him."

"Of *course* it did," Meghan said.

"I know. But Y chromosome, remember. Male idiocy. And so he may be up there spoiling for a fight because he's had to ask for help."

"Perfect logic," Dave said. "So you leave me behind and he picks on Ned?"

"He won't," Ned said.

Again that new response after he spoke, the unexpected deference.

"I'll get my bag," his mother said briskly. "Ned, take a jacket, it'll be cold out there."

The kitchen emptied of adults. Kate lingered a moment. "Want the sweatshirt back?"

He managed a crooked smile. "What's under it?"

"Me, I guess. But a T-shirt, too."

"Drat. Only reason I woke everyone was to see if you'd flash your legs again."

"I figured." She cleared her throat. "I'd feel stupid saying, 'Be careful,' you know."

"Go ahead, I won't tell anyone."

"You scared?"

"Yeah."

She looked at him. "Be careful."

He nodded.

UNCLE DAVE PARKED THE CAR where Kim pointed, by the barrier that separated the road from the jogging path. He turned off the engine and they all got out.

"Keep your cellphones on," he said. "I'm right here."

"Ready to limp to the rescue?" his wife said.

"Kim, don't be funny."

She smiled at him, the moonlight caught it. Ned saw his mother watching as Aunt Kim gave her husband a hug and lifted her face for a kiss. "Sorry, love," she said. "But I'm right about this and you know I am."

Dave still looked like he wanted to argue.

Ned walked around the barrier with his mother and aunt, following the beam of his flashlight down the path. It was farther than he remembered. The moon was ahead of them as they went. Clouds moved quickly, obscuring and exposing it, and stars. None of them spoke. This would be, he realized, the first time the two sisters had been together since his mother was a teenager.

In a way, it made him wish he weren't here. Then he realized something: he didn't have to be. There was nothing important he brought to this, once he'd woken up knowing that Cadell was calling. Aunt Kim could sense the man as easily as he could.

He was here as a buffer, he decided. To *let* them be together. Or maybe to hold a flashlight.

He kicked a pebble on the path, heard it skitter away. His aunt, on his right side, said quietly, "Not usually a good idea to talk about kids when they're there, but I haven't had a chance to tell you I really like my nephew."

His mother, on Ned's other side, made no reply. Ned kicked another stone. It was quiet up here, and cold. He kept expecting to see the tower ahead, round and roofless.

Meghan said, "None of your own. Was that a choice?"

Something difficult seemed to have entered the night.

"Not directly," his aunt said finally. "Result of a different kind of choice, back when. I would have liked children. So would Dave. Teach them basketball, whatever."

She was talking in a clipped way. Not her usual tone, Ned thought. As if she was controlling her voice.

The silence that followed made him nervous. He cleared his throat. "Yeah, post-up moves and all that, I guess."

"That's it," Aunt Kim said. Her voice was almost inaudible.

"Adoption was a no?" his mother asked.

Another dozen steps. Ned played the beam ahead of them. He really did wish he were somewhere else now.

His aunt sighed. "Oh, Meg. This was all so long ago. It would have felt like dodging something, sneaking around it."

"What? You thought you *deserved* to be childless?" His mother's voice was sharp.

"I deserved something for a decision I made. This was it."

"And you know that, Kim? You *know* that's why you couldn't?"

"Oh, sweetie. Meg. Yes, I know it."

His mother swore in the darkness. She didn't apologize, either. Ned kept his mouth shut.

He heard a snorting, scuffling sound to the right. Shone the beam quickly that way, but there was scrub and brush off the path, and he saw nothing.

He looked ahead again, and there was the tower at the end of the path, with the moon behind it and empty space beyond, where the land fell away.

His mother stopped, staring at that roofless ruin, the ghostly solitude of it. He and Aunt Kim had been here before; she hadn't.

"I could quote Browning," he heard his mom say.

"I thought of that too, Meg, first time," his aunt murmured.

"I didn't," Ned said. "Mainly 'cause I have zero idea what you're talking about."

Both of them smiled, exchanging a glance. "You will one day," his mother said. "It doesn't matter. Let's go."

She called Cadell's name, loudly, and walked straight up to the barrier that ringed the tower.

Ned was wondering what they'd do if he wasn't here, when a darkness on the far side moved and became a shape. He saw the Celt come over to them, on the other side of the makeshift fence.

"Why here?" Meghan Marriner asked. No other greeting.

Cadell shrugged. He was holding his left arm. "I thought I'd rest. It is a place I know. Then I realized it could be a problem to go down into the city like this."

Ned shone the beam on his shoulder, and winced. The bandage had ripped apart. The shirt was soaked in blood. There was blood on the hand holding his shoulder, too.

His mother said nothing.

"Ned, bring the light over. You'll have to hold it for me." Aunt Kim sounded angry. "You, on that rock, sit down. If I do this again you will undertake not to fly?"

The big man looked down at her. Ned saw him smile. He knew what was coming before the man spoke.

"No," Cadell said. "I can't do that."

"So we do this now, and then do it again?"

He stepped over the low fence and went to sit, as instructed, on the rock. Ned remembered wolves here, the last time.

The Celt said, quietly, "I expect nothing of you. I am grateful you came." He looked at the three of them. "Only the boy? Where is the warrior?" Amusement in his voice.

"Dave? Waiting in the car."

Cadell laughed aloud. "You feared for his life. Wise of you."

Aunt Kim had been reaching for his shirt. She stopped.

"Truthfully? My fear was that he would have killed you, even if he tried not to. And as I understand this, we'd have lost Melanie when he did. Next comment?"

She sounded like his mom, Ned thought. Really precise.

The man sitting on the boulder stared up at Kim, as if his eyes could penetrate thoughts through the dark. Ned kept the flashlight beam on his shoulder; he found himself breathing faster.

"You actually believe that? What you said?" Cadell murmured.

"I do."

The Celt seemed amused again. "You don't understand what you're dealing with yet, do you?"

"I think I do. I think we all do by now. I think the failure's yours."

She had taken a pair of scissors from her sister's hand and began cutting away the shirt. Uncle Dave's shirt this time. Cadell's had been sliced away in the villa the first time this was done.

His deep voice was quiet. "Not every man who fought at Waterloo or Crécy or Pourrières was a warrior. Being at a battlefield doesn't mean anything in itself."

"True. You begin to sound less of an idiot," Kimberly said. Her hands were busy as she spoke. "There are even men I have known— three or four of them—who could certainly best my husband, but I am not persuaded you are one, with a wrecked shoulder, especially."

"You make me want to test him, for the joy of it."

"I know I do. That's why he's by the car. This is about Melanie."

"Melanie is gone," Cadell said. "You must accept that. It is about Ysabel. Everything always is."

"No. For you and the other one. Not for the rest of us," Meghan Marriner said. She handed Kim sterile wipes to began cleaning the wound again.

"We're sure he missed the brachial?" Ned's mother asked.

Her sister nodded. "He couldn't have moved the arm. There's no major muscle implicated. This is just an infection risk. The knife was in his boot."

"You up to date with your tetanus shots?" Meghan said. "Got your immunization record?"

Aunt Kim laughed. Cadell said nothing. Ned watched his aunt's hands moving quickly, exposing the wound. "I can't suture out here, obviously, and I still don't think he needs it."

"Clean, debride, antibiotics."

"Yes."

Cadell remained silent through all of this, sitting very still. Moments passed, the wind blew. It really was cold. Then, softly, the man who'd called them here said, "You have never seen her. You have no way of realizing what this is. What she is. You will say you understand, but you do not. The boy knows."

The air I breathe is her, or wanting her.

Aunt Kim looked at Cadell. She hesitated, choosing words, it seemed. "Yours," she said finally, "is not the first love I have known to last for lifetimes. It isn't even the second. You will forgive me if I value one of us more than your passion."

Ned blinked. It wasn't what he'd expected. Cadell took a breath. Then the Celt smiled again. "I begin to wonder if I should pity your husband."

"He'd say yes, but I don't think he suffers so much," Kimberly replied, her hands packing the wound with gauze. She looked into her patient's eyes again. "And he could give you the same answer I did."

Ned watched Cadell gaze at his aunt. Then the Celt turned and stared at Meghan, and finally at Ned himself. Aunt Kim wrapped the wound in silence. Ned held his light steady and looked up above it at the tower and the stars.

Impulsively, he said, "Why did you put that skull and the other thing under the cathedral?"

Cadell looked at him. He actually seemed surprised. "Why do you think I did?"

"I have no idea why you did it."

"No, I mean, why do you think it was me?"

Ned felt himself flushing. "Well, I mean . . ."

"He told you I did?"

This kept *happening* with these two. He could never get his balance. Now he was trying to remember if Phelan had actually said so, in as many words.

"He led us to think so."

"And why would I have done something like that?"

"To . . . to bait him. Because he was searching for you?"

"Down there? Really?"

Ned swallowed.

"There's been nothing there for a thousand years," Cadell said.

"So . . . so what would he have . . . ?"

"He wanted to bring you in. Obviously."

"It isn't obvious at all."

"Of course it is."

"But why?"

"He sensed you, read you as someone linked to this world."

"Before I knew it myself? 'Cause I had never—"

"That can happen." It was his aunt, interjecting. "Happened with me that way. Someone knew me before I understood anything."

"But why would he *want* me?" Ned protested.

Cadell's voice was surprisingly gentle. "He looks for ways to balance matters."

"He threatened us with his knife!"

"One of his knives," Cadell said dryly.

"He never once asked for . . . he never . . ." It was hard to form thoughts suddenly, cause words to make sense. He was trying to replay that first morning in his mind, and he couldn't.

"The Roman? Ask for something?" Cadell was still amused. "That he would never do. He sets events in motion, and takes what he can use."

"He said you like to play games."

"That's true enough."

"He kept telling me to stay away. That there was no role for me."

The smile remained. "Do you know a better way to draw a young man? To anything?"

Ned felt anger surge. "The dogs outside the café? Was *that* you?"

"That was me."

"Playing games?"

"I told you I didn't expect you to come out. Neither did he."

"This makes no *sense*!" Ned cried. "When would he have had time to steal those things? And get them to the cathedral? Why did it *look* like him?"

"Not difficult. He made a bust of himself long ago, for her. You could have thought of that—which of us is the sculptor?"

Ned swallowed.

"For the rest . . . we both sensed you as soon as you arrived. I was curious, he was more than that, it now seems. He needed you more. It wouldn't have been difficult to learn who your father was—and where he was going that morning, Ned."

First time he'd ever used Ned's name.

"I imagine, if you bother to check, you'll find the two things were stolen from the museum storage the night before you found them. He had them with him and was watching to see if you went inside the cathedral that morning. If you hadn't, he'd have tried something else. Or not. He'll never have only one thought, you know."

"Oh, God," Ned said.

"Should we believe you?" Meghan Marriner asked quietly.

Cadell looked at her. "You've given me a great deal, coming here, and I'm grateful. A debt. I have no reason to lie."

There was a silence. The round tower rose above them. A backdrop.

"I told him something," Ned said. "When he left."

"And that was?" Cadell's voice changed, a rising note.

Ned drew a breath. "I told him I'd sensed her . . . Ysabel . . . in the cemetery."

That tension again, as if the air around them were a stringed instrument, vibrating.

"And now you're angry with him and telling me?"

"I feel cheated."

Cadell shook his head. "He does what he can. We don't fight the same way."

"He can't fly, or summon spirits," Kimberly murmured.

"Neither of those, no."

"And he has to be there when she's summoned?"

The big man nodded. "He's at risk, otherwise. There have been times she's come to me simply because he wasn't there."

"Unfair," Meghan Marriner said.

"Why would it be fair?" He turned to Ned. "You must hear what I am trying to say: everything else, everyone else, is insignificant. It is about her. It always has been since he came through the forest."

Ned looked away, fists clenched. "Fine. None of us matter a damn. I get it. Well, now I've told you both. Keeps it even."

"He kept it even, too," Kim said, still quietly. "At the villa. Wounded himself."

Cadell laughed. The amusement angered Ned now. "I wouldn't have done that, I confess it. He's a different man."

The Celt stood up, shirtless again, the bandage white in the moonlight. You were made aware of ease and power as he moved. "I must go."

"Does it matter, what Ned said about the cemetery?" Kim asked.

"Of course it does. A place she's been?"

"You'll go there now?"

Cadell nodded. "I may even meet him there. Which would be amusing." He glanced at Ned. "I'll tell him he's disappointed you."

"You can't fight each other," Ned said quickly.

Cadell smiled. "I know. She forbade that, didn't she?"

He turned to go down the slope that would take him towards the city. He stopped and looked back. Phelan hadn't done that.

"Move away from us," Cadell said. "Let it go. You'll hurt yourself. It doesn't have to happen."

Then he went from them, disappearing down the path.

NED'S MOTHER PACKED her kit. When she was done, they started back the way they'd come. Ned didn't use the flashlight, the moon seemed bright enough. He walked ahead, could hear his mother and aunt behind him.

"You understand all this, I guess?" his mother said.

Aunt Kim walked a few steps without answering. "Some. Not the details, but I know things like this can happen."

"You know, because of before?"

"Of course."

"And Ned's . . . like you?" His mother's voice was tentative.

"Not quite the same, but yes. You know the family stories, Meg. You grew up with them."

"I know. I don't like them."

"I know."

Stars overhead and the wind. Ned put up his jacket hood. He was still trying to deal with anger, this new feeling of having been abused by Phelan that first morning. A con job, a guy doing the shell game on a sidewalk table. Drawing him in with that underground deception. Then telling him to go away, in the cloister—just another way of luring him?

He remembered the man's fury, coming down off the roof. Surely *that* had been real? Maybe . . . maybe Ned had moved faster, ended up closer, known more than Phelan had expected?

Right. Like he was going to figure this out, however hard he worked at it.

He put his hands in his pockets. Tried to see it from the other man's point of view. Outnumbered by Cadell, who had the spirits with him, Beltaine coming, far less power than them, *needing* to know where the summoning would be, and then this kid with a link to their world shows up . . .

Ned sighed. He could see it.

He just couldn't get past the anger. This version of the story made him feel so naive, so stupidly young. He forced himself to remember Phelan at Entremont, telling them how to leave, and when, to save their lives. Cadell wouldn't have killed them there, but Brys would have. And he could have, that night.

It was hard to stay angry, and as hard to let go of it.

He heard his mother again. "Kim, do you have any idea how difficult this is for me?"

"Of course I do."

"I wonder. I can't lose Ned the way I lost you."

That got his attention.

After a few more steps, his aunt said, carefully, "Meg, I was changed, I wasn't lost. Maybe it was my fault, but I didn't have enough in me to make it easier for you. By the time I did . . ."

"It was too late. Old story?"

"Old story," his aunt agreed.

He heard only their footsteps on the path for a while. Then his mother said, quietly, "Did they die? Your friends?"

Ned strained to hear. This was *all* new to him.

Aunt Kim murmured, "One did. A darling man. Saved everything, really. One stayed there. One . . . found what she was, and joy in the end. Dave and I came home."

"And were punished?"

"Oh, Meg. Don't let's go there. I did something important. You pay a price, sometimes. Like you, when you go to war zones."

"It's not the same thing. Nothing near."

"Near enough."

He heard his mother make a sound that could have been laughter, or not. "You're being a big sister. Trying to make me feel better."

"Haven't had much chance."

The same sound again.

"I made it worse for you, when you came back, didn't I?"

Aunt Kim said nothing. She couldn't, Ned realized: she'd either have to lie, or admit that it was true, and she wouldn't want to do either. He felt like an intruder again, listening. He quickened his pace, moved farther ahead. He took out his cellphone and dialed his uncle. It was picked up, first ring.

"Where are you?"

"On our way back. It's okay."

"Everyone?"

"We're fine. It was pretty intense."

His uncle said nothing.

"Honestly," Ned said. "We're fine."

"Where are Kim and your mom?"

"Just behind me. They're talking."

"Oh."

"We'll be there in a few."

"I'm here," his uncle said.

He hadn't been, for all Ned's life. It was a nice thing to hear. He said, "We won't have a lot of time. We have to *focus* now, to get her back." His math teacher talked about focusing all the time.

His uncle cleared his throat. "Ned, I was going to say this before we went to bed. You need to think about the possibility that we won't. We'll do what we can, but it isn't always poss—"

"Nope," Ned Marriner said. "Uh-uh. We're getting her back, Uncle Dave. I'm getting her back." He hung up.

He found himself walking faster, the urgency inside him strong suddenly, anger and fear. He needed to run, burn some of it off.

He heard a sound ahead of him.

Same snuffling, grunting as when they'd come this way. He stopped dead, breathing quietly. His mother and aunt were well behind him now.

He was about to turn on the flashlight when he saw the boar in the moonlight.

It was as he remembered it. Huge, pale-coloured, nearly white, though that was partly the moon. It was alone, standing stock-still in his path—as it had the last time, in the laneway below.

The animal returned his gaze. He knew by now this wasn't a simple *sanglier* like those that had rooted up the field beside the villa.

There was an ache in his chest, as if too many things were wanting release. He said, "Cadell's gone. He went down the other way. So's Brys. The druid? He's really gone. I'm sorry. There's just me."

He had no idea what he expected. What happened was that, after a moment, the boar turned its back on him.

It turned and faced east as Ned was—as if rejecting him and all he'd said. As if saying *just me* meant nothing to this creature, or worse than nothing. As if he didn't mean anything at all, wasn't worth looking at.

It did look back once, though, then trotted away—surprisingly agile—into the brush beside the path and was swallowed by the night.

"And what the *hell* did that mean?" Ned Marriner said.

They came up beside him. "What is it?" his mother asked.

"That boar, same as before."

His aunt looked around. "It's gone?"

He nodded.

Kimberly sighed. "Let's go, dear. Don't make yourself crazy trying to understand all this."

"Can't help it," he said.

But he walked on with them, and at the end of the path they turned right and came to the barrier and went around it. Dave was on the other side, leaning against his car. Kim went forward and put her arms around him, her head against his chest.

They heard her say, "I told him you could have taken him apart."

Dave Martyniuk chuckled. "You did? Good thing I stayed behind then, isn't it? You tired of me? Ready for widowhood?"

"He was trivializing you, honey. I didn't like it."

Dave kissed the top of her head. "Trivializing? Kim, I'm a middle-aged lawyer who plays Sunday rugby for the district team and can't move for two days after."

Ned heard his aunt laugh softly. "Yeah, so?" she said. "What's your point?"

"That does remind me," Ned's mother said brightly. "I really need to review the quality of security being sent out with me. What good's a gimpy rugby player in Darfur anyhow?"

Dave Martyniuk looked at her, over top of Kim's head, which was still against his chest. He grinned. "Fair question."

Meghan shook her head. "No, it isn't. And you know it."

"I know it too," Ned said. "I saw you this afternoon, remember? That was no weekend rugby thing."

"You haven't seen our team play," his uncle said. "Ned, you want your uncle killed soon as you meet him?"

Ned shook his head. "Not in a hurry for that, no."

Dave said, "The truth? I do know how to fight. I've made sure I still do. But this one—both of these—are in their own league, their own world. I talked a good game in the villa because I wanted them taking us seriously, but I'd have died up there if he wanted me dead."

Silence. They were completely alone at the end of the road, in the middle of a night.

"What'd he wind up doing?" Dave asked.

Meghan said, "Kim cleaned him up again, then Ned told him he'd sensed Ysabel in Arles. He's going there."

Dave looked at Ned. "Why did you do that?"

Ned shrugged. "I told Phelan when he said goodbye. Guess I was being fair."

"Think anyone else will be?"

Ned scuffed at the gravel. "Maybe not."

Kimberly let go of her husband, stepped back a little. Her hair was very white in the moonlight. "I've decided not to like her," she said.

Uncle Dave pretended to be startled. He looked at Meghan. "What? After all these years!"

Kim punched him in the chest. "Not my sister! I adore my sister."

"I haven't deserved that a whole lot," Ned's mother murmured.

"Not the point," Kim said.

"Shouldn't it be?"

Her sister shook her head. "No. And the one I don't like is Ysabel."

Her husband laughed aloud, startling Ned. "Oh, God. Don't let her know," he said. "You'll completely ruin her life this time around if she finds out Kim Ford feels that way."

His wife hit him again. "Be quiet, you."

Dave was quiet. It was Ned who said, after a moment, "Don't hate her. Don't even dislike her. She's outside that. Even more than they are."

The other three looked at him.

"Can't help it," his aunt said stubbornly. "The two of them play this game of hide-and-seek and then the loser gets killed for her? I don't like it, that's all."

"You haven't seen her," Ned said. "It . . . makes a difference. It's what they're all about. I don't think she has a lot of choice either."

"Hold on," his mother said.

They turned to her. The moonlight was on her face.

"You didn't say one would be killed, Ned."

"But I did," he said. "That's what she . . ."

He stopped. His heart was suddenly hammering again.

"You didn't, dear," his mother said, very gently. "Neither did Kate. I wrote it down."

They were staring at her.

Meghan Marriner looked at her son.

"You said *sacrificed*."

CHAPTER XVII

S unrise, the first gift in the world. Promise and healing after the hard transit of night. After a darkness beset with beasts—imagined and real—and inner fears, and untamed, violent men. After sightlessness that could lead one astray into ditch or bog or over cliff, or into the clutch and sway of whatever spirits might be abroad, bent on malice.

Morning's pale light had offered an end to such fears for centuries, millennia, whatever dangers might come with the day. Shutters were banged open, curtains drawn, shop doors and windows were unlocked, city gates unbarred, swung wide, as men and women made their way out into the offered day.

On the other hand (in life there was almost always another hand), daylight meant that intimacy, privacy, escape from the unwanted gaze, silence for meditation, the solace of unseen tears on a pillow—or of secret love on that same pillow before, or after—were so much harder to claim. Rarer coinage, in the clear light.

It is more difficult—much more difficult—to hide and not be found.

BUT SHE *WANTS* to be found. That lies at the heart of this. She is prepared to become angry that they have taken so long and she remains alone.

Unfair, perhaps, for she's made this difficult, but they are supposed to love her beyond words, need her more than breath or light, and she has spent a second night outside and solitary, and it has been cold.

She is not unaccustomed to hardship, but neither is she immune to longing. Seeing them both at Entremont when she came through to the summons has kindled need, desire, memory.

She would not let them *know* this, of course.

Not yet, and only one of them, after. But these sensations are within her now and, lying awake, watching stars traverse the open space to the south, as if across a window, she has been intensely, painfully aware of them, of lives lived and lost.

And of the two of them, somewhere out there, looking for her.

She isn't certain why she'd said *three days*. No need to have done so. A small hard kernel of fear: it is possible they might not find her in time. She knows herself very well, knows she will not back away from this. Is aware that having arrived now in this place she has chosen she will not go forth again. Will not make it easier for them, or for herself.

If one of them needs her enough he will be here.

෴

Meghan Marriner, showing no signs of fatigue, had taken Greg to the hospital at first light. She'd said last night she was going to do it, was not the sort to back away from that. Steve drove them in the van.

Kate, briefed over breakfast, was at the dining-room table poring over Melanie's notes and the guidebooks she'd accumulated. Ned, at the computer, was googling as fast as he could type and skim. He'd had about three hours' sleep, he was running on adrenalin, aware that he was probably going to crash hard at some point.

They were looking for clues based on what his mother had realized by the car barrier last night. Kate had gone pale when she'd woken in the morning and they'd asked her about it. But she'd remembered the words exactly as he had.

Up at Entremont, setting the two men their task of finding her, Ysabel hadn't just spoken of killing.

She'd said the loser would be sacrificed.

They had nothing else to go on. Had to treat this as what they needed it to be: a clue to what might be happening.

Ned typed a different search combination: *Celts + Provence + "places of sacrifice."* He started finding things about *fées* and fairy mounds and even dragons. Dragons. Not much help, though from where he sat he was a lot less inclined to dismiss all that than he would have been a week ago.

There really was too much junk online. Personal pages, Wiccan sites, travel blogs. Stuff about witches and fairies—folk beliefs from medieval days. He skipped past those.

Further back, it looked like the Celts had merged their own gods with the Roman ones. Right. Conquered people—what else were they going to do? Except they did believe in human sacrifice. In worshipping skulls. They hanged sacrifices from trees, he read—that didn't help a lot. Trees were everywhere.

They performed rituals on hills, high places, which offered a little more, but not a lot. Entremont had been such a place, but they'd been back already, and Ned was certain Ysabel wouldn't have returned to where she'd been summoned. There was that other ruined hill fort—Roquepertuse, towards Arles—but Kim and Kate had gone there yesterday.

He clicked and typed and scrolled. Earth goddesses linked to water, pools, springs—Ned had been at one of those, and so had Cadell, at Glanum. Nothing. Goddesses were associated with forests—*all* the deities were, it seemed.

Much good that did them.

He found another site, read: *"They usually began with a human sacrifice, utilizing a sword, spear, a sickle-like knife, ritual hanging, impaling, dismembering, disembowelling, drowning, burning, burial alive . . ."*

He shook his head, looked away from the screen, over his shoulder. Kate had Melanie's notes and books spread around her on the table, was scribbling like a student with a teacher lecturing. Ned turned back to the computer.

The Romans, it seemed, had been shocked and appalled by all of this. Had banned human sacrifice. Sure, Ned thought, the Romans who were so gentle and kind themselves.

He tried other word combinations, found another site. Read: *"A Celtic oppidum must have been as gruesome as a Dayak or Solomon Island village. Everywhere were stakes crowned with heads, and the walls of houses were adorned with them. Poseidonius tells how he sickened at such a sight, but gradually became more accustomed to it . . . "*

He didn't know what a Dayak was. Entremont was an oppidum. The word just meant a hill fort. They were back to that. He checked the top of the page for the source of this one. Some Englishman, in 1911. Well, what was *he* going to know? A cup of tea with his pinky extended and opinions on two thousand years ago.

Ned swore and gave up. This wasn't his thing, it was making him nervous, and he didn't have a sense it was leading anywhere. He scraped his chair back and went out on the terrace. His father and uncle were sitting there, coffee mugs on the small table.

His dad glanced up. He looked worn out. "Well?"

"I'm wasting time, there's way too much. I mean, that's what they *did*—sacrifices. So it could be anywhere."

His uncle sighed. "Yeah, Kim thinks so too. Get yourself a coffee, you must be beat this morning."

Ned shook his head. "I'm fine, I just want to get *going*."

"Have to have destinations first, don't you think?"

The glass doors opened.

"All right," said Kate Wenger. "Here's what I think. There's no point checking every Celtic site in the books."

"Tell me about it," Ned said.

"I am, listen. If we're right, this whole find-me thing instead of a fight is because Melanie's inside Ysabel, right?"

"I still don't know how that's possible," Edward Marriner said.

"It is," Uncle Dave said. "Go ahead, Kate."

Kate was biting her lip. "Fine. Well, my point is, if the search is happening because of Melanie, then the one thing we can do is focus on places *she* knows about. For Celtic sacrifices. Right?"

The three of them looked at one another.

"Google is not my friend?" Ned said.

No one laughed. "Only if Melanie googled something and made a note. That's what I'm thinking," Kate said.

She had his McGill sweatshirt on again, over her brother's shirt, and jeans.

Ned's father was nodding. "That's good, Kate. It gives us something logical."

"Were they logical?" Uncle Dave asked.

"Melanie is," Edward Marriner said.

"And so's Kate," Ned said. "So what's in her notes? About Celts and rituals or whatever?"

"I found two places we haven't been to yet."

"We have three cars," Dave Martyniuk said. "Only two? Give me one more."

Ned cleared his throat. "I'm going back to Aix," he repeated. He'd told them last night.

"Why?" Kate asked, but softly.

Ned shrugged. "To the cloister. I'll let you guys be logical. I need to go there."

None of them said anything.

GREG, NOT EVIDENTLY THE WORSE for two rabies injections with more to come over the next while, courtesy of Dr. Meghan Marriner, found the name of one of the sites amusing.

"Like, if the Celts were illiterate or whatever, why'd they name something Fort Books?"

Ned's mother was in a mood. "I'll make the next shot hurt if you don't cut the jokes, Gregory. And I know how to do it."

"He called Pain de Munition, east of here, Painful Munitions," Steve declared.

"Ratting me out?" Greg said indignantly, but he looked pleased to have it recalled.

Fort de Buoux, apparently, was about forty-five minutes north, a hilltop off a rough road, nothing near it, a walk and climb to ruins—with a sacrificial altar at the summit. It sounded like a place where you could take an impressive photograph. Or hide.

The other site was farther north and west, more touristy, starred in all the guidebooks—something called the Fontaine de Vaucluse. A place where water gushed out of a mountain cave at certain times of the year. Melanie had noted that Oliver Lee wrote a section for the book describing the place from ancient times, through the nineteenth century, up to how it looked today. Some Italian poet had lived there in medieval times, but it had also been a Celtic holy site.

That figures, Ned thought, having googled goddesses and springs of water, caves and chasms in the earth.

"I'm still going into Aix," he said again, as Uncle Dave and his father started sorting out who'd be in which car. He was beginning to come to terms—a little—with the fact that the others would listen to him and do what he decided.

More or less.

"Not by yourself," his mother said.

"I'm not in danger, Mom. Brys is the one who was after me."

"Not by yourself," Meghan Marriner repeated, with a firmness that really was kind of impressive. It wasn't a voice you could argue with; it didn't actually *occur* to you to argue.

Ned ended up in the city with his mom and dad.

Dave was driving Kate and Steve to Fort de Buoux, Greg took Aunt Kim to the fountain. The idea, again, was to be in touch by phone, meet up if anyone found anything, or come back here for mid-afternoon to figure a next step if nothing happened.

It could actually have been funny in a different time and space, walking into town between his parents. Ned half felt like asking for an ice cream or a popsicle or a ride on the merry-go-round near the biggest of the fountains.

The cathedral was open but the door out to the cloister was locked. The guide who had the key and ran the half-hourly tours was coming in only after lunch. Ned didn't even think of having his dad try to pick the lock. Not here. He wondered if his mom knew her husband could do that.

They went through the medieval streets back towards the main drag, the Cours Mirabeau. On the way they passed the café where he'd gone with Kate. He saw the chair he'd used to block the dog attacking him. He didn't say anything to his parents about that. His father was looking stressed enough.

On the Mirabeau, lined with cafés on one side and banks on the other, shaded by enormous plane trees, he stopped. The feeling was becoming almost familiar.

"She's been here," he said.

"How do you *know* that?" his mother demanded. His logical mother, exasperation in her voice.

"Jeez, Mom, I have no idea. I just do. Same way, sort of, that I knew Cadell was at the tower last night, I guess."

"Why 'sort of'?"

She didn't miss a lot.

Ned fumbled for words, looking at the tourists sitting at small outdoor tables. They seemed to be enjoying themselves. Why not? People dreamed of coming here, didn't they? Of sitting at a café in the south of France in May.

"It isn't exactly the same," he said finally. "I don't get her as an aura like the other two, or Aunt Kim. Or my own."

"You can see your aunt, inside?"

He nodded. "If she's close enough, and isn't screening herself. Same with them."

His mother sighed. "And . . . Ysabel?"

"Different. I just have a feeling she was here, like she was at the cemetery."

"Why?"

"Jeez, Mom."

She frowned. "I take it that eloquent phrase means we lack an answer?"

He nodded. "Yeah. We lack an answer."

"Maybe because of Melanie," his father said suddenly. "Maybe you're picking up Melanie, not Ysabel."

"Ed! You're as bad as they are."

His father still looked strained.

"Let's have lunch," his mother said, after a moment. Ned saw her looking closely at his dad. "We have to wait, anyhow."

They picked a café near the end of the street. The inside looked flashy in an old-fashioned way, lots of green and gold, but on a day like this it was way nicer outdoors.

His father bought a newspaper next door. He found a report on the return of the skull and the sculpted bust. No details that seemed to matter. The police hadn't any idea who had returned them, other than that it had been a man in a black leather jacket, on a motorcycle.

Grey, Ned thought.

"At some point," his father said, mostly to himself, "I'm going to have to call her family."

His mother looked at him again. Then she surprised Ned a bit by reaching out and squeezing her husband's hand.

Aunt Kim called as they were finishing lunch. The Fontaine de Vaucluse was jammed with tourists on a Saturday morning in spring. It was theoretically possible (Ned's father relayed) that Ysabel might be hiding in a tourist shop among lavender sachets and olive oil samples, but unlikely. Kim and Greg were heading back to the villa.

They phoned Dave. He reported that the three of them were still climbing about and around Fort de Buoux. No one else was there at all, it was windy, and there was a pretty compelling altar right at the top. As advertised. But the "no one else there" included any sign of a red-haired woman Kate was supposed to recognize if she saw her.

They were about to work down the steeper, wilder side of the hill, to see if there were any caves or recesses where she might have ducked out of sight, out of the wind. They'd head back after that.

"Be careful," Ned's father said to his brother-in-law. "Watch your knee." He hung up.

"He can't go clambering around rocks with that leg," Meghan said.

Edward Marriner shrugged. "What am I going to do? If he can't, he can't." Worry was written on his face. He looked older. Ned didn't like seeing him like that. It made Ned feel fragile, somehow.

They went back to the cathedral. Ned walked into the dimness and past the baptistry on their right. He saw the grate covering the floor there. He didn't stop. Nothing there now, nothing to see. It had been a trick, anyhow. Items borrowed from the museum, now returned.

The cloister door was open. There were three people outside, with a severe-looking guide. She had stopped in front of the squared corner pillar by the far door to the street. She was lecturing, and pointing. The visitors, holding cameras, looked bored.

Ned went left, away from them, towards Ysabel.

He was beset with complicated feelings. Too many associations. It was less than a week since he'd first come here.

The rose was gone. Not a surprise, but for some reason it disturbed him. He wondered who would have taken it. Maybe just the gardener? He wished, suddenly, he'd thought to bring flowers.

His father had a small digital camera and was taking snaps of the cathedral walls and the roof where it came down towards the cloister. A different sort of shot, about lines and light. Ned was glad to see him working. It was hard to see him so distressed, so obviously helpless. It made Ned feel as if he was the one who was supposed to make everyone else feel better.

His mom had gone over to the tourist information on the wall. She'd put her glasses on and was reading. Ned remembered: a diagram showing how the cathedral complex was laid on top of the Roman forum, another one identifying the figures on the columns here. Saint Peter at one corner, a bull, an eagle, David and Goliath. The Queen of Sheba.

He let himself slide slowly down, back against the wall, until he was sitting on the tile flooring in front of her. He looked at the sculpture. So little there, so much implied. A hint, an echo.

He knew what his mother was going to say. What else *could* she say, reading what was posted on the opposite wall? The Queen of Sheba, it said.

He watched her coming over, putting her reading glasses back in her purse, taking out sunglasses. Her hair was really red in the sunlight, darker when she crossed into shade. She came up and stood beside Ned and looked at the worn, pale sculpture in front of them. She shook her head, and sat neatly down beside him, legs extended, crossed at the ankles. She took off her sunglasses and looked some more.

"She was beautiful," she murmured.

He swallowed. "Who?"

"Ysabel," she said.

Ned began to cry.

She looked at him quickly. "Honey, what . . . ?"

"You don't . . . you don't think it's the Queen of Sheba?"

His mother handed him a Kleenex. "Ned, dear, with Melanie gone, and what I've seen in less than a day, I'm not going to doubt you here."

"Honest?"

She made a face. "Don't fish, child."

Ned had to smile, even as he struggled for control. He wiped his eyes. "I . . . it matters a lot to me that you believe me."

His mother didn't smile this time. "Because I didn't believe your aunt?"

"Partly that. Not all."

She touched his cheek. "Someone still has to be logical here, Ned."

"I'd volunteer," his father said, coming up. The three tourists and the guide were still on the far side. "But I'm not sure where I parked my logic."

"Well find it," his wife said. "I mean, Ned may be using some kind of intuition or psychic thing here, but you and I can't. We don't have it. This can't just be about oracular pigs, or reading bird entrails, like the Celts did."

"Romans did bird entrails too," Edward Marriner said. "A whole class of priests was trained in it."

Ned saw his mother stick out her tongue at his father. He had *never* seen her do that. "Fine, be that way. But they didn't do human sacrifice."

"True enough. Other nasty bits."

"I'm sure. But we still have to try to *bring* something to this, you and I. We have to think. Ned does his thing, whatever it is, or Kim does, and we—"

She stopped, because Ned had stood up.

He was replaying a phrase in his head, over and over like a tape loop: *they didn't do human sacrifice.*

And then, like some kind of silent explosion in his mind, he locked onto the other thing his mother had just said.

Oracular pigs.

He felt himself starting to tremble.

The boar. Seen below the villa, above it under the moon. He saw it again in his mind, turning away from him, rejecting him.

But no. Not away. Turning *for* him. The slow, calm movement, looking back both times at Ned, then ahead again, before moving off.

He took a deep breath. He looked at the sculpted column, at Ysabel, then down at his hands.

"We better get back to the house," he said. "I know where she is."

THEY WERE WAITING for him to speak, assembled in the villa again. Ned felt shaky; his hands were sweaty. This was too large, it felt *massive*. But he was also sure of himself. He was absolutely certain, in fact.

"Go ahead," his father said.

Edward Marriner's voice was quiet, his eyes calm. He didn't look weary or worn down any more. He'd been like that since Ned had spoken in the cloister and they'd started back for the van, and home.

Ned does his thing, his mother had said. She was looking at him from across the dining-room table, hands in her lap, no notebook, just waiting.

He cleared his throat. "We were . . . we were really close to it last night. Mom was. When she reminded us of the word Ysabel used."

"Sacrifice?" Uncle Dave said.

He was sitting in the armchair by the piano, leg up on a hassock, an ice pack on the knee.

Ned nodded. "Yeah. So we did the obvious thing and started thinking about Celtic sacrifice places that Melanie might have known about. And that was close to being right."

"What did we miss?" Kate Wenger asked. She was still wearing his sweatshirt.

"One thing, and something else no one but me could have known. No one missed that, except me."

He looked at his mother. Aunt Kim was leaning on the door-frame behind her, where her husband had been the night before.

"The Romans did at least one human sacrifice here," Ned said. "And Melanie knew it, because she *told* me about it." He looked at

Greg, and then Steve. "That time I was really sick? When you two went up to the ambush site to look for a photo spot?"

They both nodded, said nothing.

Ned took another breath, let it out. "That's where she is. Ysabel, Melanie."

"The mountain?" Steve said.

"Yeah," Ned said. "She's up on Sainte-Victoire."

"It's a big mountain, Ned," his father said. "There's a lot of ground to cover up there. And I—"

Ned held up both hands. "No, Dad. I know exactly where. Because all of this, *all* of this, is about Melanie now, I think. The changed rules, searching instead of a fight. They didn't expect that. And she's hiding in a place she knows I know about. *We had to know, too.*"

"We're putting a lot in the idea that Melanie's . . . spirit, whatever, is inside Ysabel," Edward Marriner said.

"We can do that, Ed," Aunt Kim murmured. Her arms were tightly crossed on her chest.

No one said anything for a moment.

"All right. Fine. You said you know the place, Ned. Where?"

His mother's first words since they'd gathered back here. She was gazing at him, that calm, attentive expression he knew.

So, looking at her, he said, "She's at some chasm. Melanie called it a garagai, it's somewhere near the top."

"And she's there because . . . ?"

It was almost as if this had become a dialogue between the two of them. She used to quiz him like this, for science or social studies tests, when he was younger.

"Because she told me about it. That's where the Romans, Marius, threw the Celtic chieftains down a pit, a place of sacrifice after the battle, so they couldn't ever be reclaimed to be worshipped and help the tribes."

"Oh, God," said Kate. She put a hand to her mouth. "They even *talked* about that, at Entremont, the three of them."

Ned nodded his head. "Yeah, they did. I thought about that, too. Melanie knew we were there. I'd called her, remember?"

"Is that the second thing?" his mother asked softly. "You said there were two."

"No. The garagai is in her notes. The other thing was entirely me. I . . . twice at night, I saw that boar when I was by myself, and both times it . . . both times I think it was signalling me. I didn't get it, till just now. Till you said something in the cloister. I don't know why it was doing that, but I'm pretty sure."

His uncle sat up, shifting his leg. He had an odd expression on his face.

"What kind of boar?" he asked.

"Huge one. Almost white. Greg saw it when Brys stopped us on the road."

Greg was nodding his head. "Really big," he said. "I could have wrecked the van, hitting it."

"Go on, Ned," Uncle Dave said.

Ned looked at him. "I don't know if anyone will believe me, but I think it was pointing to something, both times. It came out, waited for me to see it, then it turned around and faced the mountain and looked back at me. And then it went off. I didn't know what was going on. And . . . and this is weird, but the first time was before Beltaine. Before anything even happened. I know that doesn't make sense."

"Time can be funny in these things," his aunt said.

"So you think she's by this chasm," Ned's mother said calmly. "All right. Good. That's our first stop tomorrow. We get directions and go look."

Ned shook his head. His hands were trembling again.

"Mom, no. I have to go now. One of them's going to figure this. They've had so much longer with her, with Ysabel. They heard her say *sacrifice* too. And they know that place."

"Ned . . ." his father began.

"Dad, I'm *really* sure. I'm shaking with it, I'm so positive." He held up his hands to show them.

His father looked at him. "That's not what I was going to say. Ned, I believe you. There's something else. You're forgetting."

"What?" Ned said.

It was Steve who answered him. "Dude, you can't go up that mountain."

"I have to."

"Ned," Greg murmured, "we saw you there. You looked like you were dying, man. I haven't seen anyone throw up that hard since . . . since whenever."

Ned stopped. He took a steadying breath. He swore. Neither parent said a word.

He *had* forgotten. Or, he'd half remembered because he knew he'd been sick when Melanie told him about the garagai, but he'd blocked out what it would mean to go back there. To climb.

Even the recollection made him feel ill, right here. He shook his head. "Doesn't matter. I have to try. I need to go, like, right now." He was almost twitching with the need to be gone.

His father's tone was gentle. "It's past four o'clock, Ned. You can't do it in the dark."

"Won't be dark. I'll get my sweats and I'll run. I'm a runner, Dad. I can do this. And maybe"—a sudden thought—"maybe I'll be better when I get higher up? My problem was the battlefield. I think."

He looked at Greg and Steve.

"And maybe you won't," Greg said, shaking his head.

"Dude—" Steve began.

"All of you *listen!*" Ned said. He heard his voice rising. "Melanie is *gone* if we screw this up. Look, I'll take four Advil or whatever, and sunglasses, and my phone, and I'll run. Please stop arguing. We can't argue. We need to move. I have to know exactly where this place is."

Kate Wenger, without a word, got up and went to Melanie's maps-and-books file on the computer table.

Ned was looking at his mother. He saw something in her eyes that went so far beyond concern he couldn't even put a word to it.

"Mom, please," he whispered. "I need your help."

"I know," Meghan Marriner said. "I just don't want to give it."

He looked at her. She shook her head. "I can't *begin* to tell you how little I like this. What do you plan to do when you get up there, if you get up there?"

"No idea."

She let herself smile a little. "Well, that's honest."

"I'm being honest, Mom."

Meghan looked at him another moment, then turned to her husband with a crisp nod. "Ed, get your two Veras in here, while Kate's looking for maps. If they live here they may know."

Her husband shook his head. "Let me try something else first."

He crossed to the desk beside Kate and checked a phone number on Melanie's corkboard, then dialed.

Ned found that he was breathing hard already—it looked, amazingly, as if they were going to help. But he was remembering the mountain now: Pourrières, and the worst feeling of his life. That screen of blood, filtering the world, and the smell of it.

His choice here, no one else to blame. Sometimes, he thought, life was easier when you had people to stop you. Maybe that was something parents were good for.

His father said, "Oliver? Ed Marriner. Am I interrupting anything?" He waited for whatever reply he got, then said, "I won't keep you long, before drinks."

The Englishman answered something, and Ned's father managed a fake laugh. "Well, if you have one already, I needn't rush. But I have a question that's come up . . . something to photograph, maybe. Do you know a place called the garagai? Up on Sainte-Victoire?"

Another pause, a longer one. Oliver Lee was launching into a story, Ned guessed. Ned could picture him, reading glasses on their chain over his chest, drink in hand, holding forth.

Edward Marriner opened his mouth to interrupt, closed it, then plunged in, "Well, yes, I've read a bit about all that, and I was thinking of going up to have a look." He paused. "I know it is a climb. Yes, I've heard it gets windy. But . . . Oliver, do you know where it *is,* up there? Have you been?"

The room fell silent. Edward Marriner looked at his son, his brow furrowed. It never unfurrowed. "You haven't? So you wouldn't be able to give me directions?"

He looked over at his wife. "Yes, of course, we'll chase down a topographic map, or I can call the mayor's office. They've been helpful." He stopped. Lee was saying something. "No, no, it is hardly a shocking confession, Oliver. My people told me Cézanne never climbed it either." He paused again. "Yes, of course, I'll give your regards to Melanie." He looked at Ned again. "No, I think I'll let you tell her that yourself, Oliver." Another small, forced laugh. He said goodbye and hung up.

Ned looked across the room at his mother. She was gazing at him, *staring* at him, really, with an expression he couldn't remember seeing before. As if he were a stranger. It bothered him. He tried to smile at her, but didn't really succeed.

"Ned?" It was his aunt. "Two things. If you're right, and there's urgency here, it's because one or both of them may get there first. And they may do that by tracking you."

"They were going to Arles," he said.

"Yesterday evening. Ned, they both seem to think you're a key to this. You'll have to screen yourself when we leave here. But you need to let it go at times, you can't hold the screening too long."

He hesitated. "I was kind of counting on the screen to help me with . . . my problem there."

"I thought you might be. But you still need to let it go some of the time or you'll make yourself ill."

He cleared his throat. "Phelan told me that too, last night."

"Kim, what if they're watching us? From out there?' Meghan gestured towards the windows.

Her sister frowned. "I don't think . . ." She looked at Uncle Dave.

He shrugged. "Might be. They know where we are, they know we're looking. Either they're tearing around searching everywhere, or they're checking us at intervals. Checking on Ned to see if he's doing anything."

"Could they have anyone watching for them?" Steve asked.

"Don't *think* so," Kim said.

"But we aren't sure," said her sister briskly. "All right, assume they are watching, what do we do? And first of all, how do we find out where he has to go?"

"I can tell you that," said a voice from the kitchen door.

They turned.

Veracook, in her usual black dress, was standing there. She'd spoken in English.

"You . . . you speak our language?" Edward Marriner said. He looked a bit stunned, as if too many things were happening too fast.

Vera smiled a little. "The owners are American. I learn a little."

"But you never . . ."

"You always speak French." She shrugged.

Kimberly walked towards her. "Do you . . . do you understand what we're talking about here?"

"Climbing the mountain?" A slight flicker of the eyes.

"That, and why." Kim's voice was direct. "Why we need to go up."

Vera looked at her. Nodded her head. Her own voice was cold. "Something happened on the Fire Night. I had rowans by the windows, to protect the house. She should not have gone out."

"She had to," Ned said. They were speaking French again. "It was my fault, but it was before sundown. It shouldn't have been Beltaine."

Veracook crossed herself when he said the word.

"How do you know about all this?" Meghan asked. She looked as unhappy as Ned could remember.

Again that shrug. "My grandmother. She told us stories. All of my family, we put out rowan on that night, and on the other night, in autumn."

Another grandmother.

It was Dave who asked the question: "You said you can help. You know where this garagai is?"

Vera nodded. "But it is a bad place. And it is already late today."

Ned's father surprised him then. "It'll be later if we hang around talking. My understanding is we need to get up there fast. Please tell us how."

"It is the girl? Melanie?"

"Yes," said Edward Marriner.

"She is gone? From the Fire Night?"

A hesitation. "Yes," he said again.

Another sign of the cross. "You should not go inside this, then," she said.

"We *are* inside it, Mme. Lajoie," Ned's father said. "Please, tell us what you know."

"Who will go?" she asked.

"Me," said Ned.

She looked at him. "You will take rowan for protection?"

"I'll take anything you want me to take," he said fervently.

She nodded, grim-faced. "For the girl, I will tell how you go. It is not far from the cross at the top, or the chapel. But you must be careful. It is easy to fall if there is wind."

"Oh, wonderful," said Meghan Marriner.

Ned ignored that as best he could.

Kate sat at the dining-room table with paper and pen and gestured for Vera Lajoie to sit beside her. She did so.

Then she proceeded to give extremely precise directions to the mountain chasm where Marius of the Romans had sacrificed a number of Celtic chieftains twenty-one hundred years ago.

NED WAS STUDYING the directions, in Kate's very neat handwriting. He lifted his head, saw his mother looking at him. "This," she said, "is hard for me. I really want to forbid you."

"I know," he said.

"Or I want to come."

He smiled a bit. "I'll be running, Mom. Uncle Dave has a bad leg. Steve can't run. Greg for sure can't."

"I can," said Kate.

"No!" said Meghan and Kim, simultaneously.

"Don't even think it," Meghan Marriner added. Kate bit her lip. Meghan looked at her sister. "Kim, can he even do anything?"

Aunt Kim had her arms folded across her chest again. "Honestly? I don't know. I don't think either of them mean him harm."

"But you don't know."

"We *can't* know, Meg."

"Even with what you . . . ?"

Her sister shook her head. "I have next to nothing here. All I can tell you is that I do think Melanie's gone if one of them finds her. And that Ned *is* inside this somehow."

"I accept that. But I'm also his mother, Kim. You can't imagine—" She stopped. Shook her head. "Oh, dear. I'm sorry."

Kimberly's eyes were bright. "Don't be. I have no children, but I *can* imagine what it might be like to let him go. I've seen it done."

"Let's do this," Ned said, as confidently as he could. He didn't think he was fooling anyone. "Who's driving me?"

"Hold it," said Greg. "If they might be tracking you, we need to do this carefully."

"I'll screen myself," Ned said, "starting now. And we go out in two cars. Even three?"

"But if they're watching the house?" Steve asked. "Like Dr. Marriner said? They'll see you leave. They don't care about the rest of us."

"Ned and I swap clothes," Kate Wenger said suddenly.

They looked at her. She stood up from the table.

"What do you mean?" Ned said. "You aren't wearing anything that belongs to you, anyhow."

Kate made a face. "Don't be funny. I mean we'll hurry out to two cars, but I dress like you, you wear the McGill thing . . ."

"That's my own sweatshirt."

"But they've seen me in it, last night and today, if they *have* been watching. You wear my brother's white shirt under it, I put on that uncool windbreaker of yours, and your baseball cap."

"It isn't uncool," he protested.

"Hush. She's right, Ned," Kim said. "It makes sense."

"All right," said Dave. "One car goes west or north, somewhere—the one that looks like it has Ned in it—and the other takes him to the mountain." He smiled at Kate. "Very good."

"Good?" she said, tossing her head. "It's heroic. I *never* wear baseball caps."

Ned's father sighed. He looked at his wife, then at Ned. "Oliver said the same thing as Vera, you know. It's apparently dangerous off the paths, Ned."

"Falling off a mountain is the least of my worries," Ned said.

"As to that," said Aunt Kim, "here's one thing."

She took off the only bracelet she wore, the silver one with the green stone. "I have no idea if this will help, but there's a chance."

"What is it?" It was Meghan.

Kim looked at her. "A gift, a long time ago. It connects to all this, I guess you could say. It may help with the sickness. Or not. But it won't hurt."

Ned took the bracelet and slipped it on. He felt nothing, though the metal was cool on his wrist.

He shrugged. "Let's do this," he said again.

Vera came back from the kitchen. She was holding leaves, a bunch of them, tied together. Gravely, she gave them to Ned.

"Thank you," he said.

He wasn't about to say no, was he? He looked down at his aunt's bracelet. Made a face. "I mean, like, what would have been wrong with a machine gun, eh?"

No one laughed.

His mother was staring at him. That same expression as before. As if Meghan Marriner were looking at her child and seeing someone she didn't quite know, or else she was memorizing his face.

"Mom . . ." he began.

She shook her head. "Go," she said.

CHAPTER XVIII

I n the van, wearing Kate's brother's shirt and his own McGill hoodie over jeans, Ned did his best to focus. He had his small runner's pack with him, would change into sweatpants and a T-shirt as soon as they hit the road east.

He'd screened himself before going out the door, so had Aunt Kim. Checking within, neither of them had sensed the presence of either of the two men—which wasn't anywhere close to conclusive, he knew.

He'd taken three Advil and brought half a dozen more, and his sunglasses. Thinking now about how he'd felt the last time they went past the mountain dragged his thoughts pretty conclusively away from the scent of Kate Wenger on the white shirt. He felt scared.

Kate—in his blue-and-white rugby shirt and the slandered windbreaker and retro Expos baseball cap—was with Uncle Dave and Steve in the red car. Greg was driving the van. Ned's father was up front, and Aunt Kim was beside him in back—because his aunt *would* be with Kate, not Ned.

Kate had worked this out, too. Detail person. Geek. Long legs. He had her written-out directions in his backpack. Front flap pocket. He'd put the rowan leaves in there, too.

Ned's mother had stayed in the villa. He wasn't sure why, but the hug she'd given him at the door was fierce. Fierce enough to make him more afraid.

Greg hit the remote control and led the other car through the gates. They went down the roadway towards the street. They would split after the first turn there: the red car west and north to Entremont, the van to Sainte-Victoire.

"You have your phone?" his father said, from the front seat. He'd asked that already, in the house.

Ned nodded. "Got it, Dad, yeah."

"It's charged?"

"Yes, Dad."

"You'll call if *anything* comes up?"

"I will."

This wasn't the time, Ned thought, to be hung up on sounding like an almost-adult.

"Ned," said his aunt, "listen to me. If one of them gets to you, either one, and he orders you to stop . . . honey, you have to stop. They won't be at their best if they decide she's up there. Don't assume you're safe."

He looked at her. "I won't," he said.

Won't be at their best. One way to put it.

His father, looking back at the two of them, swore softly.

Then, a moment later, for a different reason, Greg swore, much more loudly, and hammered the brakes.

Ned looked back quickly, but Uncle Dave wasn't tailgating. He skidded the red car to a halt behind them.

Ned leaned forward and looked out the front windshield.

"Oh, God," he said.

His aunt was already flipping open her cellphone, speed-dialing, and then, with more urgency than he'd heard from her yet, she snapped, "Dave, do *not* get out! Stay in your car!"

He looked at her. His father turned around.

"No!" Aunt Kim said. "Dave, this is *not* for you. Stay there!"

But by then, Ned had unlocked his own door, slid it back, and stepped into the road himself.

He was really, really angry.

For an instant, he wondered why it had been so important that his uncle stay in the car. He wanted to ask, but didn't have time. It occurred to him that there were a lot of questions you might have and never learn the answers to. He wasn't even sure why he was in the road himself, with so much fury. He heard his father shout his name from behind. A long way behind, it seemed. He walked in front of the van.

"Hey, you!" he yelled.

The boar, blocking the road, didn't move.

It didn't even look at him. It was gazing past Ned, past the van, off into the woods beside the road, as if oblivious to his presence.

It really was massive. The size of a small bear, practically, with short, matted bristly hair, more grey than white. The tusks were curved and heavy. There was mud on them, and on the body, caked and plastered to the hair. The boar was dead centre in the road, and there was no way around it.

"Get out of here!" Ned shouted. "Damn it, *you're* the one who showed me where to go. What are you doing?"

The animal didn't move. It didn't even seem to have heard him. It was as if Ned didn't exist for it. As if . . .

Ned was about to shout again, but he didn't. Instead he took a deep breath. Then he released his screening.

When he did that, the boar turned its head. It looked straight at him, the small, bright eyes fixed on his. Ned swallowed.

"I'm here," he said, not really knowing *what* he was saying. "I listened. Figured it out. I'm going up. Let me go."

For a long moment it was very still on that country lane. No sound from the cars behind Ned, no movement from the creature in front.

No movement. They were stuck here, blocked. And Ysabel might be up on the mountain, and time mattered. They needed to *move*. Feeling a hard white surge of anger, Ned brought his two hands up, palms together, extended. He levelled them at the dirt road beside the animal. He shivered. A flash of light exploded from him and struck sparks from the ground, spraying dust and gravel forward.

The boar looked at him another moment, then it turned, unhurried, undisturbed, and trotted through the ditch and the underbrush and into the trees.

"Sweet Lord," Ned heard Greg say, behind him. "What is going *on*?"

Ned hustled back into the van. He pushed his door shut. "Drive!" he said. "Fast, Greg. I have a feeling it just let them know where I am. Maybe more than that."

He checked within for the presence of the two men; found nothing. He put his screening back on.

"Why would it do that?" his father said. "Jesus, Ned. And how did you . . . ?"

"I don't *know*." Questions, no answers. "But I have to beat them there. Let's go."

"Does it *serve* them?" Edward Marriner asked. There were deep, parallel lines creasing his forehead.

"Not that creature," Aunt Kim said.

"Then what . . . ?"

"Don't know," she replied. "Go, Greg."

Greg shifted into gear, hit the gas. He ran the stop sign at the bottom, taking the corner hard to the left. At the main crossroad he turned left again. Looking back, Ned saw Uncle Dave signal and turn the other way, going just as fast.

Ned pushed off his track shoes and undid his belt, wriggling out of his jeans. Aunt Kim handed him the sweats and he worked his way into them. He put his shoes on again and laced them. Took a swig of water from his bottle. He should stretch, he knew, but it wasn't going to happen. He took off the McGill sweatshirt and Kate's white shirt. He pulled on his Grateful Dead T-shirt. Maybe not the very best logo for today, he thought. He stuffed the hoodie into his pack. Vera had said it would be cold on the mountaintop.

Where he was headed, with the sun going down.

GREG SPOTTED the brown sign. He slowed at a slight curve, and then they saw cars in a lot beside the highway.

"Do it fast," Ned said tersely. "Just slow down, I'm going to jump out, you keep going."

He was having trouble talking.

He was pretty sure he was about to be sick again. Wanted to get out of the van before that happened—and his father or his aunt stopped him from going.

Advil, rowan leaves, a supernatural screening, his aunt's bracelet. Not a lot of good, any of them, or all of them together. The world was tinged towards red again here by Mont Sainte-Victoire, where two hundred thousand people had been slaughtered once upon a known time.

He took a breath, and told himself it was *not* as bad as before. That there probably *was* some benefit from the combination of things he was using. Enough to let him function. He hoped. He put his sunglasses on.

"Ned, you okay?" Aunt Kim asked.

"Yeah," he lied.

His father looked back at him. Edward Marriner's face was drawn and fearful. Ned's heart hurt to see it. "I'm fine," he lied again. "I can do this. I have my phone."

Cellphones, solution to the problems of the world.

"Go!" Greg said, angling the van onto the shoulder, just behind a parked Citroën. He pushed the door-lock button.

Ned shoved his door back and jumped out with his pack. Shoved the door shut and scooted among the parked cars, keeping low.

He had no idea why he was doing this, as if someone might actually be spying on him here. It felt ridiculous, but on the other hand, after that encounter with the boar, he realized—more than ever—that he hadn't a clue how to deal with any of this.

He took a fast look at the big signboard showing the various mountain trails, noted the symbol that marked the way to the cross at the summit, and then he started running.

One thing he could do. A thing he was *good* at. He was on the cross-country team, he was keeping a training log here, he could go fast for a long time.

Assuming he didn't throw up from the pain behind his eyes.

It's manageable, he told himself. *Run through it. She's up there. And there's no one else who can do this.*

Not that this meant that *he* could do it.

The trail began at a smooth slant upwards, gravelled, wide. People were coming down, some dressed for a picnic with packs and baskets, others wearing serious hiking gear, carrying sticks. He saw some kids; they looked pretty tired.

He glanced up, a long way, to the summit with its cross. The chapel would be just below that, and left. He couldn't see it yet. He settled in, as best he could, to his pace. It was hard, because he hadn't warmed up at all and because he felt dreadful. The smell was the worst; it was everywhere, more than the pain or the sickly red hue the world had taken on. David Letterman should do this one, he thought: *Top ten reasons not to climb Mont Sainte-Victoire . . .*

Through everything there was fear, a sense of urgency that kept pushing him to go faster. He checked his watch. It was supposed to be a two-hour walk-and-climb. He was going to cut that in half, or better, or break himself trying.

Unlucky thought. Pain lanced like a knitting needle behind his right eye. Ned cried out, couldn't help it. He staggered, almost fell. He twisted to the right off the wide path, out of sight, and was violently sick in the bushes behind a boulder.

And then again. It felt as if his stomach were trying to force itself inside out. He was on his knees, leaning against the roughness of the big rock. He forced himself to breathe slowly. His forehead was clammy; he'd broken out in a sweat. He was shivering.

Another slow breath. And with it, through pain and nausea, Ned felt anger again, hard as a weapon. It was weird, a little frightening, how much rage he was feeling. He shook his head in grim denial, though there was no one to see, no one to be denying.

"Uh-uh," he said aloud, to the mountain and the sky. "No way. Not going to happen." He wasn't leaving this time, he wasn't going to call and have Greg drive him back to take a shower and lie down and have everyone in the villa tell him at least he'd tried, he'd done all he could.

It *wasn't* all he could. He wouldn't let it be. You could do more. When it mattered enough, you did more. There were stories of mothers lifting *cars* off kids trapped under them.

"Not going to happen," he said again.

He wiped sweat off his forehead with the back of one hand. She was up there. He knew it as surely as he'd known anything. And there was only him here, Ned Marriner. Not his aunt—whatever she'd done once, she couldn't do it now. Neither could his uncle. His mom could treat refugees in the Sudan but she couldn't get up this mountain in time or do anything at the top if she did. Ned was the one linked to all this, seeing the blood, smelling the memory of bloodshed.

You didn't *ask* for the roles you were given in life; not always, anyhow.

He realized that he was clenching his jaw. He made himself relax. You couldn't run that way, and he had running to do.

He swung his pack off, fished his iPod out and put the buds in his ears. He dialed up Coldplay. Maybe rock would do what bracelets and rowan leaves couldn't.

He shouldered the pack and stepped onto the path again. He must have looked pretty alarming because two people—a husband and wife, it looked like—stopped suddenly on their way down and stared at him with concern.

Ned straightened, managed a wan smile. Popped off his buds.

"You are all right? You should not be going up now!" the woman said in French, with a German accent.

"It's fine," Ned said, wiping at his mouth. "Bit of a bug. I've had worse. I do this run all the time. Training." He was surprised at how good he'd become at lying.

"It will be dark," the man said, shaking his head. "And the climb is harder above."

"I know it," said Ned. "Thanks, though." He put the earbuds back in, turned up the volume.

He ran. Around a curve he reached back for his water bottle in the side pocket of the pack and rinsed his mouth, then splashed some on his face without slowing down. He spat into the bushes. His head was still pounding.

Not going to volunteer for an Advil commercial, he thought.

Amused himself with that. Just a little. He was in too much pain for more. He wondered about the screening he was doing—when the draining effect Phelan and his aunt had warned about would kick in. He had no idea.

He ran, twisting through and past weekend climbers making their tired way down the mountain at day's end. Above him, way above, he could see the big cross at the summit. He was going there, then left, down a ridge, up another, down to the right.

Or so Veracook had said.

One woman looked at her watch as he approached and gave him an admonishing sideways shake of her finger, that gesture the French loved. His mother, he thought, should take that one up.

He *knew* it was late in the day. He *knew* it was going to be windy and get dark . . . this wasn't being done for the joy of it. Maybe he should have printed leaflets to hand out to all the finger-waggers.

He ran. After almost thirty minutes on the steady upward slant he realized two things. One was that he was feeling better. He didn't have that overwhelming sense of the world rotting all around him. He'd hoped that getting above the level of the battlefield would help, and it seemed to be doing that. He felt like offering a prayer.

His head hurt, the world was red-tinted, even behind sunglasses, but he didn't feel any more as if he was going to empty his guts with pain in response to putrefaction.

The other thing, less encouraging by a lot, was that there was someone behind him—and it was Cadell.

The Celt was just suddenly *there* when Ned did one of his quick inward checks for an aura. Nothing, nothing, nothing . . . then there he was: golden inside Ned's mind, as in life.

And coming up the mountain.

They won't be at their best, his aunt had said. Meaning something a lot worse than that.

She had ordered Ned to stop if they came up to him, either of them, and told him to leave. He'd known she was right about that and he knew it now. They might mean him no harm, but that was only if he didn't get in their way. They were alive in the world to do one thing only: find her. Two hundred thousand people and more had died in a single battle between these two. What was a Canadian kid against that?

His heart was pounding, for all the reasons that had to do with running as fast as he could up a mountain, fighting pain and nausea, and pursued by someone who had so many lifetimes of white and burning need to get to the chasm first.

It had been the boar that had called them, he was certain of it.

That's how Cadell was here. He had no idea *why* the animal had done it. You sure got a lot of questions in the world, without exactly getting the same number of answers. In fact, there was a *huge* gap between the two numbers. It made him angry again. He needed that, to fuel him, drive him on, push back fear.

He looked up again. There was a wooden sign ahead, symbols on it. The sloped path gave out here to terraced, switchbacked ridges. Vera had told him this. It got harder, angling back and forth because it was steeper now. He saw people still coming down, left and right, left and right, along the switchbacks. It was going to be slower, narrower, hard to run through them. He took the first cut to the right, got out his water bottle again to drink.

His phone rang.

He fished in his pocket, saw who it was on the read-out.

"Dad," he said quickly, "I'm okay, I'm running. Can't talk."

He flipped the phone shut. He was supposed to tell them Cadell was behind him now? Was it a tough guess what they'd say?

It was pretty simple, really. Way Ned saw it, if the big man didn't catch him, he couldn't stop him or do anything to him, right? So you didn't let him catch you. It didn't always have to be complicated.

He thought of letting his screening go, but he didn't know what might hit him—flatten him—if he did. How much the screen was protecting him from the mountain. He couldn't afford to lose any time now.

And there was the other man, too. Ned didn't for a second imagine Phelan wasn't up here somewhere. Probably screened, like Ned. Cadell was announcing himself, trying to frighten Ned, maybe warn him off. Phelan was just . . . coming.

Could scare you more, that thought.

It was still bright up here, the sun setting to his right, the wind picking up but blocked a little because he wasn't completely above the trees yet. He looked back over his shoulder. There was a lake or reservoir of some kind below, glinting in the light, and another one farther beyond. He was high enough to see a long way. The view was beautiful, and he wasn't even halfway up.

There had been a fire on these slopes, Ned saw, maybe more than one. The mountain was more bare than it looked in those paintings Cézanne had done. Time changed things, even mountains. Even a hundred years could make changes—or however long it was since Cézanne painted this peak. Was that a long time or a blink of time?

He thought he knew what the two men and Ysabel would say. But he also remembered his mother and aunt on the path from the tower last night, and it occurred to him that they might think of twenty-five years as heartbreakingly long.

He didn't have answers. He amped up his music a little more and he ran, zigzagging up the mountain as the day waned towards an ending.

AFTER TWENTY MINUTES of laboured, driving work, back and forth along the terraced slope, twisting his way through the last of the day's descending climbers, he smashed, hard, into the inner screening wall he'd been warned about.

Too soon! he thought, but even as the thought came his legs gave out and Ned felt himself falling. He didn't slide, this was still more a steep hike than a climb, but he lay in the middle of the narrow switchback, exhausted, drained, and it felt for a long moment like he wasn't going to be able to get up.

And that wouldn't do. With an effort he pulled his earbuds out and rolled to one elbow. His small running pack felt massive, a burden on his back. He worked to shrug himself out of it. There was a taste of dust in his mouth. Better than blood, he thought.

Then, with apprehension coiling tightly within him, he released the screen, because there was nothing else he could do.

He cried out. Couldn't help it.

The immediate pain in his head was brutal: a vise, not knitting needles or a hammer. He'd been right, not that it did him any good now—the screening *had* been keeping at bay the full impact of where he was.

Eyes tightly closed, gasping for thin, shallow breaths, aware that there were tears on his face, Ned realized he was going to have to phone down after all. He wasn't even sure he could stay conscious till someone got here to him.

He opened his eyes, forced himself to look up from where he lay. And facing east, he saw the chapel below the summit's great cross. It wasn't even far; he'd gotten pretty damned close. They'd have to give him credit for that, wouldn't they?

There was nobody else up here. No one had heard his cry. Every sane person had passed him already, going down the long slope towards drinks and a shower, sunset and dinner, out of the wind that was blowing here.

Ned felt something else then: a pulse like a probe in his head. He made himself, moving *very* slowly, sit up. Everything took so much appalling effort, hurt so much. He looked within himself.

Cadell's aura was still there. And the pulse, the signal, was coming from him.

Of course, Ned thought. *You're clueless, Marriner. A loon.*

He'd been thinking of Cadell as chasing him, but he'd been *screened.* The Celt hadn't been able to see Ned any more than Ned had spotted him down there. Cadell was just powering his way towards the summit, not knowing if Ned was ahead or behind, or anywhere at all.

Now, though, he realized it, and he was making sure Ned knew he was coming.

I should be afraid, Ned thought. He actually felt too weak for fear, as if all he wanted to do, all he could do, was sit here among dust and stones and scrubby little bushes and let the sun go down on these slopes, and on him.

Well, he could make a phone call first. Someone would come. His aunt was in the call-back. His dad was on auto-dial, and so was Greg. Well, not really, in fact. Melanie had done that very funny nine- or ten-digit auto-dial for Greg on Ned's phone. Then Ned had rigged their phones with ringtones in the middle of the night.

He could almost smile, remembering when he'd called her the next morning at the cathedral. *"You will be made to suffer!"* Melanie had said, but she'd been laughing.

If they were understanding anything about this properly, she was somehow up above him right now, not that far.

He thought about her laughing that morning, and something in him altered with the memory. Anger, Ned thought, could drive you hard. It could ruin you or make you, like any other really strong feeling, he guessed.

Right now, it pulled him to his feet.

He realized, straightening carefully, that he could handle this pain too. It had been the *contrast*, the shock of it when the screen went down, that had flattened him. But he was really high now, far above the plain where the battle had been, and he could hold it together for a bit longer. The weakness in his legs was something else, one more thing. Like he really, *really* needed more. He could almost hear his friend Larry saying that, the guys laughing.

Cadell was coming, and he was aware now that Ned was ahead of him.

With an effort that cost him, Ned shouldered his pack again. Since when were these things so heavy? His legs felt rubbery, the way they could near the end of a cross-country race. But he'd done those races for three years now, he *knew* this feeling. It was new, and it wasn't. You could build on what you had experienced, and he'd smashed into walls running before.

That's what it was all about, the track coach had always told them. You find where your wall is, and you train to push it back, but when you hit it . . . you go through. If you can do that, you're a runner. Ned could hear that voice, too, in his mind.

Ned went through. He was almost comically slow. Walking, not running. In places here—he was right below the chapel now—there were loose rocks on the path that could send you tumbling.

He looked back. And this time he saw someone coming, already on the switchback section, steady and strong and fast.

Ned felt like crying, which was *really* not going to help. He looked ahead. There were two zigzags left, or he could climb. He wasn't sure he had the strength for that, but he was pretty certain he didn't have the time not to. He clenched his jaw—an expression one or two people would have recognized—and left the path. He bent to the slanting rock face, using his hands now.

It wasn't alpine climbing or anything like that. Any normal time, any normal condition, he could have propelled himself up this slope easily. He could have *raced* guys up here.

Now, two or three times he was sure he was going to fall. His hands were sweaty, and there was sweat in his eyes. He took off the sunglasses, they were sliding down his nose. The light wasn't as strong now, the sun low, striking the mountain, washing it in late-day colours. He still saw too much red, but not as badly as before, this high up.

Really high, in fact. He pushed himself, feet and hands, digging and pulling, gasping with the effort it cost him. His T-shirt was plastered to his body. His head hurt; it was pulsing. His legs felt as if he were wearing weights. Was this, he thought, what getting old was like? When your body wouldn't do things you *knew* it had been able to do? Another essay topic?

Idiot thought. "You're a loon!" he said aloud, and made himself laugh: the sound sudden and startling in that lonely, windy place. He took strength from it. Anger wasn't the only thing you could use.

And, falling apart or not, he was up. He pushed with his right foot at a rock. It slipped away, tumbling down the slope, but his hands were on the top now and he scrambled to the last plateau.

He was directly in front of the chapel. He bent over, catching his breath, trying to control his trembling. He was so weak. There was a courtyard, he saw through an arched opening: a well, a low stone wall on the far side overlooking the southern slopes. The sea would be beyond, some distance off, but not all that far.

He glanced back again. Cadell was clearly visible, golden-haired, cutting straight up across all the switchbacks, hand over hand through scrub and bush, disdaining the path. He wouldn't need paths, Ned thought. He wanted to hate this man—and the other one—and knew he was never going to be able to do that.

He could beat them, though.

It was easier here, on the level ground just below the last steep ridge to the summit and cross. He didn't have to go up there. If Veracook was right—and it occurred to him that if she wasn't he had done all this to no purpose at all—he had to head east, not up.

He looked ahead and saw, as she'd said he would, the mountain falling away to the south in a swooping sheet of stone just beyond the cross. The view was spectacular in the light of the westering sun, fast clouds overhead in the wind.

But that wasn't his route. The garagai was farther along, she'd said. Up one more slope, the one right in front of him, and *then* down and right along the next rock face.

He looked back one more time. Cadell was moving ridiculously fast. He saw the man lift his head and shout something. He couldn't hear; the wind was too strong. It could blow you off the mountain, Ned thought, if you were, like, a little kid, or careless.

He dropped his pack against the stone wall of the chapel and pushed himself into a run. A shambling, dragging motion, an embarrassment, a joke, and he couldn't even keep it going. The slope of this ridge was upwards again, and he was too drained, too spent. The wind from the north, on his left, kept pushing him towards the long slide south. He did slip once, banging his knee. He thought he heard a shout behind him. He didn't look back.

Fighting for breath, fighting his body, he scrambled up the last ridge. He had to go right here, south and down. He looked that way. Steep, he'd need to be careful. He saw nothing, but Vera had said you couldn't, that the cave was hidden until you were right on it. The green land far below was the battlefield, he knew. The plain below the mountain. All those dead, all those years ago. The man behind him had been there.

And the woman ahead, if she really was here.

Ned started down. Too fast, he slipped and skidded almost immediately. He steadied himself, but was still moving too quickly. He stumbled again, leaning way backwards so as not to tumble and roll on the face of the mountain. He banged an elbow and swore as he scrabbled on the seat of his pants, dislodging pebbles. He grabbed for a rock, felt his palm tear and scrape, but he stopped himself.

He saw the cave, right beside him.

The gemstone of his aunt's bracelet was bright on his wrist. He didn't know what that was about, when it had started. He didn't have time to think about it. He shifted along the rock face and saw that there was a last descent—a short one—into the cave. There was light coming through it from another side, south. Vera had said there were two openings.

And that the chasm was below it, through the other entrance.

He was here.

Ned went in, turning his face to the rocks, going hand and foot again. He slid the last bit, touched bottom, turned and looked around. He was still trembling, his legs mostly. His mouth was dry. He'd left the water bottle with his pack.

He was in a darkened space, not too large, sheltered from the wind, level underfoot. A rock roof disappeared into shadow above. He didn't know what he'd expected to see, but he didn't see anything.

He turned to look south and his jaw dropped at the wonder of it, the quiet beauty spread out through that wider opening, as if it were a window onto glory. The fields below, a glinting line of river, the land rising a very little, and falling, and then rising again across the river towards mountains in the distance, shining in the late, clear light, and then the far blue of the sea.

He walked over and looked down. Another drop, a trickier one, because the shelf below was steep, more a slope than a plateau, really. He'd been warned it was dangerous. *I'm not going to fall off a mountain*, he'd told his father.

He could fall off down there, easily. But on that slanting shelf, to his right, Ned saw a cluster of dark green bushes against the sheer rock face. They framed an emptiness, a black, a hole in the world. The chasm was here. He *had* arrived. For what it was worth.

He was very much afraid. He took a breath. Lifted his dirty hands and spat on them the way athletes did. There was blood on one of them, from grabbing at stone as he slid. He wiped it on his sweats.

"Here goes nuthin'," he said. Little kids said things like that. He was trying to be funny, for himself.

"You do not have to go down," he heard, behind him. "I am here."

CHAPTER XIX

S he came from the back of the cave, from shadow and dream to where the light slanted through the wide window of that southern opening, reaching her.

Ned hadn't thought he'd ever see her again. Her presence became a different kind of blow to the heart. He wanted to kneel, explain, apologize. He didn't know *what* to do. He was here, he had done it, and he was empty of thought, or any sense of how to act.

She walked towards him, the auburn hair bright as the late-day sunlight touched her. She was as tall as he was.

She stopped, regarding him, and smiled, not unkindly.

"It is difficult to stay down there," she said. "There is too much wind. It feels as if the mountain wants to throw you off . . . or send you into the chasm."

He nodded jerkily. He couldn't speak. The sound of her voice undid him, left him feeling bereft with the thought that he might be hearing it now and never again.

He thought of the sculpture in the cloister. Phelan's offering, showing her as half gone from the beginning, even before time began its work. Eluding as she emerged. He understood it now. You saw Ysabel as you stood before her, heard that voice, and you felt loss *in the moment* because you feared she might leave you.

Because you knew she would.

She was gazing steadily at him, appraising, more curious than anything else. Her eyes were blue, or green. It was difficult to tell, there were shadows behind her and above. There was no malice, no anger here, though he couldn't see warmth, either. But why should he have expected that? What could he possibly have expected?

"How are you here?" she said.

That, at least, he should have been ready for. But it was difficult to form thoughts that made sense. Stammering, he said, "You . . . you said sacrifice. At Entremont. Not just killing."

Amusement, the eyebrows arched. She was barefoot on the cold stone, he saw. Wearing a long, white cotton skirt and a blue blouse over it. Her hair was down, along her back, framing her face.

"I did," she agreed, still studying him. "You were there?"

He nodded.

"Unwise. You might have died, had they known it."

He nodded. Phelan had known it. He didn't say that.

"There are many places of sacrifice," she said.

They'd figured that out, too. He said, "My mother got the sacrifice part, when we told her. And . . . a boar gave me a clue."

He didn't tell about Melanie, the story she'd told him of the battle below. The sacrifice of the chieftains here. He was going to need to speak of Melanie, he had no idea how.

Her expression changed. "Your mother gave you that?" She was pointing at the bracelet. The stone was bright.

He shook his head. "My aunt. Her sister." He hesitated. It wasn't his, but, "Would you like it?"

She smiled, pleased, but shook her head, looking at him.

A long, still moment, quiet in the cave, the wind blowing outside, the sun going down. The living world so far from where they were.

Then Ysabel smiled again, but differently.

"Now I see," she said, and the tone had altered as well, changes in her voice and face, like ripples in water. Ned wasn't sure—he wasn't sure of anything—but he thought he heard sadness, and maybe something else.

"What is there to see?"

She didn't answer. She turned away—he felt it as a wound—then she lifted a hand, stilling him.

He heard it too, and was looking towards the entrance through which he'd come himself when Cadell jumped down and in.

He landed, noted Ned's presence. Then he turned to Ysabel.

He didn't speak, and the woman said nothing either, absorbing, accepting what was inescapable in his face. There was nothing hidden in him, nothing held back. Watching the two of them Ned felt like the intruder he was: excluded, inappropriate, trivial. If he was right, if he understood this at all, Cadell had died more than two thousand years ago, in the chasm below this cave.

"You have a wound," she said, speaking first.

"A knife. It is inconsequential."

"Indeed. What would be of consequence?"

Ned remembered that ironic tone from Beltaine, after the fires and the bull. He realized his hands were shaking again.

Cadell's deep voice carried a note that could only be called joy. He said, "Coming here to find the Roman before me. That would shatter this heart as much as would the sky falling at the end of days."

"Ah," she said, "the poet returns?"

"He never left you. You know that, love."

"I know very little," she said, in that voice that made a lie of the words.

"You know that I am here, and before your three nights have turned. I remember this place."

"But of *course* you do," said another voice, from behind Ned and below.

They all wheeled. But even as he did, Ned saw Ysabel's face, and he realized she was unsurprised.

They watched as Phelan pulled himself up from the slanting plateau below the opening to the south.

He stood, unhurried, brushing dust from his knees and the torn jacket, using his right hand only. Then he, in turn, looked at the woman.

"A wound?" said Ysabel.

"Inconsequential." Ned saw the bald head, the scar, the grey, cool eyes and then—with surprise—a smile.

"You heard that?" She was smiling, too.

"It is my proof of being present, love. I need to have heard that or you might not believe me."

"You would lie to me?"

He shook his head. "Never in any life. But you have disbelieved before."

"With cause?"

Phelan looked at her. Then shook his head again. "With a right to do so, but not with cause."

The brief smile had gone. There was hunger in his face, and longing, so fierce they were a kind of light.

"You were below," said Cadell flatly.

"A harder climb, yes, but I was south and had to come that way."

"It doesn't matter. You were not *here*."

Phelan shrugged. "No? Tell me, what did she ask the boy, about his bracelet?"

Ned felt the weight of three gazes upon him. He wanted to be invisible, absent, *gone*.

Then he heard her laughter. "I see. You will say that you did hear, and so came to me first?"

Phelan was looking at the other man, his eyes cold as wilderness, waiting. The light in his face was gone. There was no reply from the Celt. Phelan said, precisely, "She asked him if his mother gave the bracelet to him. Shall I tell now his reply that you also did not hear?"

Wolf on a mountain peak.

Cadell's blue gaze, returning, was as hard, though, unyielding. It never *had* yielded, Ned knew.

"It makes no matter how and where you climbed or what you heard below. You were not here to find her first."

A silence in that high place. It felt like the last silence of the world, Ned Marriner thought.

Ysabel ended it. Ended more than stillness.

"He was not. It is true," she murmured. "But neither were you, my golden one. Alas, that I am unloved, but neither were you."

And as she stopped, as that voice fell away, the three of them turned to Ned again.

It might have been the hardest thing he'd yet done, to stand straight, not draw back. Face them, breathing hard, but controlling it. He looked from one man to the other, and ended with Ysabel. The long travel of her gaze, how far it seemed to go, to reach him.

"He is not part of this," Cadell said.

"Untrue," she said, still softly. "Did he not lead you here? Will you say he did not? That you found me yourself?"

"The boar guided him," Phelan said. "The druid's."

No fire or ice now. A sudden, intense gravity that was, in its own way, more frightening. As if the stakes, with what she'd said, had become too high for fury or flame.

"It isn't the druid's boar," said Cadell. "Brys served it, not the other way around."

"I didn't know that," Phelan said. "I thought—"

"I know what you thought. The beast is older than any of us."

Phelan's thin smile. "Even us?"

Cadell nodded. The light from the south caught his golden hair.

The woman remained silent, letting them speak across her, to each other.

"And so it was the boar . . . caused this?"

Cadell shook his head. "It made this possible, at best. The boy could have died at Entremont, in Alyscamps, by the round tower. I could have killed him in Glanum where I killed you, once." His turn to smile, lips closed. "You could have killed him many times. Is it not so?"

Phelan nodded. "I suppose. I saw no reason to have him die. I helped them get away, when the needfires were lit."

"Perhaps a mistake." The deep voice.

The other man shrugged. "I have made others." He looked at Ysabel, and then at Ned again, his brow furrowed now.

Cadell said, "We could have been here ahead of him. I saw him fall, twice. The boar made this harder for him, showing us where he was going."

"And your meaning is?"

Cadell's teeth flashed this time. "My thinking is too hard for you? Really? You said the boar caused this. It isn't so."

And still the woman did not speak.

She stood as if barely attending to them, withdrawing even as she remained. Ned thought of the sculpture again, sunlit in the sheltered cloister. It was cold here now, so far above the world.

Phelan said, "There is another way to see it, if you are right—the animal bringing us both."

"Yes. I also have that thought."

"I killed you once here, did I not? With some others."

"You know you did. They were lost in the chasm."

"Not you."

"They were lost," Cadell repeated quietly.

Phelan's wintry smile. "You cling to that, among so many deaths."

"It is more than dying, there."

"Not for you, with me alive to hold you to returning. You would have known it even as you went down."

"They didn't. They were lost there."

"Yes. Not you."

"So I owe you my life?" The bite of irony.

They actually smiled at each other in that moment. Ned would remember that.

"As you said," Phelan murmured. "We could have arrived ahead of him."

"As I said."

They both looked at Ned again.

He said, in a small voice, "I'm sorry, I think."

Cadell laughed aloud.

"No, you aren't," said Phelan. "You've been refusing to leave this from the outset."

A small, maybe a last, flare within. "You don't know me well enough to say what I feel," Ned said.

A moment, and then Phelan—stranger, Greek, Roman—nodded. "You are right. Forgive me. It is entirely possible to need or want something, and be sorry it is so." He hesitated again. "It appears I did more than I intended when I brought you into this. I could not say, even now, what made me do it. What I saw."

"No? I can," said Ysabel, breaking her stillness, returning to them. Then she added, with sudden passion, *"Look at him!"*

The two men did so, again. Ned closed his eyes this time, his mind racing, lost. He opened them. And saw, in both men at the same moment, a dawning as of light—and then a setting of the sun.

Neither spoke for a long time.

Cadell made one quick, outward gesture with his good hand that Ned didn't understand. Then he pushed fingers through his long hair. He drew a deep breath. Lifted the hand, and let it fall again. He turned to Phelan.

"You truly didn't know," he said to the other man, "when you drew him in?"

Phelan hadn't moved. Or taken his gaze from Ned. He still didn't. "I knew something. I said that. Not this. How would I know this?"

Know what? Ned wanted to scream. He was afraid to speak.

Cadell, quietly, said, "We might have realized, when we saw the mother and her sister."

Phelan nodded. "I suppose." He was white-faced, Ned saw. Shaken to the core, trying to deal with it.

Cadell pushed a hand through his hair again. He turned to Ysabel. She was standing very straight now, extremely still, gathered to herself: a beauty near to stone, it might seem, but not truly so.

The big man looked at Ned for a moment, and then back to her. He said, wonderingly, the deep voice soft, "The mother has your hair, even, near enough."

At which point, finally, very late, overwhelmed as if to a cliff's edge of stupefaction, feeling that waves were crashing there against his mind, Ned Marriner understood.

Who are you?

The repeated question, over and again. The one he'd hated, having no answer. Now he did. Ysabel had given it to the three of them.

The world rocked and spun, unstable and impossible. Ned made a small, helpless sound; he couldn't stop himself. This was too vast, it *meant* too many things, too many to get your head around.

He saw Phelan looking at her.

The wide, thin mouth quirked sideways. "When?" he whispered. And then, "Whose?"

Ned stopped breathing.

She smiled, grave and regal, not capricious or teasing now. She shook her head slowly. "Some things are not best told. Even in love. Perhaps especially in love. Is it not so?"

More questions than answers in the world, Ned thought.

Phelan lowered his head.

Her smile changed a little. "You knew I would say that?"

He looked up. "I never know what you will say."

"Never?" Faint hint of irony, but a sense she was reaching a long way for it.

"Almost never," he amended. "I did not expect this. None of this. Not the searching you decreed, forbidding battle. Not the boy being . . . what you say he is. Love, I am lost."

"And I," Cadell said. The other two turned to him. "You altered the story. He led us here. The boar guided him, and us. This means?"

This means?

Ysabel turned to Ned. The clear, distant gaze. The eyes were blue, not green, he saw. And something was unmistakable now. You would have to be blind, or truly a child, not to see it: the sadness that had come. She looked steadily at him and said, more softly than any words yet spoken, "What must I answer him, blood of my blood?"

He didn't reply. What could he possibly say? But he saw now— he did see—an answer to the one question, about his being here and his aunt and his mother, and their mother and hers, fathers or mothers back to a distant presence of light down a long tunnel from the past.

Where the woman before him waited in a far, faint brightness.

She turned from him, not waiting for an answer. Looked to one man and then the other. "You *know* what it means," she said. "You know what I said beside the animal that died to draw me into the world again. Neither of you found me first. You know what follows. The chasm is here. It is still here."

What will follow, you should not see.

Phelan had said that to him, at Entremont. But Ned had stayed, and seen, and led them here to this.

"You never said there was a child," Cadell murmured.

And Ysabel, quietly, echoed him. "I never said there was a child."

"Only the one?" Phelan's eyes never left her now.

"Only the one, ever. One of you killed the other, and then died himself, too soon, leaving me alone. But not entirely so. That time. I was carrying a gift."

"You do know what it will mean, love, if we go down together there? Both of us."

Cadell, the deep voice soft, but unafraid. Making certain.

She inclined her head gravely. "We all know what it will mean. But neither of you found me, and the boy is in the story." She had never seemed so much a queen as she did then, Ned thought, staring at her.

The two men turned—he would remember this, too—to look at each other. Fire and ice subsumed in something he wasn't smart enough—hadn't lived nearly long enough—to name.

Phelan turned back to her. He nodded his head slowly.

"I believe I see. An ending, love?" He hesitated. "Past due, must we say?"

Ysabel shook her head suddenly, fierce in denial. "I will not say that! I would never say that."

She turned to the bigger man. One and then the other. One and then the other. Ned wanted to back away, against the cave wall, feared to draw attention by moving.

She said to Cadell, "Do you still believe our souls find another home?"

"I always have, though perhaps not all of us. We have had a different arc, we three. I will not presume as to my soul. Not from that chasm."

"You will search for me? Wherever I am? If there is a way?"

Ned was crying now. He did back up until he bumped into the cold stone wall by the opening to the south. He could feel the wind here.

Cadell said, in that voice men and women might follow into war and across mountain ranges and through forests and into dark, "Wherever you are. Until the sun dies and the last wind blows through the worlds. Need you ask me? Even now?"

She shook her head again, and Ned heard her say, "No, I didn't need to ask, did I? My shining one. *Anwyll.*"

Beloved.

Cadell stood another moment looking at her, *memorizing* her, Ned wanted to say it was, and then—not reaching out, not touching her—he said, "It is time to go, then, I believe."

He turned and came this way towards the opening. At the edge of the drop he paused beside Ned and laid a hand upon his shoulder. No words.

Nor for the other man, though he did turn and they exchanged a glance, grey eyes and blue. Ned, weeping in silence, felt as if he could hear his blood passing through the chambers of his heart. *Blood of my blood.*

Cadell went down then, jumping over the edge to the steeply sloped plateau. Ned saw him in the late sun's shining, the very last of the day's light, as he walked over to the low, dark green bushes that surrounded the chasm that was a place of sacrifice, said in the tales to be bottomless.

He did pause there, but not in anything like fear, nothing of that at all, for when he looked up and back, past the two men to the woman, he was smiling again, golden and at ease.

And that is how Ned Marriner last saw him, through tears that would not stop, when he took a final step and went over to his ending without a sound.

Ned looked at emptiness where a man had been. He turned his face away. He saw a pair of birds wheeling to the south, across the mountain's side. The sky was not falling, though this was a time and place where you could imagine it doing so.

He turned back, to Phelan. That one stood another moment, looking down at the chasm. Then he came forward towards the drop to the plateau. He passed close, as Cadell had. He didn't touch Ned, though. Instead, he slipped out of his grey leather jacket and laid it, lightly, on Ned's shoulders.

"It will be cold when the sun goes down," he said. "There is a tear, I'm afraid, in one shoulder. Perhaps it can be repaired."

Ned couldn't speak. His throat was aching, and his heart. Tears made it difficult to see. Phelan looked at him another moment, as if he would say something else, but he didn't.

He went over the edge, lightly down as always, landing easily, and he went to the chasm's brink as the other man had done.

Ned heard Ysabel behind him. He didn't turn. He was afraid to look at her. The man below them did, though. He did look.

"*Anwyll,*" Ned heard her say, again.

The man so addressed smiled then, standing on a mountain so far from the world into which he had been born, claimed there by sunlight, which had not changed in all the years.

He looked past Ned, to where she would be. He spoke her name.

"Every breath," he said to her, at the end. "Every day, each and every time."

Then he stepped over the rim and down into the dark.

AFTER A FEW MOMENTS motionless against the cave wall, Ned had to sit down. He lowered his legs over the edge of the drop, looking out on the end of day and at the slanting ledge where no one stood any more. He hadn't known it was possible to feel this much sorrow, so hard and heavy an awareness of time.

Until the sun dies.

The sun was going down, would rise in the morning—people had to make themselves believe that it would each time nightfall came. He remembered Kate Wenger, only last night, talking of how sunset had never been a moment of beauty or peace in the past. Men and women fearing that the dark might come and not end.

He had stopped crying. He was drained of tears. He wiped at his cheeks, felt the bite of wind swirling. Two more birds, or the same ones, wheeled down and east and out of sight again. Phelan's jacket lay across his shoulders. He looked over at the chasm, half hidden by bushes. He wished he knew a prayer to speak, or even think.

He heard a sound behind him, but didn't turn.

He was afraid, too achingly aware of what role he'd played here. He didn't think he could look at what would be in her face. His mother, Cadell had said, had her hair. Her great-grandmother was said to have had the second sight. There were family stories further back.

And his aunt . . .

Ned sighed, it seemed to come from so deep inside it felt bottomless. He had been in this, after all. It was his family, and Phelan seemed to have been aware of something—without knowing *what*—from that beginning in the cathedral, first day.

Ysabel stepped nearer. More a presence than a sound. He was painfully conscious of her. The two of them alone now. She would be looking down and remembering two thousand six hundred years. How did you come to terms with something ending after so long? Who had ever had to deal with that?

Because it *was* over. Ned knew it as keenly as the three of them had. They had collided with a wall—with *him*—and the intricate spinning had come to a close on this mountain.

He shook his head. So many ways it might have been otherwise. Brys had tried to kill him in the cemetery. He could have been too sick to climb when he got here. Either of the two men might have been quicker than Ned. Both had said these things. It was *not* preordained, what had just happened, not compelled.

Did that mean he had killed them? Or set them free?

Did the choice of words make a difference? Did words matter at all here?

"Oh, God. Ned, you did it," were the words he heard.

They mattered. They mattered so much they powered him to his feet, whirling around.

Melanie stood in front of him. With her black hair and the green streak in it, and a smile so wide, through tears, it seemed it could light the shadows of that cave.

"I don't believe it!" he said. "It . . . she . . . you're back!"

And Ysabel was gone.

He had been right, then, to see her as going away even as she stood there. Joy now, fierce and searingly bright, mixed with something that might never leave him. Someone returned, was rescued, someone was gone. Was this the way it always was?

She said, "You *brought* me back."

"I've never been so glad to see someone in my life."

"Is that so?" she said, and he heard a note, of irony, that echoed someone else, not Melanie.

He couldn't speak. He was stunned, buffeted. She stepped close and put her hands behind his head, lacing her fingers there, and she kissed him, standing on the edge of the plateau in the wind. She didn't actually rush it. There was a scent to her he couldn't remember from before. It was dizzying.

She stepped back. Looked at him. Her eyes were unnaturally bright, maybe with the tears. "I probably shouldn't be doing that."

He was still having some trouble breathing. "Only reason I came to France," he managed.

She laughed. Kissed him again, lightly this time. It felt, impossibly, as if it was Melanie doing that, but also not *quite* Melanie. Or maybe it wasn't impossible. Not after what had happened here. He suddenly remembered Kate, walking up to Entremont, the change in her, with Beltaine coming on.

"Thank you," Melanie said, still very close.

"Well, yeah," he said, light-headed from the feel of her and her scent, and the strangeness of his thoughts. Then something else registered, really belatedly. He stepped to one side, looking more closely at her.

He felt himself beginning to grin, despite everything. "Oh, Lord!" he said.

Melanie looked suddenly awkward, uncertain, more like herself. "What is it?"

He started to laugh, couldn't help himself. "Melanie, jeez, you are at *least* three inches taller. Look at yourself!"

"What? That can't be . . . and I *can't* look at myself!"

"Then trust me. Come back, stand close."

She did. It was as he'd said. At least three inches. She came up to his nose now, and no way she'd been even close to that before.

"Holy-moly, Ned! I grew?"

"Sure looks like it." No one else he'd ever known said "holy-moly."

"Can *that* happen?"

He was thinking about his aunt. Her hair turning white all at once. What his mother had refused to believe, for twenty-five years.

"I guess it can," was all he said. "We don't know a whole lot about any of this."

"I grew?" she said again, in wonder.

"You're going to be dangerous," he said.

She flashed a smile that evoked someone else who was gone. "You have no idea, Ned Marriner."

Someone returned, someone went away forever. He hesitated. "Melanie, were you *aware* of anything, when you were . . . ?"

The smile faded. She looked through the opening to the south, plateau and plain, river, more mountains, the sea.

"Just at the beginning," she said quietly. "And even then it was difficult. When . . . when I started changing, I could feel it happening, but I couldn't do anything about it. I couldn't stop walking. I could see out through her eyes at first, and hear things, but it got *hard.* Like pushing a weight up, a big boulder, with my head, my shoulders, trying to look out from beneath? And then it started to be too heavy. And after a while I couldn't."

She was still gazing out.

"So you don't know what happened here? Just now?"

"You'll tell me?"

"What I know. But . . . did *you* make her change things, have them look for her. And pick this place?"

She had started to cry again. She nodded. "I did do that. I could do . . . I knew from inside her what was supposed to happen, and that I was gone if one of them killed the other and claimed her. So I pushed the only idea I had, which was trying to get her to come here instead, and hope someone would remember it." She looked at him. "You, actually, Ned. I didn't think anyone else could."

"You understood what might happen, if they all came here?"

"I knew what she knew." She wiped at her cheeks. "Ned, I *was* her, and still me, a little. Then it got too hard and I could only wait, underneath."

"You knew I was there? At Entremont?"

A flash of the old Melanie in her eyes. "Well, that's a dumb question. What was I doing there in the first place?"

He felt stupid. He'd *called* her. "Right. Sorry."

Her expression changed. "Don't ever say sorry to me, Ned. Not after this."

He tried to make it a joke. "That's a risky thing to tell a guy."

She shook her head. "Not this time, it isn't."

His turn to look away, out over so much darkening beauty. "We should get down. This isn't a normal place."

"Neither are we," said Melanie. "Normal. Are we?"

He hesitated. "I think we mostly are," he said. "We will be. Can you walk, like that?"

She looked at her bare feet. "Not down a mountain, Ned. And it'll be dark."

He thought. "There's a chapel I saw. Just below the peak. Not far. We may not be able to get inside, but there's a courtyard, some shelter. I can call down from there."

"Auto-dial Greg?"

It *was* Melanie again. Taller, but this was her. He smiled. Happiness was possible, it was almost here. "Very funny," he said. Another thought. "Greg was pretty amazing, you know."

"You'll have to tell me. You're right, though, we should go. I'm cold. Ysabel was . . . pretty tough, I guess."

Ysabel had been many things, he thought.

He took off the leather jacket and gave it to her.

"Where'd you get this?" she said, slipping her arms into the sleeves. It was big on her; she looked like an urchin in it.

"I'll tell you that, too. We go?"

They left through the eastern opening, the way Ned had come in. Melanie winced a couple of times, barefoot on stones.

Ned stopped just outside and looked back, standing where he'd skidded to a stop, sliding down. He could see the rock he'd grabbed. It was dark inside the cave now towards the back, the light didn't reach that far. There was nothing, really, that you could see.

Melanie was looking at him, wearing Phelan's jacket. "You've changed too, you know," she said.

"Three inches taller?"

"No, you have, Ned."

He nodded. "Come on, it's just up here, then to the left."

When they topped the ridge and looked west towards the cross and chapel, standing utterly alone on the mountain, the sun was ahead of them, very low, lighting clouds. The sunset was glorious, a gift.

They lived in an age, Ned Marriner thought, when it was possible to think that way.

HIS PACK was where he'd left it against the stone wall. He pulled on his sweatshirt; it was bitingly cold now in the evening wind. The chapel was locked, so was the other long, low room off the courtyard, with a padlock. The courtyard itself offered some protection from the swirling gusts.

"I'll give you my socks," he said, "or you're going to freeze."

Melanie nodded. "Never thought I'd be happy about that kind of offer." She'd zipped the jacket all the way up to her nose, but that wouldn't help enough if she was barefoot here.

"You have a pocket knife?" she asked.

"Yeah."

She held out a hand. He dug into his pack and handed her his Swiss Army blade, then sat on a stone bench against the building and began pulling off his running shoes to give her the socks.

"They aren't the height of fashion," he began, when he had them off and the shoes back on, "but they'll—"

He stopped. She was standing at the entrance to the flat-roofed building beside the chapel and the door was open.

"How'd you do that?" he said, walking over.

"I have skills you don't yet know about, Ned Marriner."

That note in her voice. It was there again. He might have changed, but he sure wasn't the only one.

"My dad picked a lock couple of days ago like that."

A grin. "I taught him how."

"What?"

She looked really happy. "He saw me do it once, when we were shooting in Peru, and got jealous. He made me show him how."

"You," he said, "are a criminal mastermind. Here's the socks."

She took them, and went inside. He got his pack and followed. There was no electricity up here, and the long, narrow room was dark. Ned threw open the shutters to the courtyard while Melanie put on his socks. He saw a fireplace, with wood stacked beside it. The place had probably been a dormitory or dining room for the chapel once. Now it looked like an overnight place for hikers.

"Think they'll arrest us if we start a fire?"

"I could handle that," Melanie said. "If they bring shoes."

That reminded him.

He flipped open his phone and dialed his father. One ring.

"Ned?"

He felt himself smiling, despite exhaustion. A surge of emotion before he spoke. Fighting it, he said, "Yeah, it's me. Dad, I got her."

"*What?*"

"Got her back. We're both fine."

"Oh, dear God," he heard his father say. And then he became aware that his dad was crying. He heard him relay the words. Then, "Ned, Ned . . . here's your mother."

"Honey?" he heard. "You're really okay?"

"I'm great, Mom, we both are. It's going to be a really long story."

"Can you get down?"

"Not now, Mom. It's almost dark, and Melanie has no shoes. I think you guys have to come get us in the morning, with stuff for her."

"Where are you now?"

"In this building beside the chapel. We got in. There's a fireplace, it's fine. We're cool overnight. Can you meet us here first thing?"

"Of course we can. Ned, put Melanie on, your father wants to talk to her."

"I'll bet."

He was still smiling as he handed her the phone.

"Boss?"

There was a silence. Melanie brushed at her eyes.

"Thank you, sir," she said quietly. "Thanks, all of you. I'm all right, I really am. You'll see. I do need some things, if you can put Dr. Marriner on?" She walked towards a window. Ned went outside again into the courtyard. He crossed to the low southern wall, past the well.

He looked out on the darkened land. Lights were coming on below, in houses, farms, country restaurants. He saw headlights on the roads. He saw what had to be the highway, east-west. The Riviera resorts were only an hour from here. Bars and cafés and yachts along the coast of the sea, glittering with light.

He imagined a ship sailing here from Greece a really long time ago, passing dark, forbidding forests and mountain ranges that hid whatever was inland from view, leaving it shrouded and mysterious. He imagined them finding a harbour west of here, those strangers from far away, then their first encounter with a tribe, wondering if what they'd come all this way to find was death far from home, or something else.

He imagined those native warriors with their druids and rituals and forest gods, and goddesses of still pools, pictured them coming through the woods to see these strangers, wondering what they were, what they had brought here with them.

His heart was full, sorrow and joy taking all it could hold, right to the brim. He looked at the lights below, with the sun gone now. He saw the moon to his left, towards where the resorts would be, playgrounds of the world he knew.

He knew another world now. Had touched it. Would walk in both, in a way, for the rest of his life. He thought of the boar.

Hands flat on the low stone wall in the wind, he thought of Ysabel as the night drifted down.

"Come on," he heard from behind him. "I found matches, we've got a fire. Did you bring anything someone could call food?"

He turned back to Melanie, to the world.

"Veracook packed me some stuff."

"God bless her," Melanie said in the doorway.

He walked over, followed her in. The fire was going nicely. She'd lit candles, too.

"There are blankets in those cupboards," she said. "Lots of them."

"Good. We'll be okay."

Melanie grinned at him. "Sailor," she said, "you might even be better than okay."

That, predictably, got his heart beating faster. He cleared his throat, as an image, inescapable, inserted itself in his awareness.

"Melanie, my mother's there. She'll be coming up tomorrow and looking me in the eye."

"Good point. And I work for your dad, don't I? I might have trouble facing them if we . . ."

"You?" he said. "*You* might have trouble? You know my mother! You think I can get away with pretending we played Twenty Questions? Animal, vegetable, mineral?"

She laughed softly. "Only if we play Twenty Questions."

"Not why I joined the navy."

Melanie's expression altered. She looked at him a moment. "You know, you really *have* changed."

"Well, so have you."

"I guess." She smiled at him. She looked older, he thought, but didn't say. She lifted a hand and touched his cheek. Her eyes seemed darker, so did her voice, somehow.

"Ned, I have a pretty good idea what you did today. I remember what this place was like for you, when we drove here. And . . . this won't be the only night of our lives."

He cleared his throat again. "That's a pretty hot thing to say."

"Uh-huh. I know. Your birthday's in July?"

He nodded. It was hard to speak, again. Women could do this to you.

"I'll have to try hard to remember that," Melanie said. "Now, let's see what Vera put in there for you."

She went over to his pack. He stood where he was. He could remember the feel of her lips in the cave, and there was that scent he hadn't ever been aware of before.

"Um, the fifteenth," he said suddenly. "July fifteenth."

She was rummaging.

"Baguette, pâté, cheese, apples. Vera's a treasure," she said. Then looked at him over her shoulder, a smile. "I have the date in my PDA. Meanwhile, come by the fire, let's eat, and . . ." Her voice deepened again. "I'm thinking of something animal."

"Oh, God!" he said.

She laughed aloud.

Outside, the night deepened and gathered. Boars, which fed at sunrise and at dusk, came cautiously out of woods below. Owls lifted from trees to hunt. Moonlight found ancient towns and the ruins of towers, triumphal arches and sacred pools, graveyards and vineyards and lavender bushes. One by one stars emerged in the dark blue dusk, in a sky that had not yet fallen.

IN THE BRIGHTNESS of morning they were waiting outside by the wall. They saw the others coming up along the switchbacks of the northern ridge. They'd have had to start before sunrise, Ned thought, in darkness, to be here by now.

It was harder to feel sorrow in the morning, he thought, seeing his father lift his hat in one hand and wave it. Melanie stood up and waved back with both hands over her head.

You can allow yourself joy, he thought. *And even pride.* He didn't feel ill any more. He hadn't since he'd entered the cave, since finding Ysabel.

They'd all come up, he saw, counting. Even Greg and Uncle Dave, who probably shouldn't be doing two-hour climbs. His mother and his aunt were walking beside each other. Red hair and white like a fairy tale. It wasn't, though; this was his family, and he had a different kind of tale for them. He swallowed hard, seeing the two of them like that, bright against the green of the trees and the blue lakes in the distance below.

They came zigzagging with the trail. He remembered, late yesterday, being pursued, cutting across these last switchbacks, up the rock face to get here.

They didn't have to do that. He stood up beside Melanie and waited for the others to reach them along the last inclination. Just before they did, she looked at him and smiled.

It was more like four inches, he decided.

He grinned back. "Wonder if you could slam-dunk now?"

"Feels like," she said.

Then she started running, in his socks and the white skirt and blue shirt Ysabel had worn. Ned saw his father open his arms and hug her close as if she were a lost child returned.

Greg and Steve stopped beside them, waiting their turn. His mother and uncle and aunt kept coming towards Ned. He saw Kate Wenger hanging back, suddenly shy.

"Yo, Mom," he said. "You bring croissants?"

His mother, who was *not* much of a hugger, didn't answer, she just enfolded him and didn't let go.

"Whoa!" Ned said.

"No, whoa," she murmured, gripping tightly. "No way."

Eventually she stepped back, looking at him.

His aunt was smiling. "Yo, Nephew," she said. "Want us to tell you how scared we were?"

"I can guess."

"No, you can't," said Meghan Marriner, shaking her head. "You can't come close."

He looked at her. "I have a few things to tell you guys," he said. "About us. Our family."

The sisters glanced at each other.

"Which of them was the father?" Kim asked.

Ned's jaw dropped. "Jeez!" he said.

414 Guy Gavriel Kay

"We were talking most of the night," his mother said. "Fitted a few guesses together. Like a jigsaw."

"A jigsaw," he repeated, stupidly.

Uncle Dave laughed at his expression. "Ned," he said, "believe me, it was scary listening to them. We can start being afraid around now."

Ned didn't feel afraid. It didn't look like his uncle did, either. His mother and aunt were looking at him, waiting.

He cleared his throat. "She didn't tell," he said quietly. "They asked."

Meghan said, "But we were right?"

Ned nodded, looked over at his uncle. "Aha. They weren't sure. We're still okay."

"Barely," said Dave Martyniuk. "This is just a beginning."

They looked back at the others.

Edward Marriner led them up. Greg and Steve were grinning like kids. Melanie had her oversized tote now, and her cellphone and straw hat. Meghan went over and kissed her on both cheeks.

Ned looked at his dad. "Hi," he said.

"Hello, son." His father smiled.

"Take a good look around. Morning light. I don't think you can go wrong up here. A lot of options. You'll want to go look south, too, other side of this courtyard here. You shoot *from* Cézanne's mountain, not up to it?"

His father nodded. "Had that thought, climbing up."

"I had that thought a week ago!" said Melanie.

"Oh, of course you did," said Greg.

Steve snorted, and walked away, towards where Kate was still hanging back. He was dialing his phone. Ned wondered who was left at the villa to call.

A moment later the sounds of "The Wedding March" were heard in the high, clear spaces at the summit of Sainte-Victoire.

"Dammit!" said Melanie, reddening. She stabbed for the answer button on her phone. "I took that ringtone *off*!"

Steve had turned back to them. He was laughing. So was Greg. So, actually, was Ned. Did you have to be mature *all* the time?

Steve sketched an oriental bow to Melanie. "Little Bird, learn lesson of life. That which is changed can be changed back in fullness of time." He bowed again, hands pressed together.

"You are in so much trouble, the two of you," she said.

"I am really, really happy to hear you say that," said Greg. He looked at her, and frowned. "Hey, did you, like, grow or something?"

She smiled; it just about lit the mountainside.

MELANIE WENT BACK inside to change clothes. Ned's father was eyeing the view, all directions. Ned knew that expression, the appraising look.

"Later," Edward Marriner said, catching Ned's glance. "I'll come back." He laid a hand on his son's shoulder and squeezed.

Melanie came out. Seeing her in her own clothes and running shoes was a kind of shock. This was entirely her now, his father's assistant, hyper-organized ringtone warrior.

Someone else even farther away now.

It made him thoughtful. He let the others go down first. Said he wanted a moment to himself. His mother looked at him, then started back along the path with the rest.

Ned found a boulder and sat down, his back against it, looking east to the sunrise, towards the last ridge he'd climbed yesterday. Up along it, then down to the right there was a cave.

He took a deep breath. Was it all going to recede? Would what had happened slip and drift like memories did? Become something you thought of at times, and then less often as years went by? A story, your history, as you were carried forward into other stories and other moments that became your life. Other people.

He heard a footfall, someone kicked a pebble.

"You, um, sleep with her last night?" Kate Wenger asked.

She came up beside him. She took off her sunglasses. Her expression was cool.

"What kind of a question is that?" he said, looking up.

"Obvious one, I'd say."

"No gentleman would answer that."

She waited.

Ned felt himself flush. "No, of course I didn't."

Kate smiled. "Good."

She'd brushed her hair out, was wearing Ned's black Pearl Jam T-shirt this time, over jeans. She'd done that trick girls did, tying it at her midriff, for the climb. It didn't look much the way it did when he wore it.

"I prefer New York women, anyhow," he said.

She sniffed. "Don't make assumptions."

"Wouldn't dream of it."

She grinned suddenly. "I don't mind if you *dream* of it."

Ned stared up at her, unable to think of anything to say. He looked away to his left again, beyond the ridge towards the Riviera, Italy, the sun. The land below them to the south had been a battlefield once. Probably more than once, he thought. It was bathed in a long, mild morning glory.

Kate extended her hands. "Come on, we'll get too far behind."

"What's wrong with that?" he asked, looking up at her.

She smiled again. "Nothing, I guess."

He gave her both his hands and let her help him rise.

Never again will a single story be told
as though it were the only one.

—JOHN BERGER

ACKNOWLEDGMENTS

∾

L aura and Sybil, as always, on both sides of the Atlantic.

Ysabel was written largely in the countryside near Aix-en-Provence, and so it is proper to first note those who were of great assistance in our time there.

Bethany Atherton offered Villa Sans Souci, pointed us to a ruined tower, and found the garagai one windy day's climb up Sainte-Victoire. Leslie-Ellen Ray shared a professional's approach to photographing Aix's cathedral.

At the University of Aix-Marseille, Gilles Dorival offered suggestions, answered questions, arranged access to the university library, and introduced me to the wonderfully generous Jean-Marc Gassend and Pierre Varène, architects of the Institut de Recherche sur l'Architecture Antique. I am grateful for their courtesy and enthusiasm, for their precise sketches of the cathedral and the history beneath it, and for a wonderful, evocative afternoon among the still-closed-off ruins of the newly excavated Roman theatre in Aix.

Sam Kay was with me on a long note-taking drive around the mountain, came up to Entremont several times, pacing the terrain, and—with Matthew and Laura—joined me at, among other places, the Saint-Sauveur and Saint-Trophime cloisters, Les Alyscamps and the Roman theatre in Arles, and at Glanum. "You have to use this place in the book," from both boys, became a motivating refrain. Sam also went back up the mountain again weeks after we all did, to further establish details of the route and the cave above the chasm. Matthew took photos everywhere. Sons becoming researchers marks a transition.

I read too many texts on the Celtic, Greek, and Roman presences in Provence to be comprehensive in naming them here. Let me cite Theodore Cook's *Old Provence* as memorable, along with S. Baring-Gould's genuinely charming (and undoubtedly idiosyncratic) *A Ramble in Provence*. Jean Markale's extensive work on the Celts was helpful, and so were Miranda Green, Marie-Louise Sjoestedt, Nora Chadwick (again), and the prolific Barry Cunliffe. Cunliffe's short book on Pytheas the Greek gave me a number of ideas that found their way into *Ysabel*. Philip Freeman's *War, Women, and Druids* is a tidy, useful collection of primary sources on the intersection of the classical and Celtic worlds. *Ecstasies*, by Carlo Ginzburg, a historian I have long admired, was fertile ground for concepts and images.

On the oppidum of Entremont, Fernand Benoit's monograph, *Entremont*, about the history of the site and the excavations there, was immensely helpful. So, also, was the official website at www.culture.gouv.fr/culture/arcnat/entremont/en/index2.html (in English and in French).

I hope it is obvious that it does not fall to any of these writers to bear the least responsibility for the uses I have made of history and myth in shaping this fiction.

I am grateful to Deborah Meghnagi (the presiding spirit of www.brightweavings.com) and Rex Kay for careful readings of the completed draft.

Ysabel owes much to all of these people, and so does the author.